MORE PRAISE FOR GILBERT ROGIN

"He balances wittiness and wistfulness very well . . . he should be read."
—Larry McMurtry, *Washington Post*

"Writing full of grace and intelligence"
—Eve Auchincloss, *New York Review of Books*

"I don't know anyone who has seen the imaginative environment
of the sixties more imaginatively than Rogin."
—Arthur Gold, *New York Herald Tribune Book Week*

WHAT HAPPENS NEXT?

"Rogin shares Cheever's awareness of risk, his sense that to turn a corner
of the banal may be to find oneself in a howling waste of strangeness . . .
The slapstick works as well for Rogin as it did for Salinger."
—John Skow, *Time*

"Julian Singer, in his lostness, transcends origin and place and becomes
some kind of archetypical American man. Every scrap, every line, every
joke is in the service of this artfully lifelike portrait of ourselves . . . *What
Happens Next?* is a novel of the first importance. I hope you'll read it."
—L.E. Sissman, *New York Times Book Review*

"Original, subtle, and startlingly different, Rogin's writing . . . radiates
a strength and integrity."
—Murrah Gattis, *Los Angeles Times*

PREPARATIONS FOR THE ASCENT

"*Preparations for the Ascent* ascends, and nothing can bring it down."
—Anatole Broyard, *New York Times*

"Albert would be a solipsistically inward character, mildly insufferable, if
it were not for the extraordinary grace and intelligence of Rogin's prose,
which sometimes accomplishes small, splendid feats of magic. At one point
he warns the reader: 'What follows is tender and complicated.' Exactly."
—Lance Morrow, *Time* ("Editor's Choice")

"Rogin is simply a delight to read. Witty, innovative, urbane and heartfelt,
his prose is a mine of mental gratification."
—Colin McEnroe, *Hartford Courant*

GILBERT ROGIN

What Happens Next?

& Preparations for the Ascent

Verse Chorus Press

Published in 2010 by Verse Chorus Press
PO Box 14806, Portland OR 97293
info@versechorus.com

Cover illustration and design by Mike Reddy
Book design: Steve Connell/Transgraphic

What Happens Next? first published in 1971 by Random House. With the exception of Chapters 9 and 14, the material therein originally appeared in slightly different form in *The New Yorker* (Chapters 1–6, 8, 10–13, 15, 16, 18–22); *The Reporter* (Chapter 7); and *Cosmopolitan* (Chapter 17).

Preparations for the Ascent first published in 1980 by Random House. Chapter 8 originally appeared in *Harper's*. All the remaining chapters, excluding Chapters 4, 10, and 11, originally appeared in slightly different form in *The New Yorker.*

The drawing on page 220 is by Thomas Vink-Lainas.

ISBN 978-1-891241-27-7

Library of Congress Control Number: 2010930530

CONTENTS

REDISCOVERING ROGIN

Reviewing Gilbert Rogin's novel *What Happens Next?* in *Partisan Review* in 1973, Joyce Carol Oates wrote, "Because Rogin is . . . very funny his work is in danger of being underestimated." To make a Roginesque joke, his work has been so widely underestimated, it might take a metaphysician to prove its existence. Each of his three books—a collection of stories, *The Fencing Master* (1965), and the two novels here (assembled mostly from published stories), *What Happens Next?* (1971) and *Preparations for the Ascent* (1980)—went out of print in short order. His deaccessioning from the public libraries of America proceeded apace, so that many of the copies available on used-book aggregator Bookfinder.com are "ex-library." Nor, at the time I discovered Rogin's work in 2008, were there any of his books in the New York Public Library's circulating branches—in his native city, where his work is set! A lonely one copy of each turned up in the NYPL's noncirculating CATNYP database, along with the plaintive software query to my "Gilbert Rogin" search, "Do you mean 'gilbert groin'?" (I think Rogin would appreciate that anagrammatical query, since he both anatomizes libidinal adventures and plays inventively with language.)

Of course, most writers suffer the fate of obscurity, but most have not had such an enviable literary career. Between 1963 and 1980, Rogin published 33 stories in the *New Yorker* and others in *Esquire*, *Harper's*, and *Vogue*; he won an Academy Award for literature from the American Academy of Arts and Letters (in 1972, along with Harry Crews, Paula Fox, and Thomas McGuane); and his novels have received high, sometimes rapturous, praise in reviews. Besides Oates's lauding of his "unique vision" in *What Happens Next?*, Anatole Broyard, the *New York Times*' primary reviewer at the time, found the book's "sardonic dialogue" superior to Donald Barthelme's and its portrait of marriage on a par with John Updike's Maple stories. Poet and critic L.E. Sissman, writing in the *New York Times Book Review*, declared at the outset of his review, "I think Gilbert Rogin has written a great novel, the first one I've run across in quite some time." Nine years later, his next and last book, *Preparations for the Ascent*, received less attention, but Mordecai Richler, admitting in the *Times Book Review* that he was not familiar with Rogin's work, found it "subtle, original, and refreshingly intelligent." And in his 1979 introduction to the English translation of Polish novelist Bruno Schulz's *Sanatorium under the Sign of the Hourglass*, Updike himself—after comparing Schulz to Kafka and Proust—invoked one of Rogin's *New Yorker* stories, linking the two as "writers in a world of hidden citizens" who "work with an excited precision, pulling silver threads from the coarse texture of daily life."

It was in that canonized company that I, happening upon Updike's essay in his collection *Hugging the Shore*, first heard of Rogin's fiction. His name, however, I knew well. When I started working as a reporter at *Sports Illustrated* in 1987, Rogin had recently departed as managing editor, the magazine's top post, after a 30-year career there, and his name still echoed in the halls. He then moved to the science magazine *Discover* and later to a lofty Time Inc. corporate editorial position, from which he retired in 1992. (Among other accomplishments, he helped Quincy Jones found *Vibe*.) Updike's anointing sent me to my *Complete New Yorker* DVD, where I found Rogin's stories, before later seeking out his books from the above-mentioned used-book site.

The questions that pricked me amid the amassed encomiums were "How does such a lauded writer disappear so thoroughly?" and "Is he really worthy of resurrection?" Or, to put it in another anagram of his name, "Lit gig reborn?" I wondered if Rogin, born in 1929, might be a male analogue to Paula Fox, six years his elder, whose out-of-print oeuvre in adult fiction had been revived by a Jonathan Franzen essay declaring her novel *Desperate Characters* to be "obviously superior to any novel by Fox's contemporaries John Updike, Philip Roth and Saul Bellow." I doubt I'd venture that far into hyperbole, but could Rogin, like Fox a chronicler of New York City angst, have been unfairly overshadowed by better-known peers?

I worked backward from the most recent book, ending with the short stories, which, while skillfully rendered, seemed to be a warm-up for the two novels. Those books, as is clear from their binding together here, essentially comprise one long narrative of a marriage and its entropic dissolution; Julian and Daisy in *What Happens Next?* become Albert and the similarly floral Violet in *Preparations for the Ascent*, and the later book largely picks up in chronology where the other one ends. (Strangely, in the latter, Rogin doesn't change the name of the wife's wastrel ex, Skippy Mountjoy, or those of the family dachshunds, Josh and Jake.) The protagonist, no matter the name, is a (presumably autobiographical) middle-aged, Jewish, Manhattanite male, a magazine writer of eclectic intellectual interests and eccentric habits. If Stendhal defined the novel as a "mirror being carried down a highway," Rogin's carrier stares at himself in the mirror while lugging it up West End Avenue to his therapist's office or to Madison Square Garden for a basketball game. He moves from place to place in accord with his daily duties as husband and son, lover and friend (only rarely as employee), hilariously hyperobservant of the world around him while pondering his "immobilized," abstracted personality ("the Apollonian and Dionysian sides of character being of equal strength"). "The trouble with you, Julian," his wife tells him in *What Happens Next?*, "is that you have no outer life."

Rogin's dialogue is often slightly stylized, which heightens the humor. In *Preparations for the Ascent*, Albert, separated from his wife, moves mere blocks away and can see her building from his.

> "Oh, God," his mom had said when Albert told her where he had moved. "You can hear her hair dryer from there. Couldn't you have put more ground between yourselves?"

"It wasn't premeditated," Albert said. "It was a supervenient turn of events. If you visualize the marriage as a ship that has broken up, you will see us as two shipmates clinging to opposite ends of a large piece of flotsam."

"I see you as two idiots awash on a delusion," his dad said.

There are echoes of Woody Allen in both the heady nature of the jokes and the slapstick of what little action actually does occur. He bangs heads with his dachshund; he extricates his stepson from the locked bathroom by delivering "a well-aimed kick at the doorknob, remembering—ah! too late—that he is barefoot"; he demonstrates to his wife the most efficient route to answer the telephone in the living room from the bedroom—"if you take the first turn a little wide, you'll be able to negotiate the second without decelerating. Please observe."

But there's much more than jokes and pratfalls going on here, as we are reminded on almost every page by the fineness of Rogin's observation. His descriptions can be beautifully lyric (a New York sky that is blue "like the air in which Giotto's lamenting angels hover"); slyly critical (a Southern California hotel room so "grandiose" it looked "as though it had been built and furnished with an eye to the future, for the race of giants we would become"); and poignantly tactile (he remarks of his dachshund Josh, linking him with his stepson, Barney, and wondering if he's neglected them both, in an efficient, lovely elision: "How old and scruffy he is, like Barney's football, which had been kicked around the P.S. 41 schoolyard for years.")

Pinpointing why an author fails to find his audience is largely speculation, but perhaps Rogin's problem was timing. He was writing at the very apex of the market for protagonists who were middle-aged, Jewish, Manhattanite male intellectuals/writers and musers. The urtext in this genre is Saul Bellow's *Herzog* (1964), with cohorts Mailer, Malamud, and others doing variations on the theme. In October 1971, the same month *What Happens Next?* appeared, the influential critic Morris Dickstein identified "many years of imitation and, finally, glut in Jewish writing," and Dwight

Macdonald, in November of that same year, declared *Portnoy's Complaint* (1969) "the Jewish novel to end all Jewish novels (which it unfortunately hasn't)." Even as WASPy a writer as John Updike satirized the genre and its practitioners in *Bech: A Book* in 1970, which appeared on the National Book Awards shortlist with Bellow's *Mr. Sammler's Planet*. In 1980, *Preparations for the Ascent* had the bad luck to enter a cultural world which had just the year before feted the works of similar, better established writers mining the same vein: Malamud's *Dubin's Lives* and its inventively musing libidinal biographer, Roth's *The Ghost Writer* and its fantasizing historical revisionist Nathan Zuckerman, and even Woody Allen's *Manhattan*. A cursory glance at Rogin could have convinced us that we'd heard it all before.

What unifies Rogin's novels is voice and humor, but some critics of the day were flummoxed by his "inaction" heroes and the lack of a traditional plot or character development. A reviewer in Philip Rahv's journal *Modern Occasions* griped about *What Happens Next?*, "Mr. Rogin seems . . . resigned to recording the nonevents in Singer's life." In *New York* magazine's review of *Preparations*, novelist Evan Connell wrote, "[From Albert's] behavior you can hardly tell where he is or what he is doing. Nothing changes." Even Richler admits about *Preparations*, ". . . though I both enjoyed and admired it, and even laughed out loud more than once, I'm not sure I understood it" before asserting, "I'd rather be baffled by Gilbert Rogin than read a story made plain by many a more accessible but predictable writer."

Read today, Rogin's books seem fresh, the author possessed of a turn-of-the-21st-century comic sensibility more than a fundamentally Jewish one similar to his peers from the 1960s and 1970s. Obsession, and particularly self-mocking self-obsession, rather than neuroses per se, is what characterizes his protagonists. The criticisms mentioned above—that Rogin is merely recording nonevents or that nothing changes in his books—are identical to descriptions of *Seinfeld*, an equally brilliant depiction of contemporary social manners that famously presented itself as "a show about nothing." And it's no stretch to imagine *Seinfeld* mastermind Larry David in his current show, *Curb Your Enthusiasm*, holding, as Albert does, an "operative number" of thirty-one, by which he finds "patterns" in his life, to the point that he performs actions in its multiples—sit-ups, pages read, even executing one hundred twenty-four strokes while making love to his girlfriend ("'I can see you moving your lips,' she says midway").

Furthermore, Rogin's experiments with narrative and self-reflexive techniques anticipate strategies adopted by the contemporary literary generation. The late David Foster Wallace's fondness for footnotes finds an ancestor in one chapter of *What Happens Next?*, when Julian uses them to record his parents' reactions to the story he's written about them. The result is a Russian doll of a read, in which he unpacks age-old parent-child anxieties while questioning narrative reliability, almost sentence by sentence. A later chapter relates an argument between Singer and Mountjoy almost entirely in police-report diction ("Singer inquired of Mountjoy who the hell he thought Singer was"), studded with excerpts from their grade-school comment cards. Other chapters feature diagrams (lunch-table accoutrements being used as chess pieces), mathematical formulae (calculating the point C at which his and his psychiatrist's sightlines would meet), *Heartbreaking Genius*-like references to the book itself ("Regard it here in eleven-point Garamond"), and numbered lists ("The bad things that happened on their vacation . . ."). Rogin's work, it seems to me, deserves that most clichéd of compliments: ahead of its time.

More evidence resides in the first pages of *What Happens Next?*, from a story originally published in 1966, in which one of Singer's TV-producing cronies envisions a game show in which a celebrity panel has to guess the problem a contestant faces ("I'm in love with a woman, but I think she's after my money") then "give the contestant two, three minutes personalized advice and comfort." The producer says, "We're liable to come up with television's lowest ebb." Perhaps not even Rogin could have envisioned *Big Brother*, but the show he conceived would fit into today's lineup nonetheless.

In the end, Rogin's books deserve to be read and reread for one simple reason: they're funny. Along the way, feel free to be wowed by his pinballing imagination, his linguistic dexterity and his masterly ability to see clearly what is right in front of our faces but remained unnoticed until he pointed it out.

And what happened next to Rogin, after *Preparations*? Why did we not get a continuation of the characters' story past middle-age and into their dotage? In *About Town*, his 2000 history of the *New Yorker*, Ben Yagoda sums up Rogin's literary fate in, appropriately enough, a footnote: "Soon after publication of [*Preparations*], Rogin submitted two stories to [fiction editor Roger] Angell, who told Rogin he was turning them down because they seemed to go over familiar ground. The criticism had a shattering effect on Rogin, and subsequently he has written no fiction."

That this was a great loss to literature will be evident to the reader of these novels, but at least their journey back into print after 30 years and more is a happy occasion. In preparing to publish a version of this essay in his comedy journal, *The Lowbrow Reader*, editor Jay Ruttenberg also became a Rogin fan and tracked down the writer himself, who happened to live a few blocks away in Greenwich Village, retired but hale and delightedly stunned to be rediscovered. Their meeting eventually resulted in the publication of the first Rogin story to see print since 1980, alongside my appreciation of his work in *Lowbrow* #7. Jay's efforts also brought Rogin's work to the attention of Steve Connell at Verse Chorus Press, which joyfully corrected the crime of the books' disappearance. Now bookstore browsers can find the author on the same shelf with Roth, where he belongs, and the libraries of the world can be rightfully repopulated with Rogins.

Jay Jennings
Little Rock, Arkansas
August 2009

WHAT HAPPENS NEXT?

To Ruth

1

In the morning before the fall of light, on his way to the bathroom, Julian Singer, overweight, acquiescent, having fewer aspirations than heretofore, discovers his stepson Simon, nine years old, in his pajamas among the dogs in the passage outside Singer's bedroom. All three are lying, inviolable, it seems, purples and browns predominating, on the old, eviscerated puff that, Singer has often been told, covered Simon on Barrow Street.

"What are you doing down there?" Singer says.

"What do you always want to make me suffer for?" Simon says.

"Suffer! What do you mean suffer?" Singer says. "What do you know about suffering?"

Singer returns, grieving, to bed, where his wife lies, wearing a gray T shirt that is too big for her, with "Boston Patriots" written on it.

"Simon's picking on me," he says. "Do I deserve it?"

Before he leaves for school, Simon comes to say good-bye. Singer is sleeping, having another harrowing dream. Simon bends down to kiss him. Without opening his eyes, Singer reaches up and embraces him. Ah, Singer thinks, how could groping Isaac have been so ignorant?

Going uptown, Singer descries, on the Avenue of the Americas, Bruce Binder, an industrial designer, bearing down on him in his small convertible. Singer tries to flee by doubling back on Spring Street and running north on Sullivan Street, but Binder overtakes him. As he sullenly accepts Binder's offer of a lift, Singer realizes that he has miscalculated; he had thought Sullivan was one-way the other way—a familiar failing.

Binder, whom he knows slightly, is telling Singer that sooner or later he, Binder, is going to commit adultery. Singer recalls that he may owe Binder a wedding present; he had gone to the reception at the Hampshire House, the Cottage Room, and had a handful of salted nuts. "I know me," Binder says, unconvincingly. Binder looks fairly mournful, Byzantine; he reminds Singer of some dim pendentive figure.

"I fired my mother last week," Binder says. "Julian, I was at my model-maker's. When I return to my studio, I find a message my mother has taken that So-and-So has called and so forth—a show-type girl I had had kind of a great relationship with on the Coast once.

" 'Ma, the number,' I say to my mother.

" 'What number?' she says to me—a fox.

" 'What number! What number! The number to call her back up with!' I say to my mother. Julian, I'm perspiring quite freely now.

" 'Bruce, believe me, sweetie, the party didn't leave a number,' she says to me.

" 'Ma, can it, and tell me the conversation substantially as it took place,' I say to my mother.

"Julian, the girl was something *else*. Moreover, she turns out to be Jewish. I knew there was something familiar about her. Julian, my mother told her I had gotten married recently. I say to my mother, 'Ma, how many times have I told you to forget you're my mother? You're my secretary. You're fired.' Julian, I had to hire her back. After all, she's my mother."

Binder drops Singer off at the Y.M.C.A., where he goes swimming three times a week.

Ah, Singer thinks, adultery. Blinds drawn at midday. Hear the ice-cream truck in the street! What is it playing—"Amapola"? If

I had only had the presence of mind to head *south* on Sullivan, I wouldn't have been tempted.

Singer encounters Skippy Mountjoy, Simon's father, in the shower room of the Y, which is vaulted and has more or less the same dimensions as an old railway coach, and is equally dusky, full of velleities and sorrows. Singer has never seen Skippy undressed; nor he him, to the best of his knowledge. Skippy is un-circumcised, slighter than Singer, paler, too, and has several promi-nent bruises here and there; Skippy drinks, and Singer presumes these are the result of traditional (comic?) falls. Skippy recalls in-evitably to Singer Simon, naked, frantically leaping past Singer's bedroom doorway on his way to the bathroom as though clearing an abyss. "Don't look!" he had cried. Singer wonders, Why is he ashamed to expose himself to me? This is the image I retain of him, he thinks—white, thin, exultant, aloft.

"You're not a member of the Y," Singer says.

"Why are you so concerned with form, Julian?" says Skippy.

At Tiffany's, Singer runs into Eleanor Barker; six or seven years ago, a photograph of her astride a five-gaited gelding, liver chestnut trimmed in white, sixteen hands, adorned his dresser mirror.

Singer has bought a tape measure in a silver case for his wife's thirty-sixth birthday. "Do you really think it's chic?" Singer says.

"You must love your wife very much," Eleanor Barker says, measuring his nose with it.

"I've never had less than an affectionate thought for you, Ee-zie-Beezie," Singer says. She had once stood naked (too) in his bathroom on Lexington Avenue at lunch time, he remembers with some yearning, swinging the pannier of lettuce over the tub like a censer.

Singer, an editor and writer, has lunch with Moritz, a di-rector of commercials, industrials, and institutionals, and Bloom, five years in daytime programming with a major network, in from the Coast, on the third floor of the Port Arthur, a Chinese restaurant. Climbing its narrow stairs, they are almost engulfed by a procession of descending Chinese in very long overcoats, and Bloom rolls his eyes. The Chinese had evidently been attending what Singer's father would have called a "function"; from the second-story landing, Singer sees upon many tables the involved and mysterious remains of their lunch, conventionally overhung with streamers of bluish smoke. If my mother were here, Singer thinks, she would say, "It must have been a very festive occasion."

The lunch is on Bloom, who, as he says to Singer, has said to himself only recently that Moritz and Singer got to meet one another, strike up some sparks. Moritz looks at Singer and does a thing with his eyebrows like Groucho Marx. Bloom slips his watch out of a vest pocket and hands it to Singer. Moritz fondles a bloodstone, a charm, hanging from the watch chain. "What's that—a fried marble?" he says.

"Get a load of the inscription," Bloom says to Singer. This reads, "To Buddy Bloom from Buddy Bloom, Five Years Devoted Service."

"I deserved it," Bloom says.

After an interval, Bloom says he is going to send Singer and Moritz a book he ordered five copies of at Pickwick, after hearing it described by a big *macher* in a conference as the kind of *Lilies of the Field* thing that's lying around untouched by human hands, begging with open arms to have its movie rights picked up for a song, song and a half. "Get a load of the plot line," Bloom says. "It'll refresh you." He relates it.

"So then what happens?" says Moritz.

"It's a very sensitive property," Bloom says. "The happenings are little. I see a universal ending, however. There she is in the clearing, in the woods—"

"Tweet, tweet," says Moritz. "Rustle, rustle in the underbrush."

"—rocking her little, illegitimate baby, and you pull the camera back, back, back or up, up, up, whichsoever, until all you can see of them is an insignificant dot in the midst of the universe."

"Why don't we do a film about alienation?" says Singer, who

has been drinking more beer than usual. "Why must the guineas have a corner on all the real alienation that's going around these days?"

"You're talking about something of a higher ebb, Julian," says Bloom.

"I see a party," says Singer. "They're all looking for someone. They know he hasn't left, but they can't find him."

"Where's he at, Julian?" Bloom says.

"He's lying under the coats on the bed," Singer says. "After the last guest leaves, the host and hostess find him there."

It had happened that way to him, Singer thinks, years ago— but is it a universal experience?

"Smiling enigmatically," says Moritz.

"I see an E.G. Marshall," says Bloom, "but younger, but thinner."

"With lips," says Moritz. "A younger, thinner E.G. Marshall with much lips."

"What's with this lips?" Bloom says.

"For smiling enigmatically, Buddy, it's a help," Moritz says. "You've got to keep thinking visual in this medium."

"*Garçon*," says Bloom.

"Buddy has a very real flair for languages," Moritz says.

Moritz and Singer walk along Canal Street together, agreeing it looks like snow. Wind turns the pages of cut-rate notebooks on sidewalk stands. Bloom had said he had to attend a conference. "I better hop a hack, *mes semblables*," he had said.

"Do you think Bloom really means to do a film?" Singer says. "Last month when he was in, he was talking about a TV package aimed specifically at homemakers."

"Buddy's a survivor," Moritz says. "He never lifts two feet off the ground at the same time. If Buddy can survive good in fillums, Buddy'll make fillums, and if Canal was a block north wouldn't it be Grand?"

Before taking Simon to Dr. Seidel, the dentist, Singer goes around to see Jay Donohue, to whom he hasn't spoken in six months, an estrangement dating from about the time he heard

Donohue had said several unwarranted things about him in his place of business, the Cuppa, a coffee-house—principally, that Singer had failed him in a time of personal crisis. Lately, Singer had been told that he and Donohue were being extremely puerile and that Singer should act his age and make a peaceful overture. "But I hold absolutely nothing against Jay," he would say. "In the Ovid paraphrase, '*Causa latet; vis est notissima.*'"

Donohue was formerly Singer's best friend, as Donohue always asserted. For instance, he would frequently say, "As my best friend, you have let me down." Moreover, Donohue had named his infant son Julian. "As Julie's godfather, you have certainly let him down," Donohue would say, too. Singer couldn't get the hang of the role of godfather, which he thought ill-defined, Donohue not only being an apostate but having often apostrophized the late Pope in this vein: "John, you'll have to lose a little weight if you want to ride in the Belmont." Nevertheless, this past Christmas Singer had bought Julie Donohue a share of Continental Can and announced his intention of purchasing an additional share each Christmas until Julie was twenty-one.

Singer and Donohue had met in New Jersey, in the Army, among the pines and the effusions of coal gas. Donohue, who had returned from Korea and was awaiting his imminent discharge, was one of the firemen for Headquarters and Headquarters Company; his fires invariably died out while he read *Tender Is the Night* in one gloomy fireroom or another, or called Vincent of Mamaroneck, a bookmaker with whom he placed bets on the pro baskets. After Donohue was reduced to private first class for telling his barracks sergeant he had foul breath, Singer arranged for him to be assigned to PIO, where Singer was NCOIC. There, Donohue spent the days drinking heavily sugared coffee, practicing his penmanship, in which he took great pride, composing wisecracks that he hoped to fit into his conversation in civilian life, and carrying on about the Blue Fairy, a character of his own invention, who, he said, had the power to reveal to the nescient crowd, from whose number Donohue excluded himself, its pitiable nature. Singer learned it was futile to expect Donohue to do anything more in the way of work once Donohue knew that he, Singer, had succumbed to his unremitting charm. "I am, quite frankly, the first *Übermensch* out of Belle Harbor," Donohue would say. "I am Jayzie-Dayzie, the Crowd Pleaser. I bloop singles over life's drawn-in infield."

The Cuppa is not open for business when Singer arrives. Donohue is seated at the counter, exhibiting one of his smooth shaves, drinking coffee out of a container, and opening an envelope, which contains bad checks. Save for a spotlight over Donohue's head, the room is dark; Donohue's stool rises out of the unexceptional refuse of the previous night. Singer feels as though he has wandered onstage, a feeling that is heightened when a porter and the espresso-machine man enter separately. During the speechifying that follows, the porter asks Singer to pick up his feet so he can sweep beneath them, and the machine man mutely fills tea balls at Singer's elbow.

Donohue says, "Just how aware are you of Hubert Humphrey's capabilities? You would be doing yourself a great disservice if you underestimated them." Then he says, "I may have to cut this short, inasmuch as I'm expecting a couple of fellas from the Bureau to drop by. I'm helping them out on a certain matter you'll be reading about someday." Next, he says, "A Marciano could never lick a Clay. You may disabuse yourself of that notion. Kid'd win it big." Finally, he says, "What I might as well tell you, as long as we're together, is that you're a cheapskate in considerably more meaningful terms than being a bad tipper, that you have no sense of social obligations, that you are rude — in the second dictionary definition — and that you have an upper-middle-class, upper-West Side, Jewish-Ethical Culture outlook."

"I hadn't realized that," Singer says.

"I'm amazed," Donohue says. "It's general knowledge. I venture to say I could name twelve or fourteen people who are abundantly aware of it."

"Who?" Singer says.

"Eleanor Barker, for one," Donohue says.

"Eezie-Beezie?" Singer says. "I hadn't realized that, either."

"I had expected you to say, 'Well, that's the way I am,'" Donohue says. "Now I'm merely astonished. You're absolutely insistent on your right to be unaware, aren't you? Be that as it may, it no longer concerns me. I happen to have sufficient evidence to confirm my belief that I'm significantly on the move nowadays.

I've been having dinner, with some frequency, with an attorney who sails with John Lindsay—you probably wouldn't recognize the name if I chose to disclose it, as he stays in the background—and only last week I met Bobby Kennedy at a cocktail party, and he listened quite closely for more than ten minutes to what I had to say. Very frankly, Julian, I don't think there's a place for you in my life any longer. You'll have to excuse me now. I have to make a few phone calls. I'm trying to get ahold of my architect. I might as well tell you, I'm opening a Cuppa East."

It's my fault for being swayed by popular opinion, Singer thinks. I hadn't realized how successfully I had forgotten him. Now, when he has made it clear that I should despise him, I know I will not be able to forget that I forgive him.

"What am I supposed to do about Julie's Continental Can?" Singer says. "I'm custodian under the New York Uniform Gifts to Minors Act."

"That's for you to decide," Donohue says. "Robert," he says to the machine man, "make Julian a nice cappuccino."

While Dr. Seidel, the dentist, is working on Simon, Singer sits before an electric heater in the waiting room, reading *Photoplay*. His mother had taken him to Dr. Seidel (Uncle Harry) when he was Simon's age, Singer remembers. The chart depicting huge, ruined teeth (pyorrhea!); the view of the Hotel Ansonia, through whose windows voice coaches in negligees could be seen passing back and forth; and Dr. Seidel's sweetened breath link Singer, inadequately, with Simon. The dental assistant tells Singer that his mother had had the next appointment. "She had to cancel because of a conflict with her French lesson," she says. " 'C'est la vie,' Mrs. Singer said. I told her she'd be missing you two. She said to tell you both to wear something on your heads, as it was going to snow."

Somewhat later, Singer hears three anguished screams. He can't tell whether or not they are being uttered in a dream—has he fallen asleep?—but they are evidently calls for help to which he is not responding.

When Simon comes out of Dr. Seidel's office, the remains of tears shine like scales on his cheeks.

"Did Uncle Harry hurt you?" Singer says.

"It's an imperfect world," Simon says. "Us Jews were born to suffer."

"You're not Jewish," says Singer.

After dinner, Singer plays the piano, largo, with a great deal of pedalling, while he sings Christmas carols with Simon, although Christmas has passed.

> "Good King Wenceslas look'd out,
> On the Feast of Stephen;
> When the snow lay round about,
> Deep and crisp and even.
> Brightly shone the moon that night,
> Though the frost was cruel,
> When a poor man came in sight,
> Gath'ring winter fuel."

Ah, Singer thinks, as he pounds on, that "fu-oo-el" recalls old assemblies, descants, innocence, and so forth. For what may be the first time, Singer pays attention to the lyrics, and is greatly moved by the moral account of the monarch, page, and poor man.

"Please don't take any offense or anything, Julian," Simon says, "but are you aware that you're crying?"

"I am?" Singer says.

"Are you tired of living?" he says.

Singer turns from the music to look at Simon, who steadfastly returns his gaze. He is acknowledging our secret, Singer thinks. He knows that we will never get together, that as we grow older we will grow farther apart.

While Simon is taking his bath, the doorbell rings. Singer answers it; Skippy Mountjoy is in the vestibule. Skippy is no longer admitted to Singer's apartment. Bernice, the baby-sitter, who greatly outweighs Skippy, had given him the bum's rush when he arrived half in the bag one night while Singer and his wife were at the Crandon Park Motel, on Key Biscayne, celebrating their first wedding anniversary. "Mr. Singer, Mr. Mountjoy got to pull himself together," Bernie Bear had said when the Singers came home. (What about my sober rages? Singer thinks. Am I being un-Christian?) Skippy is allowed to enter as far as the vestibule, where, as though in a kind of dingy lock, he has low (conspiratorial?) conversations with Simon by the mailboxes.

Skippy is mantled with snow. He is carrying a stack of used books like firewood, keeping the topmost in place with his chin, so that his face is somewhat raised to Heaven. The books are *Strait Is the Gate*; *Palgrave's Golden Treasury*; *Four Years in Paradise*, by Osa Johnson; *Britain: An Official Handbook, 1962 Edition*; *Cuba: Prophetic Island*, by Waldo Frank; *The Bridge of San Luis Rey*; and *Webster's Encyclopedic Dictionary*.

"But he's gotten his presents," Singer says, holding the door open with his hip to accept the sodden books. "Christmas is past."

"What am I supposed to do with them?" Singer says, putting the books down on the coffee table, where a sansevieria is dying in a *chinoiserie* pot. "He said they were for Simon, but Simon's too young to read them and this one *no one's* supposed to read." He thumbs through *Britain: An Official Handbook*. "It's all about domestic hollow ware and Transport Users' Consultative Committees."

Singer's wife takes it from him. She looks at the end papers, which have been defaced by a child with a purple crayon.

"What are *you* crying for?" Singer says. "What's wrong, Eezie-Beezie?"

"Whozie whatzie?" she says.

Singer answers the telephone.

"Julian? Bruce. Binder."

"Yes."

"Julian, do you happen to recollect that particular topic we were discussing this morning?"

"Yes."

"Julian, it's been preying on my mind consistently. Do you think I should make an overt move or something, or let circumstances do with me what they may, or what?"

"That's for you to decide."

Singer sees a note on the pad by the telephone, which reads,

Singe-
r is a
lier
and
pennie-
less.

"Julian, am I rationalizing? Just tell me that."

Singer finds a second note stuck into the frame of his dresser mirror, where he used to keep Eleanor Barker's photograph. It reads,

Life is
nothing
to you
realy.

"Simon, get out of that bathtub," Singer shouts before the bathroom door, and gets no reply. "Simon, I'm telling you to climb out of that tub this instant. You've been in there forever." There is still no response. "If you don't come out by the time I count three, I'm coming in after you. One. Two. Two and a half. Two and three-quarters. Two and seven-eighths. Here I come, ready or not." Singer flings open the door. "Three!" Simon is lying face down in the tub. "Simon!" Singer cries, stooping. Simon rises slowly out of the grimy water. He is wearing his snorkel and mask, through which he looks at Singer, astonished.

After Simon is in bed, Singer gets a telephone call from Buddy Bloom.

"Julian. Buddy Bloom. Listen, Julian, Buddy wants you to do this contestant thing for him up here at the Plaza right away, *molto* quicko. We're in the midst of rehearsing my cockamamy game show. I've got to do a runthrough for the big *machers domani*, and there's a very real dearth of contestants. Everybody's letting me down like I'm a sinking ship or something. All I've got is Arnold."

"Arnold?"

"My mother's chauffeur. You'll meet him. He's delightful as a human being. Arnold drove Mother in from Westport to be a celebrity for me. Celebrities I've got. Moritz is a celebrity. Julian, Buddy needs you bad."

Singer takes a cab to the Plaza, and in Bloom's suite, with its extensive view of the snowy Park, is introduced to Arnold, the Negro chauffeur, and Mrs. Bloom.

Bloom says, "In the developmental phase, we're calling it 'So You Think You've Got Troubles.' "

"Buddy, it doesn't scan," Moritz says.

"Ritzie, I'm the first in my neighborhood to admit it," Bloom says. "Frankly, the show's derivative. We're liable to come up with television's lowest ebb, but we're satisfying the basic appeal of the game show—it has a basis in genuine reality. Wha' hoppen ees thees: the contestant has a problem, like Arnold's here is 'I'm in love with a woman, but I think she's after my money.' We have to exercise great care about the type problem. We don't want anyone appearing with a terminal case of medulla oblongata or anything. A guffaw about death is in very bad taste. The problem is flashed to the studio audience and to the mouth readers at home. Then the panel of celebrities tries to guess it, à la *What's My Line?* The money is very little, and there's absolutely no quiz element at all in it."

"I was never personally involved with the little old organ-grinder, or whomsoever, on *The $64,000 Question,*" Moritz says. "I mean, I find out you know more than me—than I?—I quit."

"Whether the panel guesses the problem or not, they give the contestant two, three minutes personalized advice and comfort,"

Bloom says. "I foresee a panel composed of a Dr. Joyce Brothers, a Helen Gurley Brown, maybe a Lenny Bernstein, for someone a little bit masterful."

"What's my problem?" Singer says.

"First of all, you're not you, for our purposes," Bloom says. "The way we do this is we give you a *nom de* show purely at random. Say, for convenience' sake, you're Humboldt Current or somebody, you're married, you have one child, and your trouble is 'I don't get along with my boss, but I can't afford to quit.' Julian, don't worry, it's going to be loads of fun. Just put yourself in Humboldt Current's shoes for five minutes, and remember, Buddy says, 'You're saving my life.' "

"This is all new to Arnold," Mrs. Bloom says in Singer's ear, nudging him with an elbow. "Look at him. He's getting a big kick out of it."

The panelists, Mrs. Bloom and Moritz, sit on a couch behind a coffee table. Bloom, the moderator, sits in a chair at one end of the couch, with an empty chair beside him for the contestants that Bloom indicates Singer should occupy.

"Blah, blah, blah," says Bloom. "And, blah, blah, blah. So you think *you've* got troubles! Just listen to our first contestant, Mr. Humboldt Current, who's married and has one child. How do you do, Mr. Current, and let me introduce our panel, blah, blah, blah."

Mrs. Bloom and Moritz fail to guess Singer's problem. Bloom tells it to them.

"Mr. Current," says Mrs. Bloom, "what sort of work is it you do?"

Ah, Singer thinks, I should have been thinking about that.

"I work in the flower shop here at the Plaza," Singer says after a moment. "We specialize in the centerpieces and other floral décor for the various functions here."

"I see," says Mrs. Bloom.

"Ma," says Bloom. "Sparkle, sparkle."

"Now, just what is it about this employer of yours that's causing you this distress?" Mrs. Bloom says.

"He's always picking on my creations," Singer says. "Like today, he said I was out of touch with mimosa."

"An aesthetic judgment," says Moritz.

"I'm terribly sorry," says Mrs. Bloom.

"Ma," says Bloom, "you've got to play for a few *farshtunkene* guffaws."

"Mr. Current, I don't think you have a problem," says Moritz. "I think you're being very immature and unduly sensitive. No offense, Mr. Current, but have you ever considered you might be a trifle paranoid? Buddy, can we go that far? What do you think?"

"This is all very amoebic, Ritzie," Bloom says. "We're groping for a shape here. Let it play."

"Perhaps your root problem, Mr. Current, is that, subconsciously or no, you're ashamed of your name," Moritz says. "Have you ever thought of changing it?"

"I wouldn't pursue that, Ritzie," Bloom says. "The name in this instance is purely fortuitous, an *entremets*."

"I think Mr. Current has a valid point about the mimosa," Mrs. Bloom says. "It's very delicate to handle, I so happen to know."

"I don't think Mr. Current has given his problem sufficient thought," Moritz says.

"Moritz, you're asking me to intellectualize when I feel it in *here*," Singer says, clutching his stomach.

"That's the zinger, Julian," Bloom says.

"Have you ever experienced some person yanking your mimosa out of your frog because he has no understanding?" Singer says. "What do you know about personal relationships? What do you know about the creative process? What do you know about art?"

"He's wonderful, Buddy," Mrs. Bloom says. "He's so overwrought. Arnold, pay attention. Remember when it's your turn. You *do* have a problem, don't you, Mr. Current?"

"I've got many problems, Mrs. Bloom," Singer says.

"Can I be of any help, dearie?" says Mrs. Bloom.

"We're not set up for that kind of colloquy in this particular show, Ma," Bloom says. "Mr. Current, sincerely, I'm sure the panel is only trying to help you, and that there's no personal animus involved whatsoever. Blah, blah, blah. So you think *you've* got troubles. Our next contestant has… You get up now, Julian. Arnold, you come forward."

"I think you're going to have to rethink this, Buddy," says Moritz.

"That was a very poignant bit Julian did with his stomach," Bloom says. "Ooh, I felt it."

Before he goes to bed, Singer takes Josh and Jake, the dachshunds, for their walk. "My friends the dogs," he says, calling them so he can fasten their leashes. As is his custom, Singer intends to lead them down Sullivan, across Spring, past the lighted windows of the S. S. Bocce Social Club, Inc., and the Regular Republican Organization, Second A. D. West, to a place where a few meagre tufts of grass grow out of cracks in the sidewalk by the public scale—a spot he calls Poo Gardens. The snow has stopped, but the wind is blowing it about like spindrift, and the moon is revealed. Josh plunges off; Jake refuses to budge. Singer pulls on his leash, but Jake is adamant. "Now, Jakie, why can't you be a decent fellow and take an invigorating stroll with your brother and me—and I?" Singer says. Jake looks up at him. "God damn it, Josh, quit tugging," Singer cries, then gives a tremendous yank on Jake's leash. Before Jake's collar breaks, Singer, horrified, hears him choking. Singer drops to his knees in the snow. Josh, in the meantime, has wound his leash around the standard of a No Parking sign. All this, Singer thinks. It would never play. "Jakie, please don't run away," he says. Jake jumps up to lick Singer's face at the same instant that Singer reaches down to embrace him, with the result that Singer is struck a terrific blow in the left eye by Jake's nose, knocking him flat. Lying thus, embedded in the snow, quite out of sight, Singer is faintly aware that his face is being laved by the persistent strokes of the dogs' great, steaming, loving tongues.

2

"I am withering on the vine," Daisy Singer told her husband, sitting on the plush couch (from the Salvation Army) that she said, when she was in the dumps, was bluebottle-fly blue. "Whither thou goest . . ." Singer said, and Daisy shot him between the eyes with her water pistol. That night, he had been to a dinner at the Plaza—the Terrace Room—on the occasion of the tenth anniversary of the magazine for which he worked. It was, too, the tenth of these dinners that he had attended, and, as usual, he vowed between the *petite marmite* and the *mousse de poisson* that it would be his last. When the eleventh rolled around, he and Daisy would be dining at home in Malibu, or near there—far away, certainly, and by the sea. Singer's knowledge of Malibu was limited to fleeting glances; he had been driven that way once or twice by an outfielder, one of the Angels, he was interviewing. No, it wouldn't be time to eat yet, Singer, who was fairly precise, reflected; he had failed to take the time zones into account.

Singer had married Daisy shortly after the eighth dinner, when he was thirty-three and no less disappointed than he had been at thirty-two. He had felt he might actually leave the magazine once he was married, and go on, like a dusty, ardent, footsore nineteenth-century hero, to less frivolous things; he might do something in life—write a book, for instance, speak for his age.

Singer infrequently admitted to himself that he had got married so he would be able to quit; he didn't want to wind up, if things didn't pan out, all alone with many empty pages of Corrasable Bond, rolling cheerlessly hither and thither in his typing chair like an invalid.

At the dinner, he sat in the back, near a torrential fountain that largely drowned out the speeches. Despite his tenure, Singer hardly knew his tablemates; they seemed to be chiefly ad salesmen named Sandy. On his left was one of the libel lawyers, who kept writing notes inside matchbooks and passing them clockwise; they never reached Singer. On Singer's right was an elderly proofreader, wearing a lot of garnets, who rose in the midst of the address by the managing editor. For a moment, Singer thought she was going to climb on her chair and harangue her colleagues. On what, Singer wondered — the misuse of the serial comma? Immorality in the copy department? Next, Singer feared she was going to get sick on the centerpiece, for she was deeply bowing in that direction. Instead, with a great "Hoo," she blew out a candle that was stuck among the flowers. "It was about to set fire to the mimosa," she said, retaking her seat. Singer turned to contemplate the falling water, which reminded him of the celebrated fountain by Hubert Robert at the Princesse de Guermantes'; he had been trying to get Daisy to read Proust instead of spending her time "snooping around the department stores," as she invariably put it.

Two hours later, when Singer, having walked home in the rain that had been forecast, let himself into their apartment — one old, lofty room distinguished by a grand piano and a crystal chandelier — a very large dog with slanty yellow eyes was sitting by the door. As he took off his rubbers and advanced, it held out a paw. "Hello," Singer said, shaking it. "Whose dog are you?"

Daisy was sitting on the couch, looking at *Elle*.

"Hello, Daisy," Singer said. "Whose dog is it?"

"I don't know," she said. "You're home early."

"They were choosing up teams to slide down the banisters to the Palm Court," he said. "What's with the dog?"

"What's with the tone of voice?"

"It's merely my tone of perpetual astonishment," Singer said, putting his rubbers on the classified section of last Sunday's *Times*, which he had previously laid out on the floor next to the front door. "You don't read French," he said, sitting beside his wife. The dog sat on the other side of the coffee table, looming over it, gazing with peremptory intimacy at Singer. "Please tell me about this dog."

"I suppose Gerda Winters was there in one of her dresses from Design Research," Daisy said.

"At another table."

"Was she one of your girl friends?"

"Now that you mention it, you've asked me that before."

"Once again, all together now, was she?"

"In a way."

"What's this 'in a way'?"

"It's a manner of speaking," he said.

"Without communication."

"Not every question admits of a yes-or-no answer. There are shades."

"Shade is not enlightenment, Julian."

"Daisy, there are over four hundred comedians out of work. She was one of my girl friends, but a long time ago."

"How long?"

"Around 1960."

"Six years is not a long time. Why did you like her?"

"I don't know. It must have been convenience or circumstance or something. That's the way those things used to happen."

"The way it happened with me," Daisy said.

"Why are you always so defensive?"

"Because you're so offensive. And remember, Julian, a good defense beats a good offense every time."

She went to the piano and began to play and sing:

> "Ah, how sweet, ah, how sweet,
> how sweet it is to love.
> Ah! Ah! Ah! how gay is young desire!"

After a while, Singer said, "It keeps looking at me. I think it expects me to do a trick."

"His name is Jimmy," Daisy said. "He followed me home."

"I thought Jimmy was what you were going to call our son, if and when we have one."

"I got tired of waiting."

"But you can't keep it. It belongs to someone else. It shakes hands. It's too big. Stop eating my rubbers, you!"

"Do you know," she said, "you've never once made love to me the way you did the very first time? That was the only time you ever really wanted to."

"A cat would be a better pet."

"We might as well play gin."

"You've won the last four games," he said. "It's too discouraging."

"Don't you think *I've* been discouraged? I've been under zero for two years. How do you think it feels?"

"I'll play if you get rid of the dog."

"I only let him in because it was raining," she said.

They played Hollywood, and Singer won all the boxes.

"A triple schneider," he said in his Peter Lorre accent. "I have been rewenged."

It was then that Daisy said, "I am withering on the vine."

When they were in bed beneath the acanthus wreath on the ceiling—the counterpart of the one above the piano, from the center of which their chandelier, a wedding present, was suspended—Daisy turned to Singer in the dark and said, "Please change the score." He stuck out an arm and found that her cheek was wet. A few minutes later, he watched her get out of bed. She lay along the wall, so she had to push herself to the foot of the bed like a downhill skier poling at the beginning of his run. There, by the loom of the piano, it was darker, and she disappeared, as though, indeed, she had dropped out of sight. For an instant, one of the dog's eyes, reflecting an otherwise undetectable light, shone like a dragon's. Singer heard the door close and presumed that his wife and Jimmy had gone.

Toward morning, Daisy returned. Singer didn't ask her what she had done with Jimmy, for he felt vaguely at fault. Subsequently, Daisy got Baby, a calico kitten, from Bide-A-Wee.

"She has Siamese blood," Daisy said.

"How can you tell?" Singer said.

"If you say something to her, she'll talk to you. That's a characteristic of Siamese cats. Say something to her, Julian."

"What could I possibly say?" Singer said.

Daisy next found little Butter in front of the Butterick Building.

"How can you be so positive she doesn't already belong to someone?" Singer asked.

"If you have anything nice to say to Butter, she'll close her eyes," Daisy said. "Cats always close their eyes when you talk to them, if they like what you say."

These two cats frequently raced across Singer's upturned face while he was sleeping. "Daisy," he would say. "I don't think it's fair."

"Look out, Julian," Daisy would reply, "here they come again."

One evening, a few months later, after Daisy had lost her ninth consecutive game of gin, Singer told her that she now owed him a hundred and thirty-seven dollars and fifty cents.

"You're doing it on purpose," Daisy said. "You're trying to do me in. You know I can't go on this way."

"I play to win," said Singer.

"It's the way you win," she said. "Other people don't win the way you do. You win with an overbearing manner."

"I'm not overbearing. I'm an aesthete."

"Julian, you're simply not an aesthete."

"What am I?"

"You're a monster. Furthermore, I quit."

"You can't quit. You owe me a hundred and thirty-seven dollars and fifty cents, and you have no way of paying me back. We have a joint checking account, but I'm the sole depositor. To all purposes, Daisy, you're an indentured servant."

"I quit," she said, flinging the cards toward the piano. "The game is *tutto finito*. The marriage is *tutto finito*. The joint checking account is *tutto finito*." She took her handbag from the top of the jelly cupboard that served as her bureau and, opening it, began to throw her charge-account cards and plates toward the piano, too.

"Daisy, you can't speak Italian," Singer said.

"Thatsa what you think," she said. "*Addio*, Lord & Taylor. *Addio*, Saks Fifth Avenue, you sweetheart. Mmmm. Mmmm." She kissed the plate. "I'm going to miss you. *Addio*, Bergdorf's, Bonwit's, Bloomie's. . . . Baby, Butter, come to Mama. Me and my cats are checking out."

"Stay," said Singer, under the piano, picking up the playing cards, which had cherubs riding bicycles on their backs. "I'll go."

Singer moved in with his parents for the time being. The following week, he went to Boston to do a story on a basketball coach. His hotel room overlooked Commonwealth Avenue, and toward evening he would stand at the window, saying, "Is awareness enough?" Below, on the mall, were statues of statesmen and generals and so forth, so green and worn in the serene residue of light they might well have been erected on the bottom of the sea, great, slow groupers nibbling at their pommels and at the blank bronze pages of their open books.

The day before he left Boston, Singer got a message to call a Mr. Gross in New York. Mr. Gross turned out to be Daisy's lawyer and wanted to discuss terms of settlement. Several weeks later, when Singer was in Tampa interviewing a lady golfer, Mr. Gross phoned him at his motel on Dale Mabry Boulevard, where painted snow lay heaped on the letters of the air-conditioning signs. Mr. Gross wanted to know when Singer was returning, for he had to sign the separation agreement and a power of attorney for the Mexican lawyer. After speaking to Mr. Gross, Singer went down to the heated pool and leafed through his often incomprehensible notes, searching for a lead and an ender.

The day Daisy left for El Paso, she called Singer at his office and asked him if he would feed Baby and Butter while she was gone. "I'd have asked someone else," she said, "but you're the only person I can trust, and they love you." She added that she would leave the key under the doormat. Singer said it wasn't necessary, as he still seemed to have his.

Late that afternoon, on the crosstown bus, slowly heading for the apartment, he wondered what sort of note Daisy would have left him. He decided it would be jocular, and began framing a suitably dispassionate reply. The discovery that there wasn't any note, merely a can of cat food on top of the piano, and the sight of Baby, asleep in her accustomed place on the piano bench, brought Singer, unexpectedly, to the verge of tears.

Baby jumped off the piano bench, and Singer, holding the can of cat food much in the manner, he thought, that Adam used to be depicted, eyes turned to Heaven, with the unbitten apple, sat down. Open upon the piano was sheet music, its covers bordered with abundant laurel—"Salve, O Rosa, Amabil Fior," evidently the last piece Daisy had played. If Singer had ever heard it, he could not remember how it went. Above his head, the dusty chandelier hung from its leafy canopy, the crystals as obscure as cocoons. "From time to time, I would climb the ladder and polish them with vinegar," Singer said gravely, under his breath, as though reading from his autobiography. Looking for Butter in her favorite places, Singer saw, on either end of the mantelpiece, the gilded chevaliers still drawing their swords, and on the sills of the high windows, through which now shone faintly ecclesiastical light, the sweet-potato vines he and Daisy had planted and the Jerusalem cherry he had got her at the Grand Union for their first wedding anniversary. "After its original fruit had fallen," Singer murmured, on his hands and knees, peering under the couch, "it had never borne more."

After abandoning the search for Butter, Singer sat on the couch with Baby in his lap. In the fireplace before him was a vase of dried plume celosia; remains of gastropods were embedded in the marble top of the coffee table, upon which were an empty ashtray from a restaurant in Mayfair and half a cup of cold coffee. "Love never altered this room, Jack Donne of the Town," Singer told the cat.

Then Daisy phoned.

"Why are you crying?" she said.

"I can't find Butter," he said.

"Don't worry. She always turns up."

"Did Mr. Gross get you a room at the El Paso Hilton?"

"Yes."

"Does it look out on a little park?"

"Why?"

"There's an alligator in a fountain down there. I used to see it from my window. You've always been fond of dumb animals."

"Why are you always looking out of windows?"

"I once did a story in El Paso—the Sun Kings. It's a baseball team. Whatever happened to Jimmy?"

"I don't know. I went into a coffee shop to try to lose him, but he kept waiting for me on the sidewalk. He wouldn't go away. Then I found that in the back there was another way out."

"I didn't mean that you had to get rid of him right away."

"I was trying to please you, Julian," she said. Butter materialized on the mantelpiece. "Daisy, Butter's back," he said. "I'll be along, too," she said. "You're not going to Juárez?"

"I'm still at the East Side Airlines Terminal. I have a feeling I'm going to schneider you."

"Play and weep."

"Wait up."

"I may not be here," he said.

"Oh."

"I've got to go home and get my toothbrush."

"For one night, Julian, use your finger."

"I'll buy one at the drugstore. It's nearer."

"How could I have ever left you?" she said.

But Singer didn't leave. He went into the bathroom and filled Daisy's water pistol. Then he stood by the front door with his back against the wall, holding the gun before his heart, the barrel pointing up, like a melancholy duellist at the point of turning, and waited, trembling, for his wife.

3

Julian Singer and his wife, Daisy, lived on the third floor, in the rear, in a renovated brownstone in Greenwich Village. Their bedroom overlooked a deep garden that rarely was visited by sunlight. In mid-October, the poplars were becoming bare; a few petunias lingered; and the chrysanthemums were not yet in flower, principally on account of the drought. Singer, in whom black bile generously flowed, worked at home, at the foot of the great brass bedstead in which he and Daisy imperfectly slept. Above his desk, which trembled whenever he erased something, was an old hand-colored engraving showing a walrus on a floe. The ignorant artist had endowed the beast with soulful, utterly human eyes and a human nose, so that the effect, Singer thought, was rather of a man somehow imprisoned in a walrus suit, or of an unhappy hybrid. When Singer looked up from his work, he frequently found himself encountering the gaze of this unfortunate, apparently incompetent creature, which (who?) seemed to be imploring him to do something about its condition. "But what can I do?" Singer was wont to say, almost out loud.

Lately, however, he had totally abandoned it to its arctic fate, and had taken instead to gazing out the window at the birds that appeared in the garden. Many years ago, Singer had been an unsuccessful bird watcher; indeed, once in the heart of the Ramble, in

Central Park, he had become so bedevilled by a treeful of autumn warblers, his inability to identify them, that he had to go home to bed, and he had forsworn bird watching. Nonetheless, he still had his old Peterson (now that his interest had been rekindled, he had purchased the Second Revised and Enlarged Edition) and a pair of binoculars his father had bought for him at a duty-free shop, while on a Caribbean cruise.

From September 20th until October 16th, Singer, vigilant, neglecting his work, his desk unshaken, had, with the aid of these glasses, which almost always hung about his neck on a black ribbon, spied a brown thrasher, a yellow-throat, many chickadees, a yellow-throated vireo (?), a thrush (sp. ?), three blue jays, a northern white-breasted nuthatch, two Nashville warblers, several ruby-crowned kinglets, a common goldfinch, a black-throated green warbler, a sparrow (sp. ?), a fox sparrow (?), a tree sparrow (?), a towhee, a hairy woodpecker, an olive-backed thrush, and a warbler (sp. ?). The "?" denoted that his identification was suspect; "sp. ?" meant he was uncertain of the precise species. As is evident, he was particularly inept at determining the sparrows, which stayed near the ground, in the shadows under the rhododendrons, and were furtive and similar.

Singer was astonished that any birds chanced to alight in the garden, which belonged to his landlords, Alan and Paul. He assumed that the birds were largely migratory, flying south on long, perilous, exact, and obscure journeys. Passing over the city, had they descried this speck of green from their great, fluent height? Why had they chosen to tarry here? Some remained for hours; others flashed by, like scraps of paper at the mercy of the wind. Alan and Paul's cats, weary of watching television, stalked them. On October 10th, one managed to catch a chickadee.

Singer had entered the birds in what he called a house list, noting, too, the date, time, and weather of each observation; he intended eventually to compile supplementary day lists, which would have significance after several years. In the past, he had kept a life list, place lists, and year lists, in addition to innumerable day lists. The following, for example, is his day list for March 3, 1946:

THE RESERVOIR AND THE RAMBLE
Total: 16. Sunny & clear.
Temp. 48°. Slight wind.
12:30 p.m.—1:30 p.m. at Reservoir;
3 p.m.—5 p.m. in Ramble.

	1.	Pigeon
	2.	English sparrow
(25)	3.	Starling
(200)	4.	Herring gull
(19)	5.	Mallard
(66)	6.	Black duck
(1)	7.	Pied-billed grebe*
(1)	8.	Sparrow hawk
(1)	9.	Scaup (sp. ?)
(2)	10.	Robin
(10)	11.	Purple grackle
(2)	12.	Fox sparrow
(3)	13.	White-throated sparrow
(10)	14.	Slate-colored junco
(1)	15.	Downy woodpecker
(1)	16.	Blue Jay

*Seen at 20 feet in Reservoir, diving,
swimming, and flying. All marks
observed. Small size noted.

After he had given up looking at birds, Singer had made up girl lists, recording, by month and year, and in one great master list, all the girls he had slept with, and the number of times he had slept with each. The following, for instance, is his month list for February, 1959:

Eleanor Barker	3
Alice Walker	5
Angela Moody	1
Sylvia Friedman	1
Elayne Lubow	1
TOTAL:	11

He had stopped keeping up the girl lists in May, 1963, for Daisy had been the sole entry for four months running, and it was clear that they were going to get married, and that he was going to be faithful.

Prior to his resumption of birding, the only list Singer had been making was one in which he set forth the minute fluctuations in his weight. For example:

August 23, 1965 : 175
” 24 ” : 175
” 25 ” : 174
” 26 ” : 174½
” 27 ” : 173¼

On October 17th, which in 1965 fell on a Sunday, Singer awoke and lay for an instant on his back with his eyes shut, futilely listening for any "lisping dreamy *zoo zee zoo zoo zee*"s, "well-enunciated *witchity-witchity-whitchity-witch*"es, or "*I wish to see Miss Beecher; please please please ta meetcha.*" Instead, he heard Daisy saying, "Fourteen and three-quarters."

"Fourteen and three-quarters what?" Singer said.

"Inches," Daisy said.

"Why?"

"I'm finding out how far apart we've grown."

"I see," said Singer, who didn't, and opened his eyes. Directly above his nose was one end of a tape measure. Looking to his right, he saw that Daisy was holding the other end above her nose. Abruptly, she released the tape and it whizzed back into the case. She said, "This morning the distance between us, measuring from the center of your nose to the center of mine, was precisely fourteen and three-quarters inches. Yesterday, when I succeeded in taking my reading without awakening you, the distance was only fourteen and one-quarter inches. Therefore, we are incontrovertibly growing apart. I sometimes get the feeling, Julian, that marriage was your second choice in life, and that you turned to it only when you found that you were failing in the mode you originally preferred."

At that moment, a little yellow bird, a warbler, flew in the window and perched on the shade of Singer's desk lamp, whose base was an apothecary jar upon which was written, "Elect: Diaphaenix." (When Daisy had first seen the lamp in Singer's apartment on Lexington Avenue, she had added, "And restore responsible government to City Hall.")

"Where the hell are my binocs?" Singer urgently whispered, rising.

"Binocs!" she said. "Julian, the bird's *nearby*."

"Daisy," he said, stealthily approaching the desk, "we happen to have very high ceilings. Please don't horse around. For God's sake, gently hand me my binocs, and if you find it absolutely necessary to converse, keep it sotto-voce."

She found the glasses and delivered them to him. He took them wordlessly, without averting his eyes from the bird, rather like a surgeon accepting a hemostat.

"All right," he said. "Now, Daisy, hear this. Get the Peterson from the radiator cover and open it to the warbler plates. Are you ready? Here goes. Absence of wing bars—"

The warbler left the shade and began flying around the ceiling. Singer tracked it with the glasses.

"No eye-ring or conspicuous eyeline. What is it, Daisy?"

"Who the hell knows?" Daisy said.

Singer let the glasses fall to his chest, where they hung, suspended by their ribbon, and whisked the Peterson out of his wife's hands. "Jesus Christ, Daisy, you're open to *spring* warblers," he said. "This is October! Do me a favor, will you, and kindly turn to autumn warblers." He gave her back the book.

" 'Confusing Fall Warblers,' " she read.

"My sweetheart," he said.

The bird landed on the brass headboard. Singer tiptoed up and grabbed it.

"Do you think it might conceivably be a Philadelphia vireo?" Daisy ventured, turning pages.

"Will you please, please, *please* stop hacking around," Singer said. "Just hand me the book. You know, you're really pushing our marriage, Daisy. You're engulfing me with a sense of despair, sort of. . . . Jesus, it's struggling." Singer ran to the window.

"Its feathers are falling out all over the carpet, Julian," Daisy said.

"Do me a favor and shut up," he said. The bird was dangling upside down as Singer, anguished, clutched it by the legs. He released it finally, and it flew over the garden and out of sight. Singer sat down at his desk, holding his head in his hands. "You see what I mean, Daisy," he said. "Nothing *works.*"

"Did it go, '*Chi, chi, chi,*' and so forth?" Daisy inquired.

"I doubt it," Singer said.

"Did it have a beady black eye?"

"*Mezzo mezzo,*" he said, disconsolately.

"I do believe it was an immature Wilson's warbler," she said. "Peterson says they have 'no outstanding marks of any kind.' Like you, my darling."

"It was sitting in my own bedroom, and I'm going to have to put it down as a probable," Singer said.

"Why don't you take the feathers up to the Audubon Society?" Daisy said, stooping to pick them up. "Maybe they can identify it for you from them."

"How am I going to explain how they got in my possession? There's a law against capturing songbirds without a permit."

"But you were trying to *set it free.*"

"It's difficult to establish intent."

"Maybe it'll come back," she said. "You never know, Julian. It could be flying in circles."

"It's going south, Daisy. It's undoubtedly over New Jersey by now. Where does Peterson say it winters?"

"Central America."

Singer envisioned the mutilated bird beating over the Caribbean, perhaps at such a height it could divine the marbled earth's imperceptible curve, at night the hemispheres of its black eyes containing the reflection of the heavens, descending at last into one of the green, rainy republics, or, more likely, unable to keep up with its fellows, overwhelmed by an electrical storm, plummeting into a suburb in Virginia. This last imagination caused Singer to clap his right hand over his eyes.

"Get rid of the glasses," he said, lifting them over his head much like an archbishop divesting himself of his pallium, and thrusting them at Daisy. "I'm unworthy."

That afternoon, Singer's mother came to visit, her bracelets formidably rattling, bearing gladioli from Irene Hayes ("A little ray of sunshine," she said they were), a number of lampshade patterns, and what she termed "a surprise." This turned out to be a sheaf of Singer's old piano music.

"You two live in the *dark*," she said. "And, of course, need I say there are the *stairs*. Just guess where I found them, Julian?" she said, referring here to the music.

"I give up," Singer said.

"But you didn't even *try*," his mother said.

"Guess, Julian," Daisy said.

"In, in, in . . ." Singer said.

"He's blue," Daisy explained.

"Oh, well," Singer's mother said. "In that case." Humming, she began whipping off lampshades and trying out the patterns.

"What would you think if Julian and I decided to go on tour?" Daisy asked her mother-in-law. "He would tell jokes and I would dance."

"Oh, do you dance?" Mrs. Singer said. "I once won a tortoise-shell cigarette case in a ballroom-dancing competition aboard the old *Berengaria*. It was a ballroom dance, in that differently colored balloons were tied to the ladies' ankles and the band began to play and in the end whoever had the last balloon that was still intact won the prize. You should have heard the popping. The men were stepping on them all along. It took quite a bit of maneuvering to survive. Fortunately, I was wearing a full, nearly floor-length gown, and was able to waft my balloon under my skirts and so confuse the couples around me. I was too quick for them. That was before I met Mr. Singer, of course. With Mr. Singer as my partner, I would have undoubtedly been one of the first to be eliminated. The young gentleman who was my dancing partner that evening, a customers' man from Short Hills, took these long, *long* strides, and whirled me out of harm's way."

Singer sat down at the piano and played Solfeggietto in C Minor, by K. P. E. Bach. "Remember that baby, Ma?" he said.

"Ah, dear me, yes," she said. "You played it much better when you were ten. You had more *feeling* then, I recall."

The following morning, Singer awoke before Daisy, and discovered to his horror that they were as much as (approximately) three feet apart. He sidled up to her and feigned sleep. At length, she awoke, too, and through his tremulous lashes he watched her reach under her pillow for the tape measure.

"Julian," she said. "Do you know we're only seven and one half inches apart this morning? We've come together again, my darling."

"I've told you I loved you all along. Who listens?"

"Love," she said, sighing, "is here, is there, is everywhere."

"But mine's true-blue," Julian said. "I can prove it to you, too. We were married on October 20, 1963, and I haven't slept with another woman since January 19, 1963."

Daisy said, "Is it because you don't want to, or are you trying to set a record?"

The next day, Singer sat squarely at his quaking desk, a fresh sheet of paper before him, a ball-point pen poised hopelessly in the air. Having abjured bird watching, he was composing the first item in a new list, called, simply, "Thoughts." Each day, he would put down a significant concept that had come to mind in the previous twenty-four hours. He had been at it nearly twenty minutes now but had been unable to come up with anything; it seemed that everything he thought of had already been stated, and more happily. He relit his cigar. Something was amiss. He groped about his waist. *Where is my seat belt?*

He wrote:

Why aren't I growing up? My contemporaries are the stream. I am the bank. They go on; I remain, undermined here, built up there, dreaming. As they rush by, they gaily shout: You may look different, but we know you.

On October 20th, he couldn't think of a blessed thing. Daisy, coming upon the page in his absence, wrote in the empty place:

Thinker, today is our anniversary.

I could stop here; it isn't an inappropriate ending. However, there is always one more thing to say—an *esprit de l'escalier*.

Dreams. Who can listen to an account of another's dream? What an excruciating experience! Even the helpless dreamer usually gives up midway. He has had this resplendent, intense, harrowing, verisimilar vision, which only a few hours before shone behind his eyelids, as though with his eyes shut he had looked directly at the sun. But it is fading away. He cannot remember exactly how it went. You see, there were so many incidents and ambiguities. It was so emotional, too. And he had these insights. But he is not a storyteller; indeed, even the accomplished novelist, accustomed to dealing summarily with life, throws up his hands when a dream is set in front of him. Alas, it is too rich, a muchness. He'd like to tackle it, but (he chuckles) he is on a diet. With an index finger, he slyly samples the icing and recommends it.

The dreamer, hearing himself relate the dream discovers how conventional, how humdrum it is. He cannot transmit the mystery. He begins to skip the duller parts; he forgets this or that; he backtracks; he loses his way. The listener's attention has long since wandered. The dreamer mumbles on. He is downhearted. His inept recital has superseded the dream in his memory. He swears that next time he will make a point of remembering. He will keep it to himself, savor it. But who can withhold such strange things?

On the night of October 21st, Singer has a dream. He is sitting by the pool at the Beverly Hills Hotel. The sun has gone down behind the pink stucco wall that encloses the hotel, and the air has grown chilly. The water is nearly violet. Although the last swimmer left the pool an hour ago, the water is still rocking, lapping against the tiles (as it does, at this very instant, against the world's numberless shores, Singer thinks, making a mental note that in the morning this might be the basis for his next Thought). Singer is listening to U Thant, who is reclining in the chaise beside him. U Thant is telling him about the true state of the world. The pool is closing. They are the only guests left, he and U Thant. The cabaña boys are slowly collecting the mats, piling them into a great, uneven tower. Although he realizes it is a unique opportunity, and that he is privileged, Singer cannot keep his mind on what U Thant is saying. He has hidden a girlie magazine under one of the mats (which one?); if the cabaña boys find it, he will be asked to leave the hotel. He thinks, How much more of this is there? Will I never awake?

4

I tell my father of my intention to write about him, and that I expect him to hold still for an interview.

"You'll have to hurry, Julian," he says.

Uh-oh, he's back with death again.

"You're only sixty-nine," I say.

"Mother and I are going on a cruise the eighteenth instant," he says, delving into his pocket and handing me a carbon of his itinerary done on onionskin.

When I complain it is too faint to make out, he says I never even send them a postcard.

I fear he will die at sea and, wrapped in the flag he loves, be tipped over the rail between one illegible island and another.

We are sitting in the Park by the shuffleboard courts. I detect that my father has been imperceptibly turning, like an hour hand, in order that the sun's rays might smite him flush on the forehead.

I ask, "Do you think we look at all alike?"

"You have the stronger chin," he says. "If you'd only stand up straight. Would you like me to run through my life?"

I ceremoniously open my notebook.

"I was born in Lutzin, in Latvia," he says. "It has another name now. I have four memories of this little town. The first is walking with somebody by a fence behind which gooseberries are growing. I pick several and proceed to eat them, and they are like nectar. My second memory is it is a very cold winter's day. I have done something or other. I am being kept in. Am I being punished? I recall my mother coming, covered in shawls. My third memory is that I am at my grandfather's house. Behind his bench—he is a cobbler—is a high window. I walk through it into a garden, in which tall sunflowers are growing, from which I pick the seeds—"

"If they are tall, how can you reach the seeds?" I ask.

"How can I?" he says. "I forget my fourth memory. I knew it last year, I feel certain. I have five memories of coming to America. My first memory is the train to Libau stopping in a forest and my sister getting off, for a reason which escapes me. I don't see her get on, and when the train starts I am worried that she has been left behind. My second memory occurs in Liverpool, where I see a sign advertising oranges nine for a penny—"

"But surely you can't read English?"

"I am afraid I am mistaken then," he says. "My third memory is having a little playmate on the ship, and my impression that he is going back to Europe at the same time I am going to America. My fourth memory is riding away from Castle Garden in an open cart. It is my sixth birthday. In the streets are innumerable shouting people, and I believe they have all gathered to celebrate my birthday."

"But they are calling you 'greenhorn' and so forth," I say.

"I am inclined to agree," he says.

I am leaning against my father's shoulder, and he has his arm about me.

"Why haven't you told me the fifth memory?" I ask.

"I did," he says, "but you had fallen asleep."

Several days later, I call my father up and ask him if I may continue the interview.

"Was that good stuff I gave you?" he asks.

I assure him it was. I suspect he is in the foyer, in his voluminous pajamas; above his bowed head is an engraving of the Bridge of Sighs. If I don't ask my questions at once, he'll miss the eleven-o'clock news, which is the last news broadcast he listens to—but I falter.

He prompts me: "Do you want me to go on in the same vein?"

"Today I would appreciate it if you would tell me how you regard yourself."

"I am inclined to be roguish," he says.

"No baloney," I say.

"You don't know me in my extra-parental guise," he says. "I'm quick at repartee. I'm known for that. I have a way with language. I've developed a capacity in English superior to most of my circle—a wider vocabulary, an easier flow. On a couple of occasions, fellow-attorneys have asked me, 'Are you a Harvard man?' Are you in fact putting down everything I say?"

"I am, but I'm going to change it."

"But who could possibly be interested?"

"That's not the point."

"My life is inherently ordinary."

"I didn't marry a nobody." This is my mother speaking.

"She listens on the extension," says my father.

She is unlit rooms away, in her bed; upon the headboard are painted roses.

"I won't interrupt further," she says, "but I just want to say that once, in a corridor of the New York County Courthouse, an attorney of no small repute stopped your father and told him, 'You're a formidable opponent.' That's all I've got to say."

"I can hold my own with most of the boys," my father says. "I know I've done a first-rate job in the representation of people. Lately, however, I don't feel like working as hard as heretofore. You feel like easing up. Only yesterday, emerging from the subway en route to the office, I found myself saying to myself, 'Good God, this is the same pattern.'"

"He is unswerving," says my mother. "Oops. Pardon me."

"I am a well-organized human being," my father says. "Curiously, many years ago, Mother and I were at some seashore, walking along the boardwalk. We met a fellow-stroller—perhaps it was that Mother was acquainted with his wife (sh-h-h, permit me to finish)—who read character. Straight off, he told me I was well organized. I was astonished at the accuracy. No doubt, he divined my nature by the way I was dressed, my phiz."

"I thought I told you we set it up beforehand," my mother says. "It was a joke."

"Is that right?" my father says. "I was on the point of saying that life has gone along in a successful pattern. I have never suffered any deprivation. Mother hasn't been denied anything to think of."

"A house in the country," says my mother.

"I have accumulated reserves, which is a great comfort," my father goes on. "Furthermore—"

"Lawns."

"—I think I've been a worthwhile member of society in that—"

"A flower garden."

"—I haven't solely devoted myself to my own affairs—"

"Badminton."

My mother, much younger, stands on one foot like Mercury, her racket raised. A hit? A miss? Presumably, my father is on the other side of the net; at least, I imagine it is he whom I hear chuckling in the dusk.

"—and well-being. I've done something to justify my place as a human being. As I look it over, I find my life has been a rewarding one. I'm satisfied, or, more precisely, I'm not dissatisfied."

"What he's trying to say is that he's not greedy," says my mother.

"I'm an amiable person," says my father.

"He thinks the cup's half full; I think it's half empty."

"You're a gloomy romantic," says my father.

"I'm unrealistic. He keeps me realistic. He doesn't allow me to express myself."

"Ah," says my father.

"You see," says my mother.

"I've missed the news," says my father.

"Don't blame me," I say.

"You may blame me, if you wish," my mother says.

In a while, we hang up. I imagine my father feeling his way along the dark, crooked halls to the bedroom and getting into his bed next to my mother's. They pull the little beaded chains that turn out their lights and, as is their habit, shake hands across the abyss that separates their beds.

I write my father a letter at sea:

Dear Dad:
Here are some more questions:
1. Are you obedient to a moral code?
2. Do you dream? If so, how much? Are your dreams disquieting? Do they have any great themes?
3. When was the last time you shed tears?
4. What do you regret?
5. What are the kindest words a stranger ever addressed to you?
6. Eight years ago last December, I am nearly positive I saw you at the bar of the Woodstock in the company of a woman wearing a black suit, whose partly revealed bosom you were steadfastly regarding. Please comment.

Love,
Julian

My father's reply, postmarked Fort-de-France, Martinique, reaches me two days after my parents' return:

Dear Son:
In re your queries:
1. I believe in a world of law, but I realize man's infirmities. I dislike ruthlessness, unkindness, and dishonesty. What I do, I do to the utmost of my ability. I am considerate within limits. Never regard me as a paragon.
2. I dream incessantly. The majority of my dreams are peaceable, and they are mostly topical.
3. I don't usually surrender to emotions. The last occasion on which I wept must have been in a movie house.
4. The few times I spanked you, I felt so guilty. It was cruel, and I have never got rid of this great sense of remorse.

5. Once, on a flight from Indianapolis, where I had gone to address a meeting of United Cerebral Palsy, I sat next to a six-year-old boy, with whom I had a conversation. Luncheon was served, and I cut up his chicken for him. When we parted at the airport, this little shaver said to me, "You're a good man, Mr. Stinger." (You notice he didn't get our name quite right. Don't you think that made it all the more affecting? Mother, who has good instincts, doesn't.)

6. I have never been in the Hotel Woodstock.

Love,
Dad

P. S. Thanks for the mystery. Alas, I find I no longer care who kills whom, much less why.

P. P. S. Did I ever tell you that my father, whom you never met, wrote, too? I don't know what, but I think it was poetry. Otherwise, you are dissimilar. You were hovered over during the first part of your life, and have all the stigmata of the artist: essentially self-centered, forbidding, a nonconformist. You were not a friendly child, and smiled rarely, but when you did it lit up your face so. My father was a very decent, gentle, literate human being who was ground down by economic pressures. He was slightly built and never considered strong, but I remember him carrying me in his arms when I fell in the wagon shop on Cherry Street.

My father sits in his undershirt, his head in the sink. My mother stands above him, washing his long, distinguished white hair. I lounge against the tiles, taking notes. Oh, boy, this is it.

My mother, rubbing the steam off the medicine-cabinet mirror, discovers me at work.

"I thought you were done with him weeks ago," she says.

"I've dreamed up some more questions," I say.

"He's at it again," my mother says in my father's ear, over the running water.

"Who's at what?"

"Julian's here, gathering material for his biography."

"It's not going to be true," I say.

"Enunciate," says my father.

"Oh," says my mother.

"First of all, may I ask you what sort of a marriage you two have had?" I shout.

"Beautiful," my father mutters from the depths of the sink.

"But you're entirely different."

"Compromise," my father says.

"For your father I forsook my career on the legitimate stage," my mother says.

"I've developed a great tolerance and understanding," my father says.

"I've found out how to deal with him, too," my mother says, gently pushing my father's face underwater. I hear him gurgling and sputtering.

"What's he saying, Ma?"

"That he's always loved me, that he'll love me till the day he dies," she says, letting go.

It is 11:20 p.m., the news is over, and the lights are extinguished. My mother and father lie in their beds, the covers up to their chins. I am sitting in the dark at my father's feet.

"Dad," I am saying, "remember when you used to push me in my stroller along the river and sing to me about the crocodile? How did it go?"

My father makes no reply.

"He must be in dreamland," my mother says. "Has he told you about the time I was appearing in *Aloma of the South Seas* and he waited for me every night at the stage door, even when it was raining? Once, he gave me a spray of little green orchids."

My father sings faintly:

"Croc, croc, croc, crocodile . . ."

"Oh, we thought you were fast asleep," my mother says.

"Croc, croc, croc, crocodile,
Swimming in the shining Nile . . ."

5

Julian Sing-song Sing-along, as his stepdaughter Cassie, who is ten, calls him, is in the hospital, where he has had his appendix removed, and today his mother, his wife, his sister, and his sister-in-law are all gathered around his bed feeling sorry for him and trying to cheer him up, but Julian has fallen asleep and is dreaming about his end—in fact, that of mankind as well. In some manner not clear to him, the atmosphere of the earth is imminently to be drawn off. One episode of the dream takes place in the country, where Julian, from a secondary road, sees houses burning freely; they have been set afire by a deranged person, and the fire companies are no longer responding to the alarms. Another episode takes place in the offices of the New York *Times*; a kindly editor is showing Julian a copy of that day's paper, with its tiers of dire headlines, and explaining that the *Times* is now being printed in London, as the great majority of the New York staff have stopped coming to work. "Julian, did you know you were talking in your sleep?" Julian hears his mother saying.

"Ah, so. Velly intelesting," he says, not bothering to open his eyes. "Any good rines?"

"I thought it was pigeons," his sister, Barbara, says.

"What was pigeons?" his mother says.

"Julian talking," Barbara says. "It seemed to be coming from the sill, and it was kind of musical."

"Why visit Julian if you're not going to pay attention?" his mother says.

"If it was musical, it couldn't have been Julian," says Daisy, his wife. "He can't carry a tune."

"As a child, he sang like a little bird," his mother says. "Or was that you, Barbara? One of my children had the gift."

What had the headlines said, Julian wonders. The old editor's hands had been trembling. Was he afraid, or was it simply age, disease, drink?

"*I* thought it was Russian," says Juliet, Julian's sister-in-law, who's up from Silver Spring for the day.

"Julian can hardly speak a word of *French*," Daisy says.

"I mean, I thought it was the old man in the next bed."

"He's Italian," Daisy says.

"I'm sorry," Juliet says.

"It was definitely Julian," his mother says, "but it was very indistinct. What *were* you dreaming about?"

Opening his eyes, Julian discovers the women still assembled about his bed like a pedimental group, and in the same positions as when he fell asleep. Through the windows at their backs, partly screened by the great white chrysanthemums that stand in a vase on the radiator cover, he beholds the Queensboro Bridge.

"Bing Crosby and I had got up this impromptu act in the locker room at Pebble Beach," Julian says. "Bing sang 'Red Sails in the Sunset' and I did impressions."

"That sounds very nice," his mother says. "I had no idea you could do impressions."

"But I didn't know who I was impersonating," Julian says.

"Julian always had better dreams than I did," Barbara says.

"You had some perfectly good dreams," her mother says.

"*I* never had a single, solitary dream in my whole life," Juliet says. "I would so like to have one sometime, but it's not an area where making an effort does any good, is it?"

The nurse's aide puts Julian's lunch on the bed tray and cranks up the bed.

"Daisy, did you remember to feed the c-a-t-s?" Julian says.

"Isn't he something?" Julian's mother says. "He's implying that—"

"Just putting you on, Ma," Julian says.

"Cats?" his mother says. "Well, all I can say is I'm glad you got rid of those grimy little dogs."

"But we haven't," Daisy says. "Cissy and Fuzz belong to Alan and Paul."

"Do I know them?" Juliet says.

"Our landlords," Daisy says. "Julian's minding Cissy and Fuzz while they're gallivanting around the world on a Norwegian freighter. If it ever thaws, Julian's supposed to plant five hundred tulip bulbs they left behind in their refrigerator."

"Five hundred and *fifty*," Julian says. "I'm never going to make it."

"I certainly hope you're being compensated," his mother says. "But I'm not going to go into it now, because you're convalescing. We're here to cheer you up. Who knows a good joke?"

"Cissy and Fuzz live in the basement on top of a lot of old piled-up chairs—some Louis—like mountain lions," Julian says, gloomily regarding the remains of his individual beef pot pie.

"The cats get through to Julian," Daisy says. "He thinks they don't get enough affection. He wants Cassie to go down to the basement three times a day and stroke them. That, more or less, is his conception of love."

"I just think it's time she learned there's more to humanity than banning the bomb and integrating," Julian says.

"She puts water in your humidifier," Daisy says. "Julian bought a humidifier for his plants."

"Daisy, Julian's getting all the jello in his lap," his mother says. "Do you think he'd think I was butting in if I asked him to let me feed it to him?"

"A few days ago, I was carrying Fuzz in the back yard," Julian says. "She was lying in my arms on her back, like this, and . . . Please, someone, listen to me."

"Shut up for a minute, Julian," Barbara says. "We're all supposed to be thinking of jokes."

"I can never remember any," Juliet says. "Isn't there some other way we can make him feel better?"

"There—you see?" Julian's mother says. "Another spoonful fell."

"He's not very well coordinated," Daisy says.

"Fuzz's eyes rolled back as if she were undergoing a mystic, prophetic, or poetic ecstasy," Julian says. "But it was only the birds."

"What birds?" Juliet says.

"This man comes into the first-class bar on an ocean liner carrying a cakebox under his arm," Barbara says. "He's well dressed, nice-looking—about forty-five or six, I'd say, but careworn; here, there, a touch of ruin, like rust, if you know the sort. Well, anyway, the bartender, an athletic, Irish type, asks him what he would like to drink, and the man says that in the cakebox he has a turtle that can recite poetry and if the bartender would be so kind as to buy him a very dry martini he will ask the turtle, whose name happens to be Bob, to say 'Invictus.' "

"I don't think I know it," Juliet says. "Am I still going to be able to get the joke?"

"Of course, the bartender, who has no powers of imagination at all, thinks the man is around the bend, to say the least," Barbara continues, "but he figures it's worth a very dry martini to find out what's going to happen next. He has this cunning. So the bartender makes the man the martini, and the man opens the box, and from it removes this weensy green turtle, and the turtle opens its weensy pink mouth and says,

> 'Out of the night that covers me,
> Black as the Pit from pole to pole . . .'

"At that moment, there's a god-awful shipwreck, and the ship goes down, and everyone drowns except the man and the turtle. Or is it the bartender and the turtle? Well, I *hope* it doesn't make any difference. Anyhoo, the turtle and this person are sitting on a hatch cover that's floating in the middle of the ocean, and Bob says . . . No, the person says . . . Oh dear, I seem to have forgotten whatever it is whoever it is says."

"It'll come to you in a minute," her mother says, "if you close your eyes, let yourself go limp all over, shake your hands out like this, and think of something reassuring, like . . . Well, like lilacs? Why not?"

"If I'm thinking of the right story, it turns out to be very droll," Barbara says.

"Anyway, they were flying overhead," Julian says.

"I just don't understand him anymore," his mother says. "He might as well be talking in his sleep."

"Julian gets more enigmatic every day," Daisy says.

"You know, I think Bob must have been a frog," Barbara says.

"It was the birds, everybody," Julian says. "Flap, flap."

"Yes, we heard you. The birds," Daisy says. "But what's the point, Julian?"

"Fuzz was looking at them," he says. "That's what made her do that with her eyes. I was mistaken. I had thought it was something marvelous."

There were birds in the dream, too, he remembers—black birds with white eyes. Great flocks of them were walking about on the road underfoot, not bothering to fly, casting their white eyes up at him when he unintentionally stepped on their toes.

"Look at Julian, everybody," Barbara says. "He's grown more dejected. Somebody *do* something."

"Crank him down again," says his mother, which she does, then wheels the bed tray away and, with a facecloth, removes bits of jello from the sheets.

"It so happens," says Juliet, "that I have an item in my pocketbook that's quite entertaining, I think. Julian, you remember Belinda? She's just a week older than Cassie. Well, the other night for homework Belinda had to compose what she referred to as 'imaginative sentences' using the following words: 'sincerely,' 'money,' 'beautiful,' 'committee,' and 'author.' I copied them out. I'm going to read them to you now. Are you ready?

> The letter and handwriting told the story. The last words touched her heart—"Sincerely yours."
>
> The girl with her saddened face reluctantly handed the money for her overdue books to the greedy, beady-eyed library woman.

The beautiful colors on the jungle bird lightened my heart.

The committee with their dreary faces had done a good day's work. "Now to start the long walk home," they said.

The author winced as he told himself, "My days of writing are over, but I'm proud of my accomplishments."

"I thought they were so terribly comical. Aren't they terribly comical, Julian?"

"But why did the author wince?" Julian says.

"Belinda's daddy said the very same thing," Juliet says. "And Belinda said, 'The teacher said we were supposed to write quality sentences and use good descriptive words.' So Daddy said, 'What the hell is a quality sentence?' Pardon my French. And Belinda said, '"The red barn is in Ohio" is not a quality sentence. "The battered red barn full of tired old horses is in Columbus, Ohio" is. I thought "wince" was a good descriptive word. Don't you, Daddy? And because we had mince pie for supper, one thing led to another.'"

At one point in the dream, Julian remembers, he had unexpectedly come upon Daisy crouched naked in the bathtub like primeval man in a cave. Indeed, she was nearly in darkness, not having turned on the light but depending upon that which came in the window, for it was then nearly evening. She was intently shaving her legs with his razor, ruining his blade, and the faucet was dripping melodiously. It was absurd, considering what she knew was lying ahead—that there would soon be nothing left to breathe—but since she hadn't looked up when he entered or given any other sign that she had noticed his existence, he had gone away without speaking to her.

"I know a diverting story," Julian's mother says. "It isn't a joke, but it's very amusing nonetheless. It's all about Emma. Emma, Juliet, is a maid who many years ago had a post in one of the embassies in Washington. Of course, by the time she came to me she was an old spinster who resided in a hotel. You can imagine. But in those days they were trained, and lived a very circumscribed life. She told me once that she had worked for a period for people who summered at Murray Bay. Late one night, when her work was done, she opened the kitchen door to regard the northern lights. There was supposed to be a display of the northern lights that night, you see. Her people found her gazing out of the kitchen door at the sky and asked her what she thought she was doing. 'I'm looking for the northern lights, ma'am,' Emma told them. 'Close that door this instant, and consider yourself reprimanded,' she was told. It was another era then, of course.

"Well, one day last week Emma just turned on her heel and dropped her key on the foyer table. I mean *dropped*, from a *height*. You could hear it *ring out*. In a word, she left me. I can tell you. I really don't think we'd been communicating adequately. I had specifically told her to do the closets, and when I returned from my art class the shelves were still coated with dust. 'Emma,' I said, 'I thought we had agreed that you were doing the closets?' She said, 'I did them.' Then I said, 'But the shelves have simply not been touched.' Then she said, 'I did the outsides.' She was with me for five years. But, actually, I was glad. I was liberated. I don't believe the to-do about the closets was the real reason Emma departed, however. You see, a few days previous I had handed her her Christmas money. It was a substantial sum—more than I'd ever given her—and when I presented it to her she curtsied. Can you believe it? It was inadvertent, naturally, but, you see, she was so terribly embarrassed at having curtsied in front of me I do believe she felt compelled to leave."

"Did she get to see the northern lights before she had to close the door?" Julian asks. "What I mean is, were they really out that night, after all?"

"You know, the thing is she never said," his mother says.

Julian falls asleep once more and finds himself back at the *Times*, in the sports department, reading the A.P. wire, which, since no one is there to cut it, is accumulating behind the machine. The stories are coming over very slowly and haltingly, and are nearly illegible, as though a little child were punching them out. Julian notices that Baseball Commissioner Eckert is being quoted as saying that in the "ntaional interxset" the major leagues will adhere to their schedules as long as it is "humanely posziblxe." Then the scene shifts, but when Julian awakes he cannot recall what took place next.

He watches his mother and Daisy playing a hand of gin on his bed tray. "Was I lying on my back?" he says after his mother has won.

"When was that, Julian?" Daisy says.

"If you sleep on your back, you'll have bad dreams," his mother says.

"*When*?" Julian says. "When I was sleeping."

"So solly," Daisy says. "Me forget to rook."

"I'm sure I would have noticed," his mother says, "but we were saying goodbye to Barbara and Juliet. Next time you feel yourself getting sleepy, remind me and I'll keep a lookout and let you know."

"I'm going to let you do something for me *now*, Ma."

"Yes, Julian?" she says, rising. "I'll change the water in the mums?"

"Better. You can comb my hair."

"Don't," Daisy says.

"Why not?" says Julian's mother. "It's unruly."

Shutting his eyes, Julian inclines his head toward his mother.

"Do you think I'll ever find his part again after all these years?" she says. "I'll just shave your sideburns while I'm at it. You look like a Puerto Rican."

"Back off, chief," Julian says, reaching up and gently taking the comb from her.

"He's unconventional," she says, going to the window and re-arranging the chrysanthemums. "Yellow would have been more cheerful, wouldn't it? That's really what I had in mind, but I let a little man dissuade me."

"Have you heard Julian asked Miss Simoncini to kiss him in the recovery room?" Daisy says.

"Miss who?"

"A nurse."

"Well, did she kiss you?"

"No."

"I don't see why she couldn't have kissed him," Julian's mother says. "Perhaps just on the cheek." She turns to Daisy. "Do you?"

It would have been a very thoughtful gesture."

"Mother's going to her art course," Julian says.

"I was just getting my things," she says. "He's always trying to get rid of me."

"What are you doing?" Daisy says.

"This year Mr. Klaber's giving us linear perspective."

"Oh."

"One should have a thorough grounding, but I so hope he'll give us our heads and let us do a still-life before long—one with fruit, if not flowers, as he's promised."

Julian shuts his eyes again and imagines a room full of elderly women wearing hats, all drawing streets converging on vanishing points; Mr. Klaber, who has metal taps on his shoes, is looking over their shoulders, repressing sighs. When Julian opens his eyes, his mother is gone. "She's left?" he says.

"She had a choice?" Daisy says.

"I didn't mean it that way. Daisy, see if she's still waiting for the elevator?"

"What for?"

"I don't want her to leave with the wrong impression."

"Then do something about it."

"But I'm an invalid."

"Miss Simoncini said it was good for you to take walks."

Julian gets out of bed, hobbles from the room, and heads irresolutely down the corridor in his pajamas. Before the elevators, where one corridor intersects another, a great convex mirror, like those sometimes found on perilously winding roads, is attached to the wall. In the mirror Julian sees Miss Simoncini approaching.

"Where do you think you're going?" she says.

"I'm trying to reach my mother."

"Without your bathrobe?"

"Aw."

"We don't have any free shows on this floor. March right back to your room and don't come out again until you put it on."

"But it'll be too late."

As Julian is returning to his room, he hears his mother, from behind, saying, "Do you want me to give you a hand?"

"No, but you may draw alongside, so you can catch me if I fall."

"Oh, Julian, you've grown too big. I could never support you."

"Ma, you know why I love you so much?"

"Why?"

"Because you've got a classy sense of humor. I thought you said you were going to your art class."

"Well, you see, I was going to be early, so I said to myself, 'I might as well sit on the bench in front of the elevator bank for a while,' and then I heard your voice from so far away, and I thought I had nodded off and was dreaming, but I wasn't, was I? You're right, Julian. I do enjoy a good laugh."

When they enter the room, Julian's mother says, "Look who I've got, Daisy."

"I was lost," Julian says, climbing back into bed, which seems, he thinks, to be unnaturally high, nearly inaccessible.

"And I found him and brought him back," his mother says.

After Julian's mother has left, Daisy says, "I think I'll be going, too."

"Daisy, stay."

"Why? You're only going to go back to sleep again, and then when you wake up you're going to ask me to tell you what you looked like when you were sleeping, what position you were lying in, and whether you said anything interesting. I'm sick of watching you while you sleep, Julian. At times, I think you married me in order to have someone on hand to observe your life and comment on it—lend it gravity—as if you weren't convinced who you were and had to be perpetually defined. And I'm sick of the way you're hotsy-totsying through life, leaving a trail of spilled jello, trying to make the nurses, and reserving your feelings for little plants and animals. I'm b-o-r-e-d with you, Julian Sing-song Sing-along. Why don't you come off it, let go, take another step, change a little?"

"Change to what? Why do you always speak in abstractions?"

That evening, Julian and Daisy are sitting in the solarium by a pink Christmas tree; all about them are discarded morning papers.

"Daisy," Julian says, "did Cassie walk the dogs?"

"You no wolly, Missah Jurian."

"Did she feed the cats?"

"And she did her homework, and practiced her guitar, and the humidifier's steaming away like the *Queen of Bermuda*."

"I keep thinking of Alan and Paul in that little salon with the sepia photomurals of fjords, surrounded by nuns, running out of conversation."

"We only saw two nuns on board, so I don't see how they could possibly be surrounded."

"The trouble with us, Daisy, is that you look at things mathematically. Did you know that Alan told me, before he started around the world, that the high point of his life was when he auditioned at Juilliard? He sang 'Drink to Me Only with Thine Eyes,' and the auditors broke into applause, which he said was exceptional. That was twenty years ago. What do you think it was that Bob, the turtle, said, if anything? What am I going to do with all those tulips? What am I supposed to change to?"

"Oh, Julian, do you remember that night when we had that sensational fight in bed and I got so mad I said I was going to turn out the light and go to sleep, and I reached behind me for the switch but I couldn't find it, and I kept searching and missing and searching and missing until you began to laugh and I started laughing, too, and then we couldn't ever stop?"

"Yes, but then what happened?"

"Be that way, Julian."

"But I've always thought of myself as a lighthearted individual. Did I ever do my Jolly Green Giant imitation for you? 'Ho, ho . . .' Uh-oh, Miss Simoncini's lurking outside the solarium. So solly, time for visitahs to dly teahs and go home now."

"Julian," Daisy says, putting on her coat, "perhaps you can do the Jolly Green Giant if you and Bing perform again tonight."

After he walks his wife to the elevator and watches her descend and disappear, Julian—bent over, tenderly holding his incision—shuffles toward his room, feeling disabled and incapable. Ahead of him, beyond an empty phone booth, the walls of the corridor converge. By its sheen, length, and dimness, the corridor suggests to Julian a passageway on a lower deck—D or E, possibly—of an ocean liner. What would happen, he thinks, if it suddenly tilted and the liner plunged—noisily, at first—to the bottom of the sea? *That* was it, the last scene of the dream he had when he fell asleep after Emma had been searching for the northern lights—Cassie had vanished, presumably overboard. They had been by themselves, at night, in the cockpit of a great white yawl running before the wind. He had the impression that below a numerous crew was sleeping. At one point, Cassie had said, "Daddy, look at all the colored lights," and he had glanced over the side and seen spots of phosphorescence in the wake, betraying anatomies. When he looked up, Cassie was gone. He began shouting, trying to arouse the crew so that they could help him jibe, but no one appeared on deck.

"Stand up straight," says Miss Simoncini, overtaking him. "You look like an old man."

"I can't," Julian says. "I had an operation."

"What do you mean, you can't?" she says, taking hold of his shoulders and pulling them erect. "There."

"Miss S.," Julian says, "are you mad at me?"

"Why should I be?"

"Because I asked you to give me a kiss in the recovery room."

"You're too much," she says, leaving him behind.

"Hey, Miss S., you going to tuck me in tonight?"

"Who do you think you are?" she says, without looking back.

Julian goes into the phone booth and calls home. Cassie answers. "Cassie?" Julian says.

"Who?"

"Julian Sing-song Sing-along."

"Oh, herro, Jurian, me no lecognize you light away."

"I've been sick," Julian says.

"Ma says you need cheering up. Shall I tell you a story?"

"I'd be very much obliged."

"It's about this secretary who falls in love with her boss."

"What's her name?"

"Her name is Josephine Lacarté and she's twenty-four years old."

"Is she pretty?"

"Yes, except she wears glasses. Her boss's name is Eric Lankhart. He is thirty-eight years old and his company is Beechwood Products."

"What do they make?"

"Spoons."

"So then what happens?"

"Well, the boss, who is married, starts going out with the secretary, and the boss's wife, who lives in the suburbs and whose name is Henriette Lankhart, finds out and starts getting inflamed and infuriated. Then the company starts failing. You see, they've found a new substance they can make spoons out of called Matella, only Beechwood Products doesn't have the secret formula. So Beechwood Products doesn't make much profit any more and Eric Lankhart has to lower the salaries. So Josephine Lacarté starts complaining because she's not getting enough salary, and she says she won't date Eric Lankhart anymore. Eric gets real mad at her. Josephine says, 'I don't need you any more.' Eric says, 'Where are you going to get your money from?' Josephine says, 'To tell you the truth, I'm married.' Meanwhile, Henriette has plotted that she's going to get a divorce. So Eric and Henriette have this fight, and she takes a plane to Mexico to get a divorce, and Josephine has broken up with Eric and gone back to her husband, whose name is Carl Lacarté, and now Eric is left alone and has no one. The End."

More than a month has gone by; there's been a thaw; the earth releases its store of sentimental odors. Julian and Daisy are in the back yard, desperately planting tulips. Daisy, dressed in Julian's old blazer, which is out at the elbows, is kneeling at her husband's feet putting bulbs in the holes he is making with the bulb planter. It is rapidly growing dark, snow is forecast, and they still have a hundred and seventy-five tulips to go. As he digs, Julian encounters bits of colored glass, clamshells, masonry, pieces of restaurant china; once, he inadvertently uncovers a long green shoot and is unreasonably moved. Cissy and Fuzz entwine themselves about his legs. In the house, the dogs are barking.

Cassie runs into the yard. "I've got the flashlight," she cries, shining the beam beneath her chin and making a ghostly face.

"Get back," Julian shouts. "You'd only impede us."

Cassie retires in tears.

"Daisy, are you aware that you put that one in upside down?" Julian says.

"Don't feel bad," she says. "Think of the nice red tulip that'll be blooming in China."

"Saints prayzarve us," he says.

"Julian, why did you ever marry me?" she says.

"Because you make me laugh," he says.

6

My mother and father and I are out for a row. My father and I are seated side by side, he plying the right oar, I the left. My mother is reclining in the stern, taking the sun in moderation.[1] My father's shirtsleeves are rolled to the elbows, in accordance with his custom when he engages in manual labor, such as drying the dishes,[2] and he is wearing a necktie I gave him for his birthday. I had asked my mother what color I should get. "Something in the blue family," she told me.[3] My father is rowing more vigorously than I, perhaps to show that at seventy he still has plenty of jism. Whatever the case, I refuse to contest him in this respect. As a result, we are going in circles.[4] Of course, from time to time I am rowing solely with my left hand; with my right I am taking notes. For the past few months I have been gathering material on my father's life, with an eye to writing him up for posterity.

"Dad," I say, "tell me how it happened you two met."

"In the summer of 1923,[5] I went up to Lake Mohegan—" my father says.

"You didn't start out right," my mother says.

"In the winter of 1922, I went to a sorority dance at the Hotel Majestic," my father begins anew. "On the dance floor, I spotted[6] your mother, who was wearing a green dress."

"I hadn't the faintest idea," my mother says.

"She captured my eye," my father says.

"If you want to see that dress, I never destroyed it," my mother says. "The only thing missing is a spray of yellow flowers . . . She was a beautiful seamstress."

"What Mother means is 'good.' "

"Is the adjective in the wrong place?"

"No, the wrong adjective."

"Reseda green," my mother says. "I was very vivacious. I had all my dances booked."

"In the summer of 1923, I went up to Lake Mohegan," my father continues. "The Mohegan Inn.[7] At that time, you went there to meet your contemporaries, and there I spotted[8] your mother for the second time. She was being squired around by a big, burly guy with a prognathous jaw. He was the lifesaver, and the only one allowed to take a boat out at night."[9]

"He wasn't the lifesaver," my mother says. "He took me to see the Shuberts, to whom he was remotely related, but I didn't want to be in musical shows."[10]

"At any rate," my father says, "he subsequently went into bankruptcy and is now dead."

"I was at the end of some romance," my mother says.

"I saw her in the dining room," my father says. "I saw her coming down the steps, but it wasn't until she was settling her bill in the lobby that I mustered the courage to approach her.[11] She was wearing a dress with a palm leaf design."

"Paisley," my mother says. "He said he had spotted[12] me at the Hotel Majestic. I was flattered. Can you imagine, nearly half a year had passed. He asked me whether he might not get in touch with me in the city. I said I was in the telephone book."

"Big shot," my father says. "On our honeymoon we took the night boat to Boston and the train to Portland, Maine, and then some conveyance to Lake Sebago—"

"He's seen all your artistic photographs," my mother says to my father.

"You keep snapping away," my father says.

"He wrote me a poem at Lake Sebago," my mother says, "which I remember yet:[13]

'Pine-laden groves, a strip of beach,
Sunbeams dancing on the lake,
A paradise gone all too soon,
The cradle of our honeymoon.' " [14]

"You're not pulling your weight," my father says to me. [15]

NOTES

[1] "Really," my mother says to me. "Must you put us in a rowboat?"

"I seem to recall you enjoyed having me take you rowing," my father says. "Remember, in the mist, the loon?"

"Because it gratified you," my mother says. "He enjoyed applying himself to the oars, or so he said."

"I see," my father says.

"Rowing is not very interesting," my mother says.

Picture us, if you will, three abreast in the dark, save for the tiny reading light shining above my head. We are flying to Miami—night coach. I am thirty-seven, my life is half over, and I am doubly suspended, you will agree, between the kingdom of heaven and that of earth. Last week—was it?—my wife left me; or, as she contends, I left her. I'm fair-minded: who knows who left whom first? My father and mother said come to Miami with us and we won't bring it up. I have brought my MS on board and am reading it (softly, so as not to disturb our fellow-passengers, who lie all about us, like casualties, their seats tilted back, asleep) to my parents, in order, by their amendments, to arrive nearer the truth, I suppose—and to keep them, as well as me, from dwelling on what has happened to me and, in a sense, on what hasn't.

"In that case, may I suggest the following?" I say to my mother. " 'The first at Merion is a 360-yard par 4 with a dogleg to the right. Bordering the fairway are numerous bunkers renowned as the "White Faces of Merion." Tall Japanese pines conceal the green. It is a glorious day late in summer. Here and there one may discern marmoreal clouds. A threesome composed of my father and mother and I are strolling toward the tee, exchanging light banter the while. My mother has the honor.' "

"Too many literary flourishes," my father says.

"Really," my mother says. "We're playing golf now."

"Your mother was a remarkable putter," my father says.

"I had very steady hands," my mother says. "I was like a stone."

"A rock," my father says. "She was at home on a green."

"But I don't recline in a boat," my mother says. "I'm not terribly at home in water. I would never in a million years be able to save myself if we tipped over."

"In a million *million*?" my father says.

"Oh, God," my mother says.

"She swims the sidestroke," my father says.

"Exclusively," my mother says.

"Languorously," my father says.

"I don't know how to breathe," my mother says.

"What she means," my father says, "is under water."

"I can exhale," my mother says. "But then there's inhaling, you see."

"In the stern," my father says, "your mother would be sitting tensely."

"I would be sitting tautly," my mother says. "And I'm not inclined to seek out the sun. If it shines down directly on me . . . He, on the other hand—"

"I'm a heliophile," my father says, rather proudly.

"I wear big, floppy, summery hats in vivid colors," my mother says.

"What in the world for?" I say.

"I'm not talking," my mother says.

"Sun shows age," my father says. "Mother's preoccupied with age."

"You purposely said that," my mother says.

"That came out solely because it's a statement of fact," my father says.

"Precisely," my mother says.

"Precisely what?" my father says.

"Precisely why you shouldn't have said it," my mother says.

² "I would prefer if you substituted for 'such as drying the dishes,' 'such as mending broken china,' " my mother says. "That's his forte."

"Aw, give me a break, Ma," I say.

"He's a chip off the old block," my father says.

"I have my reasons," my mother says, not joining in the merriment.

"She's concerned about my image," my father says.

"I want to show you something that was broken into many pieces and he mended it," my mother says. "I defy you to ferret out the joints. I defy anyone."

"All you need is infinite patience," my father says. "I'm infinitely more patient than Mother."

"Too," my mother says.

"What's that supposed to mean?" my father says.

"Who knows?" my mother says. "It just slipped out."

³ "Blue for blue eyes," my mother says. "Give your readers a helping hand."

"Don't be obscure," my father says.

"Of course," my mother says to me, "they were bluer once— French ultramarine . . . Why do we have to dredge this all up now if you're not feeling up to it?"

I suspect she is going to press my hand, so I begin to withdraw it. However, she notices.

"We'll finish by the pool," my father says.

"On the other hand," says my mother, "I'm told it's good therapy. Resume, I'm listening."

⁴ "No, we're not," my father says. "My seamanship would keep us from going in circles. I'd maintain our heading. The moment I noticed . . . It's not in keeping with my makeup. I'd backwater. The moment I'd have noticed, I'd have rectified it. In the Navy I was on the cutter crew."

"Oh, God," my mother says.

⁵ "Must you say the year?" my mother says. "I never tell years and I don't recall dates. It's just in a vague way that it all happened

in the past."

"It's fiction," I say. "I made it up."

"It's not going to work," my mother says. "If it's fiction, why should it be fact?"

"That's a good line," my father says to me. "Did you make a note of it?"

"And if it's fact," my mother goes on, "why do you fictionalize it?"

6 "I wouldn't use 'spotted,' " my father says.

"You spot birds," my mother says.

"I'd use a synonym," my father says.

7 "Stop," my mother says. "Hold everything. Be considerate. Use your imagination. Make up a hotel."

"Crystal Lake," my father says. "Crystal Inn."

"How did you ever dredge *that* up?" my mother says.

"I don't know," my father says. "It just slipped out. Crystal Lake. Crystal Inn. It has a ring."

"Too bad this isn't more interesting," my mother says.

I say, " 'The suite, situated on one of the uppermost stories of the Ritz, has a favored prospect; namely, the Public Garden. Indeed, the actress, the second lead in *Aloma of the South Seas*, which is trying out in Boston, is seated by the window, inattentively regarding the swan boats below. It is a glorious day late in summer. Here and there one may discern marmoreal clouds. The young man pacing about the room shall remain nameless, but he will become one of the most renowned outfielders in baseball history, compiling a .317 lifetime batting average, hitting for power, and being the possessor of a truly great arm as well. The ballplayer—his team has an off day—has asked the actress to marry him and he is impatiently awaiting her decision. The door of the suite opens and a chap named Singer, a young theatrical lawyer, stands on the threshold....' "

"That was the least worthy play I was in, I should say," my mother says.

"It was a trifle," my father says.

"You had to wear one of those sarongs," my mother says. "It

was a lighter play. It wasn't a comedy so much . . . I guess it . . . I don't know. It really doesn't matter anymore, but *Aloma of the South Seas* wasn't a serious play. Wouldn't it be all right to say 'in the twenties'? They all say that. 'In the twenties.' 'In the thirties.' Don't you see, it's so long ago."

8 "Excuse me," my father says. " 'Spotted' again. 'Saw' would be more in keeping."

"You spot planes," my mother says. "Why doesn't he rest his eyes until Florida? I always find life improves when I rest my eyes."

"I'm willing to stipulate the rest of this," my father says.

"We want you to know that you have two loyal allies," my mother says to me. "We want you to know that we feel everything has worked out for the best in the wash."

"We're not bringing it up," my father says to my mother.

"Did I mention any names?" my mother says.

9 "That lifesaver was a very good-looking chap," my mother says. "He wasn't the man with the prognathous jaw. The man with the prognathous jaw came up with your father. He was one of his friends from Auld Lang Syne, a social and literary club."

"He had a very prognathous jaw," my father says.

"And a guffaw like a donkey," my mother says.

"Dead now," my father says.

"Don't say that," my mother says. "Everybody's dead."

"Who was the lifeguard, then?" I say.

"You've just got to know everything about everything," my mother says. "Strangers will read this. They don't care."

"What *was* the name of the chap?" my father says.

"After all," my mother says to me, "the lifesavers had jurisdiction over the boats. You're not being explicit. You make it sound like being out on the water means one actually has to submit."

"His name is on the tip of my tongue," my father says.

"I know his name," my mother says, "but I won't repeat it."

"He died, the poor guy," my father says.

"He's dead," my mother says. "But must you say the year?"

"If I'm seventy," my father says, "how much farther away can *you* be?"

"Why, I could be almost anything, couldn't I?" my mother says.

"I see," my father says. "I'm fact, you're fiction."

"That's a good line," my mother says.

"Ah, Cozzie, that's wonderful," my father says.

"*Cozzie*?" I say.

"This isn't going to work," my mother says. "Why not call it Lake X?"

"Crystal Lake," my father says. "Crystal Inn."

"I know you can't be vague," my mother says. "The doctors want to know your age. It really doesn't matter."

10   "And that was another chap altogether," my mother says. "I had studied drama. I couldn't sing a note. That was someone else took me to see the Shuberts. A very young fellow."

"So was I a very young fellow," my father says.

"You were," my mother says.

11   "He was terribly shy," my mother says.

"I was reserved," my father says.

"He waited until the last minute," my mother says.

"I wasn't the aggressive type," my father says.

"Such is my fate," my mother says.

12   " 'Spotted,' " my father says.

"You spot—" my mother says.

"He's going to change it," my father says.

"She didn't come from a good family," my mother says to me.

"Your mores were dissimilar," my father says.

"Too bad this isn't more interesting," I say.

"When you've had a few days of sun," my mother says. "By the pool would be nicer. But out of the glare."

13   "The Bay of Naples," my father says.

"The Bay of Y," my mother says.

"We didn't stay at Lake Sebago," my father says. "We went

right on through."

"Chalk it up to experience," my mother says to me. "Writers need experience."

14 "I hardly call it a poem," my mother says.

"It's doggerel," my father says.

"You thought it wonderful then," my mother says.

"One's taste gets refined," my father says. "I recollect his name now."

"Whose?" my mother says.

"The lifesaver's," my father says. "Norman Meltzer."

"It wasn't," my mother says. "All these years you've had it wrong. Norman *Meltzer*? His name was . . . His name was Z."

15 Unanswered questions:

  a. What is memorable about the loon?

  b. When they played golf, what did my mother go around in? My father?

  c. Do Crystal Lake and the Crystal Inn exist other than in the kingdom of my father's mind? If so, where are they and did my parents ever go there? Moreover, if such is the case, did anything of note happen in their room? Within the public rooms and upon the porches? On the lawns, in the groves? On the beach? Upon the water?

  d. What is the derivation of Cozzie? (Cozzy? Cahzzie? Cahzzy? Kozzie? Kozzy? Kahzzie?, etc.) Its usage?

  e. Who was the lifesaver?

  f. Who was *Nor*man *Meltz*er?

  g. What is the quality or nature of my parents' love for one another?

  h. What have they made of me? What will become of me?

7

For a time in my life, upon coming home of an evening, it was my custom to peek in the bathroom to see if anyone was standing in the tub full of murderous impulses. Principally, I had in mind Mr. Buxbaum, or Moody, or both. Mr. Buxbaum was a fight manager whom I had inadvertently discredited. In our last telephone conversation he had whispered, "You cut off both of my legs—*above the knees.*" Mr. Buxbaum invariably whispered to forestall hypothetical eavesdroppers; moreover, since he feared his phone was tapped, he made all important calls from pay stations on subway platforms. Indeed, immediately following Mr. Buxbaum's intelligence, there was the great, resonant rumble of a departing train, reminiscent of the organ chord called a stab, which underlines momentous passages in soap operas.

As for Moody, I was, now and again, sleeping with his wife—his second. I had slept with his first, too, when he was wed to her, and when he remarried I slept with his third as well. I consider Moody my best friend and whenever he said his home life was sheer hell, I sagaciously nodded. I had lain in his bed in squalid surroundings (he was a spy then and often out of town)—for instance, an unfinished cup of coffee and an equally unfinished martini on the bed table; likewise Moody's cleaning not taken out; dust devils under the bed when I finally, sadly, reached for my

shoes—and, like Moody, I had very often nearly said out loud:
What am I doing here?

Mr. Buxbaum was somehow related to my father and had been
in the fight game most of his life, although, more often than not,
his fighters let him down. "They're a bunch of tomato cans," was
the way Mr. Buxbaum put it. But boxing was in his blood. "I used
to be a former fighter," Mr. Buxbaum once had occasion to whisper to me. For a period there I took out a second's license and carried the bucket for him. "Like everything else, there is a right way
to carry a bucket and a wrong way to carry a bucket," Mr. Buxbaum said, stressing the fruits of his wisdom. "I will now demonstrate the right way." We were in Boston—the Lennox, prior to its
face lifting—and Mr. Buxbaum dexterously picked up the bucket
and set off with it down the long, tenebrous corridor, me at his
heels, observing his style closely. Being a faster walker than the
average, Mr. Buxbaum soon outstripped me. From somewhere in
the gloom, I heard him distantly muttering, "See. See."

I first met Moody on June 19, 1952, while we were waiting our turns in a barber shop on the Via delle Vita in the city of
Rome. To my genial inquiry, "Are you a fellow American, by any
chance?" he replied, "I am a Fulbright scholar and a poet." I said
it would be an honor to take a gander at his poetry one of these
days. It turned out June 19, 1952, was the day, as he so happened
to have a sheaf on him; he produced the works, neatly folded, from
a pocket.

A sampler from the poetical outpouring of Francis X. Moody,
Jr.:

A GUIDE

The carp at F. (regarde, regarde)
Within an ornamental sheet of water,
Tumult after the loaf on Sunday
Until (la, la grosse, la grand-mère)
A whale in the pond
Rises (le grand-père) and devours. . . .

"Would 'F.' stand for Fontainebleau, by any chance?" I asked, looking up from his typescript, which was impressively free of erasures and interlinear corrections.

Being *prossimo*, Moody was in the chair. "Suppose I said it would?" he civilly rejoined, but judging from his reflection in the mirrored wall, he was greatly vexed.

"Why the secrecy?"

"Ah," he trailed off obscurely.

The truth is, I had nearly broken his cover. Moody, of course, was no more a poet than you or I, and the works were doubtlessly composed by a melancholy GS-6 at a metal desk a little ways outside our nation's capitol.

The following is a description of Mr. Buxbaum and Moody in my apartment, a nicely furn 1½: Moody, well shaven, sprucely attired in a deep-blue, box-loomed worsted, is astride my window sill, left leg in, right leg out, right hand lightly supporting the up-raised window—a mode of entry he presumably had occasion to resort to in his line of work. After ascertaining that I'm not at home, he adroitly puts his right leg in, too, momentarily admiring his shine, and tiptoes to the bathroom. Mr. Buxbaum is standing in the tub, his hat—moderately soiled, medium low crown, pinch front—in his right hand. He transfers the hat to his left hand in order to shake Moody's hand.

"Buxbaum," Mr. Buxbaum whispers.

"Moody," Moody says.

"Don't stand on ceremony," Mr. Buxbaum cordially whispers. "There's room for plenty more."

Moody joins him in the tub.

"He cut off both of my legs," Mr. Buxbaum informs him. "*Above the knees.*" With the edge of his right hand he saws away at both of the indicated places.

"He's sleeping with my wife," Moody says. "My second. I have good reason to believe he slept with my first as well."

"He is given to sudden, sweeping, unresearched, supercilious, and exceedingly harsh generalizations about persons and states of affairs," Mr. Buxbaum whispers—irrelevantly, you will agree.

"He demands a great deal of others, dismissing them summarily if they do not come up to his wildly exacting standards,"

Moody says—a highly colored opinion, "but he feels that others should love *him* just as he is. Granted he is fond of some few in spite of their failings, but most people he dismisses for faults no greater than his own."

"Shall we be seated?" Mr. Buxbaum interposes. "It might be a longish wait."

They sit, vis-à-vis. Moody plucks at his trouser legs to preserve their creases.

"He pursues his own line of thought and indulges his own moods pretty much regardless of the interests and humors of others," Mr. Buxbaum goes on in the same tiresome vein. "His attention wanders immediately if someone tries to discuss a concern of theirs which does not interest him. Do you think you might hang my hat on the faucet? Hot or cold, *cela n'a pas d'importance.*"

"In point of fact he is rigid," Moody says, "and cannot see when a plan or theory of his violates a larger, more important principle, even its own purpose."

"He treats persons and circumstances too much as functions of his own well-being," Mr. Buxbaum whispers.

"For what, outside of himself, does he ever extend himself?" Moody asks. "What excites his pity or concern enough to extract any money, time or special effort somewhat taxing to himself?"

"He seems not to take into consideration the fact that other people are also possessed of human qualities," Mr. Buxbaum whispers "—the ability to think, and to feel; to be hurt, really."

"I believe we've already gone into that in slightly different form," Moody says.

"Granted," Mr. Buxbaum whispers. "It was set forth purely for emphasis."

"In the theater, during intermissions," Moody continues, "being taller than the average, he, without subtlety, attempts to look down the fronts of women's dresses."

"In the subway," Mr. Buxbaum whispers, "he takes pains to choose a seat opposite a woman—preferably thirty years of age or under—and endeavors to look up her skirt."

The natural light begins to fall, and Mr. Buxbaum and Moody gradually grow silent. Mr. Buxbaum contemplates my matching bath towel, face towel, and washcloth, which hang with a rich drapery effect, smacking of Largillière. Moody is momentarily diverted by my electric toothbrush, one of the earliest models. Mr. Buxbaum asks Moody if he so happens to have a deck of playing cards on his person, so they might play a few hands of gin—a fifth of a cent a point, so nobody can get hurt. Moody replies in the negative. Mr. Buxbaum then gives his attention to my diminished, shapely bar of soap, aqua in color, molded in the matrices of my palms. He next asks Moody if, like himself, his muscles are growing stiff and his circulation is becoming impeded, as evidenced by a loss of sensation in the extremities. Moody replies in the affirmative. Mr. Buxbaum then outlines several calisthenics which can be performed in the seated position, and which expressly allay the preceding. Mr. Buxbaum and Moody execute them by the numbers, Mr. Buxbaum reciting the numbers. Once or twice, Moody asks him to speak up. Moody next inquires of Mr. Buxbaum if he has anything on him to read. Mr. Buxbaum replies in the negative, adding that he is a great reader, nonetheless. Moody advances the opinion that the former is a pity, to which Mr. Buxbaum concurs, subjoining, however, that it may all be for the best; by turning on the light they would lose the element of surprise. Mr. Buxbaum then suggests that Moody might take a short nap, with Mr. Buxbaum standing watch, as Moody would do well to conserve his energy, as he might have to call on it if there was any rough stuff. Moody drops off. Mr. Buxbaum wonders what's on television, then takes out his fountain pen, unscrews the top, bends over Moody and pensively touches up a place on his right jacket cuff where the fabric has worn away, revealing the underlining. The best blue-black. Indoors no one would be the wiser.

A commentary on the foregoing: The cuckold is supposed to cut a sorry figure, the adulterer a dashing one, but there are exceptions to every rule. Oh, what a wretched adulterer was I! May I take just a moment to refute a widespread misconception? Faint heart, I have found, *does* win fair lady, as well as others less praiseworthy; but afterwards . . . I will elucidate in a paragraph or two. Even in the shade of *le petit mort*, I would, for example, imagine at that very moment, Moody on one knee in a hotel corridor, his eye to a keyhole, concerned about his trouser crease, and I would be utterly discomposed. (Suppose Mr. Buxbaum, giving yet another lesson in the art of carrying the bucket, suddenly came 'round the bend!) Why then, ill-suited as I was to adultery, did I keep it up? For one, isn't life made more tolerable by a portion of unreality? For two, permit me to think it was on account of the word "illicit"—its anagoge. Illicit. Il-lic-it. It is pleasing phonetically—a rustle unexpectedly terminating in the voiceless alveolar stop; but what enchants me is its symmetry. Regard it here set in eleven-point Garamond: the slender *l*'s escorted on either side by the yeomanly *i*'s; the *c*, with its sorrowfully bowed head, similarly embraced; the final sparred *t*, like a masthead, promising great, hopeful voyages. The row of Lombardy poplars at the rear of my garden, which I am looking at now, nearly rewrites it: a short tree; two tall ones; a short one; one bent over by a recent storm, which I have neglected to stake. Alas, for my *t* I must overlook a harbor.

The following is the promised luminous exposition: I appear in the third person singular under the name of Julian Singer; he is slightly overweight, has frequently been told he has no mechanical ability whatsoever, and leads what he considers to be a semi-secret life. It is several Aprils past. Singer is in the rent-controlled apartment of Alexander and Eleanor Barker. Barker, an ad salesman who is known to his friends and business associates as Sandy, is at Pinehurst. Eleanor, whom Singer refers to as Eezie-Beezie, is lying in bed, Singer beside her. Above their heads is a mounted sailfish Sandy caught.

Singer is saying to Eleanor: "Is he the type of person that's liable to come back early? I mean, suppose he's playing very poorly, would he tend to become discouraged?"

Eleanor says: "When he's discouraged he flings his club high in the air and cowers, his hands on top of his head, and shouts, 'Dear God, please don't let it break.' "

"His head?"

"The club."

"He wouldn't give up the game on the spur of the moment, though?"

"He's really not all that mercurial."

"But it might rain a lot. I happened to read in the *Times* this morning that occasional rain was forecast for the south Atlantic states."

"When it rains they play bridge."

"Oh."

A few minutes later, Singer hears from the corridor the elevator door opening; next, fateful, approaching footsteps.

"It's not *him*!" Eleanor cries, feeling Singer jumping. She is too late. On the way up, Singer bangs his head against the sailfish—the caudal peduncle—which falls on them, also smashing the bed lamp.

"Mommy," Singer wails in the dark.

"Oh, for Christ's sake," says Eleanor.

"What happened, Eezie-Beezie?" says Singer.

"You dislodged his fish. Get it off me, you idiot."

"I can't see. Turn on the light."

"It's busted."

"I'm getting out of here," Singer says, removing the fish from his chest and climbing out of bed. "Where the hell are my undies? I think I'm bleeding. Oh, my God, I've been stabbed or something."

Eleanor has got out of bed on her side and turned on the boudoir lamp.

"I told you it wasn't him," she says. "Don't you think I know his springy step?"

"I tell you, I'm bleeding. Look. Blood. No, here. My right ear lobe."

Eleanor hands him a flowered Kleenex. Then she inspects the sailfish, which rides upon the disordered bedclothes.

"Its eye's dropped out," she says. "You've got to help me find it, Julian."

She gets down on her hands and knees. Dressing wildly, Singer waits until she sticks her head under the bed before tiptoeing to the door. As he leaves, he hears Eleanor, muffled, saying, "If you don't help me glue the goddam eye back, I'll never let you sleep with me ever, ever again."

Sandy Barker never caught me while the crime was blazing, although he vainly loitered outside of —— East ——th Street one lunch hour. Eezie-Beezie had heedlessly left the Manhattan Telephone Directory open to the page bearing my name, address and phone number—the whole circled in pencil. However, while Sandy was keeping —— under surveillance (a job more suited to Moody's talents; but he never tumbled) Eezie-Beezie and I were just around the corner at —— Lex., where I had moved since the phone book had been published, lunching in the rosy chateaux of our skin, in the Continental style—knives in our right hands, forks, inverted, lightly grasped, in our left. That night, after Sandy had given his wife an account of his fruitless vigil, she decided to leave him, but before she could get out the door he was on her heels. The race revolved, in the main, about their bed, with many reversals of direction and fate. It was unequal, Eezie-Beezie being handicapped by the two-suiter she was carrying. When she threw in the towel, Sandy whacked her around a little bit, as Mr. Buxbaum would have said. Happily, Sandy was not, as Mr. Buxbaum would also have said, a bang-ger.

As Mr. Buxbaum once told me, "If you're a puncher, you're supposed to get in there and *setz.*" At the time, Mr. Buxbaum, myself, and Hardcastle, Mr. Buxbaum's featherweight prospect, were in Mr. Buxbaum's roomette on the Montreal Limited en route to Montreal, where Hardcastle had a fight. (He lost.) It was an especially lurid night and we were passing at a great rate through the Hudson gorge. Hardcastle was sitting on the bed, holding a transistor to one ear, like a sea shell; Mr. Buxbaum was pushing back his cuticles, and I was appalled by what I could make out of the scenery.

"I was only after one thing," Mr. Buxbaum was saying, " —the truth. When I was interested in it, I spent weeks, months trying to find it. I was tracking it down. I was like that animal who is suspicious and moves carefully through the forest."

"What animal?" Hardcastle asked.

"How should I know what animal?" Mr. Buxbaum said. "But I find I'm an *alter cocker* and have got no closer, no closer. I wanted to get something done before I died."

"You have," I said.

"Baloney!" he said. "I wanted to put a little scratch on this old stone before I left it, like the boys in the war. They didn't know from nothing so they left their names all over the joint."

This brings to mind a journey of a similar temper I took with Moody, when he left the -.-.-. and was in what he called "security." We were en route to Vegas and beating T.W.A. on the champagne. At the time, I was terminating my affair with Moody's second wife, as he was about to marry his third. The champagne had made Moody effusively sentimental and he was carrying on at a great rate about his father, Francis X. Moody, Sr., a scratch golfer, deceased since Moody was age three-and-a-half. Moody told me that when he was age four and his mother took him to his father's grave and told him his father was lying under the dirt, he got on his hands and knees and tried to dig his way down. He then related that his father, Francis X. Moody, Sr., had played ten games for the Giants, as a second baseman, but quit for his first love, golf, where he found the camaraderie more to his taste. Moody said that John McGraw had sadly shaken his head when Moody's father informed him he was leaving the team, and said, "Francis, you got the dandiest pivot on the double play I ever seen." This recollection of his father's prowess dimmed Moody's eyes; mine, likewise. Later I had the opportunity to look up Moody, Francis Xavier, in the *Baseball Encyclopedia,* which lists everyone who played the game. In between Monzant, Ramon Segundo, who pitched for the Giants from 1954 through 1960, and Moolic, George Henry, who appeared in a single game for the Chicago White Stockings in 1886, there was nobody.

The following is a truthful relation of my overnight stay at the summer home of Ira Lubow, M.D., my psychiatrist. Since I am uninvited, I arrive under some pretext—I got lost in Dutchess County and while making a wrong turn in their driveway I got a flat? Whatever, I find the Lubows at home, by their pool. Elayne, Ira's wife, is reposing in a chaise, fashioning a bow for Alistair's topknot. Alistair is her Yorkie. Ira, wearing a black velour sweat-

shirt and swimming trunks with competition stripes, is slowly circling the pool with the skimmer, removing flowers and insects.

"Last week he got up in the middle of the night to do it," Elayne
says after the introductions. " 'Ira,' I said to him, 'just where the
hell do you think you're going at three a.m. in the morning?' He
said to me, 'Gotta cleana pool, Elayne.' My husband's exceptionally neat. You've been in his office. Did you dig the décor? I'm the
artistically inclined Lubow."

"It helps me unwind," Ira says, leaving us for the shallow end.
"It's a very soothing operation."

"Oh, what a sicky world we live in," Elayne says to me, tête-
à-tête. "You should hear what Ira has to listen to every day. By my
color scheme and accessories I at least provide him with a reposeful setting."

"May I speak freely?" I ask. Ira, pensively holding a drowned
dragonfly—*Libelulla pulchella* (Drury)—to the light, seems to be
well out of earshot.

"It ends here," she says.

"What does he say about me?"

"I didn't quite catch your name."

I tell it to her.

"He's never mentioned it . . . Ira, Alistair's fallen in the pool
again. Drop the skimmer and *do* something."

I hang around until an invitation to dinner is forthcoming; after a bit of deft stalling over Ira's mulled wine, I'm asked to spend
the night. At 2:30 a.m. I proceed down the corridor to the bathroom, per prearrangement. In a moment or two, I hear Elayne's
code knock. I let her in and relock the door.

"Hi," she whispers. "It's me."

"He never mentioned me *once*?" I whisper, attempting to help
her out of her bathrobe, turning one of the sleeves inside out, her
arm still in it.

"Never," she whispers.

Somewhat later, I happen to glance out the bathroom window.
In the moonlight, I see Ira gravely wielding the skimmer, making
his way for perhaps the thousandth time to the shallow end.

Commentary on the foregoing: Ah! my moment of anagnorisis. I didn't clap my brow or fall upon my knees; I briefly considered both, but rejected them as being out of character, more suited to hagiography. In their place, with tender susceptibility, I thought of my fellow man: *videlicet*, Mr. Buxbaum, attending to his cuticles in the Hudson gorge; Moody, reflectively twirling his champagne glass at (approx.) thirty thousand feet; others in similar places and attitudes of pessimism, delusion, self-debasement, etc.; myself fleeing Eezie-Beezie's is another example.

Moody, smartly arrayed in a close-felted Glen check, and his No. 3 were guests at my wedding; Mr. Buxbaum gave us a champagne bucket.

Three consequential years pass. I am awakened early in the morning by a telephone call. The caller identifies herself as Gloria, who, I recall, is either Moody's No. 1 or Gloria Kumrisch, whose husband was a let cord judge at the Nationals one year.

Gloria says she's in Coconut Grove, Florida, and has been thinking about me.

"We trayzher yer letters," she says. It's Kumrisch, I fear. Had I written her?

"Ah, yes," I say.

"So, anyway," she says, "watcher know, sport?"

"I'm married," I say.

"You mean you got a wife beside you an' aivreethin'?"

"An' aivreethin'," I repeat with quiet or patient submission. Indeed, as I write this I hear my stepdaughter, aged fourteen, running in place in pursuit of physical fitness; my stepson, aged twelve, at the piano playing "Cobbler, Cobbler," by Louise Christine Reeb (do you know it?); my wife on the phone, conversing in confidential tones with Mr. Mandelle, her therapist; my dachshunds at one another's throats.

"You!" Gloria says. "Maireed!"

"How's Hans?" I say. That's the tennis nut.

"Mr. Jibloney?" she says. "I told him goom bye, thanks fer nothin' in '63–'64."

Why reproduce the rest of this tiresome conversation? Nonetheless, when I hang up I am as perturbed as I ever was when cheerlessly cast adrift in the many beds of other men's wives. In a way, I feel I have finally been found out. *"We"*? She said, *"We trayzher yer letters."*

There are places such as the Fraternal Clubhouse and Academy Hall, where meeting rooms are available; certain hotels will give you a very reasonable rate on a suite if you promise not to use the towels or slip between the sheets; and a number of restaurants have facilities for private parties.

The following is the minutes of the third annual meeting of the Sisterhood:

Present: E. Barker, G. Kumrisch, A. Moody, G. Moody, J. Moody, E. Lubow [and five or six others whose names I respectfully decline to publish here]. Secretary—A. Moody. Mrs. E. Lubow, President, in the Chair.

The annual meeting of the Sisterhood was called to order at 7 p.m. on March 7, 1967, in the Longchamps—affectionately known to many of the Sisters as "Longies"—located at 1015 Madison, by the President, Mrs. E. Lubow.

Following the roll call, the minutes of the previous meeting, held on March 8, 1966, were read and approved.

Receipt of the following communication was reported by the Secretary:

(a) From Mrs. Helen R. Mendelsohn of Altadena, California, inquiring as to the correct procedure for establishing a "West Coast" chapter of the Sisterhood, there being three or four "gals" who have met the requirements for membership "out this-away."

The Secretary was directed to acknowledge this communication and ask for full particulars.

The Secretary reported receipt of an application for membership made by Mrs. Gabrielle F. Long of this city. Although Mrs. Long has been eligible since "sometime in June, 1956 as a *ghastly* consequence of one of those *wi-ild* 'Village' soirees," the precise identity of the " 'gentleman' in question" has only come to light in recent months, she ably confesses, as a result of intensive therapy. (At this point, there were commiserative murmurings from the membership.) It having been established that the application has been made in accordance with requirement, the Secretary was directed to mail ballots for election to all members in good standing in accordance with the provisions of the By-Laws.

Mrs. E. Barker then tendered a report of an incident involving "him," which took place on the night of January 3, 1960, and all present had "a good laugh." A motion to accept this report was carried.

It was moved by Mrs. G. Moody that a committee be formed to investigate the feasibility of the Sisterhood taking one or more Field Trips to the *loci* of various assignations, as many of these historic old buildings are being torn down. It was moved, and carried, that the vote on this question be taken by *Yeas* and *Nays*. The vote was taken, accompanied by "gales of laughter," with the following result:

Yeas 9—Nays 3. The motion was carried by six votes.

The chairman referred to a proposal submitted at the last meeting that Mrs. G. Kumrisch be directed to call "him" when he would assuredly be abed with "her," and "try to get a rise out of him." It was moved, seconded, and carried by uproarious acclamation.

A vote of thanks was accorded to Mrs. G. Moody for completing the first volume of the *Official History*, which recounts—with original letters and other illustrative documents introduced into the text—his "exploits" through 1959.

There being no further business, the Chairman declared the meeting closed.

Respectfully submitted,
Angela Moody
Secretary

I climb out of bed and with my bare feet grope for my slippers.

Digression on the foregoing: This has always seemed to me a fateful step. Will the floor invariably be there, for instance? Why do so many make this move so heedlessly? Presumptuously in any number of cases? I, for one, feel I am taking my chances and expect anything or, not quite conversely, nothing. As I lower my foot—whichever—I recall colored plates from childhood: for example, the first creature stepping ashore at the end of the Silurian age; Columbus landing composedly on the beach at Fernandez Bay.

By mischance, I step on one of the dogs. Although I assume my wife slept through the phone call, she now perceptibly awakens.

"Just where the hell do you think you're going?" she says.

It is, as I have recently implied, a question few can intelligently answer.

"To the kitchen," I succinctly reply. "I'm going to eat an apple."

"An *app*le!"

"*Vogue*, I believe it was, says an apple before bedtime induces slumber."

       On the kitchen counter my stepdaughter's homework is outspread. I peruse it.

The following, which catches my eye, is the answer to Question 5: "We took copper and heated it. It turned grey and soft. We burned magnesium. It flared up and turned white and flakey [*sic*]. We burned platinum. It got hot but there was no change. We put some sulfur on a quarter and burned it. The sulfur hardened on the quarter and the quarter got darker. When we burn things they combine with the oxygen in the air. When the oxygen and the metal we heated combined, in no case was there any new matter created."

I read it twice to myself, twice more out loud in a breathy, fairly reverent tone and with a suitable mid-Atlantic accent, my eyes unaccountably abrim, the victim of unclassified emotions.

My stepdaughter steals up behind me. She is wearing a white terry-cloth robe that was once worn by little Hardcastle. After he was washed up, Mr. Buxbaum and I covered the red letters of his name—which, in a gentle arc, as though symbolizing his slight rise and fall, adorned the back of the robe—with adhesive tape, and in such an anonymous state the robe subsequently clad other tomato cans of the lighter weight classes whom Mr. Buxbaum handled.

Many a time, at the tail end of the procession leading to the ring, had I followed that shabby, masked robe, borne on the shoulders of one nonentity or another.

"God," I say. "This is fundamental, immutable stuff."

"It's probably all wrong," my stepdaughter informs me.

8

Every third Thursday, Julian Singer went to the barber shop in the arcade beneath his office building to have Franco cut his hair. This Thursday Franco talked, much as usual, about Mazzinghi and Del Papa, the fighters, and Fano, on the Adriatic, where he was from. He had gone back last summer, and on his return gave Singer a gift of a seashell and a small stone he had picked up on the beach. He had written "Fano 1967" in a surprisingly fine hand on these, and they now lay on Singer's desk.

When Singer returned to his office, his secretary came in.

"A Claire Singer, who said she was once married to you, called," she said, taking the pencil from between her teeth, where she carried it like a cutlass.

"Really?" Singer said. "What did she say?"

"That she'd get back to you perhaps."

"Didn't she leave a number?"

"She said she didn't know where in the world she was going to be."

"And how did she sound, would you say?"

"She had a very nice manner of speaking."

"Well, she always had that."

That evening, Singer was taking his stepson, Simon Mountjoy, to a track meet at Madison Square Garden—the Millrose Games. Beforehand, Singer hadn't approved of the necktie Simon had chosen.

"He looks like some kind of faggot," Singer had told Daisy, his second wife, helping himself to a brandy.

"It's handwoven," Daisy said.

"He's got stripes he can wear," Singer said to Daisy. "You've got stripes," he said to Simon. "Wear a stripe or something with a little figure. Doesn't he have anything with little figures? When *I* was eight, *I* had little figures. Pairs of mallard on the wing. Beautiful. Dry flies. Irish setters—the heads. Doesn't he have horses' heads?"

"It was the whole horse," Daisy said.

"What's wrong with all those little whole horses?" Singer asked Simon.

"It's been given to Goodwill," Daisy said.

"You see . . ." Singer said to Simon. The boy looked uncertain. ". . . how they wear you down," Singer went on. "Giving your favorite tie away to a Puerto Rican when your back's turned."

"But I like *this* one," Simon said.

Singer put his arm around his stepson, careful not to spill his brandy. "You don't want to look like a little faggot, do you?" he said.

"Why do you always have to be so improbable?" Simon said.

"Dear heart, it's im*pos*sible," his mother said.

"A Puerto Rican youngster wouldn't wear a tie with little horses on it," Singer said. Simon had gone over to his mother. "Is he going to pick something else out?" Singer asked. "The meet's not wholly compulsory. As a matter of fact, I could do with some steam." He made a show of looking at his watch.

"Why *don't* you take a little steam?" Daisy said.

"A little steam," her husband repeated dreamily, draining his glass. "Elevator operators at the Y take the tickets off my hands. Puerto Ricans. Be very grateful." He said next, "I know for a fact he has stripes."

"We're not going?" the boy said to his mother.

"Your stepfather wants to take a steam bath."

"But haven't we got tickets?" Simon said to his mother.

" 'Sole judge of truth, in endless error hurled; / The something, something, something of the world,' " Mrs. Singer quoted to Mr. Singer, who looked fairly blank.

"But haven't we got tickets?" Simon said to his stepfather.

"Come along, Simon," his mother said. "We're going on a stripe hunt," and they left the room.

Singer went around examining the pictures and book titles as though it were someone else's apartment.

After Singer and his stepson took their seats in the loge, Singer kept looking about for the beer vender. When he saw him, he whistled through his teeth. The man came over and Singer motioned him to bend down.

"Drop around every fifteen minutes, chief," Singer whispered, winking, slipping him two dollars.

"What did you tell him?" Simon asked.

"That his fly was open," Singer said. He reached over and adjusted the knot in Simon's tie—now gold with a blue stripe.

"Are you going to get drunk again?" Simon asked.

The band, which had been playing a galop in quick tempo, abruptly stopped. Singer pointed to the pole-vaulter poised below them at the head of the runway.

"He'll never make it," he said.

"Why don't you want him to?"

"You're not following me, Simon. You're a little sentimentalist. Personal feelings don't come into play here. What's it to me whether he clears the height or doesn't clear it? You see, what it boils down to is, well, essentially—can he make it. I say he can't. But then I'm older than you. But feel free to disagree."

"But you don't want him to."

The vaulter knocked the bar off on the way up and the band resumed playing.

"What did I tell you?" Singer said.

He had screwed up the speech about the pole-vaulter, he realized. When it came to philosophy . . . Well, there you are.

After his third beer, Singer endeavored to think of something else to say to his stepson. "Do you want a coke?" is what he finally said.

"They have Pepsi," Simon said.

Then they grew silent. A mile relay race was in progress.

"Do you think you could beat them?" Simon asked.

"Hardly."

"Were you a fast runner?"

"I got two Thirds," Singer said. He recalled for a moment himself—oh dear!—dressed all in orange, out of breath, far behind.

"My father was the captain of the Harvard track team," Simon said.

"And now Daddy Skippy is a little alcoholic and—what is it?—temporary industrial help."

"My father's an erratic social drinker," Simon said.

"Of course," Singer said. "You see, as your mama's therapist has rather conventionally expressed it, I'm insecure."

"And now you have to make a reparation."

"Yes, I know all about that."

After his fourth beer, Singer asked Simon to kindly excuse him for a moment please.

"Are you drunk?" Simon asked.

"What it is is I'm older," he said, rising. "I'll be back in 'arf a mo'."

Singer uncertainly climbed the stairs and was wandering around in a dim tunnel when he thought he spotted his first wife, Claire, but it wasn't she.

If it had been, he thought, he would have said to her, smiling, "I'm looking for the little boys' room."

And she would have replied, "I'm looking for the little girls' room."

"You never went to these things," he would have said next.

"Did you ever ask me?"

"You know I don't remember those things. I'm with my son. He's my stepson, really. He's the fastest runner in his class. Well, he's the second fastest. It's hereditary."

"You have a load on."

"Otherwise, we could go have a drink or something, somewhere."

At this stage, he would have reached out for her, possibly, although, as in the past, he wouldn't have been sure if that was what he was doing—reaching out for her or making an indefinite gesture.

"Oh, it's much too late in life for that," she would have said, perhaps fending him off. "And even so, Carl's taken me."

"The nut fixer with the fur hat? But that's unprofessional."

"But I stopped."

"But I didn't know they did that."

"They did what?"

"That if you stopped you could sleep with them. Say, did you ever ask if you could sit up? Don't you remember, you said you were going to stop if he didn't let you sit up? Did you sit up?"

And she would have said at last, indistinctly, "I sat up."

"Well, there you are, you see."

He could hear the band playing distantly, and, occasionally, shouts and applause. It crossed his mind: Millrose—a mill, a rose. The mill, white and reflected in the water, and rosebushes about it. In the evening, the air would be dark green like the stream, so that the roses glowed darkly red. He would have liked to tell Claire this, but she would have said first, "I'm really not going to be able to hold out any longer."

And "What do you like about it?" he would have said instead. "The darkies running around in their underwear? Huh? Huh?"

So she would have left him again.

As Singer got back to his seat, there was a great roar.

"He made it," Simon told him.

"What are you talking about?"

"The one who missed before who you hate."

"Has my chum with the beer been back?" Singer stood up, looking for him, and was told to sit down. He turned and saw it was an elderly man wearing a car coat yelling at him. "Why don't you shut up?" Singer said.

"Can't we go home?" Simon said.

Singer told his wife before they went to sleep, "Then this youth, the All-Irish-American boy . . .Well, he wasn't *exactly* a youth. He must have been eighteen or nineteen. But he was an inch taller than I am. Check that. Make it an inch and a half."

"And how much did he weigh?" Daisy asked.

"He was wearing a maroon pullover his old mither made," Singer went on. "Black shoes coming to those points . . ."

"What color were his socks?"

"He had a big broth of a head. A biz admin major at Manhattan College was what he was. Straight C-minuses. He stuck his face in mine."

"But he was in the row above you, you said."

"No, he came down to my row and put his face up against mine. 'That's my father you're telling to shut up,' he said. His father turned out to be the old man in the car coat. 'That's my father you're telling to shut up.' "

"What did you say?"

"I didn't say anything. What did I have to say to him? It was his father. I thought he might start something."

"That old man?"

"The boyo. I thought he might get cute."

"What would you have hit him with?"

"I'd've gut-punched him," Singer said.

"Is that what you hit Simon with?"

"You know very well I always hit Simon on the arm up here. But he sat down. Or, it may have been, I sat down. Be that as it may, we sat down."

"My hero."

"Now what I'd like to do is relate a passing thought I recently entertained, if I may," Singer said. "It was, I think, on the order of a reverie. It's that I was contemplating Millrose—the word by itself—while we were enjoying the meet together, Simon and I, and it came to me . . . Well, a mill and a rose! And next I imagined a white mill—whitewash—by a stream, which was so slow-moving and very dark green, and all about the mill there were these rosebushes that hadn't been tended in ages, with abundant red roses on them. Hundreds of roses, Daisy! You should've seen them all. In my mind it was evening. At that time, the way it is, roses appear to be burning steadfastly in a way, and the stream was the same shade as the air and the leaves of the bushes so that there were no lines between them. You see it, don't you? You don't think it's too conventional? How does it strike you?"

"It's a weensy bit banal," she said. "Where'd you read it?"

"I made it up."

"It's not like you."

"I really did. Why do you say that?"

"Because I know who you are."

When Singer and Simon had come home from the meet, Skippy Mountjoy and Daisy were sitting on the floor, crying. Skippy had all the clothes he owned on his back: a woolen shirt and a pair of pants with a piece of clothesline serving for a belt—except that he had his shoes off, and he and Daisy were gluing the soles back with epoxy.

"Bad as all that?" Singer said to Skippy, getting himself a drink.

"What are you crying for?" Simon said.

"Kiss Daddy Skippy good night and buzz off," said Daisy.

"And how was the meet?" Skippy asked.

"The best part was where he made it," Simon said.

"Made what, dear heart?" his mother said.

"Simon had the hots for a pole-vaulter," Singer said.

"What are you crying for?" Simon said.

"Isn't someone supposed to tell him?" Singer said. "Isn't it the way they're to be reared?"

"We were watching a movie on TV," Daisy said.

"But you don't boohoo at movies," Singer said. "Did she boohoo at movies when you were married to her?" he said to Skippy.

"Someone died at the end," Simon said.

"Got married, more likely," Singer said.

"Simon, get us some string to tie Daddy Skippy's shoes so they'll adhere, and then buzz," Daisy said.

"I, for one, would like to know who did what at the end," Singer said.

"Nobody did anything," Daisy said. "It's icky poo."

"Oh, God," Singer said. "Ickiness rears its icky head."

"It was the movie Skippy and I went to the night we learned I was, oh, pregnant, but we'd already seen it."

"Was that me?" Simon said.

"Man the pumps!" Singer said. "The icky poo is up to the gunwales." He picked up one of Skippy's shoes.

"It was me, wasn't it?" Simon said.

"No, I believe it was Bishop Sheen," Singer said.

"I don't think it's up to me to say anything," Skippy said.

"It never was," Daisy said.

"You see, no end of ickiness as far as the eye can see," Singer said.

Daisy took Simon off to bed.

"Anything lined up jobbie-wobbie-wise?" Singer said to Skippy.

"There are one or two things if I were well turned out."

"Say, I never *did* follow what exactly transpired with your wardrobe?"

"It's not that edifying . . ."

"If you don't mind, I'd rather you didn't lecture me," Singer said. "You take a ten and a half?"

"Not without three pair of socks."

"I may have a surplus of loafers."

"I don't think I'm the loafer type."

"You'll never know unless you try them on."

Singer left the room, coming back momentarily with the shoes and several pairs of long black socks.

"I'd use a form when you wash them out," he said.

"I'm sure they're not my style," Skippy said, putting the shoes and socks on and walking experimentally up and down. "What do you think?" he asked Daisy, who had just returned. "Are loafers me?"

"They say 'you' to me," she said.

"You don't think they make me look a bit too trainee?"

"All they need is a good shine," Singer said.

"You see," Skippy said, "I still have my youthful features."

He showed them his profile.

"I wouldn't go dancing in them if I were you," Daisy said.

"You don't think my ankles look too fat with all these socks?"

"Why don't you take Skippy for a little steam?" Daisy said to her husband.

"Too late for steam," Singer said.

"Are Daddies Julian and Skippy going to say good night to him?" Daisy said.

"After you, Daddy Julian," Skippy said.

"Won't have it, Daddy Skippy," Singer said, bowing him out and bringing up the rear.

They stood about in the dark at the foot of Simon's narrow bed.

"Oh, Siiiiiiiimon," Singer sang softly.

"Simon, Simon, Simon," Skippy sang up the scale.

"Si-si-si-si-si-si-siiiiiiiiiimon," Singer sang.

"Simon, Simon, Simon," Skippy sang down the scale.

"Simonimonimonimonimeeeee," Singer sang.

"Simonimonimonimonewmeeeeeee," Skippy sang.

Listening, enchanted by Simon's perfect breathing, it crossed Singer's mind again: a mill, a rose. Oh dear!

"Sleeping," he whispered.

"Asleep," Skippy whispered. In a moment, he added, "Two would be enough."

"Two for God's sake of what?"

"Socks. Weensy bit on the tight side. You sure you wear a ten and a half?"

"If you don't want them, say so."

"No, it's just that I got to keep up me dignity. You know how 'tis. No, I suppose you don't."

"I know all about it," Singer said. A little later, he added, "Might as well kiss him now. You don't mind?"

"By no means."

"Won't embarrass you?"

"You wouldn't happen to have any spare garters lying around?"

"That's unlikely."

"Boy, do you stink of el beltos," Simon, awakening, said to Singer.

"Here, my turn," Skippy said, bending over the bed.

"I'll buy you a shine," Singer said.

"Where you going to get a shine around here, it's midnight?"

"We'll take a cab."

"Daddies, come back," Simon said.

As the cab went through the Park, Singer said, "I saw this person at the meet I thought was Claire, who I used to be married to, except it wasn't. She doesn't even reside here any more. She's on the Coast somewhere, it seems, last I heard. Newport. One of those places out there, with all her little Westies. We're *hahd*ly in touch. The whole thing just fell all to pieces at the end. All. To. Pieces. But perhaps you've heard the exquisite story."

Skippy, lounging in a corner, smoking one of Singer's cigars, gave no sign.

"The nitty-gritty," Singer went on, "is I never had a chance. She didn't know who I was, whatever I am, *whom*ever I am. Perhaps she did by her lights, but she didn't make allowances. You've got to make allowances. And she never forgave me for not at first letting her know who I really was or that that was all there was. But, I mean, you see, I'm me. I'm the man I always have been. But she said that wasn't fair. Persons change. So as it was we had nothing to say to each other, and who can remember if I ever loved her? What the point is is the same thing's happening with me and Daisy, who you've had some dealings with, and what about it? Am I to change? I, who am what I am? I'm not tootin' mah horn, but you recognize that basically I have good instincts. Daisy keeps insisting I be different, nonetheless. Well, we can all be better than we are, but I don't ask *her* to. At this point in life, we are who we are, aren't we? You don't expect something from somebody that they're not. Do your best, that's what you do. But it's a two-way street. Of course, in your case, it was another thing altogether. You were on the sauce . . . And it started out to be such a nice day. Franco gave me a trim, and then I was taking Simon to the meet. I'm not at ease with abstract concepts. But it did start out to be such a nice day, and I was looking forward to it."

"There's not going to be any shine place open," Skippy said gloomily.

"To come back to what I was saying for 'arf a mo'," Singer said.

"Back? To what? What do you want me to come back to?"

"What I've been saying. What else can you come back to?"

"But what do you want me to say? You said it all."

"No," Singer said. "Who's right?"

"What is it you want of people?"

"Who's right?"

Emerging from the Park, the cab stopped for a red light. "Then I'm sorry," Skippy said, opening the door on his side and getting out.

Singer told the driver to take him home instead.

"What'd you and Skippy talk about?" Daisy said after her husband told her about all those roses.

"You know I can never think of anything to say to him."

"Must you always glorify yourself in one way or another?" she said.

"We're two bugs in a rug, aren't we?" he said. "Where is your famous smile? Why aren't you nicer?"

She reached up and turned out the light.

"Oh, I forgot," he said in the dark. "The mill was also reflected in the water, in case you're interested."

9

I am on my knees, bowed over the tub, giving the dogs a bath. They stand serenely in the water like Théodore Rousseau's cows. I address them.

"You're a good 'ittle doggie, Joshie. Jakie, Joshie's a good 'ittle doggie, isn't he, Jakie? Are you a good 'ittle doggie like Joshie, Jakie?"

Daisy, my wife, washing her hair (Bronze Goddess is the current mode) in the sink, interrupts to say she doesn't want me to write about her any more.

"If you can't define our relationship any better, forget about it. Get yourself some new characters. I'm sick of being separated, reconciled, divorced, packing, unpacking, watching you pack, watching you unpack. I don't want to be involved with this crumby guy. You make me sound as dead as you. I want someone to bend me backward. You don't say anything about love or what really happens between two people. You never commit yourself to any kind of explanation of what's actually going on. You never take me dancing."

"But I can't dance."

"You can do the slow ones."

"Daisy, you're a good 'ittle mommy, Daisy. You're a good 'ittle mommy, aren't you, Daisy?"

Fridays I cook dinner for me and Cassie, my stepdaughter, who is thirteen, because Daisy goes to group therapy.

"Do you want your lamb chops on the pinkie-winkie side or on the rosy-wosy side?" I ask Cassie, who is looking for split ends.

"Do you notice anything different about how my face looks?" she says.

"You're wearing eye liner at your age?"

"No."

"Jesus Christ, mascara?"

"No."

"Daisy's Blush On?"

"No, no, no, no, no."

"Zo?"

"It's that I look so pretty."

"Oh."

"You don't love me."

"What do you mean I don't love you? I do so love you."

"You always put Mommy in your stories and you never put me in."

"I did so put you in a story."

"Once. Three years ago."

"Mommy says she doesn't want to be in my stories any more."

"*Really?*" Cassie says, delighted. "Then you can write about *me* now."

"What do you want me to write about?"

"About this girl who has two kittens, Hero and Leander, and lots of different boy friends, and goes to Nightingale-Bamford."

"Guess what, Cassie-Assie?" I say to her the following Friday, over our junkets.

"Are you going to let me read it myself?" she says hopefully. "You're going to read it out loud," she says resignedly.

"The name of the story is 'Irises,' " I say, removing the paper clip from the MS with a flourish.

"Don't do me any favors or anything, but would you read it

slowly and distinctly and with a lot of expression?"

"*Ne* worriez *pas.*"

"And say 'ahrange' not 'oarange.' "

"*Je* swear. I'm going to start reading now. Are you ready?"

"I'm ready."

"*The former ambassador, nearly seventy, very well shaven, sat at a metal table on the terrace, listening to the tea orchestra playing 'Jeannine, I Dream of Lilac Time.'* "

"How does it go?"

"Once, when I happened to favor you with my rendition of 'Going Back to Old Nassau,' you told me I couldn't sing."

"I take it back."

"I don't know how it goes."

"Hum it. I don't mind so much when you hum."

"But I never heard it. It's an old song."

"How can you use it in a story if you can't even *hum* it?"

"I make things up."

"It's not fair."

"May I continue?"

"You may continue."

"*Warships of different nations, decked with bunting, floated on the silky bay.*

" '*I dislike imposing my double life on you,*' *the ambassador was saying to Dr. Battles, 'particularly since we should like you to come to dinner later this week.'* "

"He's cheating on his wife," says Cassie.

" '*Miss Kenyan is scarcely an encumberance,*' *Dr. Battles said, smiling at the young lady in the orange shift—*"

"Ahhrange. You swore."

"*Ahhhhhh*range."

"Is she me?"

"No. Sh-h-h. You come in later."

"*—who was the third person at the table. 'What a lovely iris you're wearing.'*

"*Dr. Battles no longer practiced; he had a dark beard which, it was said, implied thwarted violence, and a reputation for gallantry.*

" '*Bunny gave it to me,*' *Miss Kenyan said. 'Just think, we've been friends exactly a week and he's given me a different-colored iris every day.' "*

"Who's Bunny?"

"Please. Do me the courtesy of letting it unfold."

"What country does this all take place in?"

"I never say."

"Is it a tale of the supernatural?"

"I'm plunging ahead."

"Dr. Battles twisted his ring, an heirloom, and the ambassador winced, but the latter's distaste was evidently not transmitted to his hand, with its eminent veins, which tenderly enclosed Miss Kenyon's hands. At any rate, she had turned away so that her face might more directly receive the final rays of the sun.

" 'Miss Kenyon's from Nottingham,' the ambassador said. 'Where they shot the arrows, as she would have told you if I hadn't mentioned it first. She's here on holiday. Perhaps Dr. Battles will go swimming with you tomorrow, if he isn't otherwise occupied.'

" 'Oh, would you really?' she said, still facing the sun, her eyes lightly, but somehow gracelessly, shut. 'Dr. Battles, don't you think it awfully funny that Bunny should choose to live here and not know how to swim? I really think it's awfully funny.'

"Dr. Battles, who had occasionally gone swimming with the ambassador from the narrow, rocky beach which fronted his villa, said, 'I would have been delighted, Miss Kenyan, but I've already committed myself. A few of us are going up into the hills after butterflies.' "

"The ambassador lied," says Cassie.

"Only a little white one."

"But you've led me to believe he was going to be the hero."

" 'Oh, really?' said Miss Kenyan. 'You don't say. Butterflies?'

" 'Dr. Battles pursues fleeing beauty in his fashion,' said the ambassador.

" 'Do you stick those little pins in them? I think it's awfully nasty, don't you, Bunny ?'

" 'I believe they are nearly or already dead then,' the ambassador said. 'So it hardly matters what one does to them.'

" 'Ooh, look at me, I've really got to run along now,' Miss Kenyan said. 'I'll be late for my appointment at the beauty salon if I

*don't. The sea does awful things to my hair, Dr. Battles. What color
iris will you be bringing me tomorrow, Bunny ?'*

*" 'I'm afraid I've given you one of every color I have in my
garden. We shall have to start at the beginning again. Does that
make you sad?'*

" 'Listen to him,' she said.

*"After she had left, the ambassador said, 'I regret to say, I for-
give Miss Kenyan everything, for she has the sweetest, warmest
breath I have ever inhaled in the dark. At times, I think it must
be the essence of youth. I've suggested to her that if she bottled it,
she could become rich overnight, if no more beautiful. I have these
moments of fondness, Doctor. Do you think it's at all serious?'*

" 'No, but it might be catching.' "

"No offense," says Cassie, "but that speech didn't exactly grab
me."

"And why not?"

"It's too pseudo-sophisticated and everything."

*" 'Which reminds me, do you think it was wise, at your age, to
take up butterfly collecting? At the least, it wasn't chivalrous.'*

*" 'To capture imaginary butterflies, which, as you may well be
aware, are never as pretty as the real ones, only taxes the mind,
which gets far too little exercise here, Bunny.'*

*" 'I told Miss Kenyan that Mother used to call me that because
I was so inquisitive, which, of course, is untrue. I was never referred
to by any term of endearment whatsoever, even as a child, but Miss
Kenyan so wanted to be able to call me something. I didn't have
the heart to disappoint her.'*

"Bunny?"

"Sniff, sniff, sniff? Wobbly little nose?"

"He would have chosen something else."

"What might that have been?"

"Oh, I really don't know. It's your story."

" 'But why did you tell her you couldn't swim?'

*" 'Simply because I am ashamed of my body, Dr. Battles. Be-
fore Miss Kenyan and I make love, which, by reason of circumstance, must be during the day—and on this coast there is always
such a great outpouring of light—I always draw the blinds. Thank
God, for some reason, old men still apparently feel all right.' "*

"Is this going to be dirty?"

"I sort of resent that. I don't write dirty stories."

"I don't care for the way the ambassador expresses himself."

"Is that right?"

"It's phony and stuff."

" *'Perhaps, though, that is because we cannot accurately touch ourselves. Alas, we can see so terribly well. At times, in these past years, I have thought of the man who was dissatisfied with the quality of his image and kept purchasing new mirrors. So much dissembling, Dr. Battles. It seems hardly worth it. I confess I even contrived the foregoing example. But I still have curiosity. It's nothing more than that. It never was. My wife is after me to write my memoirs. She has fixed up a room for that purpose, giving on the garden.'* "

"You said you were going to write a story about *me*. Where am I?"

"We're nearly up to you, sweetheart."

" *'The paper she got me is still in its wrapper—dark blue, pelagic even, light cockle, grain long.'* "

I say, "Aren't you going to ask me what the hard words mean?"

"No," my stepdaughter says.

" *'It amuses me as little to look back as it once did to look ahead. I have nothing to pass on but a respectable garden—those old, hidden, twisted tubers—and some exaggerated follies. I have had no ideals and less greatness, but perhaps you will not be entirely unkind to me in your anecdotes, Dr. Battles. Can I give you a lift?'*

"*When they had gone a few blocks, the ambassador pulled to the curb and said, 'This, I believe, is the beauty shop where Miss Kenyan was bound. I'm going to see if she's done yet. We can buy her a last drink before nightfall.'*

" *'A door swinger,' said Dr. Battles.*

" *'A grand finale,' the ambassador said.*

"*He got out of his car and stepped into the shop. A moment later he reappeared, got in and drove off, gathering speed along the coastal road, which was bordered by apricot trees, their fruit glowing feebly in comparison to the lights strung about the warships, which had just been turned on.*

"The ambassador said finally, —"

"Are you still paying attention?" I ask.

"I can't control my attention."

"It's boring."

"Sh-h-h."

"It's probably no good."

"Shush."

" *'The proprietor, whose name seemed to be Mr. Adam, said, in reply to my inquiry, 'Excellency, no Miss Kenyan no have no appointment this night at no time at all.'*

" *'Perhaps,' said Dr. Battles, fiddling with his beard, 'it was another salon she had in mind.'*

" *'Fortunately, it wasn't,' said the ambassador."*

"She's cheating on the ambassador," says Cassie.

" *'Come swimming tomorrow,' Dr. Battles said. 'I have discovered a place where we can spear octopus to our heart's content. The water is exceedingly shallow, too.'*

" *'I can still dive over my head,' the ambassador said. 'If I didn't know your hidden faults, Dr. Battles, I'd think you were as great a fraud as I am.' "*

"I know what happens," says Cassie. "They both discover each other swimming."

"You happen to be wrong."

"*When he got home, the ambassador went into his garden, accompanied by a procession of his wife's cats. His wife, who fixed her grayish hair in a single, broad braid, came out, too, to watch him kneeling among the flowers.*

" *'You can't possibly see what you're doing,' she said. 'It's nearly dark.'*

" *'I'm labeling the irises,' he said. 'I'm going to dig most of these up, just saving one plant of each variety. In their place, I'm going to put in some new ones I'm ordering, so next year, at this time, we shall have many more colors.'*

" *'Listen to him,' said his wife, addressing the cats that sat marbled, godlike, on the dusky lawn. 'He should live so long.' "*

"I don't think that line is appropriate," says Cassie.

"Why?"

"She sounds like your mother."

"That line happens to be in there for the purpose of irony. If you had been listening you would have realized that it was an echo of another line that was said before."

"But don't you think it's a little bit too Jewish?"

"And, in case you're interested, that's the end of the story."

"Oh, that's thrilling. But you didn't put me in."

"Ah," I say. "But I did. You're his wife."

"I'm whose wife?"

"The ambassador's?"

"That old bat's *me*?"

"Many years have transpired, darling. The cats are the great-great-great-great-great-great grandchildren of Hero and Leander, and that old bat went to Nightingale-Bamford, and one of her many boy friends grew up, married her, and was subsequently appointed ambassador."

"I don't want to be in your stories any more," says Cassie.

"What am I going to write about? Don't you want me to make a living?"

"Why doesn't she divorce that creep?"

"Because they're happily married."

"No, they're not. He goes out with other women."

"But she doesn't know about it."

"That's how much you know about women. Write some more where she leaves him, Daddy."

"*The next day, as the ambassador, wearing his bathing suit beneath his robe, and carrying his snorkel, mask, and trident, was waiting on the lawn for Dr. Battles to come by in his car, Michel, the ambassador's man, came down the path with two cases.*

"*'Just what do you think you're doing with those?' the ambassador said. 'I'm not going anywhere.'*

"*'I am,' said his wife, who had followed Michel. 'I'm leaving you.'*

"*'But why?' the ambassador asked.*

"*'Because you don't know anything about love, or what really happens between two people. You've made me as dead as you are. I want someone to bend me backward.'*

"*'Ruthie, you're a good 'ittle mommy, Ruthie. You're a good 'ittle mommy, aren't you, Ruthie?'* ”

"I was not moved by the story at all," says Cassie. "The characters did not seem like real people, and it was therefore hard to get involved in their lives and everything. Although there is very little description, the descriptive ability seems to be on a high level throughout. The narrative ability is not on so high a level. In summary, I would say the story wasn't true to life, the characters were poorly drawn and unsympathetic, the plot wasn't too gripping and was overly bittersweet, and the irony was heavy-handed."

"I'm sorry," I say, going to wash the dishes like Melville reflectively wending his way to the Customs House.

"No," Cassie says. "You're not 'sorery.' You're sahr-ry."

"And another thing, Mr. Matzoh-ball," says Daisy, returning from group, "I'm sick of all your old girl friends in Sausalito and Laguna-oona reading your stories and sending you little notes with sprays of forget-me-nots on them: 'Tell me (and please *do* tell me) is that fact or fancy about you and your wife? I *do* hope all is well.' ”

10

As, toward the end of his thirty-seventh year, Julian Singer swims around Slough Pond, his mother stands in the little parking area beside his rented car, its paint job scored by branches—a testament to his careless driving. From her vantage point, a path descends to the nearby shore, where Singer's wife is catching up with the *Times*; today she is working on the day before yesterday's.

Although Singer's mother is in the shade, she is shielding her eyes with her right hand. "Oh, look, look, isn't it marvelous?" she exclaims. "He's got such rhythm. He doesn't miss a stroke. He never stops. What endurance. But does he always do it clockwise?"

"He breathes on the left side," Singer's wife says.

"Oh, my," his mother says.

"So if he went around the other way," his wife continues, "he wouldn't be able to see the shore and he'd be swimming all over the place."

"He was always exceptionally dreamy," his mother says.

"Solving the world's problems," says Singer's father from the bushes, where he is changing out of his wet bathing suit.

"Can you see him now?" Singer's mother asks Singer's wife. "I seem to have lost him."

"He's in a cove," Singer's wife says. "He'll be heaving into sight in a moment."

"Bravo!" his mother cries when he reappears. "Think of doing it every day. What a wonderful thing to be able to do such a thing."

"Where is he now?" says Singer's father, emerging from the bushes.

"Out there," says Singer's mother.

His father directs his gaze along the far shore, finally descrying his son's minute figure—his arms mostly; silvery splashes as he withdraws them from the water.

"He's at two o'clock, Mother," Singer's father sings out, and sits down on a prominent root and carefully dries between his toes.

Singer's mother says, in reference to her son, "He was wonderfully adept at picking up marbles with his toes. One, two, three— how many? All the different colors."

"When he was seven—" Singer's father says to Singer's wife.

"Eight," Singer's mother says. "I knew I should have brought the binocs."

"Whatever," Singer's father goes on. "When we visited him at camp, he was in First Area in swimming. They had four of them, demarcated by lemons. Fourth Area was for the most proficient youngsters. Everyone was swimming merrily about. He remained on the bank shivering, all bent over like a question mark, with a characteristic scowl."

"Solving the world's problems," says Singer's mother.

"What a skinny marink!" says Singer's father, putting on his socks and sandals. "Now he could play Tarzan."

"He's overweight," Singer's mother says. "All those sandwiches you give him for his lunch," she says to Singer's wife. "He would be better off if you made them open-face."

"I'm going to scout around for kindling," Singer's father says. "Your supply is depleted."

"He's famous for his fires," Singer's mother says in reference to Singer's father. "But aren't you going to keep him in view?" she calls after Singer's father as he strides off into the woods. "Yoo-hoo, he must be rounding the homestretch." Singer's father vanishes. "I've said something wrong, haven't I?" Singer's mother says to Singer's wife. "And last month Dad chided me because I pointed out that there was no doorman in your new building."

Later on, she says, "What a panorama!"

Singer's wife tears out an ad, lays the *Times* aside, and closes her eyes. Damselflies hover above her knees.

"I know a marvelous diet," Singer's mother says. "Don't you think we could interest him in it?"

Getting no reply, she says, "Imagine, one day last week I decided to go to the Barbizon for a swim, but they have a sign which says a person who is unable to swim at the deep end may not use the pool. This was a bit of a setback, as I always like to be able to put my foot down, so I asked the attendant whether I could go in if I confined myself to the shallow end. I told her I would be on the honor system. You see, I can only swim a few strokes without becoming distressed. The attendant said it would be much better if I took some lessons. But when I approached the young man who gave the lessons he was loath to take me on when I told him how unsettled I become if I can't put my foot down. But I wish to sign on as a private pupil, I told him. 'You can swim,' he said. 'But you lack the right attitude.' And there and then he told me to immerse myself in the pool. Naturally, I began to lower myself in at the shallow end. 'Oh no, you don't,' he said. 'You come up here.' What he meant was the deep end. Then he took hold of a long pole and told me to set out for the shallow end. I set out along the side of the pool, so I could hold on if the need arose, but he said I had to veer into the middle. 'Suppose other people were between you and the side,' he pointed out. He held the pole just beyond my grasp and instructed me to keep my eyes glued to the tip-top, and I began swimming, and he began moving away. 'Don't look at the part nearest you,' he reminded me. Before I knew it I had swum the whole length, which shows that if you only extend yourself you can attain your goals. But he wouldn't let me linger in the pool for recreational swimming. He probably had me summed up as someone who was a menace. The concept of the pole was that he wanted me to set a distant goal, but, really, what distant goals are there for me? He probably had me summed up as someone too old to be trustworthy in the water."

Singer's father comes out of the woods, his arms full of dead boughs. "Is he in sight?" he asks.

"I believe he's making his finishing spurt," Singer's mother says.

Singer's father sets the wood down and conspicuously dusts his hands.

"What a panorama!" he says in a little while.

"He's coming ashore," Singer's mother says to Singer's wife. "Have you got his towel ready?"

Raising his head out of the water, Singer says something indistinct and continues swimming.

"He's passing on by," Singer's mother says.

"I couldn't read him," Singer's father says to Singer's wife. "Could you read him?"

"I couldn't read him," she replies.

"He's fading into the distance," Singer's mother says.

"Where is he going?" Singer's father asks.

"Around again," Singer's wife says.

"He'll turn in to a prune," says Singer's mother.

When Singer is done swimming, there is no one to greet him. He climbs, dripping, to the car. His father's bathing suit is spread out on the hood to dry. He sees his mother and father sitting close together in the back seat, unaware of his approach. He wonders what they are doing in there, and ridiculously clears his throat. His mother turns in his direction and rolls down her window.

"Your lips are a vivid purple," she says.

"I swallowed a water strider," he says. "What ever happened to What's-Her-Name?"

"It was time for her jog," his father says, his face joining Singer's mother's at the window.

"Her *what*?"

"She told us that every day she jogs to the highway, where you pick her up," his mother says.

"But she doesn't," he says.

"One-point-one miles," his father says. "She said you told her jogging was good for the heart."

Singer gets behind the wheel. His mother tells him to spread his towel on the seat so it won't get wet. Singer drives through the woods toward the highway. His father tells him to stop so he can retrieve his bathing suit from the hood. Singer says he'll get it for him. His father says he's still spry enough to retrieve his own bathing suit.

Before long they get a glimpse of Singer's wife, jogging on the crown of the narrow, sandy road. She looks back at them over her shoulder and sprints out of sight around a bend. Singer steps on the gas and in a moment is driving on her heels. His wife staggers and claps a hand to her side. He puts on the brakes. She stops, turns, and regards him through the windshield.

"I've got a stitch," she says.

He sticks his head out of the window. "Don't sit down," he says. "Walk it out."

She goes obediently up the road, alternately in sun and shadow. They follow in the car.

"If you ask me, she's out of shape," Singer's mother says.

"She needs more distance work," Singer's father says, smoothing back his hair.

"She lifts her knees too high in the air," Singer's mother says.

"Yes," his father agrees. "Far too much knee action."

A moment or two later, Singer glances in the rearview mirror and finds that his mother and father are fast asleep. He pulls off the road, comes to a stop, and observes his wife departing—illuminated, obscured, illuminated, obscured, illuminated. He wonders, momentarily, what he has done with his life. She sits down in a fairly dark place and he approaches her on foot.

"I swallowed a water strider," he says, sitting next to her.

"Don't expect me to ask you what it tasted like," she says.

"Don't tell me we're back there again," he says.

"No, we've never been where we are now," she says, rising. "Take me deeper into the woods, Mr. Macaroni."

"But they're sleeping."

She offers him a hand.

"But what happens if they awake?"

"And along the way you may tell me about the water bug," she says, "and how your hands appeared underwater, and whether nature presented you with any fresh, ingenious metaphors, and if once more you reviewed your life."

Hand in hand, they wend their way, he slightly to the fore.

"The water strider tasted very fishy," he says.

"Did you let that branch fly back in my face on purpose?" she says.

11

Julian is a capable and interesting child. He is fairly quiet in manner, but his mind is busy. He often delights us with his fine memory and clarity of insight. After our day in the country last autumn, Julian identified every leaf, shrub, berry, and bit of bark that we brought back with us. Julian is not only agreeable himself but is often a peacemaker among those more prone to have social friction. There is but one thing in regard to Julian that gives me special concern, and that is his careless posture. Perhaps the home can help us, in order that his body may be as erect as his mind is alert.

Julian Singer has arranged to meet Skippy Mountjoy at the information booth on the upper level of Grand Central, at 8:25 a.m., so they can take the eight-thirty-seven to White Plains, where Mountjoy is to appear in court. Singer arrives on time and finds out the track: no Mountjoy, as Singer had reason . . .

Singer imagines Mountjoy sleeping one off in a vestibule. Singer is aware that he usually thinks the worst of people, but does the fact that he often thinks the worst of himself, too, excuse him in any way, shape, or form? And, after all, Mountjoy *has*, in point of fact, lain in vestibules; even, once, five years ago, in Singer's vestibule, when Singer had just married Mountjoy's wife, and it hardly ever stopped raining; in the morning, Mountjoy's bare feet by the radiator. On their way out, everyone stepped carefully over him in turn—the children, too—pretending, Singer conjectures, that Mountjoy wasn't there or was somehow inviolable. Of course, for Mountjoy to have elected to spend the night in Singer's vestibule— wasn't he saying, in effect, that as far as he was concerned Singer was of no consequence?

Killing time, Singer gazes at the representation of the heavens on the ceiling. No, he corrects himself, as the imprisoned king rightly observed, time is killing me.

More probably, Singer decides, Mountjoy's seated in a luncheonette, sugaring his second cup of coffee, wearing that pale overcoat several sizes too big for him someone gave him, and poorly shaven. A luncheonette in a subway arcade—*that* would be consonant with his style.

Skippy is always a helpful member of the group and has splendid attitudes. However, at times he seems nervously tense. He is musical, but his attention varies, and he should have special help to get his voice up. Skippy is mastering his carelessness in art, which used to occasion many lost results.

The day before, Singer's secretary had told him Mountjoy was in the reception room. Singer found him in a Barcelona chair, with two or three days growth, the ghastly overcoat buttoned to his throat.

Singer went up to him and asked if there was a draft.

Julian is a sensitive, gifted child, artistic and original. He is bright and sympathetic. This is evident in his intense love for animals, which he not only enjoys having about but also draws most skillfully on all occasions. His creative ability and originality are also expressed in the most delightful poems and stories. These are often about animals, too. He is a quiet child, but deep and sincere in his nature.

Mountjoy winked.

Singer said he didn't seem to be feeling any.

Mountjoy said he didn't seem to be wearing a tie and that he didn't wish to be the source of any possible embarrassment.

Skippy is a child of subtle nature and varied abilities who needs sympathetic understanding in order to give out his best. Like many original, creative individuals, he is exceedingly sensitive and cannot flower in a forbidding atmosphere. In music he has poise, humor, and dramatic ability. His voice is low, but he is usually in tune.

Singer asked Mountjoy if he minded if Singer remained standing.

Mountjoy said that Singer saw before him . . . He asked Singer what *did* he see before him.

Singer said that, be that as it might, he was afraid he was going to have to be getting back to the old . . . and he reminded Mountjoy that first impressions count and to be sure to shave for the judge, if not for himself.

Mountjoy asked him kindly not to be so condescending.

Singer asked Mountjoy kindly to recall that it was Singer who bailed him out of the Westchester County Penitentiary in Valhalla, of all places, the bond being in the sum of two hundred and fifty dollars, after Mountjoy's No. 2, whom Singer had never had the pleasure, had charged Mountjoy with assault, and wasn't it time to turn over a new leaf.

Julian is a highly intelligent child, honest and sincere. He is capable with his hands, and most artistic and original. He is a quiet and reserved boy, with great latent power. His contributions in class show depth of thought and common sense. Julian has made several delightful contributions in poetry, showing a lovely imaginative ability.

Mountjoy said as it so happened it had nothing to do with the sauce.

Singer said as it so happened he couldn't think of any thing to say.

Mountjoy said for the millionth time it was *she* who concussed *him* with the large pot of ferns, which, Singer may have recalled, figured in the case.

Singer said he really wasn't interested in who was in the right.

Mountjoy said that, howsomever, it would be *him* whom they would be sending to Grasslands, of all places, for observation, and that Singer's attitude was once more indicative of his insensitivity to his fellow-man.

Singer said that once more Mountjoy had misconstrued him, and that what he meant was that in the eyes of the law it no longer made any difference who threw what at whom how many times.

Mountjoy asked Singer for five for a room.

Skippy shows progress, though I feel he is capable of better work. We must encourage greater pride in achievement and workmanship. He has strong likes and dislikes, and once he has made up his mind it is difficult to get him to admit the right of the other side. He seems happily adjusted, though he is not a good mixer. Skippy can carry a tune when he sings alone, but when he sings with his classmates he has difficulty in singing accurately.

Singer said he was fiving him to death and that he'd think more highly of Mountjoy if he didn't wave his arms about so.

Mountjoy asked Singer why he felt obliged to shout at those less privileged than him.

Singer said than he.

Mountjoy said Singer was way out of touch with himself.

Singer went ho, ho.

Julian is a thoughtful, serious child, but at times he seems almost wistful. He should be encouraged, as he is one of those to whom a word of encouragement and recognition of good work means a good deal. He has been growing rapidly and needs to watch his posture. Julian seldom smiles.

Mountjoy said very well, ho, ho—adding that three would do.

Singer reminded Mountjoy that he'd be rotting in the Valhalla can if Singer hadn't . . .

Mountjoy told Singer that he no longer had the right to choose when he might abandon him, and that he was rotting, yes, yes, rotting, here, here.

Singer inquired of Mountjoy who the hell he thought Singer was.

Mountjoy said his fellow-man.

Singer asked him how he reached that striking conclusion.

Mountjoy said because he felt Singer cared.

Singer asked about whom.

Mountjoy said about Mountjoy.

Singer said no, that he rather gathered he did it, meaning springing Mountjoy, for himself.

Mountjoy said, well, good for him.

Singer said that what it was was that Mountjoy's plight per se didn't matter any more; what did was, repeatedly, the act of resurrection: bending down, bending down, bending down.

Mountjoy said he was full of it and was still trying to ingratiate himself with the Gentiles.

Singer said that, be that as it might, he was afraid he was going to have to be getting back to the old . . . and that there seemed to be little further to be gained, and that he would be seeing him, on his two feet, in the a.m.

Mountjoy said it wasn't fair to keep letting him down so he could pick him up.

Singer said that wasn't his impression.

Mountjoy shrugged.

Singer made to leave.

Mountjoy, rising, said it was somewhat awkward, but he could use two until the a.m., and, not so fast, he would repay him out of his next relief check and they'd be all squared away.

Singer reminded Mountjoy that he owed him, hmm, in child support, at, hmm, thirty-five a week—that's, hmm . . .

Mountjoy said, hmm, one thousand eight hundred and twenty dollars per annum.

Singer said, hmm, hmm, for four *anni*, and one, two, three, October—no, from the twentieth—November, December, three, four, and two weeks in March, hmm, hmm . . .

Mountjoy told Singer you had to break it down into weeks, which, hmm, hmm, made it seven thousand nine hundred and eighty.

Singer reminded Mountjoy that he owed him in the neighborhood of eight thousand dollars in child support, and if one cared to project his future from his past they'd never be all squared away in this world.

Mountjoy said Singer was a scrounge and a lousy hard determinist, and that, furthermore, *liberum arbitrium indifferentiae*, and that his understanding when he signed the separation agreement was that it was just a formality, given the bag he was in, and that Singer was lacking in maturity to throw the support thing at him now, and that if he felt like doing the bending bit, bend somewhere else.

Skippy evidently prefers to remain in the background and appears to find greater satisfaction in listening than in taking part. He will pay attention to criticisms or suggestions, but rarely makes use of them. At times he is too readily satisfied with mediocre results, although of late he is beginning to check his work before letting it falsely represent his ability.

At eight-forty, Singer is turning a shoe this way and that, inducing reflections; Mountjoy is trying to get the counterman's attention. Singer lightly closes his eyes and is appalled by hundreds of footfalls. What's said has always been drowned out by that, he thinks.

Julian remains rather quiet but gets on exceedingly well with his contemporaries. His work habits are much improved, although he is likely to go off on a tangent or pursue odd or fantastic aspects of the job at hand. It is not clear whether this is due to intellectual curiosity or to escapism. Julian has a great facility in art. This is a special gift and should be nurtured.

At nine-twenty, after the departure of the last train that would have got them to White Plains in time for Mountjoy's appearance in court, Singer recalls Mountjoy blissfully asleep that time in the vestibule, his shoes set to one side, lined up and stuffed with newspaper, his socks on the radiator cover where he had put them to dry, and the four of them, in Indian file, stepping over Mountjoy, and Singer realizes that, in a way, his foot is still suspended in the air and that he doesn't know quite where to put it down; Mountjoy shifts on his stool.

Those who require the greatest amount of work from Skippy are unanimous in their comments on his carelessness in regard to form and neatness. Skippy resents criticism on this score and refuses to see that such things are important. His occasional excellent work appears to give him an unwarranted overconfidence that he can repeat the performance at all times with little effort on his part.

12

Every so often I am made aware of how much I am my father's son—for instance, while doing the dishes. When I wash dishes, I use a cake of soap and let the water run; my head is slightly bowed, so that my forehead is resting on the cabinet above the sink, and my eyes, my wife informs me, are full of unreleased tears. This, too, is how my father does the dishes, except that he is erect. Bearing is one of his obsessions. When I was younger and tried to please him by standing up straight, he said I was having sport with him and he told me I had lordosis, which he then defined. That way I built up my vocabulary. My father also told me not to tip my chair back at the dinner table. Why did I persist? Why did he keep yelling at me? Why do I tell my son to stop tipping *his* chair back? Why does he defy me?

Lately, when my father and I talk on the phone, he doesn't say goodbye—he just hangs up. When I ask him why he won't say goodbye to me, he says he is unaware that he hasn't said it. I gather he wants me to drop the subject.

When I am seventy-one, will I neglect to say goodbye to my son for reasons that have not yet been revealed to me?

Once, I thought my father and I were poles apart. I was a dreamy boy, as he called me, as I grew to fancy myself.

We even make beds the same way—what my mother calls "the lazy man's way." That is, we don't strip the bed but tuck everything back in. My mother would just as soon my father forgot about the beds; after all, one of his favorite sayings is: If you're going to do something, do it right. Ditto the dishes. "I'd rather he'd go sculpt," she told me the other day. "Something worthwhile."

A number of years ago, my father took a ceramics class; an ashtray in the shape of a leaf survives. "He could have done things," my mother said to me recently. "It would have been an outlet."

What thoughts does my father entertain, standing at the sink as though on a parade ground? If my wife were free to investigate his eyes, what would she come up with? I imagine her giving him the once-over from several vantage points, taking his hand, leading him into better light.

Would you think anything stupendous went on in *my* head? My wife never inquires. She tells me I'm a hummer, however.

My wife won't take a shower with me. "Once the water strikes you, it never reaches me at a good angle," she says. "Besides, I have to listen to your long, boring dreams."

My father calls me up. "You're old enough to have your own safe-deposit box," he says. I have always kept my valuables in his tin. I say, great, but I want a box in *his* bank. I wish my father would take a minute to question my motives, but he doesn't. Does it even occur to him? We make arrangements to meet outside his bank. "Wear a tie, for God's sake," my father says.

My father has never asked me to meet him *inside* anything. How would it be embarrassing? I've never challenged him on this. Not long ago, my son begged me to meet him *outside* the drugstore where we were going to eat before a Knicks game. I ask you. I arrive ahead of time, because I assume my father thinks I'm not very punctual. Of course, he's beaten me there. I see him before he sees me, in his long, gloomy overcoat. He has taken up an equivocal stance to fool passersby. Has the distinguished-looking cat paused to note an architectural detail? Or, toward the end of his life, has what was unclear suddenly become known to him?

"What are you wearing a vest for?" he says, taking hold of my overcoat and flinging it open.

"I want you to be proud of me when we're with your cronies at the bank," I say.

"Why do you insist on going to extremes?" he says.

We descend together to the vault—the netherworld. For a moment, I think he is going to take me by the arm, but I am disappointed. I have always got a kick out of these excursions with my father—two men of affairs. The first time he took me to the vault, it made a strong impression. I was worthy of him, his mysteries. Smitty, the vault attendant, will be in the anteroom at the bottom of the flight of marble stairs. He always has a big hello for my father, and a word for me, too.

A strange man is seated at Smitty's desk before the vault.

"Smitty's out to lunch," my father says to me.

"Yes?" the man says to my father.

"We'll wait for Smitty," my father says.

"Who?" the man says.

"Mr. Smith," my father tells him.

"He retired last week," the man says.

"But he never said anything to me," my father says.

"He was sixty-five," the man says.

"I've been a depositor for forty-five years," my father says. The man is mute.

"Smitty was delightful as a human being," my father says. "He never failed to have a cheery greeting."

"One of nature's noblemen, so I've heard," the man says.

My father takes out his key case, and we accompany the new attendant into the vault.

"If you'll just sign here," he says, indicating the register.

"Jesus Christ," my father says, "I haven't signed in forty-odd years."

In the coupon room, my father and I sit across the table from each other. The lighting makes him look older and more tired, and I avert my eyes.

"I guess Smitty must have been getting up there," he says, slowly opening his tin.

"Dig the hunting prints on the walls," I say.

"They're tarting the place up," my father says. "Did you say you got a haircut?"

"You betcha."

"What about this?" he says, flicking the hair about one of my ears.

"It's styled," I say.

"And this?" he says. "And this?"

"You wouldn't yell at Harold Macmillan," I say. "He wears his hair full at the sides."

"I'm not yelling at you," my father says.

When he has sorted out my little pile of valuables, we leave the coupon room and he explains to the attendant that I wish to rent a box. I fill out some forms and we reenter the vault. The attendant climbs a ladder to reach my box.

"Ah, ah," my father says, "you're almost to Heaven."

While the attendant is screwing on the lock, my father and I sit by his desk in our overcoats.

"Smitty was pretty much all surface," my father says, revolving his hat by the brim in his lap.

"Hey," I say, noticing his trouser bottoms for the first time. "No cuffs! You going Mod?"

"Mother turned them," he says. "They were somewhat frayed."

The hat picks up speed.

"There's no need to wait," I say.

My father gets up. "The likelihood is he never read a book in his life," he says, and goes off.

I am in the shower, presumably humming, when the glass door slides open. I am terrified. A little white demon is standing there. It is my naked wife, who hops in.

"I am in a lofty studio by the sea," I say. "In the summertime. I can tell by the typically fine, serene light."

"More froufrou," says my wife.

"In the studio is an immense block of pale marble, with a scaffold erected about it."

"More cold water," says my wife.

"On the scaffold stands my father, wearing a groovy suit, with his shirt cuffs turned back over those of his jacket. A hammer is poised in his right hand, a chisel in his left. He is about to begin a statue."

"Of what?" says my wife.

"He hasn't begun," I say.

"You're typically obstructing the flow," she says. "Did he say bye-bye to you?"

"There was no opportunity one way or the other."

"My facecloth."

"Nothing happened."

"My eyes are closed. I can't see."

"There was little or no action or passage of time."

"Blah, blah, blah. Blah, blah, blah. Every moment we expect that our fathers will reveal their secrets to us, but they never do. Why? Because we are unworthy of them."

My mother and I speak on the phone. "I've found out why your father's been in a state," she says. "He was telling me about the outing to the vault, and it slipped out. They've started all over from the beginning with his checks. Your father! A depositor for forty-five years! He was up to check number fifteen thousand and something, but when his next batch came they had put him all the way back to one hundred and one. Imagine, after being loyal to them all these years! I told him I would certainly have brought it to their attention. He said he thought of mentioning it the next time he happened to be in the neighborhood, but he didn't want them to get the impression he suffered from false pride."

Why am I watching my father so intently? Why do I pay attention to my mother when she's yakking? Do things change?

13

It is Sunday, fairly dim and silent. My wife is asleep beside me, her hands made into fists. I suppose I am committing inimical acts in her dreams.

My mother sails through the gloom with a small shopping bag, followed by my father. She has a key. When we're not here, she pops in to thoughtfully water the plants she gave us.

"I am in the way," my mother says, rather grandly.

She sits on my edge of the bed she bought us; she gets a discount.

"I see no signs of change," my father says, picking up the clothes I let fall the night before.

"You're right," I say. "I'm the boy you made me."

My father hangs my trousers upside down from my top dresser drawer.

"*I* preserve the creases," he says.

"I recall your demonstrating that little trick," I say. "It was not enough."

"At the very least," he says, "you could drape them over the back of a chair."

"We gave you special hangers," my mother says.

"*You* did," my father says. "They were uncalled for."

"It's important to have nice, shapely hangers," my mother

says.

"All it takes—" my father says.

"Is a little time and effort," I say.

"You know how it would please him," my mother says.

"Show me again, Dad," I say. "But do it slowly this time, the way you used to, with the cuffs tucked under your chin as you open the drawer. That was the best part."

"Anyone can run people down," my mother says.

"Not the case," I say. "I'm trying to find the point at which I went astray."

"You were always a rebellious spirit and a wiseacre," my father says.

"You don't show your best face to the world," my mother says.

"I try to conform," I say.

"Then why have I found this mess?" my father says. "Things strewn all over the lot."

"Because I couldn't live up."

My mother settles her gaze upon the plants she has dropped off over the years. "Are you sure Ernestyne isn't letting their feet get too wet?" she says. Ernestyne is her maid, whom we get two days a week. "The other morning when I arose, I detected an unusual aroma in the air."

"Your mother has a highly developed sense of smell," my father says.

"Your father identified it," my mother says.

"Rotting vegetation," my father says.

"We were both watering the plants, Ernestyne and I," my mother says. "Imagine!"

My father is going about the room adjusting the pictures on the walls to make them hang straight; these are Doré plates from the Inferno.

"Oh, God, put up something contemporary," my mother says to me. "Something with splashes of color." My father narrows his eyes and cocks his head first to one side then the other.

"Their ceiling's askew," my mother tells him. "He's vexed because he can't finish his puzzle," she tells me. "Why don't you give it another—"

"Whirl?" my father says. From his pocket he morosely withdraws the page from the Magazine Section that has the crossword puzzle on it, unfolds it, and smooths it out. He sits in the chair upon whose back I might have draped my pants, and crosses his legs. I remember his shoes from when I would sit on the floor beside his chair and pat them—large, unpolished, and extraordinarily seamed.

"I may need your help if I encounter any sports terminology," he says to me.

"I'm your man," I say. "You look European this morning," I say to my mother.

"I do?"

"It's a certain cast to your eyes."

"You mean Eurasian."

"I don't."

"They're tired, is that it?"

"It's not what I meant."

"Old," she says, touching herself tentatively about the eyes. "Recesses and shadows."

"It's not really light yet," I say. "What did you bring me? Another African violet? Some brownies?"

"More newspaper clippings," she says. "Do you know how I communicate with you? By circling things and cutting them out."

"But I hardly ever get around to reading them."

"You don't have to," she says. "I imagine it."

"I'm going to lie under the bed," my wife says, evidently awakening.

"We can't stay long," my mother says.

My father tears his puzzle into little pieces; these he puts in his pocket.

"I wish I could have helped you," I say.

"For the sake of argument," my father says, "let's assume I was deficient—"

"I'm not a party to this," my mother says.

"Specifically, in what areas would you say I let you down?"

"You did the best you knew how," my mother says.

"And youuuuuu?" my wife says from beneath the bed.

"We both did what we thought best," my mother says. "By

our own lights."

"Where?" my father asks me. "Hypothetically."

"I don't remember," I say.

"Perseveeeeeere," my wife says.

"This isn't going to bear fruit," my mother says.

I join my wife under the bed.

"I cut out a quotation by Arthur Miller for you," my mother says.

"You didn't have to do that," I say.

"It's very apt," my mother says.

"Have you recalled anything?" my father says.

"I'm sorry," I say.

"I'm leaving what he said in the middle of your pillow," my mother says.

Their footsteps recede.

"I saw you reach out and touch one of your father's shoes as he passed by," my wife says.

"Would you say our parents are projections of ourselves?" I say.

My wife declines to answer, and presently I fall asleep. After long preparation, I am at last ready for my transatlantic swim. It is very early, and everything is equally gray. I am standing on a beach, naked to preclude chafing, ponderous. My mother and father, who will accompany me across, feeding me and taking turns holding my head up while I sleep upon the bosom of the deep, are in a dinghy beyond the breakers, resting on their oars. I try the water with my toe. Ah, it's cold. I have three thoughts in this position. Is the swim mere rhetoric, as it were? When I step ashore, will I be adorned with a great, stiff, golden beard? Why do I cause so much pain? Counting to my favorite number, I wade out, gingerly splashing myself, patting my face, and my parents pull on the oars. Soon I am over my head. I have two thoughts in this position. Why am I not lighthearted? Why am I not deeper, more solid? When I am borne to the crests of the waves, I can see my parents far ahead, all bundled up in the pitching boat. The wind carries their voices back to me.

"It's time to trade places," my mother says.

"You're not allowed to stand up in a boat," my father says.

"I'm in a slight crouch," my mother says.

"You're tipping the boat," my father says.

"This oar is longer than the other one," my mother says.

"You're not feathering it," my father says.

"This oar is definitely heavier," my mother says.

"We're heading back to shore," my father says.

"Let's trade oars," my mother says.

"Now we're not going in any direction," my father says.

"Water from your oar dripped on my head," my mother says.

"We're dead in the water," my father says.

"Would you say that's a blister in a formative stage?" my mother says.

"It's raining," my father says.

"What happens when the boat fills up with rain?" my mother says.

I heave myself into the drifting boat, take up the oars, and row back to the beach in the rain. My parents are huddled in the stern, their eyes cast down. I notice that a number of my pubic hairs are white. I have one thought in this position. Why don't I feel any pain?

14

Julian Singer is standing by the window in his flowing pajama bottoms, relating an interesting dream to his wife, who is still in bed, when Grandma, his mother-in-law, comes into view, moving fast and low across the garden terrace.

The Singers live in the Village, on the first two floors of a renovated Federal house. Their garden has a paved terrace and a lawn sloping up from a low, sandstone wall to a row of poplars. In the center of the wall is a concrete fountain adorned with dolphins, swans, cherubim, and disrobed women in obscure compositions, which is on the fritz. At this season sooty petunias and day lilies bloom in the borders.

Singer's wife says, apropos of the dream, "Is Norman still letting you take notes?"

Norman Silver, M.D., is Singer's latest analyst.

Singer says, "Grandma is in the garden in her faded bathrobe stealing the sweet alyssum."

Singer's wife says, "They make a lovely nosegay."

Singer says, "She's digging them up by the roots."

Singer's wife pulls the covers over her head.

"She's a flower thief!" Singer shouts.

He sneaks downstairs and watches Grandma wrap the alyssum

in newspaper and pack it in her suitcase. She is going back to Waterbury on the 12:05.

"Madam," he says, stepping forward, holding up his pajama bottoms, "do you believe the whiteness of your locks mitigates the redness of your hands?"

"I believe sweet asylum is my all-time favorite," Grandma says. "Of course, there were days when my preference was anemoneezers. I can never forget them, for they rhyme with lemon squeezers."

Singer goes upstairs and addresses the form beneath the bedclothes. His theme is extrinsicality, and at times he raises his voice. There is no response. He whips off the sheet and blanket, revealing their four pillows. From the bathroom he hears his wife imperfectly humming "Amapola." He tries the door, which is locked.

"If you don't open up," Singer says, "I'll step on Simon's violin."

Simon Mountjoy, aged twelve, is Singer's stepson. Monroe Sloat, Ph.D., Singer's physiologist, has told Singer it seems unlikely that he can have children of his own, but not to abandon hope. Singer has told Dr. Sloat that, notwithstanding, he is aware of a certain shade of regret.

"Stand back, everybody," Singer says and delivers a well-aimed kick at the doorknob, remembering—ah! too late—that he is barefoot.

Singer regards his upraised foot: disembodied, perhaps not even his, knocked off a second-rate Pietà, but nicely modeled, veins and all; larger than he would have thought, too, nearly heroic, and more yellow, with several toenails needing cutting. Where had he last noticed it? On the bottom, through shallow water? Sticking up irrelevantly at the end of a bed?

Why, Singer wonders, did his wife, naked from the bath, get down on all fours and head for the bedroom closet? Why, limping, did he open the door for her? Why did she go in? Why did he shut the door behind her? He tenderly puts on his socks.

She doesn't stir. Presumably she is still crouching in the dark beneath his neckties.

Singer tells Simon, who has joined him, that there is a mouse in the closet. Singer's wife wiggles a finger so that it is visible in the crack between the bottom of the closet door and the floor. Simon asks Singer what part of the mouse he thinks that was. Singer says it might have been its little belly. Simon says he believes it was one of its little paws. There is a commotion in the closet. Singer fears his wife has dropped one of his dumbbells on the shoe rack his mother gave him for his thirty-fourth birthday. Simon says it sounds like a fairly big mouse. Singer tells Simon to poke something in the crack and see what happens. Simon sticks a ballpoint pen in and it is taken from his hand. Singer tells Simon to try something else—for example, a sheet of typing paper. Simon does so and it is taken, too. In a moment, the sheet of paper is pushed out through the crack. Upon it is written, "Your sperm are a reflection of yourself."

"Dear heart, our view of life is misleading," Singer informs Jake, a dachshund. "Of course, we have bad seats." Singer, wearing an Ace bandage on his injured foot, is going uptown in a taxi, with Jake on his lap. Jake is getting a new home because he fights with his litter brother Josh. A researcher named Topsy Temple answered the ad Singer placed in his house organ: "Available, to the proper person, Jake, 4, a dear heart. . . ." It is raining as Singer arrives at the rent-controlled apartment house on Riverside Drive, which is Topsy Temple's address.

"We need a towel or something for our belly," says Singer when Topsy Temple opens the door. She turns out to be not half bad, although on the big side. Topsy Temple gets a bath towel patterned with *fête galante*. Singer sinks to his knees in the foyer and begins drying Jake. "When it rains, dachsies' bellies accumulate moisture," he explains. Topsy Temple sits cross-legged on the floor, in order to watch. "Don't forget their little armpits," Singer says, endeavoring to look up her skirt. "For the first day or two he might be leaving his card on the rug," Singer says after a bit. There are two uncurtained windows in the adjoining room. Singer has expectations of viewing the Palisades, but he is too low down, and the windows are simply great, melancholy oblongs of light. Jake lies on his back, saying "Ahhhhh," and regarding Singer upside down. "He has a very low rate of metabolism," Singer says, "so I wouldn't give him a whole bunch for dinner or between-meal snacks."

"Am I the proper person?" says Topsy Temple.

Singer obligingly leans across Jake and kisses her.

"I'll put on a record," she says.

Singer calls up his analyst from a phone booth near Verdi Square.

"Norman," he says. "Julian. Help, I suspect. I'm not afraid of being disappointed. I'm *confident* of being disappointed. Concerning Marvin. No, Marvin Finger, C.P.A., my accountant. He came up in more than one session. He figures prominently in my notes, Norman. I can be home in ten minutes and consult them. Granted, I'm putting you on. Notwithstanding, Marvin lost my day book, Norman. It's what he makes me keep with business expenses in it in case they question my returns. This has no bearing on persistent abdominal pains about cash flow. These are all deductible items, Norman. Marvin's supposed to leaf through it and put it in the mail. The point is . . . The point is, Norman, it never showed up this year. 'Marvin,' I said, giving him a ring, 'where's my day book?' 'Didn't Fiona shoot it back already?' he said, or words to that effect. His mouth was full of lo mein or something. He eats Chinese to go at his desk. Actually, it's a table. A reproduction his mother picked out. No, I haven't put the blocks to this Fiona. 'Then she's putting it in the mail first thing,' he said. 'I'm personally supervising the matter. Julian,' he added, 'Sean wants Arnold Palmer's autograph.' Marvin is always after me to get autographs of sports personalities for Sean, who is his son. 'Have Mickey write,' he'll say, ' "To my pal, Sean, a great little center fielder. Yours in sport, Mick." ' Or ' "To my pal, Sean, a great little playmaker. Keep making those assists, fella." That's f-e-l-l-a. "Yours in sport, Wilt." Make sure the big *schwarzer* spells Sean right.' When the day book didn't arrive in the mail, I gave him another ring. 'I'm going into New York Hospital tomorrow,' he said. 'Under the knife. It's minor. Corrective. While we're having this conversation I'm making a memorandum to get you your day book as soon as I'm on my feet. Why all the anxiety about the *ferblundget* book, anyway?' 'It's got my dreams in it for Norman,' I said. 'But they're last year's dreams, Julian,' he said. 'You already told them to Norman.' 'I want them for reference,' I said."

Since he is early for his dentist appointment, Singer goes to see *Sex in the Suburbs*, a dirty movie, arriving a few minutes before the first show. The theater is nearly empty, the light fixtures shed a wan, peach-colored glow, and a worn recording of Viennese waltzes is being played. *Sex in the Suburbs* takes place almost entirely in the corners of poorly lit rooms, in which the draperies are drawn. The characters—Jim, Sally, Bob, Irene, Mr. Stone— spend a good deal of time by themselves, anxiously rubbing their faces, reading long, crackling, handwritten letters, which they then ball up, and making telephone calls to their fellow characters, who aren't home. They also come and go a lot, putting on and taking off their coats, winding and unwinding their scarves. The men all wear white silk scarves with fringes. After a while, Singer realizes that there must only be one scarf, which the actors hand around in turn. It is evidently winter, but there isn't a single outdoor shot or view through a door or window to confirm it. Singer imagines Jim, Sally, Bob, Irene, Mr. Stone hurrying along bleak suburban streets late in the afternoon, hands in their pockets, eyes cast down, regretful.

"Mr. Singer has considerable gingivitis," Harry Seidel, D.D.S., tells Miss Topaz, the new hygienist, when Singer arrives for a perio.

After Miss Topaz has done some deep scraping, Singer tells her, "Uncle Harry thinks I'm not brushing my teeth conscientiously."

"You have definite deposits," Miss Topaz says.

"I do my best," Singer says, rinsing. "I'm just no good at brushing teeth. It's like my golf game. I don't have a repeating swing, either. You can't be a talent at everything."

"You have like a condition," Miss Topaz says.

"Would you say I'm on the hopeless side?" Singer asks.

"Some people get deposits," Miss Topaz says.

Singer withdraws his elbow, which has been resting against Miss Topaz's snatch.

Singer goes to the Y for a workout, before dropping in on his dad. The elevators in his office building are run by little, cheerless men with accents. Singer realizes he has watched them grow old, their brown uniforms piped with gold become threadbare; they have taken to wearing cheap, wavy hairpieces. As he slowly rises, Singer reflects: When I used to ride with my dad, he habitually introduced them to me, but it has been many years since they remarked on how tall and handsome I have grown.

Singer's dad's office is at the end of a dim corridor faced with grayish marble; at intervals there are doors of engraved glass, behind which shadowy figures loom, writhe, vanish.

"You've been crying," Singer's dad says to him.

"I have?" says Singer.

"Your eyes are red," Singer's dad says.

"I was at the Y," Singer says. "It's the chlorine."

"Did you have a nice workout?"

"Two different people bumped into me in the pool."

"Who had the right of way?"

"One was an old man doing the sidestroke," Singer says. "I assume I was overtaking him. 'Ow!' I said to him, 'You kicked me in the throat.' 'I haffent got eyess in ze bottoms of my feets,' he said. 'Heh, heh,' he added. He was a German. He was swimming in *my lane!*"

"Your capacity to love is stunted," Singer's dad says, interlocking his fingers to show how people should get together.

"The other one hit me on my blind side," Singer says. "I indicated to him the lines painted on the bottom of the pool, or rather, done in black tile, and explained their purpose. 'You must swim vertically within these demarcations,' I told him. Or are you supposed to swim directly above them? 'You aren't permitted to recklessly swim horizontally nor, for that matter, on your back at random. This has all been thought through. Furthermore, you have to keep your eyes open. You may not elect to possibly blunder into other swimmers. If the chlorine irritates your eyes, you must tolerate it,

144 / Gilbert Rogin

like I do'—as I do?—'or wear goggles, which are inexpensive. By the act of entering the pool, you become a member of a confraternity of swimmers. Its welfare depends upon obedience to certain rules. Let me give you some examples. Fancy bathing suits are prohibited. Horseplay is prohibited. One is not allowed to do the deadman's float.' 'You don't own this pool,' he said. He was gay."

"It becomes harder to earn praise as you grow up," Singer's dad says.

Singer uses his dad's phone to call home.

"Is she there?" he asks Simon.

"No," Simon says. "Please don't get mad or anything, Singer, but I want to ask you something."

"Ask."

"Do you have any wood?"

"Wood! What do you want wood for?"

"I want to build a doghouse for Josh—but one that he'll go into."

"I don't have any wood."

"Not even a little? I plan to keep it simple."

"No."

"Will you get me some?"

"Who do you think I am?"

"I don't know, Singer. I wish I was young again. When I was seven, I was happier."

When Singer hangs up, his dad says, "You're crying."

Miss Feltzer, the lab technician, says, "Dr. Sloat has the twenty-four-hour and won't be coming in."

Singer says, "Could I take a look this time?"

Miss Feltzer prepares a slide and puts it under the microscope. As she bends over to focus, Singer notices her rather fat, pale thighs above her white stockings.

"Be my guest," Miss Feltzer says, stepping aside.

"There's nothing there," Singer says.

"Wait," says Miss Feltzer. "There ought to be one making tracks any minute."

"Here comes one now," Singer says. "It's wandering erratically, like a dying man in the desert."

"He's not very speedy, is he?" Miss Feltzer says.

"He's gone," Singer says. "Just a lot of bubbles."

"Buck up," says Miss Feltzer.

"It's not an inspiring view," Singer says. "Do you think I'm hopeless?"

"I'd say you're somewhat below average, count- and motility-wise," Miss Feltzer says. "I wouldn't want to be quoted on your morphology. Would you like to check out a donor's?"

She slips in another slide and refocuses. Singer peers through the eyepiece.

"*Ma'rone*," he says. "Like the dance floor of a discotheque."

"Over a hundred million per cc," Miss Feltzer says. "It's got to be fabulous."

"Would you like me to do your portrait in Magic Markers?" Simon asks Singer when he gets home. "It's free."

"Why don't you do Josh instead?" Singer says.

"He always moves," Simon says.

Singer rests his chin on his right thumb and curls his fingers against his lips, except for his index finger, which he extends along his cheek; thus had his dad sat for a studio photograph before Singer was born. The photographer had retouched the waves of his dad's hair, adding romantic highlights, so that he looked as though he were bathed in moonlight.

Singer had once asked his dad why the pose was so sorrowful.

"It isn't," his dad had said.

"It's not the way you look," Singer said.

"It's how I generally see myself," his dad said. "That is, the expression is true to nature. Of course, it's no longer a good likeness. And then, my face lights up when I see you, as does Mother's."

Simon shows Singer his portrait.

"You made me look like a kid," Singer says.

"It's a mistake," Simon says.

"Is that how I appear to you?"

"I've admitted it doesn't resemble you. I've failed. Do you think Josh misses Jake?"

"How would I know?"

"Every time Josh lies down he goes 'Ahhhhh.' "

"He does?"

"But, on the other hand, he might just be thinking his life's a waste."

"I think I'm coming down with the twenty-four-hour," Singer says.

After a nap, Singer hobbles down to the kitchen to gargle with warm salt water. There he discovers his wife and Grandma, who has missed her train, pasting Triple S stamps in an album. He looks in a pot simmering on the stove.

"We're having brisket for dinner?" he says.

"No," his wife says. "I made it for Mr. Mandelle."

Mr. Mandelle is the therapist on West End Avenue, to whom she goes twice a week—once for group, once for individual.

"He's sick," Grandma says.

"You're painting yourself into an emotional corner," Singer tells his wife. "Do me a favor. Do yourself a favor. You've got a workable inner life. You don't need Mr. Mandelle any more. You can tell me what you tell him. I'm perceptive. After all, who's Mr. Mandelle, anyway? Just another well-read Jew. Where did he go? The New School? What does he do for you?"

"I'm grateful to him," she says, "like I'm grateful to Uncle Harry for doing such beautiful root-canal work and making my caps and building the permanent bridge up here. No, Julian, up here in the corner. You've got to admit it's lifelike."

"Mr. Mandelle's going for his Ph.D.," Grandma says.

Singer is five feet eleven and a quarter, his wife is five feet one and a quarter, and they are standing back to back, so that when Singer throws his head back to gargle, he can rest it on top of his wife's, which, in fact, he does. Idly agitating the salt water in his throat, regarding the ceiling, Singer fancies he is drowning.

Singer is riding uptown on the I.R.T., with a shopping bag on his lap; in it is a Tupperware Flavor Saver containing the sliced brisket—first cut. Singer told his wife that it might be kind of beautiful if he laid it on Mr. Mandelle himself. Singer perceives his gloomy, steadfast reflection in a window, his thinning hair. When last had moonbeams played there?

He limps through a dark, magnificent, and sepulchral lobby and enters Mr. Mandelle's first-floor apartment, where WPAT-FM booms from concealed speakers. Skippy Mountjoy, Simon's father, who is a lush, is squatting on the floor, doing a finger painting.

"Obviously, I won't be shaking hands," he says.

"You don't go to Mr. Mandelle," Singer says.

"Your wife's treating me to an individual for my birthday," Skippy says. "I'm afraid I can't say much for his décor."

Singer looks around disapprovingly. "I'd get him the wood myself, if I could afford it," Skippy goes on. "At any rate, I'll help him knock it together, if you like."

"Wood! What wood?"

"Keep it conversational, Julian. Mandelle's having a session."

"What wood are you talking about?"

"For Josh's doghouse."

"What do you know about that?"

"I'm the architect."

"Listen, Skippy, if there's going to be any doghouse built around here, I'll supply the goddam wood."

"Why do you always exhibit such signs of insecurity, Julian?" Skippy says, dipping a finger in a jar of yellow paint.

"Which way's Mandelle?" Singer shouts, flinging open the door to a linen closet.

Skippy points behind him with a yellow finger.

"He's not much of a dresser, either," he says.

Singer takes the Flavor Saver out of the shopping bag, removes the lid, and barges into Mr. Mandelle's office. Mr. Mandelle is seated in a director's chair, wearing a blazer with a meaningless device; he is in his stocking feet. A large girl is sitting opposite him. She has her blouse off, is hugging a stuffed animal, and is weeping. Her broad red shoulders, the arrangement of her straps reminds Singer of Topsy Temple, and he is unable to throw the brisket at Mr. Mandelle like a custard pie, which had been his intention.

"Where's the kitchen around here, anyway?" he asks.

Mr. Mandelle tells him.

"Don't move, anybody," Singer says. "I'll be right back."

In the kitchen, Mr. Mandelle's socks and undershorts festoon a clothes dryer, which hangs, swaying slightly, from the ceiling. Singer gets three plates, silverware, and napkins and finds his way back to Mr. Mandelle's office. He distributes them and dishes out the brisket.

"Eat," he says hoarsely. "Eat."

They bow their heads over their plates.

"Mr. Mandelle," Singer says, his fork trembling, "my wife understands me."

Singer holds the umbrella over Josh while he goes to the bathroom. The poo drops stately and gently steams. Singer believes he may most fairly be described as the man who walks the dachshund—formerly dachshunds; there, he is passing by again, with bad posture and no mechanical ability whatsoever, his eyes cast down. "Dear heart," Singer tells Josh, "just because we have not settled upon a solution, doesn't mean that life's necessarily a mystery."

When Singer goes into Simon's room to kiss him good night, Simon says, "If Josh could speak, what do you think his first words would be?"

" 'I love you'?" Singer says.

"No," Simon says. " 'Where's Jake?' "

"Shoot me a Kleenex, will you, Simon," Singer says.

Singer gets a call from Norman. "Your inspiration is," Singer says, "that seeing that Sean is getting up there, that, in point of fact, he is going to be all of seven, we get Joe Namath to autograph an official regulation football for the little scrapper and we leave the inscription up to Broadway. Yes, I know, S-e-a-n. Who's springing for the ball, Norman? You'll take it off the bill."

After they've been in bed awhile, Singer says to his wife, "But still, underneath it all, we're the happiest, most well-rounded couple we know, aren't we?"

"I'm not married to you," Singer's wife says. "I'm too young to be married."

"But I'm your best friend, aren't I?"

"I don't have a best friend."

"But if you happened to have one, it would be me, wouldn't it?"

"The position is open," she says.

"Anyway, I'm the most cheerful depressed person you know, aren't I?" he says.

"You've taken every single pillow," she says.

"So? You never use any."

"But you're so high up. I can't reach you."

"I'm thinking up here."

"About?"

"About if we got divorced, whether you'd let me go through the negatives so I could get a set of prints made."

The doorbell rings at 1:30 a.m. Singer gets out of bed to answer it. Skippy Mountjoy, boozed-up, is standing in the vestibule.

"You got the wood yet?" he says.

"No," Singer says.

"I thought we might roll up our sleeves and get down to it."

"At one-thirty a.m.?"

"That's all right," Skippy says, "I forgive myself."

"Did anyone ever tell you your eyes are like little black olives?" Singer says when he has climbed back into bed.

"No, Julian, no one ever did."

Singer dreams that Simon is sitting on his lap and that Skippy is sitting on Simon's lap, so that Simon is lovingly pressed between them like a flower in a book.

"Singer," Simon says.

"Yes," Singer says.

"You're sitting on my violin."

Singer wakes up his wife. "This person bumped into me in the pool," he tells her.

"What did you do about it?" she says.

"I gave him an elbow."

"That straightened him out."

"It didn't. He bumped into me again. I cut in front of him and kicked extra hard, the idea being to make him choke on my wake."

"Did he?"

"He bumped into me again. I resorted to reason. In modulated tones, I gave him my set piece about lane markers."

"How did he take it?"

"He smiled beatifically, swam over to the side of the pool, and, with his forefinger, traced S-O-R-R-Y on the tiles."

"He was deaf and dumb, the poor fellow," Singer's wife says.

"All we know is that he was dumb," Singer says.

The cats rouse Singer at 4:30 a.m. He looks out the window and sees five or six of them standing about the garden in vaguely menacing attitudes, like the lions in Riviere's painting of ruined Persepolis, and crying sadly or wearily, it seems, like long-neglected babies.

Singer, barefoot, holding up his flowing pajama bottoms, runs downstairs and out into the shadowless garden. The air is pearly, still, musky; in the old firehouse next door is a firm that occasionally deals in secondhand drums obtained from perfumers. Shouting, gesticulating, shying rotten tulip bulbs, Singer, feeling like archetypal man, drives the cats from the garden.

"I forgot to put on my Ace bandage," Singer says when he returns.

"The trouble with you, Julian," his wife says, "is that you have no outer life."

15

When you turn off Sunset onto La Cienega, you go down a great, steep slope. On the occasions that I have been driven down it at night, I have felt I was descending into a sort of netherworld and that, *au fond*, I would be somehow different—or, as Le Beau says in another context, have more love and knowledge.

I mentioned this impression to my father when I found him in the steam room, which happens now and again. He said I had always been a dreamy boy, and uneasy, and that he was often struck by how well I had done. We were alone. Steam rose between us. I told him he was misled, that I was very imperfect. He said we all fall short, not to expect felicity or, even, a moment's peace. The proper study of man, he said, is how to lose gracefully, like Lee. I said I agreed with his sentiments but didn't find his illustration apt.

Not long ago, on one of my infrequent trips to Los Angeles, I was riding down this profound hill, in the dark, in Miles Ackerman's *deux-chevaux*. I had first met Miles in New York, when he was doing a talk show on an FM station. He said he admired my work, and had read some of it on the air, without permission. "I dig your stuff," he told me. "You say what I feel." Later, I was his guest, and we discussed, I believe, Fellini. We came to have lunch or dinner two or three times a year. I got a kick out of Miles. He told funny stories about himself and filled me in on his career.

Miles wasn't the King of FM, as he styled himself, for long. In one of those cataclysmic changes, which I no longer view as extraordinary, he became an independent producer and moved to the Coast. He had made, so far, three films, all of which grossed over ten million; the last, I had read, did better than thirteen. Miles never mentioned grosses to me; with me he dwelt on what he called "our creative forces." What he might say was "You're a word man, I'm visual, but we have underlying affinities."

This evening, before leaving for dinner, we had stood by Miles' pool. He lived high in the Hollywood Hills, and we were gazing down on the city. "Describe it to me," Miles said. "Describe what?" I said. "All that," he said, gesturing. "I'm closing my eyes. I want to hear it." He remained standing, his eyes shut. From time to time he shifted his head slightly, as though the sound of my voice might come from an unexpected direction. What he heard, though, was a phone ringing in his cabaña, which he went at last to answer.

Although it may be due to a recurrent sense of my own inadequacy, I have always felt that Miles didn't dig my stuff, or, for that matter, me, as much as he professed. I was, I suspected, being kept on tap for the moment—whenever—that he would need to make use of me; and I suppose one of the reasons I kept seeing him was that I was curious to learn the role I would finally play. Another, of course, was that through Miles I had entrée, however transitorily, to *Hollywood*—all its echoes and resonances—to a world and a life of which I had once vaguely dreamed, perhaps still long at times to be part of.

Miles was driving the *deux-chevaux*. He was wearing a T-shirt with "L.A. Rams" across the front, which was too big for him, chinos, and pink go-aheads, or zoris, and with the watch he had on he could dive to six hundred feet and know what time it was.

"How do you like what Jerry is doing with my hair?" he said. Jerry, I gathered, was his stylist. Miles turned his head this way and that so I could get the full effect. By this time we were past Santa Monica Boulevard, and the lights from the restaurants revealed Jerry's handiwork. Miles' hair was longer than before and what my father would call "unsightly." "Do you think it distracts from my having next to *bupkes* on top?" Miles said. He took his hands off the wheel and, thrusting his head at me, grabbed most of his hair in two handfuls and violently parted it, disclosing his wan crown. Out of control, the car veered toward the center line. I was dazzled by the lights of the oncoming traffic. "Do you?" Miles said. "Do you?" I reached past his bowed, bared head and guided the car back. Miles took the wheel from me as if we had never gone awry.

Farther on, he indicated a restaurant up ahead. "Great curries," he said. "Used to eat there all the time. My accountant picked it up for me. I can't go in there any more. All the time I'm seeing spots on the waiters' ties. I told my accountant, don't buy any restaurants behind my back. I'm dying for a great curry and I've got to take you to a little Italian place."

Miles shortly pulled up before it—it was, of course, quite grand—and explained to the parking valet how to work the shift. Inside, he was greeted, in succession, by the hat-check girl, the bartender, and the owner's brother. Miles told each of them that he was *mezzo mezzo*. "Great linguini with white clam sauce," he said when we had been seated at a table for four, and stuffed a corner of his napkin into the neck of his T-shirt. He closed his eyes once more and gently shook his head; for a moment I thought I was going to be called upon to describe the restaurant. However, he said nothing further. I imagined him slouched in pajamas strewn with cigar ash, looking at the dailies far into the night, and becoming aware that what he was seeing didn't match his original vision.

The owner's brother approached. "The linguini with the white clam sauce, Mr. Ackerman?" he said. "You're on," Miles said. "Order a drink," he told me. "I'm on the w-a-g-o-n." When the brother left, Miles took out his wallet, extracted a set of prints which had been cut from a contact sheet, and spread them out on the tablecloth. "I want you to look at a bunch of pictures for me," he said. "I'm putting them in chronological order for you." He spent some time pushing them back and forth, as though he were playing with one of those puzzles in which the object is to align little movable squares, numbered one through fifteen. In the end, he had the photographs neatly arranged in four equal rows. There were, in fact, sixteen and they depicted two strangers—a very young blonde and a short, smiling man who was possibly Mexican.

"That one there," Miles said, pointing to the blonde, "is someone I've been seeing on the side. I might be in love with her."

"Who's the Mexican?" I asked.

"His name is Angel Moreno," Miles said. "He's from Panama. They tell me he's hung. He rides for me. I've got horses now." This last revelation seemed to depress him disproportionately. "Do you think they're me?" he said at length.

I said, "Why use him, in the circumstances?"

"You and this lawyer I've got," he said. "I show him the pictures and he tells me there's a distinct possibility he could do something through Immigration to get Moreno's temporary work permit lifted and have his *tushy* kicked back to Panama. But, you see, he wins for me."

He readjusted one of the prints.

"Let me fill you in on the sequence," he said. "In the first picture here, they're pulling up to the Sans Souci Motor Inn, in Costa Mesa, for a nooner—a portion of the sign is visible to the naked eye in the upper-left-hand corner, if you'll observe—in the little Mustang I gave her."

Miles paused. I felt obliged to make a comment.

"Nice depth of field," I said. "Who took them for you?"

"His name is Gertler," Miles said. "He has a flair. In the next picture over here, Moreno is being a little gentleman, opening the car door for her. In this one here, he is giving her a kiss. He's got lifts on, but if you examine the picture carefully you can see he's up on his toes notwithstanding. Over here now, they're arm in arm, strolling to their unit."

A waiter arrived with our order. "Stick 'em out of harm's way," Miles told him, waving his arm as he had when he encompassed the city. "In this next row," he said to me, "you'll observe that the shadows have changed around because time has passed." I was reminded of one of those elderly, shuffling guides in shiny suits, with insignificant decorations in their lapels, who lurk about the naves of cathedrals and whom you cannot shake off. "Now here the duo is en route back," Miles was saying. "He kisses her, he opens the door of the little Mustang, she gets in and so forth and so on."

His spiel was apparently over, for he stacked the pictures, put them to one side, and set the dish of linguini before him; the clams, which were on the half shell, were arrayed around the rim. He bent low over the bowl and inhaled deeply. "Great aroma," he said. "Go ahead and sniff yours. Take a real lungful, for Christ's sake." He began to wolf his food down, his chin nearly level with his plate. Suddenly he let his fork drop. He took his wallet out again. "The goods," he said. "Xerox of Sans Souci registration card." He handed me a slip of paper that had been folded many times. I unfolded it while he resumed eating. "Mr. and Mrs. A. Moreno," the top line read in a surprisingly fine hand. "Don't you think she's beautiful?" Miles said next. I saw that he had turned his attention to the photograph on the top of the pile, which portrayed the duo en route back. "Of course, it's a heck of an angle. Gertler knows his still photography."

We ate in silence. Bent, like Miles, over the linguini, I wished I were in bed, in my hotel room, reading; I had *Boswell on the Grand Tour* with me. Why had Miles picked *me* to make sense out of his life, to depict it in words, to console him? Of course, why had I called to say I was in town? I covertly looked at my watch; if I didn't get back to the hotel soon, it would be midnight in New York—too late to phone my wife.

"You remember Joan?" I heard Miles saying. I looked up and saw that his wife—his second—whom I had met once, when they had stayed at the Regency on their way back from London, was standing by the table. Joan had been an actress before she married Miles—indeed, had played in his first picture. Now she nodded to me.

"Great linguini, Joan," Miles said. He was evidently used to her turning up. "I'll have them whip you up a plate *molto molto*."

"I ate," she said, letting him seat her.

"What did you have?" he asked. He really wanted to know.

She opened her bag, took out a sheet of paper, and laid it in front of him. I could see it was a bill from a M. Russell DeWinter & Associates, for twelve hundred and fifty dollars.

"What's this, Joannie?" he said mildly.

"He couldn't find you," she said.

"Who couldn't find me where?"

"DeWinter," she said. "My detective."

"He couldn't have looked very hard."

"You weren't there."

"Where was I supposed to be?"

"In New York."

"Who says I wasn't in New York?"

"Me and DeWinter," she said. "You told me you had to go to New York, but you were somewhere else, fucking that little blonde."

"I was there," Miles said. "DeWinter is misinformed. Let me recommend a detective to you. His name is Gertler. He takes pictures and everything. A heck of a man with a long lens."

"You weren't there, you mother fucker," she said, "so you pay the mother-fucking bill."

She got up and left. The owner's brother started to come over. Miles held up his hand.

"I wasn't there," Miles said to me. "What's the date on that thing?"

I told him.

"Where was I?" he said, more to himself. "*Commendatore*," he said loudly. The owner's brother now advanced.

"I'm sorry," he began, "but—"

"Forget it," Miles said. "You got any nice melon?"

"Right away, Mr. Ackerman," the brother said.

"Make sure it's nice," Miles called after him.

I realized that Miles had been fortunate in one respect, at least; Joan had somehow overlooked the photographs and the Xerox. He had not been that lucky with his first wife, Theresa, who had caught him in bed with his dental hygienist. Miles may have been thinking along these lines, too, because he said, "Did I ever tell you about when Theresa and I got married? It was in the Essex House—or the Hampshire House. After the ceremony was over and the dancing had been going on for a while, Theresa kept getting after me if we couldn't please go upstairs to our room. I suppose she wanted to have dinner or to be alone with me or consummate our marriage or whatever, but I didn't want to leave the wedding. I wanted to keep on *shmoozing* with the guests."

He pondered this or something else for a moment, then dug in his pocket, took out his cigar case, selected a cigar, and stuck it in my breast pocket. I was about to withdraw it, to glance at the band, when he reached across the table and laid a hand on my pocket, inadvertently against my heart. It was, I suppose, the most intimate gesture that had ever passed between us.

"It's from Las Palmas," Miles said. "In the Canary Islands, and not half bad. A guy gave me a box of fifty." He went into his pocket once more, this time producing an envelope. First the view of L.A., then his scalp, the photographs, the Xerox, the cigar, and now this. What paraphernalia! He was a magician performing a trick for me, but one that was so obscure—or so poorly done—that I didn't know when to marvel.

"It's from my mother," Miles said. "She was out to see me. It comes in two parts. Read the clip first."

This was a photograph cut out of the New York *Post*, showing Mayor Lindsay and Thomas Hoving at a preview of the "Harlem on My Mind" exhibit at the Metropolitan Museum. Miles' mother had written on Hoving's neck, with an arrow pointing to his hair, "Above collar!" Similarly, she had written on the Mayor's neck and shoulders, with accompanying arrows, "Bottom of ear! Not below collar!" The letter read as follows:

Dear Miles,

Please examine the enclosed, especially of the Mayor, since your head is more like his. Long hair, a little below the ear, but not over the collar! Yours gets over the collar and meets your rounded shoulders, making the hair pushed up like this [at this point there was a crude sketch of the back of Miles' head, and these notations: "head," "no neck," "over neck meeting shoulders," "no contour"]. It just looks *old, old, old* and not *mod* or anything that a good barber would do. He is taking advantage of you. It distressed me so much because you can look so handsome. *Please* have the barber fix it and always have him *hand cut hair on neck.* Don't let him use the electric clippers ever!

So much for that. You really must be frustrated because you're taking it out on eating. I think you must have gained ten pounds when I was in Hollywood, and that always makes you look older, too, and unkempt.

You know I love you. That's why I feel I can say it.

Mom

I put the clipping and the letter back in the envelope and returned it to Miles. He laid it on top of his other belongings, next to the empty linguini plates, with their dismal litter of clam shells. He did, I realized, look old, but not on account of his hair.

"Jerry wouldn't dream of using electric clippers," he said.

The melon arrived. He took a spoonful of his. "Eat," he said. I did so. "How do you like it?" I said it was nice. "Where was I?" he said.

"When?" I said.

"When that DeWinter was looking for me. Honestly, I don't know where I was."

"I can't help you, Miles."

"Who can?" he said.

"So why," I said, "have you showed me all these things?"

"Who can I show them to," he said, "if not to my best friend?"

I suppose I should have known. Perhaps, in a way, I was.

"Hey," he said, "this English director's supposed to meet me here. They tell me he's gay. I'll be in New York in a couple of weeks. We'll have lunch."

This announcement was not unexpected. Our meetings generally ended on much the same note.

I thanked him for dinner and got up. "What's wrong with me?" he said. "How are you going to get back to your hotel? Take the car. Tell the kid I said it's all right."

"I'd rather—"

"What are you talking about? I must have six or seven of them at home. Emil'll pick it up tomorrow or something."

"I don't know how to work the gearshift," I said.

"You don't?" Miles said.

"And I thought I'd walk."

"Walk!"

"I've always had it in mind to climb the hill."

"What hill?"

"The one we came down."

"Oh, that," he said. "It never entered my mind."

"The air," I said.

A minute or two later, I was on the sidewalk outside the restaurant. In the distance rose that vast, sombre, and terrible slope, its crown somehow reminiscent of Goya's "A City on a Rock," in which winged men fly about a fantastic summit. These musings were interrupted by someone calling my name. It was Miles, running toward me, go-aheads flopping, Rams T-shirt out at the waist.

"Give me back that cigar," he said.

"What do you mean?" I said.

"Give me back that cigar," he said more vehemently.

I handed it over. He took out his case, replaced the cigar, and gave me another.

"That's a Montecristo I've placed in your hand," he told me. "It's the finest smoke on the market. You can't even buy it in the U.S.A. I don't know how I could have ever done such a thing. Forgive me. I don't know what came over me."

I noticed that the dial of his watch was glowing powerfully, as though, in fact, he were far below the surface.

Then he turned and walked slowly back to the restaurant. Before I reached the bottom of the hill, I hailed a passing cab, which took me up it and out along Sunset to my hotel.

That night, I dreamed of Miles. He was standing on the roof of a residential hotel in Miami Beach—the section known as South Beach, which is largely inhabited by elderly Jews in reduced circumstances. It was a balmy night, Miles was dressed as he had been when we were both awake, and he was slightly drunk. I was on the roof with him, as were some others. The dream took liberties with geography; the hotel we were on top of had only three or four stories, but it was on a height, and before and below us lay the width of South Beach, blocks of old stucco hotels palely colored and tumbled like seashells, and beyond that the dark, serene sea. Swaying a bit, Miles gazed upon the scene like a painter or

an emperor. "You might as well give me a trim," he said, not un-
kindly, to a young man next to him, who went and stood behind
him and, bending his knees so that he was on a level with Miles'
head, began snipping at his hair. My father now planted himself
in front of Miles and interviewed him, though he took no notes.
"Mr. Ackerman," he said, "what's your formula for making successful movies?" I was embarrassed by the question; I felt it was
trite. Not Miles. "You put a city shoe on one foot," he said, "and a
country shoe on the other foot, and then you dance." And he did
a little time step.

His meaning seemed clear enough, but why did he use that
figure of speech? Before he had stopped dancing, I recalled one of
Boswell's letters in which he had written that "speculation renders
us miserable. Life will not bear to be calmly considered. It appears
insipid and ridiculous as a country dance." I verified the wording
when I at last awoke.

If Miles came to New York in two weeks, he didn't call.
When I heard from him, a year had gone by. His latest movie was
playing at Radio City Music Hall; every time I passed, there were
long lines.

"Do you remember," he said, when I answered the phone,
"my asking you to describe L.A. to me?" I said I did. "I'm sitting
in my cabaña looking at it," he said. I expected him to continue,
but he didn't go on. "And?" I said finally. He said, "I wish you
had told me what we saw together. You never did. Remember?" I
said I remembered. "It's not the same any more," he said. "What
was there, that's all gone. Everything looks different." I recalled
his telling me, when he had displayed the photographs, how the
shadows changed around, marking time passing. I asked him what
had happened to the blonde. "Who?" he said. "The one in the con-
tacts," I said. "I'm afraid I don't know what you're talking about,"
he said. "The one with the jockey," I said. "I don't know what
happened to her," he said. "She went away. My accountant sold
the horses. They were never me." I had a feeling Joan had gone
away, too, but I didn't inquire. I realized Miles never asked about
my life. Had he ever even conceived it? "I'm having a drink," he

was saying. "I've fallen off the w-a-g-o-n. I'm by myself. It's getting dark. What do you think happened to my scenery?" I told him I couldn't tell from here. He agreed and in awhile we hung up.

Not long afterward, I met my father in the steam room I said I had walked across the Park and had gone by the softball diamond where, thirty years before, Mr. Sanders, who was the first person I knew who wore oxblood shoes, took the second grade for P.E. Children were playing ball there now, and, as in the past, Mr. Sanders was standing, motionless, under a tree in right field, as though he had never moved away. I went up to him to say hello, but veered off without speaking; he had shown no sign of having recognized me; his hair was all white. "Like me," my father murmured, "but I know who you are." I told him he didn't. I said that seeing the old diamond, with its eroded base paths, had brought home to me how little I knew of what had happened to me since I had played there. So much time had gone by. How much more I should have done. My father asked which of my contemporaries had done more. I said, *shlock* and all, Miles Ackerman even. My father said hadn't I read today's paper. He often upbraided me on this account. I said I hadn't, and he told me Miles had been killed in an automobile accident. I recalled the blinding headlights and wondered if, unappeased, he had shown his pallid scalp to someone else. I related the incident to my father, who sat erect, enveloped in steam. He said the article stated Miles had been alone at the time. He said I had always been self-centered and that in the future I should be more *engagé*. Like Schweitzer? I said. My father said that was not what he had in mind.

16

I have been alerted by my father to the fact that my mother is lying in wait for me in the drugstore where I have lunch after swimming at the Y. She's got my father's proofs; she had inveigled him into sitting for a "black-and-white executive portrait plus six glossies." "She wants you to look at them with your artist's eye," my father had said when he called.

My mother is in one of the booths, a half a cup of coffee before her. This is a prop. I feign surprise by throwing up my hands and making "O"s of my mouth and eyes. In the same way, I obligingly stagger all over my father's office when he hands me one of his rosy checks for my birthday.

"I took a chance," my mother says as I slide in opposite her.

Blowing on spoonfuls of cream-of-turkey soup, I go over the proofs. These consist of both head and bust shots, and my father is either smiling rather roguishly or pretending to be deep in thought, as though he were about to raise an index finger and say "Ah!" Perhaps he really was inspired; after all, when it dawned on Henri Poincaré that the transformations he had used to define Fuchsian functions were identical with those of non-Euclidean geometry, he was boarding a bus. By what had my father been struck? I'd ask, but he'd tell me, in the pidgin French he regularly spouts, that I was a "*petit stinquer.*"

"You didn't dry your hair," my mother says.

I raise my index finger and say "Ah!"

In the bust shots, my father is variously fondling his glasses. "He insisted on draping my fingers over them," my father had said on the phone, "although I told him that, in life, my glasses are either on my nose or tucked securely in their case in my pocket."

I point out this discrepancy to my mother.

"Your father has well-modeled fingers," she says.

In the bust shots, they are smooth, lustrous, marmoreal, as though carved by Canova. The retoucher, I realize, has been at his sly work on my father's face as well, unclouding his brow, firming up his chin, putting a gleam in his eye.

I order a B.L.T. down, easy on the mayo.

"Why have you let them do this to him?" I ask my mother.

"Do what?" she says.

"This! This! This!" I cry, jabbing at one of my father's head shots.

"What's wrong?" my mother says, alarmed. "I didn't bring my glasses."

"He's been retouched."

"Has he?" my mother says. "All our friends say they look like him."

I excuse myself and call up my father.

"Are you aware that you've been retouched?" I ask him.

"No," he says.

"Well, you have," I say.

"You have a practiced eye," my father says.

I rejoin my mother.

"They didn't drain the bacon," she says. "I took a very small bite. A nibble. Do you think any of them sum him up? I'm going to bow to your judgment."

I flip through the set of proofs again. The more I gaze upon my father's polished face, the more unfamiliar it becomes. I no longer know what he looks like; I must never have known, never will know.

"He kept up a patter to relax me," my father had said during our first phone call. "'Do you tell stories?' he said. I told him you don't push a button to tell stories. So he chattered on, and from time to time gave vent to little expressions of approval. Your mother was sitting in a far corner, out of range, making comments."

I confront my mother with this.

"They didn't want to let me watch," she says. "I told them they didn't have to worry about me, I'd be a little mouse. You see, I like to know what's going on. I'll sit in a dark corner on the sidelines, I told them."

"Were you a little mouse?"

"Oh, you know me," my mother says. "I have to express myself. He was beginning to get rather fixed in his expression. I said something that relaxed it. He was very docile, all things considered. When we arrived at the studio, one of the young men asked your father if he would like to go in and fix his hair. 'It's already in place,' your father told him."

I am at my mother and father's for dinner. Tomorrow they're going to Europe on a New York County Lawyers Association charter flight.

Suppose the photographer were seated in the maid's room across the areaway, with a long lens, watching, through our dining-room window, my father pouring salt on the fresh stains on the tablecloth, me endeavoring to put reverse English on my napkin ring, my mother very gracefully holding her arms above her head.

We had been kicking the past around when my mother said, "At Lydia Wadleigh High School, I always played center because I had such long arms." And she reached up, as though in the act of rebounding, and stared at the ceiling. I told my mother her arms seemed about average length to me, but she wasn't paying attention. My father gave me the look that meant I was letting my mother down.

After a bit, my mother lowers her arms, and the dinner-table conversation turns to the fate of her African violets, several of which are in bloom.

"I'm willing to take them home with me tonight," I say. "Believe me."

"But how will you ever manage?" my mother says.

"I'll splurge on a cab," I say.

"Must you eternally load people down?" my father says to my mother.

"I'm paying for the cab," my mother says, and trots into the bedroom, where the violets are set out on the radiator cover getting, as she puts it, the benefit of the natural light. When she's carted them all into the dining room, she begins packing them in shopping bags, but some leaves fall off, so she unpacks them.

"You see," my father says. "I say forget about them. Let them die, for God's sake."

The photographer leans forward, twisting his great lens.

"I'm more than willing to come up three times a week to water them, if someone will show me how," I say.

"Nobody's going to water your mother's African violets while we're gone," my father says. "What's going to happen is they're going to be allowed to die. Then, when we return from Europe, I'm going to buy your mother some new ones. What is it, two dollars, two dollars and a half per plant? Four, five dollars if they're blooming? So that's . . . There's seven plants, and that makes it ten. . . . And three with blooms on them. . . . All told, say, what—twenty-five dollars?"

"Please, Dad, don't do it," I say. "I'm coming up."

"I'll change the locks on you," my father says. He rises and, getting down on one knee, gathers the fallen leaves.

"I would have attended to it," my mother says, crouching beside him. By this time, however, my father has picked up all the leaves, which he doesn't seem to know what to do with. He remains kneeling, as though forever, like an insignificant figure in a corner of a *quattrocento* Adoration.

Now. Shoot. I recognize him. I am that man's son.

My mother holds out a hand, and my father lets the leaves drop into her palm.

I have an impulse to help my parents to their feet, but don't follow through.

"Did you pack my flannel pajamas?" my father says to my mother. "I hear it gets cold in the fjord country at night."

"You didn't push your chair in," I say to my father.

"*Petit stinquer*," my father says to me.

I am taking my mother and father to the airport in a Carey I hired as a love citation.

On the Van Wyck, my father withdraws a sheet of paper, folded many times, from the pocket of his drip-dry shirt—a piece of correspondence, he announces, that he found in a lockbox he had opened in connection with an estate he's handling.

I tell my mother I smell a rat.

My mother gives me a look that means I'm not supposed to disparage my father.

My father unfolds the letter; it is nearly worn through along the creases. "A communication from Chronic Diseases," he informs us, "thanking my client for a substantial contribution he made a number of years ago. I'm taking the liberty of reading the closing to you: 'You're a sincere Jew with a Jewish heart, and that means a man of great and noble spirit.' "

"What else did you find in there?" my mother asks.

"Zip," my father says.

"Zip?" my mother says.

"Otherwise empty," my father says.

We ride in silence. I can think of nothing to say to them. My father folds the letter and puts it back in his pocket. He is taking it with him to the fjord country.

"How would you like to have our subscription to the Philharmonic?" my mother says at last.

"After all these years!" I say.

"It's no use," my mother says. "If you don't want the seats, I'm going to have to abandon them."

My father adjusts the air-conditioning.

"I'm submitting myself to your father's will," she continues.

"These modern pieces they insist on playing are an assault on one's ears," my father says.

"We should make an extra effort to keep up," my mother says. "Leonard Bernstein wouldn't include them in the program unless they had merit."

"But Bernstein's left," my father says.

"The last time we went, we had *The Rite of Spring*," my mother says.

"I told your mother we had arrived at the crossroads," my

father says.

"I informed him that *The Rite of Spring* isn't modern any more," my mother says. "It was first performed in 1913."

"I said I'd be a good scout for her sake," my father says.

"You said you'd stiffen your sinews," my mother says.

"It's all the same," my father says.

"But in the middle he began casting frequent glances at the ceiling," my mother goes on, "so I took his hand and we left. I must say, however, that that Boulez is no Leonard Bernstein."

"Schonberg has praised him lavishly," my father says.

"Boulez," my mother says, "is a little fat man, and he doesn't move very much."

I kiss my mother goodbye at the International Departures Building.

"Don't worry," I whisper. "I'm going to sneak up and water them anyway."

"It's too late," she whispers back.

"He's uprooted them?" I say. My father has drifted out of earshot.

"His pictures," my mother says. "They don't look like him anymore."

"Aren't you going to order any?"

"I should have made him go for a sitting years ago," she says, "but you know me."

A week later, I get a picture postcard from my mother, showing the fjord country:

Violets are always watered from the BOTTOM! Don't use cold water. Make sure it's TEPID! Water when the soil appears very dry. From my experience, this is every other day. Once a week give them a little violet food, which you'll find nearby.

Love,
Mom

I had forgotten the pain-in-the-ass plants. I dream of an irremeable past. In the dream, I take a cab to my mother and father's.

There, I go into the kitchen. On the drain-board is a pitcher I have never seen before; it must have been broken long ago. Had my father thrown it in a rage? I fill the pitcher with tepid water and head down the hall. The blinds are drawn in the bedroom; nonetheless, it is favored with light—the natural light my mother is always pointing out to everybody. There are no violets; they won't be bought for years and years. The radiator cover is bare, and two people are sleeping in my mother's bed. My father's is empty, but has been slept in. I kneel to see the sleepers' faces better: my mother and father, breathing in harmony, her arms about him. They are terribly young; their faces are those in the snapshots obliging strangers took on their honeymoon. In front of the Antlers Hotel. At Echo Lake. In the Garden of the Gods. I am going to be born. I am going to let them down and disparage them.

17

When Singer first realizes that his wife is Space Ant, and that she has been sent to Earth from another planet, he is driving through Florida in a rented car. His wife sits beside him, a partly unfolded road map on her lap. She is wearing sunglasses with red rims and slightly convex lenses, which are in between harlequins and wraparounds. Their effect is to make her look like a giant ant. Singer tells his wife he has discovered she comes from outer space. "This is my otherworldly smile," she says, smiling. "But what is your mission?" Singer says.

Another day Singer says, "We're going to go out of our way and see what Boca Grande is like."

Singer's wife says, "You're doing this for me and then you're going to regret it and tell me that you did it for me."

Singer's wife has often mentioned to Singer that when she was separated from Skippy Mountjoy for the first time, she decided to start her life all over again somewhere else. She was living in Providence and she went to an employment agency in the Arcade that specialized in placing people in resorts. She asked if they had anything waiting on table in Florida, and was told there was a job at the Boca Grande Hotel, which she envisioned as a massive, white, frame building with great porches upon which millionaires rocked after dinner. But she got no closer to Boca Grande than locating it on a map; Skippy, tapering off, came back, with bits of toilet paper clinging to the places where he had cut himself shaving, and said he was beginning to see his way clear.

On the way to Boca Grande, Singer's wife says, "If Skippy had shown up a day later, I would have caught the eye of a millionaire in creamy flannels with dotted lines running up and down them, and he would have carried me off."

Singer says, "In that event, what would have happened to me?"

Singer drives over the bridge to Gasparilla Island, on which the town of Boca Grande is situated; the island is flat and scrubby, and there are metal signs advertising lots.

"This isn't Boca Grande," Singer's wife says. "Boca Grande is much greener, there's lots more trees, and the interior is very dense."

As they pass through the town, Singer points out the banyans and the glimpses of the Gulf afforded by the driveways that, at intervals, interrupt walls enclosing estates. A block or two beyond town several large brick buildings rise; their windows are blank, they appear empty, in disuse, perhaps soon to become ruins.

"Christ!" Singer's wife says. "A sanitarium."

"The Boca Grande Hotel," Singer says, showing her the sign.

He pulls off the road opposite the hotel.

"The lady in Providence said the girls who waited on table lived in," Singer's wife says. "Which would have been the window of my room?"

"There," Singer says. "On the top floor. You would have been able to see the Gulf."

"I would have never got away," Singer's wife says, "unless I let down my hair."

"But Space Ant *flies*!" Singer says.

"It was before I came to Earth and assumed my present form," Singer's wife says.

"There's a blue one in the fastness," Singer says.

"When you were in nursery school—" his wife says, reaching in among the branches.

"I found a thumbtack on the floor," Singer says. "The teacher praised me. She said I had very sharp eyes."

It is nearly three weeks after Christmas, and they are finally taking down the trimmings, which date from her marriage to Skippy Mountjoy. Rather, Singer's wife is; Singer points out ornaments she's missed. He has never had anything to do with trimming the tree, either, except for fixing the tin star from Mexico to the top, and that he has done because he's taller.

Singer continues, "Did I ever tell you that although I have been paid any number of compliments since—"

"For what?" his wife says. "Turns of phrase? Your neckties?"

"At various points or moments in the act of love," Singer says.

Singer and his wife are at a party. Singer is talking to a girl, whose name he didn't catch, who has paid him a compliment. "When I was in nursery school, I found a thumbtack on the floor," Singer tells her. "The teacher praised me. She said I had very sharp eyes. Although I have been paid any number of compliments since, this first, being least susceptible of flattery or other impure motives, is the best."

But Singer can no longer hear the teacher announcing that a thumbtack is lost and that everybody is going to stop everything and look for it. No other children are searching alongside him. He is off by himself, crawling somewhere, and comes unexpectedly upon the tack. "I found a thumbtack," he says, holding it out. The teacher smiles and accepts it. "You have very sharp eyes," she says. She has felt sorry for him.

"I think I'd better find my wife," Singer says, plunging off.

She is in the dining room, eating shrimp off of colored toothpicks.

"I was looking for you," he says.

"You have very sharp eyes," she says.

I do, Singer acknowledges. When I drive, I see the deer in their noble attitudes at the edges of woods, in dreams I have beheld all the different fishes streaming in the interiors of lakes, and I can see all of us growing old.

Singer is home alone and penniless; not even carfare to get uptown. He goes to the bedroom closet and gropes for change in the pockets of his jackets, summer and winter, including those he last wore years ago. Putting his hand in the pockets of his old, shiny suits, he realizes he may have been a slightly different person when he wore them, and he tries to remember who that person was.

He doesn't find a cent. He goes to the coat closet in the foyer and feels in the pockets of all his wife's coats. The pockets are surprisingly shallow, worn, even desolate, and warm, as though they still retain the heat of his wife's hands, and they are all empty. No money, no gloves, no matches, no old Kleenex. Singer wonders why he had never noticed how small her hands must be to fit in her pockets. He imagines that his hands are his wife's, he her, walking by himself, his hands in his pockets. For a moment, he has a sense of his wife's life. She was someone else, whom he fell in love with.

The foyer darkens, and he is afraid it is the shadow of her wings, and that she is hovering above him.

One night, Singer's wife tries on all her sunglasses. Singer is lying on his side of the bed, reading. Singer's wife is on her knees on the floor by her side, hidden, with her pile of sunglasses. She puts a pair on, sticks her head up, drops out of sight, changes glasses, reappears, disappears, and so forth. Singer's wife must have a dozen pairs of sunglasses, including those which betray that she is Space Ant.

Singer is reminded of one of those frantic impersonators who turns his back to the audience, does something to his hair, turns around and becomes—Jimmy Cagney! Victor McLaglen! Bette Davis! He is reminded, too, of a swimmer, rather a drowning man, bobbing repeatedly to the surface, his features progressively altered by his experience, appealing for help. Also a child playing peek-a-boo. Is his wife saying recognize me, save me, catch me? Is this the high point of their marriage?

While Singer is doing his push-ups, his wife says to their dachshund, "Josh, if you were Space Ant why would you come to Earth?"

"Why would he?" Singer grunts.

"To make you talk," she says.

"What would he want to do that for?" Singer says, getting to his feet.

"So you could tell me what you feel about me," she says.

"But it's implied," Singer says.

One morning Singer decides it's time to turn the mattress, and discovers that his wife has hidden a notebook between it and the box spring. He reads what she has written:

Space Ant is in the kitchen cooking bacon and crying. Tears fall into the pan and the hot fat pops. Space Ant sits down on the stool and turns on the radio to hear the news. She cries listening to the traffic. She thinks her mission has failed.

Singer says life is largely unrewarding, but one stumbles forward. Singer says life is hard and he has no time. Singer says life is exhausting and he goes to sleep.

Space Ant whispers in Singer's ear while he is sleeping, "Wake up loving me and I'll teach you to fly."

Skippy Mountjoy calls up Singer and tells him he's working behind the steam table in the Automat on Broadway near

Forty-seventh Street. "It's one of the most venerable in the chain," he says. "Do drop in and see me in my little bow tie." The purpose of Skippy's call is to borrow Singer's portable typewriter. "I want to knock out a few résumés," Skippy explains. "I'm beginning to see my way clear again."

Singer visits Skippy on the way to work. Skippy is stationed by the toaster. Besides the little bow tie, he is wearing a white cap with a gauze top, which is set at a jaunty angle. When he sees Singer, he winks and throws him a salute.

Singer gets a cup of coffee and sits down. In a few minutes, Skippy joins him. "They give us five minutes," he says.

"When you were married to her," Singer says, "did you ever have the impression that she came here from outer space?"

"Not that I can recall," Skippy says.

Singer's goldfish, which he owned before he got married, dies. He had won it at the Feast of Saint Anthony by throwing a Ping-Pong ball into the globe of magenta water in which it frantically swam.

"Are you still upset?" Singer's wife asks Singer when he comes back from walking Josh in the rain.

"I had it five years," Singer says.

"Five years is the normal life-span for goldfish," his wife says.

"And all the other dogs I see go to the bathroom when it's raining," Singer says.

"And?" Singer's wife says.

"The pop-up book," Singer says.

He goes on to explain that yesterday there had been a pop-up book in the window of the bookstore past which he and Josh invariably walk. The book seemed quite old, perhaps late Victorian, and it was displayed so that it was open to an illustration that showed children in old-fashioned bathing suits playing in the surf with a large dog or donkey, he has forgotten which. They are all in a bay, the arms of which are high cliffs. The children, the animal, and many of the waves popped up. He had been charmed by the scene and was about to go in and buy the book, when he stopped to classify his emotions. Why was he agitated? Because the illustration so sweetly evoked a lost childhood for which he yearned. But the scene didn't represent his past; it belonged to others, Englishmen now extremely old or, more likely, dead. He was moved by, was pining for, someone else's youth, and he didn't go in. Why did he keep deluding himself? Why did he fail to grasp the reality of his own life? However, today, as he and Josh approached the bookstore in the rain, he became aware that his heart was quickening. The subject didn't matter. What did was a clear sense of momentariness. What happened when the waves broke, everyone came out of the water, the light failed, the day ended, children grew up? However, the book was no longer in the window, and when he inquired he learned it had been sold.

"Would you like to know why I came to Earth?" Singer's wife asks.

"I would," Singer says.

"To put my arms around you," she says, doing so, "and to solace your existence."

She doesn't tell him that his goldfish died years ago, and that she had replaced it with one that resembled it, and that that one had died and had been replaced, too.

18

Singer and his wife are in the smoking section at the movies. Singer would like everyone to know he doesn't smoke, yet he has climbed up here. Singer gazes at the audience arrayed below him, the rows of dark, motionless heads; they are buried sitting up, like the Azande. Singer reflects on the struggle to liberate form from the fetters of mass—Michelangelo's *càrcere terreno*. My son is like a flame, he thinks in turn. Not my son, really; my stepson. Singer's stepson is fourteen, five-nine, one-thirty-five. These figures are relevant, because Singer and his stepson had a fight in the living room. During the fight, Singer kept yelling at his stepson to apologize. Apologize for what? For growing up, Singer supposes. I knew he'd grow up, Singer thinks, regarding the great shaft of light from the projector, but I must have thought he'd be the same—the same person bigger, a six-foot seven-year-old; this was his age when Singer first met him, got his first kiss.

Singer's stepson told Singer's wife he beat Singer up. Singer maintained it was at least a tie, since he controlled himself and refrained from hitting his stepson in the face, on account of his braces. Singer's stepson said Singer had *tried* to hit him in the face, but he had danced out of range. Singer said those were intended to be slaps.

Singer went to Medical and told the doctor it felt as if his hand was broken. The doctor, who had recently joined the company, leafed through Singer's file. Singer believed his file contained a number of notations made by the doctor's predecessors to the effect that Singer was a hypochondriac. Singer was of this opinion because whenever a new doctor laid his file aside, he looked up at Singer as though—Singer had given the expression a lot of thought—as though Singer were a nestling that had fallen from a nearly inaccessible nest. Should he try to put him back? Should he take him home and feed him with a medicine dropper? Should he ignore him, his fall being the will of Providence?

The new doctor asked Singer how he had hurt himself. Singer said he was punching his son around and must have missed and hit a piece of furniture or a wall or something. Singer thought the doctor was going to put his arm about his, Singer's, shoulders; but if he was he thought better of it, because he withdrew his hand and rested his head in it instead. The X-rays were negative.

Singer remembers his stepson, shirtless, in Provincetown, in the playground across from the Patrician Shop, making thirty-foot jumpers in the failing light.

"Let's go," Singer had said. "It's dark."

"Let's stay," his stepson had said. "I'm on."

From the corner, pale and writhing like a flame.

The metal backboard went brrannnng.

"I got a new move."

"I'm watching."

"I can get rim."

"Are you going to get good marks?"

His stepson went up for a jumper from the top of the key, his bare torso nearly phosphorescent, as though he had leaped from the sea.

"Are you?"

"I'm hot."

"Well, *are* you?"

"Don't you think I'm ashamed of my past?"

He dribbled to the other end of the court, where Singer couldn't make him out.

"It's nighttime."

"I'm deadly."

Brrannnng.

"I'm going."

Walking up the hill to the house the Singers had rented for July, his stepson had said, "Do you think I've grown any taller?"

"Since *yesterday*!"

"It's conceivable."

"A kiss?"

"No."

"Are you too old?"

"No."

"Are you wearing your rubber bands?"

Singer puts a finger in each ear to shut out the dialogue and the score, and calls to mind his stepdaughter doing a dolphin, a synchronized swimming stunt, in Slough Pond, her nipples appearing above the surface. The little flowered top of her bathing suit had whizzed by his ear, followed by the bottom, and she had come ashore naked, like Venus. Singer had been reading the sports page. It was the first time he had seen her undressed. She was sixteen. She had reminded him of girls he had never loved, and this made him love her more, from farther away, and with a sharper sense of despair. Singer's wife had told him he didn't love her daughter and that he yelled at her all the time. His stepdaughter had told a psychiatrist she had seen for a while that Singer had kicked her when she was hysterical and lying on the living-room floor. "Did you tell him it was with my *bare* foot?" Singer had asked her.

"What's wrong with your bathing suit?"

"It's not pretty."

"But you picked it out."

"Last year."

"When will you ever make up your mind?"

"I don't know. This morning, I thought: I'm going to be seventeen and I don't know anything."

"Why don't you shave your legs? That isn't esoteric."

"It's unnatural."

"All you nonconformists are sheep."

"Do you want to see me do a subalina with a half twist?"

"I want to know why you don't read."

She was already running back into the pond. Singer laid his paper aside. One white foot stuck out of the green water. I've made no effort to know her, Singer informs himself.

Singer thinks of something Murray once said. Murray and his wife belong to Dr. Moscow's couples group, which Singer's wife makes Singer go to. Singer has been to a number of analysts. "You change nut-fixers as often as your mother changes maids," Singer's wife told him. "Psychology is a soft science," Singer explained. "It may even be softer than sociology."

Singer keeps trying to leave Dr. Moscow, too. He even wrote him a letter:

Dear Dr. Moscow:

I won't be coming to group anymore. (I can't, of course, speak for my wife.) I have to do something, however symbolic, to alter my circumstances; so this stroke. I feel I've stopped growing and, like my potted palm (which, you'll recall, we discussed in several sessions), I'm withering at the tips. If I can no longer add, I must subtract. Perhaps if I hew away, I'll emerge. Group is a chip flying off.

Dr. Moscow called him up. "You're a rascal, you," he said.

What Murray had said was that he realized his marriage was a mistake at his wedding reception, when his wife insisted that he take a big bite of wedding cake for the photographer. "She kept trying to push this piece of cake into my mouth," Murray had said. "*And I didn't want any.*"

That was seventeen years ago. Singer had married *his* wife when he was nearly thirty-four, or six years ago. Actually, as Singer's wife told him the other day, they aren't really married; she had her fingers crossed during the ceremony.

Five minutes after this revelation, Singer said to his wife, "Who stole our wedding pictures?"

"You're not going to be able to see it," she said.

"Why not?"

"Because of my bouquet."

"What about your bouquet?"

"I was hiding my fingers behind it."

"But he hopped about."

"Who hopped?"

"The photographer. He covered it from different angles."

"The wedding pictures are in the bottom of a box on the top shelf of the linen closet."

Singer slung his binoculars around his neck.

"Where are you going?" his wife asked.

"Home," Singer said.

He took a cab to his parents' apartment house on Central Park West.

"I was in the Park looking for birds," Singer said when his mother opened the door.

"But it's dark," she said.

"I didn't see any," he said. "What do you know," he added, advancing into the living room and picking up an album. "My wedding pictures."

When Singer returned home, his wife said, "I just remembered. When I crossed my fingers, it was my *first* marriage."

"Let's go," Singer whispers to his wife.

"No."

"But it's no good."

"I want to see how it turns out."

"It won't get better."

"How do you know?"

"Because it's bad art, and bad art is bad all the way to the end. That's what makes it bad."

"What about a bad life?"

"No such thing. Life is *hard*. Now can we go?"

"You may."

Singer arises, goes downstairs, and sits in the lounge, which is empty except for a Negro maid setting out coffee cups, who presently leaves; this must be what a bomb shelter is like, he thinks. Singer listens carefully, but he is unable to hear the movie. After a while, he goes back upstairs and stands at the foot of the smoking section, looking for his wife. He can't find her. How had he ever found her in the first place? He leaves the theater. It is still light out—blue like a gas flame, like fishes' backs, like the air in which Giotto's lamenting angels hover.

Singer walks down Fifth Avenue, which is deserted at this hour. When he gets to Twenty-second Street, he recognizes his wife a block ahead, walking downtown, under the bare flagpoles. All the buildings are old here, with elaborate cornices, and of a similar height, so that they form two great palisades. When I was a boy, Singer thinks, my father had his office in this sombre region, his windows below Formals and above Toys, Novelties, and Key Chains. Singer thinks, too: I am as old as my father; that is, the age he was when I began to understand what he was driving at. How quickly it has happened. Is this all there's going to be to it?

Singer catches up with his wife.

"I thought you went home," she says.

"I was going to, but everything's frozen."

"I don't know what you're talking about."

"You didn't take anything out of the freezer. There's nothing to eat."

"What are you waving your hand about for?"

"Air pollution."

"You're *dispersing* it?"

"This is symbolism."

"Can we take a cab?"

In the cab, Singer says, "I'm not going back to group and I'm not going back to Provincetown."

His wife doesn't say anything.

"I'm trying to convert a work of nature into a work of man," he adds.

"What you're trying to do in this marriage is to turn me into you," she says.

"You should have married someone mediocre," he says, "someone without a gift of expression."

Singer turns away and glances out the rear window. His stepson is riding his ten-speed bicycle right behind the cab, pedaling furiously; he has his mirrored sunglasses on. Singer's stepdaughter is on the crossbar; she is wearing a T-shirt and no brassiere. They look wanton to Singer, and he opens his mouth to shout, to censure them. His stepdaughter puts a finger to her lips. Singer shuts his eyes. When he opens them, the street is empty. He hears a faint rapping on the side of the cab. It's his stepson's ring, which he made out of the handle of a teaspoon. The children have drawn alongside.

"Please be good," Singer tells them. "Please read something besides Eldridge Cleaver."

Singer can't sleep. He gets out of bed and, naked except for his slippers, goes into the living room, picks up his palm—which he owned before he got married, and which is now as tall as he is—and lugs it into the hall bathroom, where he immerses it in a pail of water with the chill off in the stall shower. Singer sits on the toilet seat, listening to the palm drinking.

A few minutes later, he returns to the bedroom, kneels by the bed, and whispers in his wife's ear, "Who stole the cuticle scissors?"

"You're going to give yourself a manicure in the middle of the night?"

"My palm is dying."

"How many times have I told you palms are bad travelers? Palms like their spots. They don't like a lot of jostling."

"I know."

"Then why do you keep carting it around?"

"It was an emergency."

"Do you want me to trim the tips for you?"

"I want you to stand by."

She gets up and precedes him down the hall to the bathroom. She is also naked.

"You forgot your slippers," he says.

She steps into the shower and examines the palm from the back; then, parting the fronds, she peers at him.

"Good morning, Mr. Tootsabelli," she says.

Later, she says, "Is that the first time you ever did it on a desert island?"

"Why didn't you stay to the end?" he says.

"I wondered when you were going to get around to that," she says.

Singer would like everyone to know that he can tell the story of his life in twenty minutes.

19

Singer's wife is washing Singer's socks in the kitchen sink and weeping prodigally. Singer watches. He is forty and marking time; he believes that in a number of respects his life is repeating itself. He pays attention to the great, submerged tangle of black socks, mid-calf length; his wife's red, vehement face; her tears dropping at intervals into the murky water. He thinks: My socks are washed in her tears. What a heavy responsibility!

Singer gets a letter from his mother-in-law, who was born in Italy. She encloses a certificate for five shares of the capital stock of the Ocean Floating Safe Company, purchased in 1920 for a hundred dollars. Singer is supposed to find out whether she's a millionaire. He dwells on the vignette: an ocean liner going down, pitching lifeboats loaded with survivors, people in the water, ships steaming to the rescue, a number of cylindrical objects bobbing on the waves—presumably floating safes.

Singer gets a letter from his mother. It goes on and on. Singer disapproves of the punctuation—too many dashes. He folds the letter and puts it back in its envelope.

Singer lies on his back, hands prayerfully joined on his breastbone, like an effigy. The phone rings. It's his father. "You will have nocturnal emissions if you sleep on your back," he tells Singer.

Singer stands at midday at the threshold of his stepdaughter's room. She is seventeen and wants to be known as Lacy Lightning. The room, like a midden, is littered with beads and small seashells, which she strings. On the windowsill, by the head of her bed, is a pot of baby's tears she has neglected to water; three alarm clocks, which cannot wake her; pills for her slight anemia, which she insists she takes, but the bottles are full; and a box of Familia—she's a vegetarian except for tuna fish and salami.

"Why are you standing there looking at me?" she says.

"I'm not looking at you. I didn't know you were here."

"Then what are you doing?"

"Taking stock."

"Again?"

Singer advances, loving, regretful.

Crunch, crunch.

"You're stepping on my shells," she says.

Singer washes his hair in the stall shower. The scent of the Castile shampoo calls to mind seven cakes of soap modeled in the forms of the Seven Dwarfs. Singer briefly ponders the passage of life, mainly his. He quotes Wittgenstein, without conviction: " 'The solution of the problem of life is seen in the vanishing of the problem.' " His stepson flattens his nose against the shower door. It is Father's Day at Singer's old school, where his stepson is a third-former and a substitute defensive end. "Don't tell any of the coaches you're related to me," his stepson says. "Pretend you don't know me. Don't hit me on the top of the helmet if you walk behind the bench. If you see any of my teachers, don't ask them if I'm contributing to class discussions. Don't reminisce about your playing days."

Singer regards the form covered by blankets on the other side of his bed. Almost certainly, he thinks, this is my wife, and if I were to rip off the covers she would appear much as she was when we went to bed. But more time might have passed, and she could be greatly aged; or someone else might be lying there; or there might be a pile of rocks.

The doorbell rings. Singer answers it. It's Skippy Mountjoy, Singer's wife's first husband, who's supposed to be an alcoholic. "Your raincoat buttons up the wrong side," Singer says disapprovingly. Skippy sways gently, like an underwater weed. "Doesn't that raincoat belong to my wife?" Singer asks. Skippy goes into the kitchen and turns on the kettle, putting his weight on the handle.

"You won't save thirty seconds that way," Singer says.

"This is *my* life you're talking about," Skippy says.

Singer gets a letter from his mother. He notes that her handwriting has got larger recently and resembles the smoke that poured out of the steamboats and locomotives he drew as a child.

Singer lies on his side, knees drawn up, hands folded thoughtfully beneath his chin. The phone rings. It's his father. "If you sleep in that position, it will lead to curvature of the spine," he tells Singer.

Singer's wife says, "What would you say if you pulled the covers off and found a pile of rocks? 'Oh, a pile of rocks'?"

Singer learns by chance that Skippy is staying with them, sleeping on the living-room couch, wrapped in a sheet, embracing the dog. How long has he been there, Singer wonders. A week? Two weeks? A month?

According to Singer's wife, every morning after the kids have left for school and before Singer gets up, Skippy drapes himself in his sheet and goes into one of the kids' rooms, emerging after Singer has left for the office.

"What does he do in there?" Singer asks his wife.

"He minds his own business," she replies.

When Singer comes home, Skippy has already had his dinner and is concealed. While Singer is in the bedroom reading, Skippy comes out to do the dishes and walk the dog. "Does he know that if he hums to him it will help him go to the bathroom?" Singer has inquired.

Sometimes Singer hears Skippy conjugating irregular French verbs with his son; or, just before Singer goes to sleep, he hears, more faintly, organ chords—Skippy and his daughter are watching television.

Singer often finds crossword puzzles lying about that Skippy has started and given up on. Singer finishes them for him.

Singer once came across Skippy's damp footprints, and followed them from the hall bathroom to his stepson's room. Singer's wife found Singer kneeling in the hall. "Are you tracking him down?" she asked.

"Get a load of this," Singer said. "He's barely five-eight and these prints have got to be five feet apart. He was running!"

"He must have heard you coming," Singer's wife said.

Singer awakens his wife. "If he's an alcoholic why doesn't he go out and get drunk?" he says.

"You're not being constructive," she says. "He wants so much to be part of the family."

"Skulking about in his goddam sheet?"

"He's trying to respect your privacy. You should see him flitting through the apartment, his sheet streaming behind him, crying, 'Who am I?' "

"Who is he? Seneca?"

"He says he's the West Wind."

Singer's wife takes Singer to a screening to which she has been invited. After the movie has been on awhile, Singer realizes that he had gone with one of the actresses fifteen years ago. "She has changed," he says to himself. "If our roles were reversed, would she recognize me?" The actress takes off her clothes, even revealing what Singer's father used to speak of to Singer as the tropical regions. Her body is a mystery to Singer. Had he ever seen her undressed? Had he slept with her? Did anything ever happen? Does she remember me?

Singer awakens his wife. "Did Skippy Mountjoy go to the screening?" he asks.

"I gave them his name," she says. "He didn't want to be left out."

Singer gets out of bed and gropes his way down the dark hall. The phone rings. It's his father. "Always swing your arms confidently when you walk," he tells Singer.

"You have no right to spy on my past," Singer shouts at the form on the couch. When his eyes become accustomed to the dark, he sees that Skippy isn't there, and that the couch is empty, except for the dog and a folded sheet. "Oh, the dog and a folded sheet," Singer says.

With the help of private detectives, Singer finds his stepdaughter in a motel on Hollywood Boulevard, which is faced with what appears to be artificial stone. She is sitting cross-legged on one of the twin beds, picking up beads with her beading needle and listening to Led Zeppelin on the portable stereo she lugged across country. Singer takes off his shoes and lies on the empty bed. "Do you like this?" she says, holding up a string of beads. "Orange, orange, violet, orange, orange, violet, orange, orange, violet, violet, violet, orange, orange, violet—"

Singer gets a letter from his mother-in-law. She encloses a certificate for thirty shares of the capital stock of the Paesano Hydraulic Power Company, purchased in 1923 for ninety dollars, and a prospectus describing its system for developing power by tidal movement. Another killing! Singer reads: "*Soggiogare gli oceani indomiti e ribelli ai bisogni dell'uomo è un prodigio di meravigliosa bellezza—*" Singer breaks into song. "*—un prodigio che esalta la potenza umana, un prodigio che onora di nuova gloria l'umana famiglia. . . .*" Tears are streaming down his cheeks.

Singer and his wife go to a restaurant on an island in the Gulf. There has been nearly five inches of rain that day, and the parking lot is underwater. The restaurant windows are ablaze with light, and as they wade toward the steps that lead up to the entrance they can make out the diners seated by the windows, who are inclined toward each other at almost identical angles and not speaking. All are over seventy. A middle-aged woman with a blond pageboy is playing an electric organ in an anteroom furnished with wicker armchairs, where couples waiting for tables are reading the *National Geographic* and *Audubon*. Singer looks over the organist's shoulder. Her piece is "The Road to the Isles—A Tramping Song." A smiling woman in a dress printed with innumerable violets approaches Singer and asks if he has a reservation. He says that he hasn't, that he didn't know one was needed. She says she's sorry; they are all full up; perhaps he would like to make a reservation for another night. Singer says he's sorry; he doesn't know.

"The theme and pattern of my life is that all of it has happened to me," Singer tells his wife as they drive off. "It has no more—and no less—necessity than may be demonstrated by the fact that it is *my* head that is attached to *my* body."

In the rearview mirror, Singer notices that the restaurant seems to be floating.

"That's the trouble," Singer's wife says.

"What is?"

"Your life. None of it has happened to anyone else."

20

Ursula Hapworth said the style was popular in Florida thirty-five or forty years ago: one story; corbie-steps; phony vigas sticking out; stucco doing for adobe; flat, tiled roof. They were called Spanish houses. She wore her red hair in an ape cut and had an English accent. "The awnings belong to a much later period," she added. Julian Singer, whom she was addressing, peered at these; they were aluminum and brought to mind huge, reptilian eyelids. After a moment's reflection, he said the house seemed to have an air of desuetude. Ursula said what it needed was a good coat of paint. "The rain marks led you astray," she said. "Actually, it's very cozy."

They looked at the house from several other angles. Singer was dazed by the evidence of sunlight, the implication of heat. "Where does the street lead?" he asked. "To the river," she said. "It's extremely wide. You can just see the other bank." In front of the house, by the street, were two lofty royal palms, in back a grove of live oaks. Any number of things grew round about. Singer recognized eucalyptus, sea grape, hydrangea. He told Ursula he envied authors who knew their taxonomy—for example, told you what the protagonist was tramping across or under. "Peeping through," she added. Singer was aware of a momentary sadness or longing caused by something deeper than an inability to classify plants; he felt as though all that could be seen of him were unsatisfactory glimpses. By the same token, these seemed to be all *he* was afforded. He imagined naked women, along the lines of Fragonard's *baigneuses*, asleep in a glade, aroused by his heavy-footed approach, scattering into clumps of—what? Mountain laurel? Rhododendron? "I'm forty-one and I really don't know anything," Singer told Ursula.

She enumerated the other plantings: areca, date, and traveller's palm; Florida birch; three varieties of pine; almond, fig, peach, lemon, orange, grapefruit, and papaya trees; jasmine, bougainvillaea, hibiscus, poinsettia, crotons; roses, tiger lilies, marigolds . . . Singer thought the garden a *locus amoenus*; Noah's ark also sprang to mind—a refuge for every kind of plant. Without the din and the terrific stench, of course. He had an impulse to leave his wife and children and hide out there, have the—"What do they call the paper down there?" he asked Ursula. "The Fort Myers *News-Press*," she said—have the *News-Press* delivered. But that would only get him through his second cup of coffee; in his reverie, the house was his and he was living in it alone. "There's also the Gulf edition of the Miami *Herald*," she said. "And these are bathing-beauty pictures."

Singer was sitting on the other side of her desk, in New York, looking through a viewer at slides of the house she was buying. They worked in the same office, but this was their first conversation. The slides she now handed him showed a redhead in a bikini posing on an empty pool deck. The pool was empty, too, except for a pair of drifting water wings. The woman in the photograph was evidently Ursula; her face was mostly hidden by a pair of enormous sunglasses, and Singer had never taken note of her figure.

"Did you ever stop to think why swimming pools look bigger in brochures than in real life?" Singer said. "Camera angle, you say? Not the case. Consider the 'vacationers' grouped in and about the pool. Ever look at them closely? If, as I have done, you had spread out a number of brochures before you, you would have discovered that the same people appear in every one. That is, members of the same cast, so to speak; their number varies from brochure to brochure. From my sampling, I have determined that there may be as few as five and as many as seventeen.

"Their identity is not so readily arrived at. Each model (for that, obviously, is what they are) has at least four changes of costume—bathing suits, cover-ups, cabaña sets, etc.—as well as any number of sunglasses, wigs, bathing caps, hats, bandannas, and snoods. Moreover, the figures who appear at the far end of the pool are often so minute as to be nearly indistinguishable. But, you ask, what has all this to do with the disparity in size between the pools in the brochures and in actuality? Just this: all the models are midgets.

"Although, for the picture-taking, the chaise longues and other pool furniture are removed and replaced by children's chairs, tables, and umbrellas, once in a great while, due to carelessness or as a joke to relieve the tedium of gaily posing at poolside after poolside or to get even with a motel owner who chiseled on the price, one of the midgets stands too close to a pool ladder and his true size is given away.

"These midgets belong to a troupe that hires itself out for this specialized line of work. The troupe travels about from motel to motel in a VW bus or stretch limo or similar conveyance, packed with wardrobe trunks, children's furniture, and photographic equipment. This busload of midgets never attracts notice. Because of the occupants' size, the bus appears empty. But if you could peer in you would see them—five, six, even seven to a seat—sleeping on one another's shoulders or reflectively supporting their chins in their tiny hands.

"The scenery flashes by unseen except by the driver, who is raised on cushions. As, huddled in their bus, the midgets crisscross the country, night and day make as little impression upon them as the passage of years. Every so often, however, the remark is made that so-and-so has got too old-looking to pose; motels stress youth at poolside. The midgets' way of saying this is, 'Nix on the pix, Gramps' (or 'Granny'); many of them have theatrical backgrounds. I haven't been able to learn the fate of these old-timers."

Singer elevated the viewer to get the benefit of the light from the ceiling fixture; his attitude suggested that of St. Francis renouncing his earthly possessions in the fresco in the upper church at Assisi, hands, eyes raised presumably to Heaven—a naked man whose depiction always struck Singer as being more representative of our essential plight than of reverence. Singer had grown weary of his tale, as he did of so much. "The bus crashes on a secondary road," he said. "Little bodies, little wigs, little chaise longues lie strewn about . . ."

Ursula had begun to weep. I know how to make people cry, Singer conceded.

A policeman materialized in Singer's lane and held up his hand. Singer stopped and the policeman came over and looked in the car window.

"Do you know," he said, "that you were traveling in a fifteen-mile-per-hour zone?"

"I know," Singer said, "but I was gently braking."

"Do you know," the policeman said, "that you were traveling in excess of fifteen miles per hour?"

"I know," Singer said, "but given time I would have been within the speed limit."

"Do you know," the policeman said, "that you have come to rest in a school zone in which there is a schoolhouse full of itty-bitty children?"

Singer recognized a school across the highway. It seemed deserted, its windows blank; grackles, he noted, were walking very stately on the lawn.

"Do you know," the policeman said, "that *I* would have been a whole lot happier and *you* would have been a whole lot happier if *you* had been traveling within the posted limit?"

While Singer was framing a reply, the policeman waved him on. He turned down a side street and came to the river for—what was it, he wondered, the fiftieth time? He was in Tampa on business and had driven down to Fort Myers to see if he could find the Spanish house. He had thought of calling Ursula in New York to get the address, but it had been two months since he had looked at her slides, and they hadn't talked again. Besides, he felt it would be more rewarding if he stumbled upon the house. However, as he came to realize, he couldn't recall what it looked like; he had passed several Spanish houses with royal palms out front and a great many rank, diverse, and haphazard plantings but was unable to tell which, if any, was the one he sought. None, certainly, aroused in him the sentiments he had experienced looking at the slides.

Industrial chimneys rose beyond the far bank. No smoke issued from them, and the buildings to which they belonged were screened from view by foliage. The chimneys put Singer in mind of columnar necks of dinosaurs looking up from their feeding. He half expected the chimneys to sway, and felt a sense of foreboding. But everything was still. Only the slow, glittering flood betrayed that great forces were imperceptibly at work. Singer reviewed his life in the hot car and tried to project it over the years that remained to him. He gathered he was probably incapable of change and that it was his portion to be denied access to the Spanish house. For one thing, he loved his family; for another, he couldn't find it.

On the way back, he saw the policeman sitting in his cruiser off the road, the door open to allow air to circulate. Singer pulled alongside. Tears were bathing his cheeks. "Not a whole lot," he told him.

"As I said on the phone, I went looking for your house," Singer told Ursula when she admitted him to her apartment. He followed her down the hall. Cats twined about his legs. "It's really a pity you didn't find it," she said. She was moving toward a source of light—a window—so she was made insubstantial. Singer noticed a mirror, but so low on the wall no one could have seen his face in it except the cats jumping. The living room was dominated by a concert grand, with great claw-and-ball feet. The Chinese, Singer recalled reading, attached religious significance to this motif, which typified a dragon's foot holding a pearl withdrawn from the bottom of the sea. Singer went over to the piano; a sonata for four hands by Mozart lay open on the rack. He wondered who had interposed his hands between hers. Who took the bathing-beauty pictures, for that matter? He glanced at her books. Pots of mysterious plants were arrayed on the window sills. How long it's been since I've been in anyone else's apartment, Singer thought; too, he had forgotten the strong, venereal impression one gets among a strange woman's things. "I may have but I couldn't remember what it looked like," Singer said. Ursula took down prints from one wall—Klees mostly. Singer regarded the paler oblongs where they'd been. She set up a projector and put in a stack of slides. "These will refresh your memory," she said. The projector advanced the slides automatically at intervals. They were sitting on the floor. "Bother," she said, "the bathing-beauty pictures got mixed in," and made as though to remove them, but Singer took hold of her hand and drew her toward him. Looking up at one point, he saw that their heaving, mingled shadows were projected against the base of the stucco walls, like the unimaginable shapes that lie ahead.

21

The Singers graded the days of their vacation, which they spent at the Sun 'n Sea Motor Inn in Key Biscayne and at the Whispering Sands Resort Motel on Sanibel Island, C+, B, D, A, B-, C+, B, A-, D, F, C. These grades reflected the weather.

During their vacation, the Singers noted license plates from twenty-eight states and two Canadian provinces.

The bad things that happened on their vacation (and which they wrote down) were:

1. No gas cap.

On the way from the airport to the Sun 'n Sea, a woman in a station wagon, in which a little boy intently turned a toy steering wheel, kept honking her horn and shouting at Singer. Motorists frequently blew their horns at him or shouted unintelligibly as they passed. Singer almost never knew why. Off and on, he appealed to his wife, who didn't drive. She reminded him that he had made her navigator, and that such appeals didn't come under her department. On this occasion, however, Singer finally understood that he was leaking gas. He parked: no gas cap.

On Key Biscayne, Singer drove from one gas station to another, looking for a gas cap.

"Make a note of the mileage," he told his wife.

"What ever for?"

"I'm going to have Hertz deduct it."

"We've only been in Florida forty-five minutes and you're already preparing to create a scene."

"But I'm in the right."

2. No Unit 21.

The Singers had come to Key Biscayne every year since 1963, when they had honeymooned at the Crandon Park, formerly the Crandon Palm. In 1965, they switched to the Sun 'n Sea. There they had always had Unit 21, which differed from nearly all the other units in that the bathroom was on a breezeway and had a louvered window. Each year, the first thing Singer did after he put down the bags was stand on the toilet seat, unplug the ventilator fan in the ceiling, and crank open the window.

This year, they had Unit 33: not on a breezeway.

"I specifically requested Unit 21," Singer told his wife, trying the bathroom light switch, which also operated the fan.

"You can still unplug it," she said.

"But the point is," Singer said, raising his voice so he could be heard above the great melancholy roar of the fan, "the point is that this unit has adjoining units on both sides, so the possibility of people having their television on too loud at night is twice what it is in Unit 21."

3. Spooky galleys.

In years past, the print above their bed at the Sun 'n Sea had shown a curve of beach, some palm trees, the wrecked hull of a native fishing boat. This year, the print showed several fantastic galleys that seemed to be rotting in a backwater, sails in theatrical tatters, oars drooping in the stagnant, faintly phosphorescent water. Singer's wife maintained that it actually glowed in the dark; Singer said she was overreacting.

Singer peeked into some other units, including 21. The galleys were hanging all over.

"What do you think made them put them up?" Singer's wife asked.

"What do you think they did with fifty-four native fishing boats?" Singer asked.

4. Portuguese men-of-war.

The ocean was choppy, turbid, and dotted with innumerable

men-of-war, so Singer was loath to go swimming. He sat on the beach in his collapsible chair, from which an accumulation of baggage tags fluttered; he had bought the chair the day before they got married and took it to Florida each year.

Singer's wife spread her towel beside the chair and sat down. "I'm waiting for a lull," he told her, "but they keep coming."

5. No binocs, no bird book.

Singer had forgotten his binoculars and his Peterson. "If you see one you don't know," Singer's wife told him, "ignore it."

6. No mask, no snorkel.

Singer had forgotten to pack his wife's face mask and snorkel. He said he was sorry, adding that there was too much sediment to see anything anyway.

7. No pajama bottoms.

Singer had packed two pajama tops and no bottoms.

8. No pumpernickel raisin, no whole-wheat onion.

Singer's favorite restaurant was Chippy's, in Coral Gables, because pumpernickel raisin bread and wholewheat onion rolls came in the breadbasket. This year, the nights the Singers were there they didn't serve any.

9. South Dixie Highway at night. The traffic had become murderous.

10. Abner's.

This was a restaurant on the South Dixie Highway, where they ate one night. Singer had chosen it on account of the modern architecture: it was walled with dark glass. Inside, large color transparencies portrayed slices of rare roast beef and succulent ribs. Their orders came in woven-plastic baskets and didn't resemble the photographs. Singer sat with his chin in his hand, looking through the dark glass at the murderous traffic and at his reflection.

11. Simon.

Singer's stepdaughter called from New York to say that Simon, his stepson, had ridden his ten-speed bike over "Santana," "Let It Bleed," and "Revolver."

12. Cassie.

Simon called to say that Cassie, Singer's stepdaughter, had spent the food money on Indian jewelry.

13. Z.

A comic strip.

14. *Bob & Carol & Ted & Alice.*

"Why do the protagonists in these movies always wear jockey shorts?" Singer asked his wife. "Nobody *I* know wears jockey shorts."

15. No upstairs at the Whispering Sands.

This was the third year the Singers had gone to Sanibel. The first two times, they had a unit on the second and top story near the Gulf; the Whispering Sands was built at right angles to the water. This year, they had a unit on the first floor.

"I can't see the ocean from my bed," Singer's wife said after Singer had put down the bags. "On the second floor, I could see the ocean."

"It's the Gulf," Singer said.

When he returned from the office, where he had gone to complain, Singer said, "I told them I had specifically requested a unit on the second floor as near the Gulf as possible. I told them to refer to my letter, which they did. They agreed that I had specifically requested a unit on the second floor as near the Gulf as possible, but they didn't have any. They said their regulars liked the first floor because they didn't have to lug their bags up the stairs."

The good things that happened on the Singers' vacation (and which they wrote down) were:

1. 9 a.m. plane.

The Singers had reservations on a 10 a.m. flight to Miami, but because Singer liked to allow plenty of time for eventualities they got to the airport so early they made the 9 a.m. flight, which gave them an additional hour in Florida, fifteen minutes of which, Singer pointed out, they wasted looking for a gas cap.

2. Brindley's.

Singer had forgotten to take pipe tobacco. Vernon's, in the Key Biscayne Shopping Center, had his brand—Brindley's Mixture.

3. Chinese hairless.

Window-shopping on the Miracle Mile one night, the Singers saw a strange dog. It was black and hairless, except for a tuft that grew out of its forehead. Singer's wife said that the dog looked as though it was made out of clay. Its owners were a man in plaid shorts and a woman who wore socks and heels. Afterward, Singer's wife said the woman must have been the man's mother; Singer said he had assumed she was his wife. The man told Singer the dog was a Chinese hairless. Singer's wife said she hadn't known Chinese hairlesses existed. Singer said he had heard of them. The man said he had never heard of them until he heard on television that a woman who owned four Chinese hairlesses had died, and that they were available on a first-come, first-serve basis. "So we went over and got one," the man said. "One was gone already. We got the second."

4. Maids.

Until this year, the Singers' chambermaid at the Sun 'n Sea had been Minerva. Each year, Minerva asked them why they didn't bring the children with them, and each year they told her they were going to bring them next year. When they didn't, Minerva would throw up her arms and chide them for breaking their promise. This time, they had another chambermaid. They asked her whether Minerva still worked there; the new maid said she did. The next day, they met Minerva by the linen room.

"I heard someone was asking for me," she said, "and I knew it had to be you. Where are the children?"

Later, Singer said to his wife, "I like the maids at the Sun 'n Sea. They do the dishes. The maids at the Whispering Sands don't do the dishes."

5. Portuguese men-of-war gone away.

For two days, following a shift in the wind.

6. Lifeguard.

At Crandon Park, the Singers met Wayne, a lifeguard they had got to know the year before. It turned out he had seen Z the same night as the Singers, at Wometco Twin II, opposite the Dadeland Shopping Center; in fact, he and his wife apparently had sat behind them. Singer's wife said she thought she had heard a familiar laugh. Wayne said he thought Z was a comic strip, too. He and his wife hadn't seen *Bob & Carol & Ted & Alice*.

7. Sandbar.

The sandbar off the beach at Crandon Park had become much bigger since last year, and nearer shore. You weren't allowed to swim to it, but, as he had the year before, Wayne let Singer swim over with him. While Wayne jogged around the bar, Singer looked for shells. Then Wayne and Singer waded to a farther bar, on the edge of the deep. On the way, Wayne told a story about another lifeguard who had been marooned on the second bar; a hammerhead had entered the channel between it and the first bar. He said the lifeguard had run about on the bar, yelling and waving his arms, but nobody could figure out what he was up to. When Singer told the story to his wife, she said Wayne had told it to them last year. She also said that last year Singer had brought her back a shell.

8. Elderly waitress.

Singer's wife said Singer gave the elderly waitress at Chippy's a hard time. Singer said that he was only kidding around. Singer's wife couldn't finish her turkey sandwich. The elderly waitress put it in a doggy bag for her, but she left it in the booth. Two evenings later, when they next ate at Chippy's, the waitress said she had run outside on the sidewalk with the doggy bag, looking for Singer's wife, but she had disappeared.

9. Unidentified bird.

Singer saw a bird he couldn't identify sitting on the end of one of the groins at the Sun 'n Sea. He waded out with his notebook and pencil to sketch the bird, which must have been fearless or exhausted, since it didn't fly away. Where the bird was, the water was up to Singer's shoulders. His first attempt was ruined when spray wet the page. When Singer came out of the water, a woman said to him, "How could you write out there? *I* couldn't do it." Singer told his wife what the woman had said, adding, "Why didn't she say, 'Why are you writing out there?' Or, 'What are you writing out there?'" Singer's wife asked to see his drawing. "You made the bird look like me," she told Singer.

10. Swimming backward.

On Sanibel, the littoral current was so strong that no matter how hard Singer swam against it he was swept back along the shore. He told his wife about it and made her watch the phenomenon. Singer roared with laughter as he streamed backward, the scenery slipping by. Singer's wife took his picture with their Instamatic.

11. Laughing fit.

On the F day, Singer and his wife were lying in Singer's bed at the Whispering Sands, beneath a collage composed of seashells, sand dollars, and starfish, when they started laughing and couldn't stop. Neither remembered what had set them off. Singer thought it might have been because of their plight—meaning the rain. Singer's wife thought it was because Singer had been loath to let her in his bed.

The pictures the Singers took at Key Biscayne showed: Singer standing by their car, a blue Impala custom coupe, in the Sun 'n Sea parking area, smoking his pipe; Singer's wife standing beneath a palm at Crandon Park in her flowered bathing suit; Singer standing on the beach at Crandon Park in his red bathing suit; Singer's wife standing in the Sun 'n Sea parking area; Singer standing on the pool deck at the Sun 'n Sea in his blue bathing suit, smoking his pipe; Singer's wife lying on her stomach on a chaise on the pool deck; Singer's wife looking up a moment later; Singer swimming ashore at Crandon Park, with just his head visible; Singer stepping ashore a moment later; Singer's wife standing by the shuffleboard court at the Sun 'n Sea; Singer standing by the shuffleboard court. One picture didn't come out.

The pictures the Singers took on Sanibel showed: Singer standing on the beach in his red bathing suit; Singer's wife standing on the first-floor walkway of the Whispering Sands; Singer making a turn in the Whispering Sands pool; Singer's wife lying on a grassy bank by the pool in her flowered bathing suit; Singer being swept backward, laughing; Singer's wife standing on the terrace of their unit; Singer standing on the first-floor walkway; Singer's wife kneeling in the surf in her orange bathing suit; Singer in his bed in one of his pajama tops; Singer's wife in her bed in a nightie with pink ribbons she had bought to wear on her honeymoon; Singer leaning against the trunk of their car before leaving for the airport, smoking his pipe; Singer's wife holding the car door open on her side a moment later.

When they had looked at the pictures, Singer remarked on how little change there had been. The years were differentiated by the cars, he said. To a lesser extent, by their bathing suits.

"Age," Singer's wife said.

How imperceptible! That is, Singer added, from year to year. One is able to believe that one looked that way last year and will look the same next year.

His wife assured Singer he was the same.

Singer wondered, speaking of bathing suits, what had happened to the bathing suit she was wearing when she thought he had drowned.

It had been the first year they had stayed at the Sun 'n Sea. Singer had told his wife he was taking a dip, but he had struck out alongshore and out of sight. When he finally returned, she was standing in the doorway of Unit 21, in a French bikini, a peach print with ruffles, sobbing.

It was the only time she had cried in Florida, Singer said. A mockingbird had been singing by the shuffleboard court, did she remember?

She said she had cried on their honeymoon, in the public library.

They had gone to the Miami Beach Public Library to read their wedding announcement in the *Times* and *Tribune*. Singer had composed it and given it to one of his wife's friends, who worked on the *Trib* and said he would take care of it. The announcement wasn't in either paper. Singer's wife said they mightn't have had room for it that day. Singer looked in the papers dated two days after their marriage; it wasn't there, either.

Now, once again, Singer dwelt on how her friend had let them down.

Singer's wife said she had cried in the public library because Singer had let her down, because she thought he would be interested in her, that he would want her, that they would go out—

"Chippy's is out," Singer said.

—that she would be able to wear her new dresses, she added.

"You wouldn't even lie on the beach with me," she said. "You brought that chair!"

She said she used to look forward to going to Florida, to having a good time. She said she had always thought he was going to change. It was she who had changed. It used to eat her heart out.

"I remember the first time I saw you," she said. "You looked like a nice person, but you didn't want to talk. I should have remembered that."

"Nonetheless," Singer said, "you cried when you thought I had drowned."

"I cried because I didn't know what I would tell your father," she said, "and I didn't know what to do about the car."

Singer said he often felt like that little boy in the station wagon—that he was wrestling with the wheel, but which way was he going?

When he had swum out of sight, he recalled, gleaming bait fish had leapt out of the sea, over his head, and there was, overwhelmingly, a sense of brightness. Terns dived, disappeared, reappeared. Light transfigured their wings. At some point, he was going to have to turn back.

22

I was awakened in the middle of the night in a motel room in Southern California by—what? I like to think it was the sound of moving water—water that, during the two previous nights I had slept there, had at that hour been still. I got out of bed and, in the dark, went in what I knew to be the direction of the picture window. It was far off. Everything about the room was grandiose—the bed, for example, could easily have slept four—as though it had been built and furnished with an eye to the future, for the race of giants we would become.

The window had two sets of draperies drawn across it, the inner thick and brocaded, of the same stuff as the bedspread, the outer diaphanous. These were in shades of green, as was nearly everything else—the upholstery, the linen, the toilet paper. Because of its great length, its dimness, and the different greens, I likened the room to a sea cave, into which I had been washed.

I peered through the draperies. My room was on the second and top floor, and I looked out on the heated pool, which gently steamed and was illuminated by underwater lights. Four couples were in the pool. Everyone was naked. Actually, they weren't, but I want you to share my first impression. I soon realized that the men were wearing jockey shorts, the women bras and panties. Later on, I wasn't so sure: one or two of the women might not have been wearing bras.

Because of their haircuts, I assumed the men were Air Force officers; some sort of Air Force conference was going on at the motel. The women all had flip hairdos, which they were trying to keep dry. They held their heads rigidly and appeared to be taking part in a water ballet rather than an orgy.

That's what I thought, trembling in my shortie pajama bottoms, in the dark, on a green carpet, in my forty-first year—an orgy. Some orgy! As I said, there were four couples. In each, the man had his hands on the woman's waist, holding her nearly at arm's length, and they glided about the shallow end that way, as though they were crouching like Groucho Marx, either so as not to expose themselves or because the air was cold. Occasionally, two couples came together to make a figure of four. Whenever a couple ventured over its head, it did so in single file, each partner holding on to the gutter, first with one hand, then the other. Nobody swam a stroke. I've noticed that people don't swim as much as they used to.

Nothing was happening. Nothing was going to happen. Nobody was going to embrace, kiss, fondle, get laid. But I was greatly affected. Here, in a sense, was a period piece, a scene from my past (not specifically, not even from old dreams or longings, but of the genre). I envied the young officers gliding solemnly through the mist in the illuminated water, inhaling fumes of chlorine and Evening in Paris, as though the last twenty or twenty-five years hadn't taken place. I didn't want to join them; I am too ponderous, too gray, too morose, and all I own is boxer shorts. Nor do I yearn for a more pristine state, of which the scene below me, like a painting on a vase recovered from a tomb or the sea floor, bore witness, and from which we have tumultuously declined. What aroused me was the rush of time: what was gone, what had never happened, what, while the officers steered their dates or pick-ups (sweethearts or wives, even—who knows?) this way and that about the vaporous pool, was going, would never happen. That, and that I might be seeing bare teat but couldn't be positive.

These feelings gave rise to an impulse to step forth and address the orgiasts from the rail of the walkway connecting the second-floor units, to acquaint them with—again, what? The order of natural things? The evanescence of human grandeurs? That I was there?

"Ladies and gentlemen," I might say, "allow me to introduce myself. My name is Singer and I have run away from home. . . ." Check that. "Ladies and gentlemen, don't be alarmed. Please bear with me for a moment. My name is Singer, I'm harmless, a *Gummimensch*, and I have run away from home. . . ." No. "Ladies and gentlemen, I am all alone up here and I want to tell someone the story of my life. Along with the opposable thumb, eloquent discourse, and a sense of history, this perhaps piteous urge to confess may be one of the few things we have in common.

"Before I go any further, I must admit that I have been spying on you from my room, and for that and for so much that came before I set eyes on you, I ask forgiveness. Night, moving water, mist—these provide a traditional backdrop to regrettable acts as well as to scenes of remission. Historical examples should not be difficult to find. But to continue. It has occurred to me that I probably was not alone in my vigil. A dozen or more guests may have stood—may still be standing—in their bare feet, in the dark, their heads slightly inclined as though before a mirror, peering through green draperies, trying to make sense out of their lives. Though my life, I like to think, is in many respects different from those of my fellow-guests, I am, in a way, their spokesman and you our common mystery: shrouded in mist, distorted by refraction, flesh indistinguishable from underwear, random, inexpressive, young.

"It has also occurred to me that the last time I looked down at such length, although, I admit, more abstractedly [*Laughter*], was one afternoon last week when my secretary came in and told me they were marching in the streets again. I got up from my desk and stood by the sealed window. Twenty stories below, students streamed raggedly up the avenue. Through the glass I heard faint, almost plaintive cries, like those of birds in the air. How high their voices were! I read their makeshift banners. I saw my wife marching in their midst; I recognized her bathrobe.

" 'I've decided it's a maxicoat,' she explained that night. 'The way it flowed around me as I walked was a nice feeling.'

"I said did she remember to call Gimbels about the man coming to repair the couch, which, gentlemen, I recommend you don't bring up when your wife's been demonstrating in her bathrobe to end the war in Vietnam, to promote the use of biodegradable shampoo bottles, or to free some *schwarzer*.

"Speaking of shampoo, may I inquire whether any of you has ever taken a shower with a beach ball? [*Laughter*] I did, for a week. [*Laughter*] It was orange, with a few green leaves and the inscription 'Your ORANGE from FLORIDA.' My wife bought it in Miami Beach for Simon, my stepson. He played basketball in his room with it, using a hoop made out of a wire coat hanger.

" 'I'm afraid I'm going to have to confiscate that,' I said one night, taking a rebound away from him.

" 'But I'm not making any noise,' he said.

" 'People live below us,' I said.

"Even as I uttered them, I realized that both of my lines were my father's; so is the language handed down, civilization preserved.

"Years ago, my father gave me an old three-drawer filing cabinet—metal finished to look like wood; it came from his office, and once contained what he calls 'various matters.' The cabinet, he said, was for my 'vast accumulation of junk.' My father is an orderly person. He ceaselessly rearranges his table setting, as though seeking a more perfect symmetry. Before he goes to bed he checks the pocket flaps of the jackets hanging in his closet to make sure they're entirely out. 'There's an ample supply of folders,' he added. These were labeled: 'Eagle Factors v. TotCraft,' 'Fein v. Fein,' 'Freibush v. Ace Braid,' etc., and evoked mournful scenes I had never witnessed, such as the prospect from my father's office forty years ago or, more precisely, my father gazing out of his office window, considering the years that stretched before him. I am reminded of this cabinet because there must be a folder in my mind labeled 'Singer v. Singer,' in which is filed all that my father felt obliged to say to me more than once. [*Laughter*]

"At any rate, ladies and gentlemen, the beach ball turned up in the stall shower. My stepson must have put it there, possibly as a symbol of his regret.

"After it had lain in the shower three or four days, my wife said, 'Aren't you going to do anything about that ball?'

"I said, 'As Wittgenstein said, "My *life* consists in my being content to accept many things." '

" 'Why did he italicize "life"?' my wife asked.

"One night not long afterward, I went to the kitchen to get a bowl of cold cereal and discovered Cassie, my stepdaughter, and a six-foot, five-inch black bass-guitarist. He was sitting at the counter, gazing at the reflection of his Afro in the toaster. One of the burners was on and his curling iron lay in the flames. My stepdaughter took up the iron and made a curl for him in back where he couldn't see. I assume I am safe in saying here is a scene beyond Wittgenstein's ken.

"The following night, I thought I heard someone in the kitchen and got up to look. No one was there, but I imagined it was my father, eating a bowl of cold cereal in the dark.

" 'I couldn't sleep,' he explained when I had turned on the light. 'I took a cab. I couldn't find the raisins.'

" 'There aren't any,' I said.

" 'No raisins! I remember a little fellow who wouldn't eat cold cereal without his raisins. What's happened? Sometimes I stand back and look at you as though you're apiece of sculpture I'm carving—'

" 'But it's done.'

" 'There's a point when it's too late to change the concept,' my father continued. 'There's not enough material left.'

"All the foregoing is true. I no longer find it beguiling to invent; there has to be a reason for everything, even if the reason is the absence of reason. This could happen to anyone.

"As long as I have you here, ladies and gentlemen, what, I ask, are my mother, my father, and I doing at Roosevelt Raceway having a few drinks in the Cloud Casino? None of us is a horseplayer. We don't bet sports. We're in the market, but as an investment. As a matter of fact, up to tonight my mother and father have been to the track only once in their lives, and that Hobby Horse Hall in Nassau, when I was six or seven and Nana came back to look after me; the stamp on the letter they sent me showed flamingos flying from left to right.

" 'We're not winners, you see,' my mother explains.

" 'I won a few quid,' my father says.

" 'The only thing I ever won in my life was a course on how

not to forget,' my mother says.

" 'I bought a paper in the morning and played their recommendations,' my father says.

" 'It was one of those lonely nights when he was at one of his meetings,' my mother says. 'Cerebral palsy.'

" 'They were a small, scrawny-looking breed,' my father says.

" 'There was a demonstration advertised,' my mother says.

" 'Not a sturdy-looking tribe of horses,' my father says.

" 'I wanted to remember things better so I went down on the bus,' my mother says.

" 'It's the fodder,' my father says.

" 'The Engineering Building,' my mother says. 'I took a seat on the fringes.'

" 'The fodder's no good,' my father says.

" 'The man who gave the course had his students arrayed on the stage,' my mother says. 'He asked those of us who were sitting on the fringes to move down front and introduce ourselves. His students had never seen us before, but later in the evening, when he called upon them to identify us, they all knew our names. They remembered who we were. Next we were told to write our names on little cards, and mine was pulled out of a hat, and I won a free course. How Not to Forget. It was held on Thursday evenings at Steinway Hall. There were ten lessons. He gave us his formula. But I've forgotten all that. I suppose I was too used to remembering things my way.'

"But what I would like to talk to you about tonight, ladies and gentlemen, is the difficulties strewn in the way of finding out who we *are*, not formulas for remembering who we *were*. For example, when you go to the doctor for a checkup, he begins by asking you a lot of questions. When you reach my age [*Laughter*], one usually is 'Do you go to the bathroom in the middle of the night?' [*Laughter*] 'Yes,' you say. 'Matter of fact, I do.' 'Frequently?' he says. 'What do you mean by "frequently"?' you say. 'Well, do you go more than once?' he says. Notice, he's not answering the question. Then, in one of those sudden shifts of mood that, in my experience, arise between doctor and patient—husband and wife, too, I suppose—at the moment when, as it were, the secret watermark of one's existence is about to be held up to the light, he becomes remote, even sibylline. You say, 'Sometimes, I suppose.' He says, 'Twice?' You say, 'I guess so. Once in a while.' He says, 'Three times?' You say, 'It's conceivable.' He says, 'Frequently?' You say, 'I believe you've already asked that.' He says, 'You're mistaken. What I'm trying to determine is whether you go three or more times—frequently.'

"You get the picture, ladies and gentlemen. The picture *I* have in mind, rendered perhaps in the manner of Bruegel, is one of millions of middle-aged men, some sleeping, some getting out of bed, some feeling their way to the bathroom in the dark, some returning to bed, but, on account of all this activity, you can't figure out how many times any given individual is going to the bathroom, as in an ant hill. 'Why are you shaking your head?' the doctor says. 'Let me get back to you on this next year after I research it,' you say. 'As you will,' he says, turning to my drinking.

"Over the years, as a result of similar give-and-takes, several doctors have told me that I'm an 'erratic social drinker.' They evidently have some basis for this judgment, but that, and its moral and physiological implications, have never been imparted to me, and I am as much in the dark about how I stand in relationship to my contemporaries in this regard as in regard to the act of going to the bathroom in the middle of the night, a journey which, whenever I undertake it of late, is fraught with an almost metaphysical weight. There are, in this vein, analyses which I have arrived at independently, but these, too, have an equivocal, even oxymoronic flavor; for instance, long ago I decided I was 'the most cheerful depressed person I knew' as well as 'a social hermit.'

"An episode illustrating or, to make a lesser claim, incorporating these findings took place in Billy Brillo's Sports Bar. This, ladies and gentlemen, is a beer bar in Fort Lauderdale, where I drank on three occasions a number of years ago—erratically, full of wary cheer, in society but withdrawn, may I say anchoritic, on my stool. [*Laughter*] Different root, of course. [*Laughter*] If, implausible as it may seem, any of its patrons or employees—even Billy Brillo himself—happen to be within earshot, they won't remember me, though possibly they will recall the silence which suddenly gripped them, and in which I joined, when the Tiger was about to throw his second dart at the little man, whose name I didn't catch, who rested his head against the board as though all at once he had grown tired of life, although perhaps it was that I had only come in, as is so often the case, in time for the last scene, or that his action was some sort of parlor trick, like 'dissolving' a quarter in a glass of beer, which, having performed it a hundred times, he undertook with the melancholy foreknowledge that he would bring it off, that nothing would change, that he would have to do it again; thus, too, we arrange flowers, make love.

"I came across Billy Brillo's Sports Bar one evening while driving around in my rented car, listening to the radio. I was in Lauderdale on business and usually spent my evenings going for drives; earlier in life, I sallied forth on foot. To say I had no destination is, I suppose, not the same thing as saying these outings were aimless. Then as now, there must have been at least an *expectation*—but of what? The manifestation of a naked woman, no matter how improbable, which lurks at the end of most of life's journeys, forever springing back, like an apparition in a tunnel of love.

"Billy Brillo's Sports Bar was in a row of stores opposite a shopping center and, from the outside, had no distinction other than its name. It was this which intrigued me. What on earth was a 'sports bar'? Did Billy Brillo really exist? (He came in during my first visit, wearing a plastic name tag with 'Billy Brillo' on it.)

"I went in and sat at the rectangular bar. At my back was a mural depicting a South Sea beach scene. I recall, perhaps erroneously, a native maiden; an outrigger canoe; a fire on the beach; a volcano or two, ominously smoking. This rather lurid work, whose motif wasn't carried out in the rest of the décor, bespeaking a mysterious change of heart, was lit by a black light suspended over my head. The bar was in the front of the room; in the back was a coin-operated pool table. This, a bowling machine, and the dart board, were evidently the 'sports.'

"I suspected I was the only stranger there. Because of the bar's out-of-the-way location, it was unlikely that tourists would stumble upon it; in fact, at that hour—it must have been seven or so, already dark—only the drugstore was still open in the shopping center, so it would be safe to say, too, that no one but me had found his

way there by chance. By their dress, most of the patrons appeared
to be Coast Guardsmen or people who worked on boats. As you
may be aware, ladies and gentlemen, Fort Lauderdale is the Venice
of America. There were, too, of course, a few women in the place.

"By the time I had finished 'spinning' two or three cans of
Busch Bavarian, as Skippy Mountjoy, my wife's first husband,
would say—the Alpine scenery on the can in marked disunity
with the mural—the crowd which had been there when I came in
had to all purposes left and been replaced by another, some of the
new arrivals entering by means of a door in the back, beyond the
pool table and the rest rooms, which, I gathered, gave on a parking lot. Among these was a tall, slouching young man with lank
blond hair, who was addressed as the Tiger. After awhile he began
dancing with a woman who was sitting across the bar from me,
drinking splits of domestic champagne. She was more formally
dressed than the others, as though she hoped the evening would
offer greater promise than was to be found in Billy Brillo's Sports
Bar. The Tiger's dancing style was notable for the number, depth,
and dignity of its dips, and seemed to belong to another age, perhaps one that predated his birth. So had I danced."

I was briefly in tears.

"Either they had a disagreement or had grown bored with
one another or, simply, the music stopped and no one put another
quarter in the jukebox—at any rate, she went back to her place
at the bar, he picked up a handful of darts and, toeing the line,
threw them one after another into the bull's-eye. It was then that
I became aware of the little man. In the interval between the time
the Tiger retrieved his darts and took up his stance to throw them
again, the little man went up to the board and stood with his head
against it, facing the Tiger. He was smiling broadly and looking
about, seeking approval or sympathy; indeed, everyone in the bar
turned to watch and there was some laughter. The Tiger threw a
dart, which entered the board by the little man's cheek. [*Gasps*]
As the Tiger was about to hurl his second dart, the bar grew, as if
on command, silent. The Tiger let his hand fall by his side, put the
remaining darts back where he found them, and went over to the
pool table to kibitz a game. Talk became general once more. The
little man remained against the board, suggesting by this position

that he had in fact been transfixed by the dart, which he seemed to be trying to see out of the corners of his eyes. I realized that I was the only one still looking at him; the others had turned away, as though he were an object of shame or a reminder of their own follies or failures to come to terms with themselves. In time, I, too, found I could no longer look at him; our eyes had met and I understood that what he was imploring me to do was to throw the second dart. It was then that I happened to glance out the rear door and saw the parking lot rise and fall. In the next instant, I realized that what I had seen was an oily swell. My supposititious parking lot didn't exist. Beyond the rear door was water; although more than a mile from the ocean, Billy Brillo's Sports Bar backed, as I learned years later by examining a map, on a canal in which the brackish water of the New River estuary stagnated.

"For some reason, this discovery profoundly moved me, and it is one that I often reflect upon, although to no particular advantage. My thoughts generally tend to the somewhat romantic notion that, at odd moments in life, unexpected prospects are disclosed, making possible divagations and reversals. These, of course, are rarely undertaken. This was one such—dark, beckoning, numinous. I also reflect on the fact that I might still believe a parking lot was out back if a distant boat hadn't been under way—for it must have been the last, most diminished remnant of a wake that caught my eye—or if the little man hadn't expressed his innermost repinings. I never went to the door and looked out; for all I knew at the time, the ocean itself, by some trick of the coastline, may have been lapping at the door. This brings up another contemplation, which, I suppose, has ultimately to do with fear of death."

I answered a call of nature.

"My third visit to Billy Brillo's Sports Bar took place several years after the first two, which occurred on successive nights, and was in the company of my wife. Such sentimental excursions are often disappointing. The bar might have changed hands and been redecorated or it might have been torn down, like so many of the largely residential hotels off Sixth Avenue, in whose tenebrous dining rooms, their lofty ceilings supported by pillars inexpertly covered with paper simulating marble, my father would take me to lunch and, bringing his silverware into line, urge me to 'unload my dogs'; by 'dogs' he meant those of my stocks in which he had no faith. My fears were unjustified; the bar was unchanged. I indicated the water, rather like, I fancied, one of Balboa's scouts, who had scrambled to the top first, must have pointed out the Pacific. Wrong ocean, of course.

"But I set out to tell the story of my life. If I may take liberties with Jung, since I am essentially the instrument of my life, I'm subordinate to it, and since I have expended myself to give it form, you shouldn't expect me to interpret it.

"Before I start a mystery, I hand it to my wife and ask her to tell me how many pages it has. I like to know when I'm nearing the end. But I'm afraid to look; I might inadvertently discover how it turns out. Could I say this about my life? Would it have any meaning? Would it be interesting? Sometimes my wife tells me a mystery has so-and-so-many pages and when I reach that point there are still pages unread; or I come to the end and I haven't yet arrived at the number she told me.

"I announce I'm going on a diet. My wife serves macaroni for dinner. 'I only put a little bit of butter on it,' she says.

"You argue I treat my life too flippantly? No more than death is dealt with in my mysteries. My life isn't founded on philosophical ideas but on temperament.

"At my age, I fear the purpose of my life is to relate it. Of course, narration gives it form, like one of those puzzles solved by connecting numbered dots. But you would need an almost infinite number. Can I say I lead my life to give me something to say? Such as it is, it's all romance. Take the constellations. Lyra could as well be Orion, be Taurus; this has all been said before.

"Let us consider the panoply of the heavens. One night last summer, lying in bed with my wife, in the country, I heard a faint whine, apparently emanating from above. A mosquito? It didn't vary in intensity or volume. Another, more sluggish insect? I imagined it was the silvery tension of celestial bodies I heard, counterpoised, as they are, by gravity—as though gravity were a series of fine wires connecting straining bodies, and these wires vibrating under tension gave rise to the whine. Then the music of the spheres, which Pericles, recumbent in the pavilion on his ship, heard with such great relief, came to mind. Shall I tell you what it was? My wife breathing in her sleep.

"Form is repetition. Revelations are lines between dots. Nothing is revealed that isn't anticipated. My wife's wheezing wasn't an explanation but a more sublime mystery. My life consists of arranging and rearranging mysteries. A happy life is one of consonance, not resolution.

"Once more it is early morning, in the country. Draw chairs round my bed. That's me, with all the pillows. As I've implied, my life has changed. I used to sleep without any pillows or piled them over my head. Now two aren't enough; I need three, four, five if I can get them. The older I become the more I aspire toward Heaven. That's my wife, clutching me as though she were saving my life—the cross-chest carry. I have been lying here, in the amplifying light, listening to the birds in the interval between one period of sleep and another. At one time, I could identify most of them by sight, but I never learned their calls. This morning they were exotic, rich, perplexing, and recalled the fabulous birds that used to sing in my dreams and nowhere else. This morning, beyond that window, birds sang and flew off, or grew silent, by the time I awoke next. Some never resumed singing—as though the house were gliding through a land of stationary birds.

"Grant me this as, however loose, a metaphor of my life.

"To literalities. My stepson assures me he doesn't smoke. What a back number I am! I tell him he shouldn't smoke because it will shorten his wind (another of my father's precepts). 'You won't be able to hold up your end in the full-court press,' I say. I come home and find my stepson waiting in the lobby of our apartment house, having forgotten his key, lounging against an abstract mural—in its own way a work as ineptly executed and inharmonious as its counterpart in Billy Brillo's Sports Bar—his hands behind his back. Take a look at him in his big-apple hat, grape T-shirt, and modified bells. The sweetness and despondency of his expression remind me of the times I have let him down; not taking him to the Super Bowl, for instance. I go to kiss him and find he hasn't shaved. I say, 'I smell something strange.' He remains mute. 'Don't you smell something strange?' I say, imploringly. He says he doesn't. The elevator comes; we enter and ascend. A day or two later, I notice a burn hole in the mural.

"My stepdaughter leaves for Maui, where she's going to live on the beach in an abandoned machine-gun bunker with Randy, a boyfriend. 'Please don't forget your bite plate,' I tell her. Weeks afterward, I come across it, lightly coated with dust. How small the roof of her mouth is! I blow the dust off and run a finger over the clear plastic matrix of her palate, tenderly exploring its corrugated surface. I hold it up to the light. Where the median ridge known as the palatine raphe has pressed against it is a channel, resembling a dry streambed running downhill, with lesser gullies—molds of the transverse plicae or rugae—branching off; at the base of this barren and eroded slope is a sort of lagoon, also dry, formed by the eminence called the palatine papilla: a fantastic landscape akin to that in which the birds of my dreams had sung, or those that make up the backgrounds of so many Renaissance paintings, where, I have read, the Old Masters, being released from the themes and conventions governing the treatment of the figures in the foreground, gave full rein to their imagination or their despair or their yearning. Like these landscapes, the bite plate was invested, or haunted, with a degree of earthly sorrow—my musings on it corresponding in mood with those of my father when he learned I was out of raisins, my reflections on your shadowy presence in the swimming pool, and so forth.

"My stepdaughter calls collect from Maui, wondering if we'd send her one hundred and eighty dollars so she and Randy could take modern dance at Maui Community College. I hesitate. 'I thought it was always your dream that I should go to college,' she says, her voice reverberating, as though she were calling from the dim chambers of the sea.

"My stepson is fast asleep in the bed which once dwarfed him and which he now fills like his coffin. He is dressed in his away basketball uniform, which is brilliant orange, so that it is as though he were 'swathed in confining fire.' '*Dentro dai fuochi son gli spirti: ciascun si fascia di quel ch'egli è inceso.*'

"My wife said she was thinking of a story she would write, if she could write. No, a novel. 'The ending is,' she said, ' "She now knew that she would give him what he most desired. She would go away." ' [*Tears*]

"Unless I speak falsely, there are any number of things that raise the human spirit more than concupiscence, but since I have already taken up so much of your time, I will mention only three: the song of a pine warbler on a hot day—that one I know, and submit that its monotonous sweet trill endlessly reaffirms life's illimitable reach and promise; the head of a well-bred dachshund; a gin spade laydown.

"Before I close, I want to tell you this: one afternoon, years ago, in a bedroom under the eaves of a mock-Tudor cottage off Kalakaua—now surely razed—I made love to a young woman. Around her neck she wore a ginger lei I had bought her the day before, and which she had kept overnight in the refrigerator. During our lovemaking, the lei was crushed between us. At the time, I thought I would never forget the overwhelming aroma of the bruised blossoms. I have forgotten it. Forgotten, too, her name, her features, any intensity of feeling. What I recall is that little white petals lay strewn on the sheet. It is as though they had remotely dropped upon the surface of a slow-moving stream, and only now, after long windings, minutely rearranged by the current, so that their meaning is no longer clear—I am postulating that it would have been possible to read the past in their configuration, as the future is foretold from tea leaves or sheep dung—are borne momentarily into view."

Imagine it is dawn, that there is no one in the pool, and that the water is changing color with the sky. At some point the orgiasts must have left, my fellow-guests let their draperies close and gone to bed. Unseen sparrows are chirping, an occasional semitrailer drones by, leaving a faint odor of diesel fumes, and the rising sun glints off two or three of the gray hairs on my chest so that they appear almost incandescent. I shuffle back into my room.

That morning, as I was getting dressed, I was arrested by my socks. They were black, as are all those I own, but darned with bright red and green thread. I examined the other socks in my bag; I found darns in violet, in tan, in blue, in orange, in yellow. I telephoned my wife in New York and asked her what the hell was going on with my socks.

"They needed mending," she said. "I was going through your

bag the night before you left, while you were sleeping, to see if you had forgotten anything."

"Didn't you have any black?"

"I was mad."

Repacking, I remembered the rolls of Life Savers I used to find in my pockets when I went on business trips, and once an applique of three roses and their leaves, embroidered in several shades of pink and green, which my wife had snipped off one of her slips and pinned to my pajama top, so that, when I put it on, the sprig would be next to my heart.

A week or so after my return, I take my father to lunch. He looks over the décor and the prices, runs through most of his repertoire of derisive ejaculations, and calls me a *knacker*. After we order drinks, the conversation unfailingly turns to my "dogs." My responses evidently disappoint him, for he reaches out his hand to rearrange the objects on the table. I beat him to it, shifting my book of matches.

1. . . . . . . My father moves his book of matches up.

This hoary riposte is scarcely seen anymore.

2. I move my book of matches up.

Embarking on a subtle scheme that will not be easy to refute.

2. . . . . . . My father moves his swizzle stick to his right.

A thoughtless interpolation.

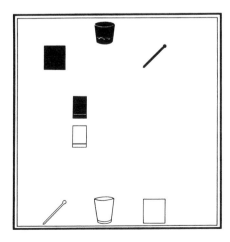

3. I move my cocktail napkin up and to my left.

For all its dour aspect, a move that reveals great ingenuity and depth.

3. . . . . . . My father moves his Red Label-on-the-rocks to his right.

Winter apparently underestimates his youthful adversary.

4. I move my cocktail napkin up and to my right.

"A mighty maze!" wrote Pope, "but not without a plan."

4. . . . . . . My father moves his swizzle stick up. ch

Aggressive but somewhat otiose.

5. I move my tall Cutty-and-water diagonally to my left.

Done with a *brio* that calls to mind a Mozart divertimento.

5. . . . . . . My father moves his swizzle stick back.

Sad necessity.

6. I move my tall Cutty-and-water up.

"Nothing exists," said Spinoza, "from whose nature some effect does not follow."

6. . . . . . . My father moves his Red Label-on-the-rocks up.

Pseudo-development.

7. My swizzle stick X his cocktail napkin! ch

A masterly concept.

7. . . . . . . His Red Label-on-the-rocks X my swizzle stick.

He is nearly reduced to *Zugzwang*.

8. I move my cocktail napkin up and to the left!! ch

Finis coronat opus.

8. . . . . . . "Would it be a burden," my father says, "to show your old dad the way to the gents'?"

A charming struggle, varnished with melancholy.

PREPARATIONS FOR THE ASCENT

To Ring, His Memory

1

Albert tells the story of his life—*that* again. Lippholzer richly hums. A composer and arranger, he is being kind enough to score it for Albert—his life, that is.

Lippholzer holds up a hand, as though shushing the brass. "Not exactly what one would call Brahmsian," he murmurs.

Albert tells him that he never represented his life as such, that cinematically speaking, which, after all, is how we're looking at it, he sees it as one that might befall a fat Montgomery Clift.

Lippholzer makes a face and unfolds his napkin. They are in a French restaurant, about to have lunch.

The reason Albert brought in Lippholzer is that for some time he's felt there's been something missing in his life. Music is what suddenly came to him, swelling, as in a movie.

He had called Lippholzer up to tell him about it.

"Please?" Lippholzer had said.

"I was watching this commercial," Albert had said. "Two young marrieds. In Miami Beach. By moonlight. They're swimming to a sixty-five-piece symphony orchestra."

"So?" Lippholzer had said.

"So when my wife and I are in Miami all I hear is sixty-five air-conditioners, every one of them on 'hi cool.'"

"I could get the London Philharmonia," Lippholzer is saying, bending his noble head to his Bloody Mary. "But for you it would be a waste. From what you're telling me, your life, it is strictly low-budget."

Albert tells him it never crossed his mind it couldn't be brought in for under a million.

"I am going to put together for you," Lippholzer says, "a woodwind quintet—a little piccolo for your comical childhood—supplemented by three trombones—so solid, your college education—two percussion, harp, four celli—how sad! how jubilant!—a bass, a guitar. These will amply take care of any moment in your life. I underscore the oboe in your case. What a pathetic instrument! When you are alone, I do the whole thing on the oboe."

Albert tells him there's going to be an awful lot of oboe.

"Do me a favor," Lippholzer says. "You do the living and leave the music to me."

A few days later, following Lippholzer's advice, Albert is on his way to the twenty-fifth reunion of his high-school class. This is to take place in the dining hall where once they lunched on tuna-fish casserole and macaroni and cheese. Albert has ridden the subway to the end of the line and is toiling dismally up the hill. The ruin I will note in my classmates will tacitly be noted in me, he muses, so I will age twenty-five years in a few minutes.

It is late May, early evening, and the trees beneath which Albert passes are in full leaf. He lifts his eyes and is made dizzy, as though he were being crushed to their massive and odorous bosoms. Not my kind of simile, granted, he thinks—but do I hear music in the air already?

Albert takes the shortcut through the patch of woods. There it is nearly dark, wilder, and his way more steep: shades of Dante, he acknowledges. He gets a whiff of the past, an emanation, he supposes, in which verdure, rot, damp, mold, earth, pollen, car exhaust, and dog do are commingled, and for an instant he is able to visualize a boy (a character, however, so nearly imaginary that the fact that he bears Albert's name and resembles him seems an astonishing coincidence) traipsing up the hill with a briefcase. What books does it hold, Albert wonders. *Silas Marner*? *Ethan Frome*, P-40s and Zeros, guns blazing, on the end papers? What expectations is he carrying about in his head?

Albert reflects: Through the years, any number of people have played the role that has become known as my life: I would but faintly recognize them, their lines, businesses. As I have often remarked, I seem to vanish behind me like footprints on a mud flat. Of course, I do not deny the possibility that my life has a hidden continuity. Oedipus comes to mind. But suppose he knew what he was up to all along. Or suppose he *once* knew but forgot. Or, even, that he was indifferent. These versions would be as tragic as the traditional one, perhaps more so.

A reunion I would more gladly go to would be one of my earlier selves, Albert reflects. He pauses on a footbridge in the woods to consider that somber assembly. (Earlier in the spring, the melting snow would have formed a torrent below him, a touch Albert associates with Boswell preparing himself for his great interview with Rousseau by pensively strolling along a similar stream, the romantic prospect giving his thoughts "a vigorous and solemn tone." Now, however, the streambed is dry and littered with trash.)

To keep my reunion manageable, Albert thinks, I'd invite who I was at each quarter of each year in my life, so that if everybody showed we'd have a crowd of a hundred and sixty or so. I can see us all, in some Crystal or Palm Room, the oldest with the youngest in their arms. This is apposite, for, being childless, I have been my own child. An accordionist is playing standards. Looking appealingly into our nearly forgotten faces, we wonder what has happened and what lies ahead.

"You call this living?"

Not Vergil, nor Laius, nor Mlle. Le Vasseur, coming to conduct Albert to the Savage Philosopher, but a postman, going downhill with an empty bag. No, not even he. It is Lippholzer, who joins Albert on the bridge. They gaze at the refuse together.

Albert asks him how come he's all dressed up like that.

"I'm doing research," he says.

Albert asks him what a scene like this inspires him to compose.

"*Bupkis,*" he says. "For nothing scenes I write nothing. Let me clue you in, it would wind up on the cutting-room floor."

At the reunion, Albert is cornered by Roger Russek. They drink sherry out of plastic cups. Except for his hair, which is entirely gray, Russek looks exactly as Albert remembers him—more precisely, as he looked when they were fellow-scientists in their senior play, *R. U. R.*, and they powdered one another's hair. Albert has the feeling that Russek never grew up, or that he is a well-coached impostor. His insistence on dredging up lurid episodes from their school days reinforces the latter impression.

"You remember Norman Greenberg?" Russek says.

"No," Albert says.

"He was with us in fifth grade," he says.

"Were you in fifth grade with me?" Albert says.

"You remember when Norman's science experiment exploded?"

"No."

"We took him to the nurse's office, you and I."

"I don't remember."

"You were leading him along and I was bringing up the rear, wiping the blood off the floor with paper towels."

"I don't remember."

"He kept saying, 'I'm blind. I'm blind.' "

"I remember," Albert says. But, he reflects, I thought it was myself, when *my* experiment exploded.

"Greetings, gates. Give me five."

Lippholzer is before them, hand outstretched. Like them, he is wearing a name tag. His reads, "Dr. Lippholzer, Music."

"How are you, Dr. Lippholzer?" Russek asks.

"Crazy. Another year, another 'Hallelujah Chorus.' I could have used you cats. My basses were nowhere."

Russek goes for a refill. Lippholzer laughs like a rhinoceros, like Dr. Johnson. "Campus character," he explains. "By the way, I couldn't help but overhearing your conversation with that person. For that I would dash off a divertimento in F minor for the bassoon and piccolo, with a soupçon of French horn thrown in for poignancy."

Russek gives Albert a lift home so he won't have to take the subway. As they drive down the Henry Hudson Parkway, Russek says, "There is no integrity anymore." Albert merely nods in agreement. It is night and Albert is smelling the incoming tide. Farther on, Russek says that he took his son up the Amazon last winter. "I always liked science," he adds. Albert pictures the Russeks, father and son, at evening, aboard a river steamer, contemplating the great, dark flood astern, the darker banks. Russek takes a snapshot from his inside jacket pocket and shows it to Albert. It is of the scene Albert imagined.

They stop at a toll booth on the bridge spanning Spuyten Duyvil. As Russek fumbles for change, the toll collector winks at Albert. Lippholzer.

"Strings in a low register!" he shouts as they drive off. "Harp and Latin percussion lightly in the background!" He bursts into song: "La-dah-dah-dah-*dum*-la-dee-dee-dah-dah-dah-*dum*."

Russek pulls up at the door of the restaurant where Albert is meeting his wife, Violet. Albert prevails upon him to join them. He can only stay a minute, he says, as he is getting up early to ride in the Park. Albert sets him there, amid fanciful mists, posting. This elegant pose cannot be sustained. If there is an illiberality among us Jews, Albert tells Russek, it is because we never learned to sit a horse; we missed out on the whole cavalry *schmear*. While everyone who was anyone in Western Europe was on horseback, absorbing grace, bearing, panache through the seat of his pants, the Jew was *schlepping* on foot. In the nineteenth century, when he finally arrived, it was by carriage.

"I never cared for history," Russek says.

They enter the restaurant. Violet is seated at the bar, bent over the *Times* crossword puzzle. Albert introduces her to Russek.

"Roger and I went to school together," Albert explains.

"Do you remember how we used to look down the front of Señora Ramírez y Ramírez' dress when she went over our *examenes*?" Russek says.

"Did we see anything?" Albert says.

"Which way is the little boys' room?" Russek says.

Albert looks over Violet's shoulder at the upper left-hand corner of her puzzle:

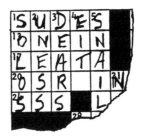

"What's this 'sudes' you've got for 'Secular people'?" he says. "Marketplace of old is 'leata'? 'Uness' is a 'Scottish county'?"

"I didn't know them," she says, "so I made them up."

Russek is passing among the tables, handing out snapshots, like tracts, of what he and his son saw from the stern.

Albert reflects: So often illusions cannot support the symbolic weight they are meant to carry; Russek's dimly perceived river falls into this category, as do my wife's definitions. The team of horses awaiting me in the woods is yet another example. Tonight I will dream that I was to drive them into Yankee Stadium for a Giants game. These absurd notes always intrude. I will be led to believe that the team—are there two horses or four?—has been tethered in a clearing, but I won't know where and I will have mislaid the reins. I will have the feeling that more time has elapsed than I have accounted for, that I was supposed to have gone after them days ago, and that by now they have dropped in their traces. In the poor, brown light with which I am going to grace the scene, the fallen horses look like a pile of old rugs. None of this will be found in anything I tell Lippholzer or will ever be orchestrated. (Nor, as in Bach—I'm thinking of "Vor deinen Thron tret' ich hiermit," composed on his deathbed—will the numerical equivalent of my name be resplendently revealed, the quavers correspond to the beat of the human pulse.)

One order of wonders might be: things seen; things unseen; things seen in dreams; things unseen in dreams.

Also, I must resist the temptations of pessimism.

A porter comes out of the kitchen with a bucket of ice. He hands it to the bartender, who empties it into a sink. The sound is of, simultaneously, a roll on a cymbal and a roll on a timpani shell. The porter turns and points to a corner table. Lippholzer again. Albert follows his finger with his eyes. A man is seated at the table, wearing a well-worn dinner jacket. On Lippholzer's cue he raises an oboe to his lips.

2

Albert says, "I was swimming with my eyes closed. Breaststroking. But before long I realized that I wasn't getting anywhere, that what I was swimming in no longer had the consistency of water."

Violet says, "What would you say it had the consistency of?"

"Let's say it had a granular consistency. I opened my eyes and I was lying on my stomach on a sidewalk on the Upper East Side, ineffectually breaststroking in several inches of snow. Some children were watching."

"It sounds to me like a dream of old age."

Shaving, naked, still wet from the shower, Albert sees in the medicine-chest mirror a person standing behind him, shrouded in steam. He holds up what seems to Albert to be a cloak, and makes to wrap him in it. Albert thinks: My time has surely come. Instead, the person starts drying Albert's back. It is Barney, his stepson, aged seventeen. "Blot, don't rub," Albert says.

"You shave too recklessly," Barney says, patting Albert here and there with the towel.

Albert slows down. Barney raises Albert's left arm, which, Albert surmises, must have been hanging by his side, dries beneath it, guides it back into place.

"If I fell in battle," Barney says in Albert's tone of voice, "he would thus tenderly arrange my limbs."

He is putting me on, Albert reflects, but the sentiment is affecting, and his choice of words and imagery shows wider reading than I had suspected.

Albert flies to Miami, speculating on futurity. Upon his return, he tells Violet of an exceptional incident. He had arrived late at night, changed into a bathing suit, put on his little plastic goggles to protect his eyes from the chlorine, and gone to the motel pool, which was illuminated by two underwater lights at the deep end. A Cuban boy of ten or twelve was in the shallow end. Although it was Albert's impression that the boy was climbing out of the pool while he was diving in, as Albert approached the wall to make his turn he saw the boy's dark, slender, headless body before him.

Violet says at this point, mimicking Albert, "There's no one else in the whole pool except me and him, so, of course, he has to do a number in my lane."

"It's not fair," Albert says.

"At the Y, the guy in front of me always gets a towel with more nap on it than I do," Violet says.

"The guy behind me gets one with more nap, too," Albert says. "Didn't he see me coming? Wasn't he going to get out of the way? His figure loomed larger."

"I was going to have to smack him one," Violet says.

"I was going to have to brush him aside," Albert says. "Instead of dropping my hand slightly below the diagonal at the point of entry, I rotated it outward—"

"So I could give him a brush in the mouth," Violet says.

"What I was going to do," Albert says, "was make contact, touch, and execute my turn all in one fluid motion. But as I extended my hand he held out his to mine."

"Like God giving life to Adam," Violet says.

"Along those lines," Albert says. "My fingers touched the tiles and I was joined to my writhing shadow."

The above discourse has taken place in bed. Dwelling on his

unresisting drift, Albert prepares to rise.

As my readers—they are Albert's too, it seems superfluous to note—Violet, and Josh, Albert and Violet's dachshund, are well aware, Albert frequently gets up in the middle of the night. My readers know because I have touched on it in previous works. Violet knows because Albert wakes her up and tells her. "I've got to go to the bathroom," he may say. (If he's not sure she heard him, he enlightens her on the return trip; e.g., "I had to go to the bathroom.") Or "I think I'll get something to eat." (Sometimes he expatiates. For example, "I'm torn between a sardine sandwich on health bread and a bowl of Granola." A corollary to this might be, reawakening her: "Nobody told me there aren't any sardines.") Or, simply, "I can't sleep." (The corollary to this, as to so much, is "It's not fair.") Josh's knowledge is presumed. Although Josh gives few signs of it, it is Albert's belief that he knows what's going on—not understands, *knows*. What else could account for his jumping into Albert's lap the other night and pleading with him to unburden his heart.

Who knows Albert best? Let's find out. "Are you sleeping?" "Yes," Violet says. "But who knows me best?" "Your readers know as much of you as you've ever acknowledged," she says. "I know as much of you as you've ever acknowledged and almost everything else. Josh knows nothing that you've acknowledged, but he knows everything else."

With that, Albert puts on his slippers and sets out for the kitchen. En route, he passes Josh, curled up on the living-room couch. Josh opens an eye—keeping tabs on me, Albert acknowledges. The kitchen light is on, and Emily, Albert's stepdaughter, is bent over the stove, stirring the contents of a saucepan with a wooden spoon. She is nineteen and lives with Sean, who's into yo-yos, in the Intergalactic College of Love. This, she has explained, is neither a crash pad nor a commune but "a whole bunch of people doing a trip separately but in the same house." From time to time she comes home to see what's in the refrigerator or if there are any new magazines, and to look at herself in the full-length mirror.

"You're cooking something at 2 a.m.?" Albert says.

"No," she says, without averting her head.

Albert approaches and looks over her shoulder. Agitated by boiling water so that it appears alive, obscured by bubbles, is something blue and white, evidently flowered.

"Then what are you doing?"

"Shrinking my underpants."

Albert reserves comment.

"Many years ago, I went with a nurse," she says, imitating Albert. "Once, when I had occasion to use her bathroom, the tub was full, and in it giant, pale jellyfish almost imperceptibly writhed. As it turned out, she was soaking her uniforms."

"I've boiled my eggs in that pan for fourteen years," Albert tells Violet when he returns to bed. She is lying on her side, facing the wall. He cups her head with his hand. Sometimes, when she is too weary or too deep in sleep to reply, she communicates by shaking her head. Now, however, the movement is so slight—the least tremor—that he is unable to tell whether she is sympathetic (up and down) or, once more, fed up to here (side to side).

It is at this point that Albert hears someone playing the piano. I must explain that Albert and Violet live on the third floor, in the rear, and that their windows look out on what amounts to an immense airshaft; that is, although there are several neglected gardens below, strewn with sooty, rain-soaked toys, they are walled in by the backs of two other apartment houses and two loft buildings, one occupied by a machine shop, the other seemingly empty save for an acting studio.

From their windows you have to crane your neck to see the sky, and Albert has never observed a woman disrobing or a migratory bird. In the day there is the whine of machinery, at night unearthly cries. When Albert and Violet moved in, they thought these were the product of passion or violence, but they soon learned that the cries came from the acting studio.

Albert called the police.

"Sixth Precinct. O'Hanrahan speaking."

"Officer O'Hanrahan, people are screaming outside my window."

"Yes."

"You can't hear them?"

"No."

"If you'll hang on a minute, I'll stick the receiver outside the window."

"That won't be necessary."

"It won't take a second. I've got a long cord. Did you hear *that*? Are you still *there*?"

"We can't do anything about it until after eleven. If it's still going on then—"

"They're actors and actresses."

"—I'll send a couple of men over."

To return to the piano music. In the drab, barbarous setting I've described, its notes glitter like a toad's eye. Albert gets up and peers through the blinds. One window is lit. Albert sees a man in pajamas playing Mozart's "Fantasy in C Minor." Actually, all Albert can see of him is his left hand, a pajama sleeve. In the cadenza, more of him comes into view: for instance, his unshaven cheek, his right hand. The sixty-fourths defeat him. He falls behind, breaks off, starts the cadenza anew. Again he cannot keep the tempo. He strikes wrong notes, stops. He will never reach the andantino. His left hand holds a chord, but it has died out or is so faint Albert can no longer hear it. Albert imagines the man's right hand supporting his head—a pose Albert is acquainted with.

The man arises and approaches the window, and Albert sees that he is him, too—that is, in the sense that he could be Albert's shadow cast across the dismal gulf. The impression is so vivid that Albert hesitates to move lest it be confirmed.

"How to account for this melancholy apprehension," Violet says in further imitation of Albert. "I never got beyond 'Little Keyboard Frolics.' "

"I did."

"How far?"

" 'More Little Keyboard Frolics.' "

A day or two later Albert gets out of bed under the scrutiny of cats. One cat is looking him over from the floor, another is looking him in the eye from a radiator cover, a third is looking down at him from the top of a bookcase, its tail swishing in front of a set of Carlyle. (It has often been Albert's lot to be thrown in among cats. No good has ever come of it.) On this occasion, the bed is not his own, and it is 1:30 p.m.

"Have they been there the whole time?" Albert says to the person still in bed, who nods. "Did they see everything?" She nods again. "Do you think they'll remember what they saw?"

"If they do," she says, "they wouldn't dream of telling my husband."

Albert thoughtfully puts on his socks.

"What are you doing?"

"I'm going."

"But you've only been here forty-five minutes."

"I've got to go to the Y."

"Go later."

"Then I'll have to swim in the small pool. They kick you out of the large pool at two-thirty. Actually, I have to be in the water by two-ten, because it takes me twenty minutes to do my laps. My record is fifteen minutes and fifteen seconds. I was younger. Also, I may have miscounted."

"Oh."

"The large pool is twenty-five yards long, the small pool is twenty, so if I start out in the large pool and am obliged to switch to the small pool, I have to do this math in my head while I'm swimming, to figure out how many small-pool laps I have to swim in addition to the large-pool laps I've already swum to make them add up to a half mile—which is how far I swim—and I lose track of what number lap I'm swimming."

"What do you do in that case?"

"I go back to the last recollected lap."

"So don't go until later and do all your laps in the small pool."

"You make more turns in the small pool than you would swimming the same distance in the large pool. There's more pushing off. When you push off you're not swimming, you're gliding. In other words, to swim the equivalent of a half mile in the large pool you have to swim . . . Besides, the water's warmer. They always keep the water in the small pool warmer than the water in the large pool, and the water in the large pool is too warm."

"Why don't you ask them to lower the temperature?"

"I do. They tell me the older members complain when the temperature is below eighty. I tell them it's the *Young* Men's Christian

Association. They tell me they can't disregard a member's feelings just because he has grown old. 'Ah, you will grow old, too,' they tell me."

"Why don't you skip the Y altogether for a day?"

"But then I couldn't weigh myself."

"Run that by me again."

"I weigh myself every day I go swimming. There's a scale at the Y."

"What would happen if you didn't weigh yourself one day?"

"It would leave a gap."

"A gap?"

"Or lacuna. Each day, I put my weight down in an appointment book. I've got books going back nine or ten years. You can spot trends."

"For one day, couldn't you put a weight down without actually weighing yourself? You could approximate it."

"I wouldn't dream of falsifying my weight."

"It wouldn't be a falsehood if you never actually *weighed* yourself."

"If I didn't weigh myself, I wouldn't put my weight down. It's an historical document. It reminds me of who I am."

By this time, Albert is knotting his tie. He is at the window, looking out.

"Do you see that apartment over there," she says, joining him. "The other night we heard someone playing the piano. We couldn't see him. The piano is out of sight."

"It might have been a recording."

"He kept making mistakes and starting all over again."

Albert muses: If my life were of my devising, through the windows of the apartment she indicated I would see the marble-topped table at which I write. Josh would be curled before my open dictionary, having leaped on the chair on which I sit while I write, and from there gained the table, as though he had sought to look up something I had not satisfactorily defined and, finding the task beyond him, given himself over to sleep. I would mark how he resembled the marble dogs that lie at the marble feet of effigies — often, in fact, support them. And I would recall that when I went to the yard to buy the stone for my table-top the man dashed a pail of water on the great, unpolished slab, revealing its color and pattern.

"But the moment passes," she says, evidently impersonating Albert.

As Albert goes down her stairs on the way to the Y, he is made aware, as he was when he climbed them, of a pervasive, musty odor. It is, Albert realizes, a smell he associates with the stairwells of poorly maintained brownstones, which, in the years before his marriage, he would ascend to see one girl or another who dished up casseroles and put Vivaldi on the phonograph while making love.

Once again it is borne in upon Albert that his life is repeating itself, only this time around he has to pause on the landings on the way up to catch his breath, and WCBS-FM has superseded "The Four Seasons." In another ten years, he thinks, I will have reached the point I am at now—between the third and second floors, on the way down—and so forth.

A man climbing up draws abreast of Albert. He is wearing modified bells and has luxuriant gray sideburns—possibly the husband. As their paths cross, the man murmurs, "My life stands revealed as a Sisyphean ordeal, with Groucho Marx as Sisyphus, a partly deflated beach ball for a boulder." The conceit isn't half bad, Albert admits, but the imitation is barely acceptable.

It would behoove me to change, Albert concludes, to see another class of girl—a stewardess, say, or cocktail waitress, with a Dynel pouf and a twenty-four-hour doorman, a girl who reads Jeane Dixon and says "shirr" for "sure."

"May I . . . ?"

"Shirr."

"Do you like it when I do this?"

"Shirr."

"And this?"

"Shirr."

"How about me? Do you like me a little bit?"

"Shirr."

"Do you agree with Kierkegaard when he says, 'It is perfectly true, as philosophers say, that life must be understood backwards. But they forget the other proposition, that it must be lived forwards. And if one thinks over that proposition it becomes more and more evident that life can never really be understood in time, simply because at no particular moment can I find the necessary resting place from which to understand it—backwards'?"

"Shirr."

"I just called to let you know that I didn't weigh myself."

"You *didn't*?"

"There wasn't any scale. Evidently, it was inaccurate, for it was taken out to be repaired."

"I see."

"I'm up in the air."

Albert goes to one of Barney's basketball games. Barney has forbidden Albert to speak to him at half time or after the game; he is also not allowed to speak to the coach or even to the official scorer to see how many points Barney got. For this, and for other desolating reasons, Albert gets on the officials. You may have heard him: "On the arm! *On the arm!*"

Barney is taken out in the second quarter and never reappears—doesn't "get any more light," as he would say. From his seat high in the crowded bleachers, Albert gazes down at him on the bench across the court, impassive, resplendent in his shimmering purple-and-gold uniform, and shakes his head. By this he means to reassure Barney of the strength of his affection—that he doesn't know why the coach doesn't put him back in, either, and that his, Albert's, life is tremendously sad. Barney doesn't respond.

That evening when Barney comes home, Albert asks whether he saw him at the game.

"I always see you," he says.

"Did you see me shaking my head?"

"You always do that."

Albert's mom calls. "As you know," she says, "I've been lying here sick, so I've had the opportunity to think about that old pile-lined coat you insist on wearing. It's unworthy of a man in your position."

"Don't give it another thought, Ma."

"But it's falling apart. It makes you look like one of those derelicts you see. Even Sean wouldn't wear something like that. You've exhausted it. Ragged pieces flap about."

"The coat has assumed too much prominence in your life, Ma."

"No, in yours. You even chose to wear it when you came to lunch with me and Dad, and we live in a conventional neighborhood. Abercrombie's having a sale on pile-lined coats. Dad's willing to forgo his lunch hour and meet you there."

"I'm forty-two years old."

"And you've been wearing that coat since you were sixteen. Are you trying to set a record at my expense?"

Violet says, "Guess what happened to me today?"

Albert says, "I give up."

"I went to Dr. Prigozy for a checkup, and he said I had grown more than an inch. Last year I was five one and a quarter. Now I'm five two and a half."

"Forty-three-year-old people don't grow."

"Won't you let something exceptional happen to me?"

"I'm calling Prigozy."

While Albert dials, the immense suburban hedges against which so many nineteenth-century ideologues, autodidacts, crackpots posed for their photographs come to mind—great, rank barriers imaginably stories high, through whose dense and mysterious foliage tram bells, footfalls but faintly penetrated.

"I hope I'm not disturbing you, Dr. Prigozy, but are you really of the opinion that it is possible to grow when you're past forty?"

Albert enters the Intergalactic College of Love. Emily and Sean live in the basement. This is his first visit. He sits on a mattress on the floor, alongside Emily, and they have a conversation. It lasts nearly an hour—by far the longest they've ever had. As they speak, it grows dark. Sean is practicing with his electric yo-yo. He does a man-on-the-flying-trapeze. He rocks the baby. He does a double-brain-twister. He does a sleeping-beauty. He walks the dog. He does an around-the-world. The fiery yo-yo swings about the darkened room like a heavenly body.

Albert struggles to his feet. "I've got to go," he says.

Emily accompanies him upstairs. In the foyer, they come to a stop before a hand-lettered notice: "Vacuum Bee, 11 p.m."

"I wonder what *that* is," she says, giggling.

Albert thinks: She could be six—an age at which I didn't know her, she me. If we had, we might have rescued each other. I want to hug her. There is no precedent. I write this in longhand, consoled by my familiar loops, my bars, my terminal strokes. These are my lineaments.

3

People lead their lives differently. You can't crouch in hides, watch them like grebes or gibbons, and draw specific conclusions. Consider, if you will, Albert requests, that man who bears such a heartbreaking resemblance to myself, weeping into his dinner tray at thirty-three thousand feet. Heading south at an airspeed of five hundred and twenty miles an hour, what grief has overtaken him? Just this: He put salt and pepper on his mashed potatoes. Then, taking up his fork, he made to plunge it into the plastic dish. Grains of salt and pepper flew every which way, including that of his impending face. He had struck a sheet of Saran Wrap protecting the potatoes, which he had not noticed. He laid down his fork, removed the Saran Wrap, and salted and peppered the potatoes anew. Picking up the fork again, he took his first bite. The mashed potatoes was banana pudding. This could not happen to everyone. Offhand, Albert would say *it* would occur once every five hundred thousand passenger-miles. The emotional reaction is less unusual. Feelings are accentuated at altitude, even in a pressurized cabin.

But who can say what will undo one? For instance, here is the same exceptional fellow sitting by himself late at night in the Sans Souci Launderama, in a Miami shopping center, shedding tears at sea level. Except for the Sans Souci, in which fluorescent tubes distribute their forbidding light on the ranks of washers and dryers, the notices advertising babysitters, lost cats, and used potter's wheels, the shopping center is dark. What's the matter? First off, the decline of Arabic numerals. He had glanced at his watch to see when his wash would be done. Although the watch wasn't new, only then did he realize there were no numbers on its face. In their place was a series of inconsequential dashes. It must have been years since he had seen numerals on a watch face. He envisioned the missing figures, was moved by the elegance of their lines, and arrived at the opinion that man had never designed anything finer, "3" and "5" having pride of place, although, he acknowledged, there might be those who would plump for "2." The several alphabets suffered in comparison, as did mathematical symbols, toasters, cathedrals. Against these he arrayed great works of nature—striped bass, roses, shearwaters, disrobed women. He pictured a vast plain upon which the pick of both classes of things was forming up, as though to pass in review, and was struck by how much he took for granted and, equally, by how much he had failed to take seriously. If you had these or similar imaginings in the middle of a rinse cycle, would you, too, be brought to grief?

Under certain circumstances, playing footsie can have much the same effect. For this demonstration, put yourself in the shoes of our hero. More literally, put yourself in his socks. Behold him, one of a party of six, sitting at a small round table in the cocktail lounge of a Holiday Inn, playing footsie with a stewardess whose name is either Lauri, Audri, or Kelli. He has slipped off his right loafer—on the principle, he supposes, that if he is right-handed he is bound to be right-footed, and he wants to give it his best shot—and is caressing one of her feet with his instep. At the same time, he is watching her face for her reaction. Nothing. He has grown old. He has lost his touch. He knocks a book of matches off the table—a ruse—and stoops to retrieve it. Beneath the table everything is murky, dismal, and tangled, like a mangrove swamp. To sort things out, he takes hold of his right leg at the knee and gropes downward toward his unproductive foot. He has been playing footsie with his own cast-off loafer. As Rousseau said, my pen falls from my hand.

Albert thinks: My dad is as sensible as the next man, but none of the above could happen to him, so it would be idle even to speculate on his responses. He doesn't own a pair of loafers. He disapproves of loafers. He considers my wearing them perverse. "Loafers don't offer enough support," he says. ("Your feet flop around in them," Albert's mom chimes in. "We brought you up to respect your feet.") When Albert's dad goes on a trip, he takes drip-dry garments, which he washes in the sink before retiring. "A moment's application," he says pointedly. Albert's dad thinks that Albert is apathetic. Albert submits that what he is, in fact, is immobilized, the Apollonian and Dionysian sides of his character being of equal strength. Albert's dad also considers it an affront to season your food before tasting it.

Although Albert's dad keeps his guard higher than Albert does his, blows do get through, as the next episode so poignantly illustrates.

Albert would have thought he had visited his dad's office only a couple of months ago, but more time must have gone by, he realizes, for how much has changed! Not in his office *per se*—that is immutable—but in the long, straight, insufficiently lit corridor that leads to it. (Albert calls it "insufficiently lit" out of deference to his dad. He once referred to it as "dismal," to which his dad took exception. He said Albert tended to be eisegetical, that the corridor was merely insufficiently lit. They don't always see eye to eye, Albert and his dad.) What's different is that the names on the doors along the way are new. In the past, they were Jewish. On occasion, Albert would come across their bearers in the men's room, absorbed in combing their hair with both hands. Operators, Albert's dad called them. Now the frosted-glass doors read: Taiwan Consolidated Corp.; Interglobal Philippine Import, Ltd.; Mitsobushi American, Inc.

"You're being overrun," Albert tells his dad.

"My secretary tells me their girls make rice in the ladies' room," his dad says in what Albert would definitely call a dismal tone of voice.

How would you like to be seventy-five and hear the rumble of furniture-laden dollies drawing near?

How would you like to be forty-three, Albert asks, and hear, first thing in the morning, a dachshund awakening, shaking himself? The sound is like that of slatting sails, and proposes imponderable voyages, whales' grandiose sighing. For an instant, another version of life seems possible. Then the blower in the machine shop next door is switched on, as it is every weekday at eight. It roars yet as I write, Albert would like to let you know. What recourse does Albert have? He could seek out the shop manager and fall on his knees. He could encourage Josh to go on the standpipe by the shop door. After the roar, a resounding crash—Barney letting his weights down in his bedroom. Before going to school he presses his body weight (one hundred and fifty pounds)—three sets of five reps. He is developing his shoulders and arm extensors so he can beat me up, Albert realizes. Following the crash, a whine. The volume increases as Albert approaches the living room. Sean is standing naked before the full-length mirror, dreamily wielding the power detangler Violet bought him for his twenty-fifth birthday.

Albert goes through the mail. It includes a rejection slip from a French publisher. "*. . . Avec nos regrets, veuillez agréer l'expression de nos sentiments les meilleurs.*" Albert realizes he is not fully conversant with *agréer*. He is about to get down the French-English, English-French dictionary when he recalls that Emily tore out nearly all the French-English "A"s and a good many of the "B"s several years ago. He cannot remember what he did to annoy her or why her revenge took the form it did, but he can still hear the terrible ripping.

As you may have noted, so far not a word has been spoken in Albert's household. The following occurs to him: If you've been confined to bed for a long time, your first steps would be weak, hesitant. The same could be said in connection with other parts of the body. Not the tongue. Albert has gone for days without speaking to anyone but waitresses and cabaña boys. When he did he was as eloquent as ever, perhaps more so. Albert is sure he is not alone in this regard. He submits that if he didn't utter a word for a year, his first cogent, mellifluous sentences would make men sit up and take notice, cry, laugh, whichever his intent. Given a year to get it right, he is convinced he could sweet-talk the thrush from his thicket, have him singing to him from his wrist. So it is with the general plan of my life, Albert recognizes, but although I have been tinkering with it all these years, it may not be workable. The possibility exists that instead of seeking solace in assonances I should be stilling the discord in the faithless arms of Lauri, Audri, or Kelli.

Albert supposes he was attempting something of that sort when he haunted the Sans Souci Launderama late at night, helping divorcées and widows fold their laundry and reciting snatches of Gerard Manley Hopkins to them above the hum, whir, whine, and clank of Big Boys. A divorcée who shall be called C—— dates from that romantic period. If it can be said that we have ruling principles, hers was carnality; Albert's is less easily expressed. What he supposes he's doing is trying to pick every last shred of flesh from his life so that he may contemplate the serene, gleaming bone. Bear in mind—Albert does—that in the end this may have a different, less consoling shape than he had anticipated.

When Albert made love to C——, he gazed down at her broad, slightly domed forehead. Almost no flesh was interposed between the skin and the frontal bone. As she struggled to be once more free of the weight of her life, what little light there was slid across the curve of her forehead, making it appear harder, bleaker, nearly phosphorescent; the illusion was that as a consequence of her exertions the skin split, revealing the bone.

Albert recalls thinking at the time that they could not be less alike but that they are heading in the same direction, she convulsively, eyes shut, he painstakingly, looking where he's going, and that at this point she is out front, and that these are the chances you take.

Nowadays Dr. Nathan Nederlander is the pilot of Albert's soul. "I'm turning the wheel over to you, Doc," he told him the other day. This drew a chuckle from Dr. Nederlander, adding to Albert's depression. Why, he asked himself anew, do I insist on playing these sessions for laughs, milking them for applause?

Dr. Nederlander is, you might say, the family psychiatrist. That is, Skippy Mountjoy, Violet's first husband, was the first to go to him; Skippy recommended him to Violet; she, in turn, prevailed upon Albert to see him. Emily *almost* saw him on three occasions: the first time she didn't have anything to wear; the second, she had, but it wasn't dry yet; the third broken appointment had something to do with hundreds of split ends. Violet, who is unhappy in love, goes twice a week; Albert once; Skippy, who is on welfare and has a drinking problem, intermittently. Dr. Nederlander considers their interlocking sorrows high above West End. When he's running late, Albert gazes out his smutty windows at the Cimmerian prospect of the avenue or takes down German paperbacks—mysteries, largely, in translation—from his shelves and blows the dust off them.

When Albert began going to Dr. Nederlander, he assumed Skippy no longer went. After Albert learned that Skippy was still a patient of sorts—asking to be squeezed in when he had overslept and it was too late to get a job running sandwiches from the Leonard Street employment agency he patronized—Albert put it to Dr. Nederlander.

"In effect, I'm subsidizing Skippy," he said, raising himself from the languid pose on the couch he usually adopts. (When Violet goes, Dr. Nederlander sits on the couch, she in the chair. Albert doesn't know Skippy's seating arrangement.)

"He has Medicaid," Dr. Nederlander said.

"But you couldn't afford to see the Skippys of this world unless you had patients like me at forty bucks a pop."

"You are covered under your wife's noncontributory major medical, which pays seventy-five percent of covered charges after a cash deductible of three hundred and fifty dollars."

"Up to a maximum of thirty-five hundred dollars in any twelve-consecutive-month period, and you only get twenty dollars an hour from Medicaid."

"But your tax dollars provide social services for innumerable unfortunates."

Albert whipped off his shirt. "Look at that," he said, indicating eruptions on his shoulders.

Dr. Nederlander put on his reading glasses. "Do you want me to recommend a good dermatologist," he said, "or are you suggesting that I compare you to Job?"

"What I'm suggesting is that no one I know pays for even a *percentage* of his wife's first husband's psychotherapy."

"As we've elicited in previous sessions, your life has become circumscribed. You should widen your circle of friends."

What made Albert think that Violet's love life might have changed for the better was her singing "The Star-Spangled Banner" at a Knicks–Bucks game. At the Garden, Albert sits on the aisle; she is to his left; the flag hangs on their right. Therefore, when they rise for the national anthem and turn to face the flag, she is behind him. On the occasion in question, Albert heard an unfamiliar voice raised in song. After a few bars, he realized it was Violet's. Although they have been married ten years, this was the first time he ever heard her sing "The Star-Spangled Banner"; in fact, he can't recall her singing anything. (In her defense, Violet says she has so sung lots of songs in Albert's hearing, not least "Happy Birthday" on a number of his birthdays. Be that as it may, her voice was foreign to him, pleasing, but slightly flat.)

When Albert said his wife was unhappy in love, you naturally assumed he was responsible. Not in this case—though, in all fairness, more than a few of her woes can be laid at his doorstep. (Forgive me if I picture them as an accumulation of copies of the New York *Times*.) No, for once someone named Owen, a New Realist she met at a film-making class at the New School, let her down.

Albert learned of his existence—and her inconstancy—in Florida. "Neither of you has any emotional content," Violet told him there. "Dr. Nederlander said I shouldn't put all my eggs in one basket. What he didn't tell me was not to put all my eggs in *two* baskets." At the time of this revelation, they were standing up to their waists in the Gulf of Mexico, a setting more conducive to sympathy than hard feelings. All the same, Albert felt that if he spread his feet any farther apart he would be able to detect the earth's curve. (While in this position Albert was put in mind of the fact that his two favorite odors are those of seas and books. If you bury your nose in the gutter of a new book, preferably a paperback, you can detect the mustiness to come; seas are best smelled when cold—no more than sixty-five degrees—and dead calm and with your nose a quarter inch from the surface. If you inhale deeply enough you can smell unseen fishes. Since my aim, here as elsewhere, is to increase understanding, it must be admitted that this hasn't been scientifically determined. Certain fishermen, however, claim to be able to distinguish the aroma of flowering diatoms, which indicates the presence of schools of bluefish. They say the odor resembles that of "a crate of honeydew melons" or of an unspecified amount of "moist cucumbers.")

In New York, Violet once told Albert, "I don't like the relationships in my life." This, evidently, was a further response to his offer to help her lay the Persian rugs that had come back from Spotless that morning—a proposal she had rejected, saying, "I don't want to put them down with you. All you want to do with me are domestic things."

"Of which relationships are you speaking?" Albert asked.

"All of them. They're too bland, too wispy, too elusive."

"Do you mean elusive or allusive?"

"I don't *know*," she wailed. "Could I mean *both* of them?"

Since they were in bed at the time, and the children were presumably asleep, having abandoned the imaginary electric guitars with which, disposed about the living room like statuary in an Italian garden, they accompany the Stones, he drew her to him.

Getting back to the Knicks game, Albert could think of nothing to make Violet break into song—even the national anthem—except that Owen had called or that she had distributed her eggs more prudently. Albert offers in evidence Exhibit A, she took up ice-skating; and Exhibit B, she took up peace-marching. Once or twice a week she announces she's going ice-skating. Upon her return she regales Albert with such tales as that the rink was mobbed with hundreds of *yeshiva buchers* gliding solemnly about in crocheted, beaded, even suède yarmulkes. (It is, no doubt, uncharitable to imagine a window being flung open in a third-floor loft in SoHo, the New Realist shouting down to the street, "You forgot your goddam skates!") Not long ago, she told Albert she was going to Washington for a peace march. "Look for me on television," she said. Albert watched on and off, but didn't see her. "I was there," she said when she got back. "If you had spotted me, you would have seen me give my secret signal."

The cease-fire agreement terminated the marches, but Albert assumes she will keep on skating into summer, when the crowds will thin. He pictures her at last, idly tracing an outside backward eight on the empty rink—a figure well beyond her capability. It is a scene he associates with that of his dad standing at a hotel-room sink, hands underwater, dreamily kneading his beloved garments of sixty-five percent polyester, thirty-five percent cotton.

My dad! Albert exclaims to himself, as much in awe as regret. A few days ago Albert paid him a visit to see how he was holding up against the Oriental tide. A firm named Fukuoka Foto now occupied the office alongside his—the corridor branches to the right at his office—so, in effect, he was cut off. He was at his desk when Albert came in, eyes nearly shut, head fractionally back; the impression was that he was sniffing the air for traces of simmering sukiyaki. The light in his office was dim, the source for most of it being the window behind him, so that when he arose at Albert's entrance he was nearly silhouetted. He seemed much thinner, eroded; he looked, in fact, like the somber coastal formation known as a stack.

Albert's dad asked Albert whether he had come from the Y. Albert said he had. Albert's dad asked Albert whether anyone had bumped into him while he was swimming and if so what Albert had said to him. They've had this conversation a number of times, Albert said they now let women into the pool on Mondays, Wednesdays, and Fridays, and what he had told her was, "You know, you're being anti-social."

"Many years ago," Albert's dad said, "I worked on a chicken farm in New Jersey. Jews, you know, have an affinity for all phases of the poultry business. When I fed the chickens, I would inadvertently step on their toes. I said, 'Excuse me.'"

Albert's dad's utterances usually have a high moral content.

They sat in silence for a bit, the gloom abruptly thickening as the sun passed behind a cloud or office building. Albert thought of pulling the chain on the standing lamp by his chair; then it occurred to him that the bulbs might have long since burnt out. He was tempted to take off his shirt and show his dad the eruptions, but that would have meant launching into a greatly revised account of the last ten years of his life, and his dad wouldn't put up with the *vie romanisée* he fobs off on Dr. Nederlander. "I have more at stake," Albert's dad would say.

"Many years ago," he started anew (he gets on these kicks, Albert reflected, his voice nearly entering the head register, as though he were speaking to him from the other side), "there used to be a place in the Bronx called Starlight Park—"

"Where in the Bronx?"

"What conceivable difference does it make? You know nothing of the Bronx. To you, it's terra incognita." Albert's dad often accuses Albert of being indifferent to his, Albert's dad's, past. "You have a habit of asking questions to hear yourself speak."

"I go days without speaking," Albert told him.

"In Starlight Park," Albert's dad went on, "there was a vast outdoor swimming pool. It was a hundred yards long—"

"A hundred yards!"

"A hundred. Seventy-five. It was vast. One summer, when I was a young man, I would go there every day to play handball. When I was through I would jump in the pool at its deepest point, expel all of my breath, and lie on my back on the bottom with my arms outspread—"

He tilted back in his chair, held his arms out wide, and gazed—Albert would say beatifically, Albert's dad would say momentarily—at the ceiling.

"—and look up."

As for me, Albert muses, looking down is my fate or forte: at women's foreheads gleaming in the dark, as I mentioned earlier; at the sidewalk to see where I'm going or, as Dr. Nederlander would say, where I've been; at the pages of a book, as at this moment.

" 'When thou at the random grim forge, powerful amidst peers/ Didst fettle for the great grey drayhorse his bright and battering sandal!' " Albert intones to a woman who has lost her husband in Vietnam, while his pathetic little bundle of laundry flies about in one of the Sans Souci dryers.

People are stirred differently, too, although—and this perplexed Marx—literature depends on and resounds with common chords. For example, Dr. Johnson contended that no poetical passage rivaled the description of the temple in "The Mourning Bride"—"How reverend is the face of this tall pile . . ." Of course, he wasn't trying to get into the pants of the Sans Souci clientele.

"I know I've bumped into you before somewhere, you know," the widow says as Albert closes his book.

In his motel room, when they've undressed, he lies on his back on the carpet and says, "Hold my legs."

"There?" she says.

"No. The ankles."

"Here?"

"But really clamp down on them. Put your weight behind it."

"You know, I hope you're not into heavy S & M, you know."

"I know. It's just that I forgot to do my sit-ups."

When they are in bed, Albert gets a collect call from Emily. "Next Tuesday is the third anniversary of the day I met Sean," she informs Albert, "and I'm getting him a mist-type styler and I wondered if you wanted to make a contribution."

Brimming with love, Albert pledges five dollars.

A moment later, the phone rings again. Will Albert accept a collect call from a Mr. Mountjoy in New York?

"I will not."

"In that case, I'll pay for it, operator," Albert hears Skippy say.

"Don't believe him," Albert says. "He hasn't got a dime to his name. He's on welfare. I have to contribute toward his psychotherapy."

"What number are you calling from?" the operator asks Skippy.

He reels off one that is strangely familiar to Albert, being his own. He pictures Skippy lolling about on his bed, negligently unbuttoning his collar, loosening a hand-blocked foulard Albert wore before he was married—Violet slips Skippy Albert's old clothes. Albert supposes there is comfort in the fact that they wear different sizes.

"If it wouldn't be putting too much of a strain on our relationship," Skippy says, "I was wondering whether, as a fellow-citizen of the Republic of Letters, you could see your way clear to wiring me twenty to get my typewriter out of hock. I'm in the middle of a sonnet sequence."

"Use a pen," Albert says. "Like Shelley."

Albert hangs up and flings himself upon the widow, as though executing a racing dive. You know, he thinks, I *have* bumped into her before, in the pool at the Y. Albert keeps this discovery to himself; he doesn't mean to have his life veer into the novelistic. In addition, he prays that she won't, like a nineteenth-century heroine, remember and cherish him as she unrolls each pair of children's socks they rolled together in the Sans Souci Launderama, he pining the while for the little, lost feet of his stepchildren. Albert reflects that his life has become increasingly like a dream from which he has less and less expectation of awakening.

After she has gone, Albert lights a pipe, takes up the "Manyōshū"—in translation—and resumes reading where he left off the night before. Cuckoos, plum blossoms, and pessimism imbue his mind. His forehead is peeling. As he absently rubs it, bits of dead skin drift down pathetically, like blossoms, or airy snow, or ash. At the same time, the smoke from his pipe rises like that from salt fires. It is vain, he muses, to expect the smoke to bear his skin upward. He would like to compare the sound of turning pages with some natural effect, but none comes to mind.

A few days later, Albert is in a Boston whaler, off Nonesuch, on the edge of the deep, watching shearwaters migrating from Tristan da Cunha to the Newfoundland Banks. They come singly, by and large, greaters mostly, with the odd Manx, ranging deviously down the wave troughs, as though searching for something. Albert fancies it is remembered fragments of their pasts. After all, they had come this way before. Perhaps they recall me from other springs, Albert reflects, bobbing here, Jewish in bearing—that is, somewhat hunched—but younger, more slender, but no less full of wonder.

Like the acrobats, usually related, who form human pillars by standing upon one another's shoulders, as we grow older, heavier, less agile, we take our place farther down until, at last, we are at the bottom, supporting the rest. There we totter about—a bit theatrically from time to time, Albert admits.

4

On the flight to Miami, Albert wins a bottle of wine for producing the oldest penny. In case you haven't flown lately, stewardesses now play games with passengers. Albert hadn't entered into the spirit of the thing. For years his dad has exhorted him to do just that—enter into the spirit of things. What a nice ring it has, Albert has come to realize; it might almost be the name of a Victorian pastime—Entering Into the Spirit of Things. Gazing down at the smoldering Everglades, he imagines the rollicksome Marxes playing it during a picnic on Hampstead Heath.

Albert hadn't expected to win; the penny he grudgingly dug out of his pocket was dated 1945. When, in its final approach, the plane enters a pall of smoke, Albert dwells on the vanity of human wishes, which his dad has had more luck impressing on him.

The girl behind the counter at the car-rental office on North Le Jeune is wearing a miniskirt. As she turns to get a form, Albert notices that the insides of her thighs jiggle, and he is mildly aroused.

"Do you and your husband like wine?" he says, flourishing the bottle and setting it on the counter.

"I'm not married," she says, "but I enjoy it in moderation."

Albert shifts his glance. Beyond a plate glass window rows of brightly colored Novas and Dusters gleam in the sun; they might have been tesserae in a great composition of which he could not see enough to grasp or which he was viewing from the wrong angle. Such is often the case. Although his dad doesn't know how to drive, he must have passed this way, proselyting, Albert concludes, for once you entered into the spirit of things, you enjoyed them in moderation. "You're forever going to extremes," his dad has told Albert. His tone suggested that this was some malarial coast Albert insisted on visiting without taking the requisite shots.

Albert feels his desire for the rent-a-car girl waning; if he is going to sleep with her he will have to talk to her, and he has lost interest in the story of his life. Whatever the rewards, being compelled to relate it yet again seems as much of an intrusion as fishing out his pennies had been.

"Then permit me to give it to you," Albert says, presenting the bottle with both hands, like a wine steward, so she can read the undistinguished label. As he does so, it occurs to him that this is the way infants are held up to view. He himself must have been displayed thus. He imagines a giant hand under his bottom, another supporting his head, his dad gazing critically down at him. Had he proved satisfactory?

Albert reflects that as his dad has grown older—he is now seventy-seven—he has become more lavish in his praise, at least that which he bestows on his surviving compeers. Where once he would refer to someone as "a wonderful guy" he now extolls him as "a warm and delightful human being." Although such citations had the virtue of being slightly more specific, they had the defect of sounding like the first drafts of eulogies. Indeed, his dad is in great demand these days as a eulogist. "I have finally found my true calling," he told Albert. "You couldn't have done it without your friends, relatives, and associates," Albert told his dad. "No, I couldn't have done it *with* them," he said. A warm and witty human being.

Albert often attends the services at which his dad is asked to say a few words. From his seat on the highly varnished bench, Albert admires how well his dad carries his years. Instead of being bent, shrivelled, diminished, his clothes hanging about him like a sack, he seems more erect, fit, spruce, as though he is streamlining himself to make his own impending ascent to Heaven as rapid and frictionless as possible.

Afterwards, mingling with the mourners on the sidewalk out-side the chapel, Albert invariably finds himself comparing the scene to the intermission of a play, and once or twice he has caught himself straining to hear the bell summoning them back for the next act. There has to be a greater resolution.

Morton Savoy, D.D.S. is usually among the last to disperse. "I guess I better be drifting off," is what he always says. Albert has the impression that each successive destination in Uncle Morty's life holds less in store and wonders when he had arrived at the turning point; further, if this is a general rule, whether he, Albert, will be able to recognize his. A gentle and painstaking soul, as Albert's dad has lately termed him, Uncle Morty is his mother's and father's dentist as well. Albert has been going to him all his life, his appointments increasingly taking on a melancholy cast; the water that perpetually runs around the basin into which he rinses now has a Stygian gur-gle. Each time he lies submissively in the chair, Albert remarks anew that Uncle Morty has aged more conventionally than his dad; that is, every six months he is smaller, except for his feet. These remain the same size but appear larger by contrast, giving him a spurious stability. If this trend continues, Albert speculates, all that will be left for his dad to eulogize will be a pair of shoes.

In consequence of their respective positions, Albert feels that he and Uncle Morty are like lovers engaged in a long, unbroken, dispassionate affair. As he worked on his teeth through the years, Uncle Morty's face hovered intently over Albert's; Albert knows it perhaps better than Violet's, and sympathetically has marked its changes.

Pursuing this theme, Albert concludes that such an intimate relationship would be more appropriate if Dr. Nederlander were the other principal, but they sit ten feet apart, Albert at point "A," with his chair inclined toward Dr. Nederlander's at an angle of 53° from the imaginary base line "b" running between Dr. Ned-erlander's chair and his; Dr. Nederlander at point "N," with his chair inclined toward Albert's at an angle of 47° from "b." If they were willing to turn their heads so that their eyes might meet, their lines of sight — "a" and "n" — would intersect at point "C."

After Albert had gone to Dr. Nederlander for a month, he asked Violet to find "C" for him.

Violet's Calculations

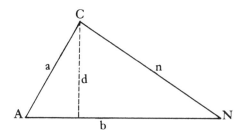

given: $b = 10$ feet
$\angle A = 53°$
$\angle N = 47°$
$\angle C = 180° - (53° + 47°) = 180° - 100° = 80°$

Applying the laws of sines,

$$\frac{a}{\sin \angle A} = \frac{b}{\sin \angle C}$$

$$\frac{a}{\sin 53°} = \frac{10}{\sin 80°}$$

From the table of functions,
$\sin 53° = .7986$
$\sin 80° = .9848$

$$\therefore \quad \frac{a}{.7986} = \frac{10}{.9848}$$

$.9848\, a = 7.986$

$$a\frac{7.986}{.9848} = \underline{\underline{8.109}}$$

Now we can find d:

$$\sin 47° = \frac{d}{a}$$

$\sin 47° = .7314$

$$.7314 = \frac{d}{8.109}$$

$d = 8.109\,(.7314) = \underline{\underline{5.9309}}\,\text{feet}$

She determined it was located at an unspecified height above an unravelling Oriental carpet 5.9309 feet from Albert. However, both Dr. Nederlander and Albert invariably turn to more or less gaze at each other, but Albert turns more than Dr. Nederlander since he is paying and wants to get his money's worth.

Albert always thought he knew where he stood—or sat—with Uncle Morty, but the last time he went to him for a perio, Uncle Morty was wearing a cerise coat. "You look like a hair stylist," Albert said.

"My colleagues felt we should be 'with it,' " Uncle Morty said fatalistically. Since his practice had declined, he had given up his office on Amsterdam and now shared a suite on Central Park South with three younger men. "Do you know how to floss?"

"Up to now I didn't even know it was a verb," Albert said.

Uncle Morty tore off a length of dental floss and held it up critically, nearly at arm's length, much, Albert thought, as his dad would display one of his mom's hairs after finding it in the bathroom sink. "Wind it around your middle finger," he said. "Did I say tight? You're not supposed to cut off the circulation."

Albert pictured himself in ten years with all of his teeth, but minus the first joints of his middle fingers. "Before we go any further, Uncle Morty," he said, "I want to tell you that if it requires a high degree of eye-hand coordination, I'm not going to be a very good flosser."

"You're snapping the floss, Albert," Uncle Morty said. "You're not supposed to snap the floss."

"Is there no room for individual expression in flossing?"

"It's not an art form," Uncle Morty said.

Neither, Albert decides a week or two later, parting the drapes, is the process of restoration, be the object a cast-iron building or a human relationship, as his mom trustingly calls it. The scene is lurid, unexpected. "Sunrise on the Charles." These words come to mind—Albert finds himself silently articulating them—as though he is reading them off a plate below the view, which his eyes have sought. This reaction is undoubtedly a result of the prospect being framed by the window and by his not immediately being able to make out what is before him—a common enough failing. Bands of garish reds, dark indefinite masses evoke a milieu more exotic than Back Bay—indeed, one suggestive of the Near East. Subject matter has less to do with this illusion than coloring, rendering. The effect is primitive, or inept, and strongly reminiscent of the gaudy rugs depicting floral arrangements, kittens, the Last Supper peddled by Lebanese Jews. Reality imposes itself. Beneath Albert's gaze the reds pale, diffuse, the water begins to move, and he succumbs to thoughts of Messianism, a life lived in deferment.

He lets the drapes close and glances down at the bed. Amanda Moran is sleeping along the near edge, as she had been when he stole out of her bedroom ten or twelve years earlier—anyway, before he got married. Suppose she hasn't stirred since, Albert reflects, peering at her face, which has agreeably aged in the interval, like an old apple. His attention is next drawn to two strands of dental floss dangling from his middle fingers. The whereabouts of the other ends is not evident; they might be clews, extending far into the past. Attempting to unravel the floss, Albert recalls being fairly drunk and naked in front of Amanda's medicine cabinet mirror the night before, remorsefully flossing. As he payed out the floss from one finger and took it up on another, he had the inexact impression that he was raising anchor at last—or was he letting more chain down?

"What precisely are you up to in there?" she had called from the bedroom.

"I'm carefully following an effective personal oral hygiene program."

"At 3 a.m.?"

"Amanda, I'm on plaque control. . . Holy shit!"

"Albert, what happened?"

"It broke."

"Come here, baby. I'll tie a knot."

Albert stumbled from the bathroom, trailing the floss behind him.

Now he removes Amanda's cats from his clothes and gets dressed. He lets the floss be and begins plucking cat hairs off his suit. I'll have to get it cleaned, he thinks, or Violet will suspect something.

He notices that Amanda's eyes are open and obligingly approaches her. "See you in ten years," he says.

"Albert, we can't go on meeting like this," she says, reaching out to embrace him or to remove an additional hair.

If Violet has tumbled, Albert muses as they drive along the Rickenbacker Causeway to see the afterglow over Biscayne Bay, she hasn't let on. Albert esteems the afterglow as viewed from the causeway, as does Violet. To see it in all its glory from a moving vehicle requires split-second timing, however. According to Violet's calculations—Albert once told his dad he had a calculating wife, whereupon his dad quoted Benjamin Constant: "Jokes appear to hold the real key to life"—on this particular evening they have to be crossing Bay Bridge, the best vantage point, at 6:12 and it is now 6:10 and Bear Cut Bridge is not yet in sight. It's going to be dicey. The speed limit on the causeway is 45 m.p.h. and they have 2.2 miles to go before reaching the midpoint of Bay Bridge. Violet says that if Albert cranks her up to 66.96 m.p.h. and holds her there, he'll hit it right on the nose.

Violet's Calculations

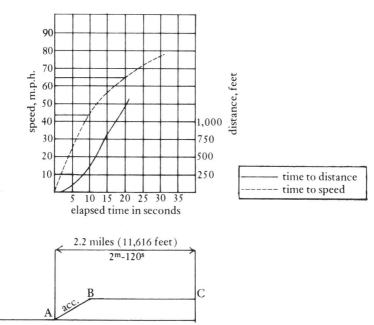

Acceleration, '70 Vega

To obtain minimum constant speed between B and C, acceleration has to be at a maximum. Ideally, instantaneous constant speed, then, would be between A and C at

$$\frac{2.2 \times 60}{2} = 66 \text{ m.p.h.}$$

CONSTANT ACCELERATION
S = distance moved in feet
V_f = final velocity (feet per second)
V_o = initial velocity (feet per second)
a = acceleration (feet per second × second)
t = time of acceleration in seconds

CONSTANT VELOCITY
S = distance moved
V = velocity
t = time of motion

ACCELERATION

$$S = \frac{(V_f + V_o)t}{2}$$

$$a = \frac{V_f - V_o}{t}$$

According to ordinates, time elapsed
between 45 m.p.h. and 66 m.p.h. is 10 seconds

$$\text{Acceleration} = \frac{(V_f - V_o)}{t}$$

$$a = \frac{V_{66} - V_{45}}{10} = \frac{(66 \times 1.467) - (45 \times 1.467)}{10}$$

$$\frac{96.82 - 66.01}{10} = \boxed{3.081 \ \frac{ft^2}{s}}$$

$$S = \frac{(V_f + V_o)t}{2} = \frac{(96.82 + 66.01) \times 10^5}{2} =$$

814.15 feet

DISTANCE AT CONSTANT SPEED
11,616 − 814.15 = 10,801.85
TIME AT CONSTANT SPEED
120 − 10 = 110 seconds
LOWEST POSSIBLE SPEED

$$\frac{10,801.85}{110} = 98.2 \ \frac{ft.}{s}$$

98.2 × .6818 = $\boxed{66.96 \ \text{m.p.h.}}$

Smoothly accelerating, Albert briefs Violet. His area of responsibility is to maintain speed, hers is to keep an eye out for the law. Events happen thick and fast.

18:10.23. *Violet*: Cop car at two o'clock.

18:10.47. *Police Officer*: Where's the fire?

18:10.50. *Albert*: Beyond the rim of the world.

18:10.54. *Violet* (sotto voce): Holy shit!

18:10.57. *Police Officer* (to Albert): Prosify that, Jack.

18:11.01. *Albert*: We're late for the afterglow, officer! We've got to be at Bay Bridge by 6:12!

18:11.17. *Police Officer* (glancing at his watch): Wind 'er up and follow me.

He gets back in his cruiser, turns on the cherry light and the siren, and shoots off the shoulder, his rear wheels tossing shell. Drafting behind him, Albert and Violet flash across Bay Bridge at 92 m.p.h., catching the afterglow at the moment of its greatest refulgence.

They park alongside the cruiser in the grove of Australian pines before West Bridge and watch the sky become drained of color and evenly darken, the bay lose its gilding—processes one would have thought would take years. The police officer tells them he is enrolled in Imaginative Writing at Miami-Dade Junior College, and presses on Albert a sheaf of poems. These he keeps in the glove compartment to rework by map light while the tires of unapprehended speeders sing in the night.

It strikes Albert that while the police officer was counting feet he had been struggling to count sheep. As with so much else, Albert has come late in life to this anodyne and has failed to master it. (Among other things he has taken up after forty with one degree of diffidence or another are adultery and loving his wife.) The first part is easy: an empty meadow. This he has no difficulty envisioning. In fact, he dallies there, enjoying the lowering prospect, which is executed in the manner of Philip de Koninck. The fence presents a problem. How is it put together? Albert has a lively imagination, a middling background in Western art, but he's not handy. When he was in the third grade, his shop teacher wrote on his report card: "Albert has good intentions, but insufficient manual dexterity to carry them out." (He's come to realize that as a moral agent, he's all thumbs, too.) He has tried erecting a number of fences in his mind, but the business of fitting the rails into the posts defeated him. His rickety creations would, he feared, collapse if more than one bobolink sat on them. At last, he threw tradition to the winds and stapled barbed wire to the posts. The first sheep—Albert knows sheep; Giotto did terrific sheep—approached the fence and leapt over. Its leg action didn't seem right. For the next sheep, he altered it. This time he realized that what was bothering him was what the hind legs did when the front hooves struck the ground. Sheep *have* hooves, don't they? He considered borrowing a Hulcher and shooting a couple of rolls of Josh jumping over a footstool, so he could analyze the disposition of his limbs. Meanwhile, the third sheep refused the jump. Perhaps he had made the fence too high.

At this juncture, he realized he didn't know enough about sheep vis-à-vis fences. He called the American Sheep Producers Association, which put him on to a major sheep owner, a sheepherder, and a retired "camp jack" who came to the phone in the lounge of DuWayne's Bowl-O-Drome & Recreation on U.S. 70 south of Richfield, Utah, where he was drinking tomato juice and beer. From those sources he learned the following: Contrary to the familiar representations, for the most part sheep won't jump fences unless they are urged to do so by man or are stirred up by a predator. This rule of thumb applies to range sheep rather than farm flocks; the latter, of course, are more docile. However, even a range sheep isn't usually obsessed with escaping from an enclosure unless pressured, and a sheep would much rather break through a fence or find a hole in it than jump over it. For this reason, most sheepmen use "L-wood" fences, which have close wire squares instead of horizontal strands of wire. The fences contain about three feet of these squares, topped with two or three barbed-wire strands, making a four-foot barrier in all. A sheep can jump from two and a half to three feet. They have pretty good explosive power (standing jump), but generally take a little run at the fence. Sheep follow a leader. If, under pressure, one sheep jumps a fence, the others will follow, but rarely in single file. They will almost always jump simultaneously. The only way sheep would line up and jump over a fence one at a time, as customarily envisioned, would be if a leader, usually under pressure, jumped the fence and there wasn't room for the others to clear it en masse.

Albert relates his findings to Dr. Nederlander, who nods

several times. "Dr. Nederlander is the only man I know who is more inexpressive than you," Violet has told Albert. "But he may be concealing his true feelings for therapeutic reasons." Nodding and allowing his eyes to close is Dr. Nederlander's entire repertory, and since at least two of the four bulbs in his ceiling fixture—in whose plate a prize collection of dead insects is on permanent exhibition—are always out, his responses seem even more minimal, more shrouded.

Bringing his head to a halt, Dr. Nederlander says, "The sheep, Albert, drop them. Try a more urban situation. Conceptualize, possibly seriatim, Bradley running his man into that double screen and getting free for the baseline jumper."

Dr. Nederlander's passions and Albert's converge at two points: the Knicks and food. In a previous decade, Amanda Moran had told Albert that on the basis of sleeping with a random sample of Jews, she had determined that their racial disquiet was food-oriented, centering around applesauce. "Your ingestion is symptomatic of your limitations," Dr. Nederlander once said to Albert. "You have almost infinitely postponed the achievement of pleasure. Deli, Albert, is a backwater in the tide of Western civilization."

Subsequent to his advice *in re* the sheep, Dr. Nederlander closes his eyes for a longer period than usual, giving Albert the opportunity to study his eyelids, which in the half-light seem unnaturally smooth, marmoreal, nearly heroic in scale.

When Dr. Nederlander reopens his eyes, Albert tells him that it so happens that after dinner Violet and he are going to a Knicks game, and that he will watch Bradley closely so he can get that move down pat.

For the first time since Albert has known him, Dr. Nederlander gives evidence of being in the grip of a moderately deep emotion. He even passes a hand over his spacious brow, and when he speaks his voice is more vibrant than customary.

"Tonight," he says, "eat Chinese."

As it turns out, Albert goes to see the Knicks with Barney, who is now eighteen. They eat at the Stage.

The game goes into double overtime and is unbearably tense.

"I'm not going to look if we shoot any fouls," Albert tells

Barney. "I'm going to close my eyes."

"I'll tell you what happens," Barney says.

"Don't tell me," Albert pleads. "I don't want to hear the truth."

"Give me your hand," Barney says, taking it and placing it on his thigh, "I'll tap it if the shot is good."

Gianelli is fouled. As he approaches the line, Albert shuts his eyes and listens to the crowd grow silent. More time passes than he would expect. Has Gianelli in fact missed? Albert thinks: Wouldn't I have been able to tell by the reaction of the fans? As the silence continues, he imagines the game is over and that everybody has left the Garden but Barney and he. Barney's ringer strikes his hand. Albert doesn't want to open his eyes, but to sit in the dark in the midst of the howling crowd, his hand on Barney's thigh.

In this respect, Albert recalls Violet telling him how she had sat for hours by her father's hospital bed when he was dying, her hand in his. From all signs, he was unconscious, but when she fiercely whispered in his ear, "I'm Violet; if you know it's me, squeeze my hand," he would squeeze it.

What follows is tender and complicated. Violet awakens Albert in what lately has become known as his room, Violet having moved into Emily's room when she went to stay with Sean's family in Nebraska, which meant that Sean's mother had to move in with his father. Albert sees his stepdaughter as a sort of Clotho, twisting here, untwisting there to maintain a mysterious symmetry.

On the morning in question—it is morning because Albert's room is perceptibly lightening, as though his bed is being raised through the high interior of the sea—Violet enters, crouches by Albert's ear, and whispers, "I can't tie my tie."

She holds out a plaid necktie of the size they had bought Barney in the boys' department at Brooks years ago. It might well be one of his: an example of what the Japanese call *mono no aware*, the poignancy of things. Albert props himself up on his pillows, puts the tie about her neck, and attempts to knot it. After several failures, he asks her to sit on the edge of the bed, with her back to him. Putting his arms around her, he ties the tie. In much the same way, he recalls, when Barney had asked him to part his hair, he made Barney stand with his back to him and bow his head. As Albert gently tightens the knot about Violet's throat, he thinks that they were never as close, as allied in purpose. As though she were prey to similar sentiments she says, "Why don't you talk about something important with Dr. Nederlander? All you talk about is growing old."

She means I omit sex, Albert thinks as he walks along the forbidding perspective of West End Avenue at midday in the company of Dulcie Barclay, whom he hasn't seen for ten or eleven years. They are on their way to the apartment of a friend of hers who is skiing in Courchevel. The ostensible purpose of the visit is for Dulcie to collect her friend's mail. The actual purpose is to have a nooner.

"This is it," Dulcie says, taking Albert's hand and leading him into a lobby evidently designed by an admirer of Balthasar Neumann. Many a time has Albert gazed up at its soaring stuccoes, sculptures, and frescoes—the whole *Gesamtkunstwerk*: It is Dr. Nederlander's building! The doorman, a greybeard who isn't on when Albert sees Dr. Nederlander, approaches. Albert wonders: Is he going to offer to serve as a guide to the lobby's splendors, or is it his portion to play an admonitory role, like Wordsworth's leech-gatherer? He stands respectfully before them, his dark uniform, upon which the piping has all but unravelled, as shiny as carbon paper. Dulcie asks for her friend's mail. The doorman retires into a murky, chapel-like recess. When he returns with the pile of mail, carrying it with both hands as if it were a relic whose keeping he is about to entrust to her, he tells her that the maid is "up there."

"The maid?" Albert says as he and Dulcie rise in the elevator. "What's the maid doing up there if she's in Courchevel?"

"She doesn't want to lose her," Dulcie says. "And if she's going to keep paying her while she's away, she might as well give her something to do so she can get her money's worth."

By this time they are in the corridor, and Dulcie is fitting a key to a lock.

"Like what?" Albert persists.

"Like cleaning the stove," she says, opening the door, "or doing the drapes."

Indeed, over Dulcie's shoulder, Albert glimpses the maid,

enveloped in a flowered house dress, standing on the radiator cover at one of the living-room windows, about to take down a Fortuny drape—or possibly, putting it up; they don't stay long enough for Albert to learn which.

"But doesn't she come on certain days?" he says as they go down in the elevator.

"I can never remember which are her ones," Dulcie says.

Albert studies the demotic avowals of love scratched on the elevator walls. What have they been done with? House keys? Human nails? Wordsworthian dim sadness and blind thoughts he dispels. If I can't look at my life as farcical, he thinks, I can't look at it—like a double overtime.

"I think my life is more prefigured than most," he says to Dulcie.

"I think the only life that interests you is your own," Dulcie says.

"Admittedly," Albert says. "But, as Constant said, 'only faintly.' "

Recrossing the lobby, Albert glances up at the ceiling and imagines his dad, with Merit in tow, arms tightly pressed to his sides, speed lines indicating his great velocity, flashing by mildly astonished cherubim en route to the empyrean.

Albert says to Dr. Nederlander the next time he sees him, "I'm almost positive the maid was Violet."

Dr. Nederlander makes no response. Only one bulb is burning overhead. Albert can hear, but not well enough to make out what it is, the classical music Dr. Nederlander pipes into his waiting room to drown out his patients' secrets and sorrows—or to provide an accompaniment for them. Unresistingly, Albert and Dr. Nederlander fall to discussing restaurants. Dr. Nederlander recommends a little French place in the West Forties. "It's not first-rate," he says, "but it's honest, and the price is right. May I suggest the cassoulet."

Albert gets up to leave. When he opens the double doors to Dr. Nederlander's office—in between which he has imagined that a very thin and determined lunatic could secrete himself—he is struck by the force of the music, a Handel organ concerto. The waiting room is empty, as it always is. Sometimes Albert fancies that Violet and he are Dr. Nederlander's only paying patients. Taking it a step further, Albert sometimes wonders if *she* actually goes.

Dr. Nederlander is saying something. "I can't hear you," Albert says, turning on the threshold.

"Bring money!" Dr. Nederlander shouts above the sonorities. "They don't honor credit cards."

Emily calls collect. She and Sean are en route to Florida to look for work in boutiques. "Do you know if Florida still makes women wear bathing caps in swimming pools?" she asks Albert plaintively.

"It was my impression that they would turn back if the law was enforced," Albert tells his dad as they walk around the reservoir. "The fate of Western civilization is balanced on self-indulgence, socio-economically speaking."

"Marx had occasion to refer to his life's work as '*Ökonomische drek*,' " his dad says, lengthening his stride.

Why does he always make me bust my hump to keep up, Albert wonders.

Lyrically flossing in the Beverly Sunset Hotel early one morning, Albert recalls his dad on the cinder path, vigorously swinging his arms, hellbent for the vanishing point. Albert's pajama top is held together by three disparate safety pins. (As he mentioned to Dr. Nederlander, Violet no longer sews his buttons, to which Dr. Nederlander responded that although it is not his practice to reveal confidences, Violet has already brought it up, that he is fed up to here with this button *drek*, and that Albert should address himself to the wellsprings of his pain.) The bathroom window is open and an unidentifiable bird is singing in the garden below. Albert grows aware that he is more or less manipulating the floss in time with the bird's heartsore measures.

Putting his raincoat over his pajamas, he descends to the garden, in which winding paths lead to pink stucco bungalows, and tracks the bird to the top of a tall, unidentified tree; what Albert *has* come to grips with is that he is an ignoramus west of the Rockies. As he is jotting down the bird's field marks in a notebook, a voice says, "All right, hold it right there."

Albert looks over his shoulder at a security man with a drawn gun.

"Hands against the bungalow, Jack," he adds. To comply without stepping in a flower bed, Albert has to assume much the same angle that his chair is inclined toward Dr. Nederlander's. As he is being frisked, he imagines the yellowing soles of a daytime game-show host pressed against the wall opposite his hands to get better purchase while *schtupping* a bottomless waitress. Just an idea.

Needless to say, the security man turns out to be a bird watcher and insists on making a Xerox of his place list for the Beverly Sunset and leaving it in Albert's box at the front desk.

Albert returns to his room and, taking his suit in his arms, as though it were an old and undemanding love partner, stretches out on the bed and idly plucks dog hairs off it, working from the cuffs up in an attempt to bring to his life what his dad, despairing, calls "a little order." The hairs had been shed by Lois Hamilton's spitz, which had compassionately licked Albert's unoccupied soles while he embraced its mistress on her kitchen floor. He had last clapped her to his bosom ten or eleven years before, but found her little changed, except that she had taken up gourmet cooking.

In the kitchen on South Mariposa, the fluorescent light gleaming in the spines of a complete set of Time-Life cookbooks, Albert had a vision of Amanda, Dulcie, Lois as great, indolent caryatids bearing him submissively upward through time—aerodynamically unsound.

Albert invites Dr. Nederlander to a Knicks game. During time-outs he reads to him from a journal he kept at Wellfleet the previous summer.

"Here's a revealing entry," Albert says. " 'July nineteen. I asked Violet to take my picture coming out of Slough Pond after I had swum around it. "But I already took it," she said. "That was *Round* Pond," I said. When I approached the place where I had started, I made her out standing in the shadows of the pines, wearing the gown she had stolen from New York Hospital after her hysterectomy, the Instamatic to her eye. "Don't take it until I'm nearer," I said, striding ashore. "I have the spot picked out," she said. "If I loom any closer I'm not going to be in focus," I said. "Stop," she said. "Unclench your fists." When she had taken my picture, she removed the gown and entered the water. Among the hyacinths I held her face between my palms, squeezing it. "You look like a walnut," I said. "I read your journal," she said. "Was it any good?" I said. "It was like reading love letters addressed to others," she said.' "

The game is in its waning minutes. Dr. Nederlander is hunched forward in his seat, seemingly brooding over the destiny of the tiny figures of the players far below. "That No. 42 is the stiff of the century," he says at last.

Later that night, Albert calls Uncle Morty at home. "Mission to Plaque Control," he says.

"Yes, Albert," Uncle Morty says.

"As I'm speaking to you, I'm holding between my right thumb and forefinger a gold inlay you cunningly fashioned for me in my youth."

"What is it doing out of your mouth, Albert?"

"It nearly went down the drain, Uncle Morty."

"What precisely have you been up to?"

"Flossing. It flew out of my mouth, describing a parabola. It whizzed around the sink like a roulette ball."

"You're not supposed to take out your rage on your teeth, Albert. Flossing isn't an outlet for repressed violence."

"I have other qualities," Albert says.

But I digress. Albert, you recall, was presenting the bottle of wine to the rent-a-car girl. He has held his pose all this while, as has she, as though they are Victorians sitting for a photograph designed to excite strong emotions. Mrs. Cameron's "Pray God, Bring Father Safely Home" and "Seventy Years Ago, My Darling, Seventy Years Ago" come to mind. Now the action flows. She accepts the wine, fills out the rental agreement; he signs and initials in both places, fingers the keys. As he drives over the Rickenbacker

Causeway, the sun sets unbeheld behind him.

Several nights later, unable to sleep because of the explosion of colliding shuffleboard discs on the court outside his motel room, Albert turns on the radio and catches the end of a newscast on WFUN: ". . . was killed and five hundred dollars is missing from the Flamingo U-Drive office on North Le Jeune." This is the agency from which he rented the car. Banal but true. Banal *and* true. Truth isn't conditional.

The next couple of days, Albert looks through the newspapers for an account of the crime. There is none. If the girl with the tremulous thighs has been murdered, there certainly would have been one. The victim must have been the elderly black who took his bag and put it in the trunk. These speculations occupy him as he walks on the beach early one morning. It is high water and the sea is as calm as milk in a pail. The high-tide line is festooned with the fuchsia sacs of Portuguese men-of-war. Albert recalls walking with his dad by the Hudson and calling his attention to floating condoms. His dad said they were balloons from waterfront bars. For years Albert had envisioned a fantastic New York in which bars on pilings, decorated with crepe paper and balloons, as though for a birthday party, lined the shore from the Sixties south. At night, from a boat, you could hear the revelry and dimly make out the roistering patrons crowded at the windows, releasing balloons. One of the great, thematic currents that flows through Albert's life has swept them to sea and deposited them at his feet to point up his dad's rectitude.

In an hour Albert will drive out to Le Jeune. The elderly black man will be hosing down the plate glass windows. Within the cascade, the girl will shimmer as in a pointillist painting. Opening the door, raising his voice so he can be heard over the water drumming on the glass, Albert will begin his life story.

When the owl awakens him, he will notice that the base of the lamp on her bedside table is fashioned from the wine bottle. The same owl had awakened Violet and him at Wellfleet. "Did you ever realize that if you had done thus and so, we wouldn't be breaking up?" she had said. The fog was particularly thick. He hadn't answered.

In North Miami, lying beneath a shake roof, hemmed in by

crotons, the bedroom reeking of burning brush, Albert will agree with Goethe's remarks on the ending of "Novelle" that a lyrical conclusion was necessary.

Last summer, on the Cape, we heard the same owl
Transmitting its great distressful vowel
From the woods. The same? she said. Not the selfsame,
He said, secretly recounting his wealth of shame.
Slumberous, he wondered if the threefold Os
Transfiguring their connubial woes. . . .

He will falter. Doggerel, like the form and substance of so much of his life. If he had the gift, he would make something of

Suppose it was the identical bird, tracking him down,

rhyming it with

grey silk dressing gown.

That was what the owl's plumage resembled, what his dad had worn years ago, when, upright and mettlesome, he had stood, indistinct, at the threshold of Albert's bedroom, believing Albert to be asleep, and gazed at him with love and terror.

The owl will be perched in a tree hibiscus, chapleted in smoke, listening to the rent-a-car girl's cries—

oh, oh, oh.

And Albert will hear

His dad, the moral scientist, intoning no, no, no.

5

Unable to sleep, Albert wanders through his dark apartment. His way is fitfully lit by little flaring lights—static electricity manifested when he touches this or that to get his bearings. The gleams put him in mind of fireflies in remote country lanes and enlarge his sadness by taking it out-of-doors and extending it backward and forward to summer; more of these behind, he acknowledges in line with Philodemos, than ahead. His distress is exacerbated by the notion that his apartment might, in fact, harbor an enfeebled firefly or two, which pathetically emerge at night, perhaps from the recesses of the piano, which is badly out of tune, some notes silent. What was there for them to *eat*? This anxiety he recognizes as a product, or portion, of his Jewish upbringing.

Albert bumps into the couch, which isn't where it was when he went to bed. He reaches out a hand to steady himself. It comes to rest on the dry billow of the open dictionary. This, too, is in a different place. Albert imagines it creeping secretly in the dark, like a great slug, propelled by the energy generated by the compression of knowledge.

He barges into his wife's room, formerly his stepdaughter's. Violet is sitting up in bed, doing her crossword puzzle. When they separated—by twenty feet—she asked him to buy an extra Sunday *Times*, so she could solve the puzzle independently.

"You've rearranged the living room again," Albert says with a note of despair.

"Sean and Emily are coming home," Violet says. They have been in Fort Lauderdale, working in a car wash.

"Where will they sleep?"

"Here."

"Where will you sleep?"

"In a little nest I'm going to make in the living room, with white wicker furniture."

Albert tenderly pictures her curled in it at dawn, as in a birch grove, and is reminded of Turgenev.

"You can sleep in my room," he says magnanimously. Formerly this had been their room.

Violet shakes her head. Albert edges forward. Violet shrinks back, clutching the magazine section to her breast.

"I only wanted to see how far you'd got," he says.

"You only wanted to make fun of me," she says.

Albert decides to go through his ties. When he was younger, his mom was always after him to "go through" things, his dad to "get rid of them," his mom's concern being material—objects remorselessly overflow—his dad's spiritual: To be found in possession of dead flashlight batteries and headless lead grenadiers made one ineligible for the Kingdom of Heaven, or its sheolic equivalent.

Albert dumps the mass of ties on his bed. There are many more than he would have reckoned, and he has the fleeting notion they may have proliferated in the dark of his closet, like some kind of tropical growth. But when he examines them he realizes that, stained, narrow, somber for the most part, they represent more than twenty years of his life—in a sense, recapitulate it. That is, as, just casting his eyes over his bookshelves, he can almost recall with a greater wealth of detail where he read such and such a volume than its contents, so, surveying his ties, he can better remember the act of buying this or that one than the occasions upon which he wore it. In *this* sense, he reflects, I am a victim of circumstance. That is, substance eludes me.

Rummaging absently through the ties, as though tossing a great, gloomy salad, Albert thinks further: If I were to contemplate hanging myself by one of my neckties, how could I ever make up my mind which to knot about my throat? Also, if I wanted to make a less drastic escape by knotting my ties together and lowering myself out the window, how many stories' worth do I possess? In the literature, has anyone marked a significant correlation between the number of ties troubled urban souls own and the stories upon which they dwell? That is, do they usually have too few to reach the ground?

Albert imagines his apartment as it would look in one of those illustrations that used to appear at the beginning of mysteries: not a floor plan but a view from above and to one side, with the ceilings removed, so that the rooms and their furnishings—easy chairs in slipcovers, lamps with pleated shades, virtu—were revealed. The tenants never were shown, nor were there signs of habitation—the cushions would be perfectly plumped, the beds neatly made; no plants, no books, no litter box. What this school of art had hit upon, Albert reflects, is that the way people live doesn't matter as much as their opportunities for entering and exiting unobserved.

This makes Albert recall a conversation he had with Violet earlier in the evening. He had gone into her room to say good night. She said that if the phone rang not to answer it (the extension was by his bed), as it would be for her. The phone was in the living room. To get to it, she would have to make two right turns: from the bedroom to the hall and from the hall to the living room. Albert said that to minimize the chances of his being awakened, he would now demonstrate how to reach the phone in the least number of rings. He lay down next to her on the bed. "It would be helpful," he said, "if you would sleep on your back on the extreme left side of the bed, with your feet more or less together. That way, when the first ring obtrudes into your subconscious you can swing your legs over the side and be fully erect in one fluid motion." He demonstrated. "Secondly, if you take the first turn a little wide, you'll be able to negotiate the second without decelerating. Please observe." She got out of bed to do so. "I'll now walk through it at half speed. You'll note that if I take the first turn too sharp, I have to pivot once, twice on my right foot, with a consequent loss of speed. I'd target for two rings, maximum."

"Don't forget to remember your dreams," Violet said. Dr. Nederlander had asked Albert to jot down his dreams. "Don't give me the whole *farshtunkene* shooting script, Albert," he had said. "Just hit the highlights."

There is no relationship between the number of rooms portrayed in the frontispieces, Albert muses, and the number of bodies to be found sprawled in them. He pictures four recumbent figures on his premises: his, Violet's, Barney's, and Josh's. Presumably, Violet would be sleeping in her room, Barney in his, Josh on the living-room couch, barricaded behind throw cushions. This wasn't always the case. In the morning, when he went looking for Josh to walk him, Albert was frequently startled to find Violet in Barney's bed or Barney in Violet's when he gently lifted the covers. Recently, he discovered Josh in Violet's bed. For a moment, contemplating the grave, hoary muzzle, Albert thought he had found himself. On this occasion, Barney was in his bed and the couch was empty. Albert checked his own bed to see if Violet had slipped into it while he had been roaming about the apartment. It, too, was empty; she wasn't anywhere.

Albert ponders the baffling distribution of bodies. It seems to him less an instance of individuals switching beds behind his back than an illustration of the effects of propinquity. The members of his household were becoming interchangeable. It was as though they exchanged molecules; Albert imagines the tiny particles of matter jumping like fleas from one to the other.

Next he turns his attention to what his mom would call "articles of décor." In Barney's room, six gilded basketball players surmounting trophies eternally hold gilded basketballs aloft. In Violet's room, a cheap plastic elephant perpetually raises its trunk. In the living room, forsythia long since minus its blossoms arches over the couch, embowering Josh. The upward thrusts evince unspecified yearning. What if the sleepers simultaneously elevated their arms (and paws)?

"The first exercise tonight is the UNATTAINABLE REACHER," Albert announces from his bed. "It is a two-count exercise. In the starting position the body is supine, palms down. On the command ONE, swing arms vertically overhead, keeping the backs of the hands turned upward, fingers desperately clenching and unclenching. On the command TWO, return arms resignedly to the starting position, sighing in unison. In cadence, this exercise is performed as follows: (1) Starting position. (2) MOVE. In cadence, EXERCISE. One, two, *one*. One, two, *two*. One, two, *three . . .*"

Listening to the Milkman's Matinée on Barney's headset radio, Albert makes his way to the kitchen to get a tangerine. Opening the refrigerator he is dazzled by the burst of light, finding it comparable to the effulgence which in the Rembrandt print reveals the stirring Lazarus, floods Christ's robes. In that case, the light presumably emanates from the Lord instead of coming from behind the No-Cal cream soda, but the principle is the same. The Renaissance provides a wealth of examples of the Refrigerator Effect—a mysterious source of light, located below eye level in the middle ground.

Albert pulls out the vegetable bin. No tangies. He is on the point of letting the door shut on another inconsolable chapter of his life when the array of eggs catches his eye. Violet has written on them, "If you can't recall any dreams, you can have some of mine." Turning the eggs around, Albert gently inscribes them in ballpoint with his multitudinous dreams. He is relating how a basketball ref, about to present him with the ball for a foul, instead whips out a revolver, when he runs out of eggs. Putting his clothes on over his pajamas, Albert heads for an all-night deli, meditating on *noctambulisme*, Baudelaire. The cashier is black, more nearly lustrously purple, *iridescent*, his cheeks adorned with tribal scars. He smirks as Albert puts three dozen jumbo on the counter, the scars silently opening and closing like fishes' mouths. Albert has the impression that he is participating in an instructive encounter—that the cashier belongs to one of those didactic tribes Wittgenstein kept invoking. Of course, he is also taking his master's at N.Y.U. Nowadays everyone is.

When Albert returns to bed and attempts to lay his head on the pillow, he fails to make contact. Investigating, he discovers he is still wearing the headset radio, and he feels his cheeks expanding in a savage smile.

When the phone rings the first time, Albert beams, imagining Violet going through the drill, negotiating the corners with a slight body lean, arms gracefully flapping. Elapsed time: one abbreviated ring. The second phone call takes a ring and a half. Emboldened by her first, dazzling run, she must have pushed it too hard, lost control, and crashed into a wall. Albert compassionately speculates whether she sustained injuries. The third time the phone rings, Albert rips the receiver off and bellows, "I was almost asleep!"

"May I please speak to Violet?" Owen, the New Realist, whose token is the plastic elephant.

"You've overdone it, Owen," Albert says. "The cuckold, as comic hero, may be derided, but not reviled. *Three* phone calls isn't funny."

"The first two were from Emily," Violet says, picking up the phone in the living room. Is she holding her separated shoulder in place, Albert wonders.

"From Fort Lauderdale? What did she want?"

"She asked me to help her place the commas correctly in a long sentence."

"She's writing?"

"A postcard."

"And the second call?" Albert says, restriking the note of despair.

"To remind me to water her avocado. I didn't know you thought of yourself in heroic terms, Albert."

" 'The modern hero is no hero,' " Albert says. " 'He acts heroes. Heroic modernism turns out to be a tragedy in which the hero's part is available.' "

"That's not you, Albert," Violet says.

"Violet, 'As individuals express their life, so they are.' "

"That's not you, either."

"Nope, Marx."

"And the other?"

"Walter Benjamin."

"Don't know him, old boy," Owen says.

"You stay out of this, Owen," Albert says.

"Are you insinuating that you're up for the part, Albert?"

Violet asks.

"My dime's running out," Owen mutters.

" '*Je suivais, roidissant mes nerfs comme un héros,*' " Albert chants.

"Albert, it's late," Violet says. "Hang up your end."

" '*Et discutant avec mon âme déjà lasse . . .*' " he murmurs before breaking off. "I'm a roomer in my own house."

"It's what you always wanted from us," Violet says. "It gives you so many opportunities for remoteness."

Returning to the kitchen, Albert reflects that for the first time in his life he has been nearly guilty of aposiopesis. He'd have to remember to tell Dr. Nederlander. Opening the refrigerator, he kneels before the devotional light. He is admiring how the Saran Wrap covering a dish of leftover bass formidably shimmers like the raiments in the Rembrandt painting of one-eyed Julius Civilis, when the phone rings. As he goes to answer it, he dimly makes out Violet, diligently barreling through the switches. Her arms *are* flapping, and as she hits the straight and accelerates he is put in mind of a great wading bird lifting off at dawn, as in a portentous dream.

"I've got it," Albert says the moment before they collide.

"I hope I'm not disturbing you."

"My dad," Albert says, holding the receiver against his chest with one hand, helping Violet to her feet with the other, drawing her to him so she can listen in.

"No, Dad, I wasn't asleep."

"I wasn't, either. I couldn't finish the puzzle. It kept preying on my mind. When you get old, words elude you. What's 30 down, for God's sake?"

Philodemos said thought would console you when you can no longer enjoy the act of love, Albert reflects, but he didn't mention words slipping away, being haunted by unfilled spaces. Fall warblers come to mind, remotely flitting, undifferentiated, his eyes spectrally tearing, recalling spring.

Violet brings him *his* magazine section. As he gives his dad the answers, his dad swears, groans, chuckles in his ear, lulling and melodious as doves. He will have to tell Dr. Nederlander about this obsessive bird metaphorizing as well. Albert lies down where Violet intends to make her nest, remembering how his dad would come into his room and sing him to sleep. Violet stretches out alongside, finding the places in the puzzle for him. Like Turgenev, looking up Albert gazes into a bottomless sea.

6

The bedroom floor creaks alarmingly when Albert does his push-ups. What if it gave way and he descended, outstretched, into the apartment below like a poorly coordinated quattrocento angel? Suppose he crashed through a number of apartments in a hail of lath, plaster, Sheetrock, excelsior, whatever's in there, his undershorts fluttering, wearing what an astonished succession of tenants took to be an insipid smile but was in fact an artistic convention.

This, he realizes, is preposterous; he lives on the third floor. Plummeting through *two* apartments to fetch up in a boiler room wouldn't be worth the pain and suffering, regardless of the sensation he caused. Worse, there might be nobody at home. To drop unnoticed through vacant rooms seems to Albert to be an act that could only lower one's spirits. He imagines such a melancholy descent, past shuddering rhododendron that had seen better days and bunched upholstery from which appalled cats shot up.

Then the idea came to him: What if one found oneself falling through one's former apartments, the earliest bottommost, as though they were embedded in geological strata? He might flash by Violet, his semi-ex-wife, and Barney and Emily doing a jigsaw puzzle of "The Death of Sardanapalus" in a newly renov 3 BR w/ wbf, A/C, brk walls, and 24-hr secu, imploring their forgiveness, signifying his inadvertence, regret, dismay, whatever, and gathering, amid a blizzard of fragmented slaves and concubines, that they had interpreted his wild gestures as an unsuccessful attempt to execute a forward two-and-a-half with a twist or similar dive with a high degree of difficulty. Mindful that Schopenhauer said you could no more express two thoughts at the same time than think them, he will strive for intelligibility in the charming duplex overlooking gdns w/clsts galore, but plunging into a darkened bedroom he makes out Violet, her face smoother, her trust intact, sleeping on her side, the fingers of her left hand clasping those of the man who lies next to her, his arm thrust between her thighs, and who Albert assumes is himself. (This arrangement of limbs is conjectural; a sheet nearly covers them. As though restoring his own ruined work, Albert fearfully extends and entwines.)

The phone rings, and he is left hanging in air.

"Albert, you're a patsy."

It's his dad, the attorney-at-law, *in re* the separation agreement. Albert pictures him in his office, light flashing off framed citations from charitable organizations, holding his ancient, heavy handset with one hand, a pencil poised in the other, in case he has to make "notations." These he always "jots down" on irregular scraps of paper he produces from a mysterious supply.

"You have an overgenerous nature," his dad goes on. "You're throwing away your future. You're depriving me of negotiating room."

Once again Albert has the impression that it is his dad and Violet who are separating, and that his vain function is to mediate their differences.

"I'm getting together with her attorney," his dad is saying, "but if that young whippersnapper thinks I'm going to traipse all the way down to lower Broadway, he . . . I know the building. No one has offices there anymore."

Albert summons up a dim lobby with cracked marble facing, his dad scrutinizing the directory as though it were a corrupt text.

"Albert, why are you breathing so hard?" It's his mom, on the extension. In fact, his dad is at home.

"I was in the midst of my push-ups."

"Don't overtax yourself in this difficult period. If you're

having dinner with us tomorrow, come before six. That way you and Dad can listen to the news together."

Albert falls through brite, lux 1½s in which he had hummed more frequently than he realized—in one sep kit a naked woman on the verge of tears, whom he can't place, is patting bacon with a paper towel—before crashing into a series of spacious 7 rms w/hi ceils and w/w cptg where his parents, ever younger, are listening to the news. How do they react to their son's barging in on them this way? In the first apartment, his mom begs Albert to shield his eyes if he intends to keep this up, as they are his most precious asset; his dad irritably turns up the volume; a comic maid drops a tray and says "Lawdy!" In the second apartment, his mom tells Albert he ought to treat himself to some decent underwear, since he will undoubtedly come under the scrutiny of strangers; his dad makes a face in response to her suggestion, but it is unclear what has displeased him, form or content; a different comic maid drops a tray and says "Lawdy!" In the third apartment, his parents stare blankly at the intruder. They have failed to associate the grieving, disheveled middle-aged man with the child in the next room; so, Albert painfully concludes, has he.

"As we periodically fall, demanding explanations from the past, like great clouds of gnats, words irresistibly rise from the pages where they had so restlessly teemed," Albert informs Violet after tracking her down in the International. Pushing her cart through the narrow aisles, he remarks how the supermarket resembles a catacomb. He goes on, talking to her back as she hefts cantaloupes like skulls: "They get in our ears, our eyes, our noses, maddening us; we submit to their high, insistent buzzing—"

"Gnats are inarticulate, Albert," Violet says, holding a cantaloupe to her ear, thumping it, listening for the resonant note of ripeness, which he has never been able to distinguish.

Albert says, "Furthermore, in the next to last apartment I caught a glimpse of myself. I was four."

She shoves the cantaloupe under his nose. "Now breathe deeply, Albert."

"You know the porcelain heron on the lamp in the living

room? I was stroking its feathers, as though I could warm it to life."

"It won't work," she says. "I tried it on you for eleven years. Can you smell it, Albert?"

"No. And don't make me squeeze any pears." He is unreasonably bereft. "I can't tell the difference."

"Oh, Albert. 'By what we do we know what we are, just as by what we suffer we know what we deserve.' "

"Who said that?"

"Buzz, buzz. Schopenhauer."

Now, *aetat.* forty-five, Albert stands in the shower energetically shaking a bottle of shampoo under the mistaken impression it is Italian dressing. It has just struck him that Violet and he have not discussed who is going to get the Instamatic. This came to him during his precipitate tour of the past, for Violet and he are still imprisoned upside down in the back of the camera, a roll started at Wellfleet the summer before not having been finished. Albert recalls posing for the last shot. "Stick your nose in my ear," he had whispered. Violet has a long, shapely nose, like the Comtesse de Noailles. "I'm not putting it in there anymore," she had hissed back. So they were condemned to hang from their heels apart—not, admittedly, for eternity, but until the emulsion deteriorated.

This puts Albert in mind of the fact that in old-timey libraries books were chained to desks. He imagines them straining to get loose, snapping in Latin. Or a group of restless scholars, books in hand, pacing around a desk, punctiliously raising or lowering their chains to allow a colleague to pass under or step over; or, lost in thought, neglecting this courtesy, so that they become bound together in a great ball; or one absently wandering to the end of his tether and being jerked off his feet, as if emphasizing that knowledge has its limits.

Parallels may be drawn with the state of marriage, Albert reflects, brushing his teeth. Before he and Violet separated, he kept his toothbrushes on the right side of the fixture; hers were on the left, and thus they lay in bed. Now Albert realizes he is so habituated to living in half the available space that he has preserved this arrangement; if she were unexpectedly to rejoin him, the accustomed holes would be free to receive her toothbrushes, and she could slip between the sheets in the dark without asking him to shove over.

So, in fact, she often had come to bed in the last days of their marriage. If she wasn't home when Albert was ready to turn out the light, he would start calling the three bars she frequented. When she came to the phone, he would say, "When do you want me to set the alarm?"

If his dad knew that this sort of thing had gone on, it would only confirm his opinion that Violet had let him down, and he would say to Albert, "You've effectively tied my hands on the alimony by mentioning a figure when I asked you to refrain from making any offers, but I'm not going to let you fork over a lump sum up front."

"I just want to do what's fair," Albert would say.

"Fair, fair, you've been fair. Now you're being guilty. What have you to feel guilty about? Who started it?"

"I told you—it was virtually simultaneous."

Albert imagines this conversation while watching his dad squeeze lemon into his tea as though he were wringing out a bathing suit, and he realizes that a disproportionate amount of his childhood was devoted to wringing out bathing suits under his dad's supervision.

"Do you want more coffee, Albert?" his mom asks.

"No."

"Just half a cup?"

"Do you know what the hardest things to get in America are?" Albert says. "A half a cup of coffee and an AM radio you can plug in. I went to a place on Fourteenth Street and said, 'I would like to buy an AM radio you can plug in. No portable, no FM, no police band, no ship-to-shore.' The clerk said, 'I have a very nice radio for thirteen dollars.' I said, 'But that one has a clock. I have a clock. I want a radio without a clock.' The clerk said, 'I'll let you have it for twelve.' I said, 'You're not following me. I want the radio for my bedside table, upon which there is already a clock. What am I supposed to do with two clocks? I want a little, plastic

AM radio you don't have to buy batteries for so I can listen to the news. I was raised to listen to the news twice a day. What's happened to those little radios? Where did they all go?' The clerk said, 'It's yours for nine-fifty. Think of it this way: a clock would set you back five, so you're getting the radio for four and a half bucks.' Insofar as a half of cup of coffee is concerned, I defy you to show me a restaurant where you wind up with less than two-thirds of a cup. Three-quarters is the rule."

"I hope you didn't let her have your clock, Albert," his mom says.

"Your mother got that clock for you by depositing five hundred dollars in a savings account," his dad says.

"She has the clock," his mom tells his father.

When Albert is getting his coat from the closet, his mom says, "Why don't you try on Uncle Arthur's overcoats?"

Uncle Arthur had died the month before, at the age of eighty-five. His three black coats hang next to Albert's, revealing nothing, as Schopenhauer noted about overcoats and men, of the man who wore them.

"Is this a new tactic in your campaign to disparage my pile-lined coat?" Albert says.

"Dad says they're too voluminous for him," his mom says.

Albert fingers a sleeve.

"One hundred percent cashmere," his mom says. "Uncle Arthur liked quality."

"He ate in the best restaurants," his dad says.

"In his overcoat?" Albert says.

"Maître d's greeted him by name," his mom says. "We had them cleaned, of course."

"What am I going to do with *three* overcoats?" Albert says.

"You can rotate them," his mom says.

"Allow me," his dad says, holding one so Albert can slip it on.

The second is bigger than the first, the third bigger still, as though for some mysterious purpose Uncle Arthur had them made so they could be worn one on top of the other. Albert goes through the pockets in case Uncle Albert left an explanatory note.

When he gets home, Albert hangs the coats in his hall closet;

they suggest the presence of three natty strangers of slightly differing size in his living room. Perhaps, hearing that he was plagued with uncertainty, Brown, Jones, and Robinson, the three faceless men who hire themselves out to philosophers for demonstrations (Smith and the King of France are other members of the firm), have arrayed themselves on his couch, their well-scrubbed hands resting on their knees.

Albert sits on the side of the bed, vaults obliquely into it, and by a series of dexterous movements contrives to wrap himself in the covers—a system perfected by Kant. But he cannot sleep because of the intense cold; Violet has the comforter pending the final agreement. *Les pardessus de mon oncle!* Albert lays the coats, which had been an ornament to so many restaurant checkrooms, on top of the blankets and springs back into bed.

The sleeves of the bottommost coat lightly embrace him. "Albert, I want to clear up this coat business for you," Uncle Arthur says. "One's not bigger than the next; what they are is smaller. As you grow older, Albert, you shrink. Take Kant, a great man. He boasted how he'd triumphantly maintained his balance on the slack rope of life for almost eighty years. In the end he was a midget like everybody else. What can I tell you, Albert? I hope you live long enough to see the Cuban embargo lifted so you can get a nice cigar to smoke. Another thing: never overlook the captain; it's not *au fait.* Slip a nicely folded bill into his palm. And don't be *too* surreptitious. You're not sneaking him a state secret, you're dining out."

This aspect of spying arises again the following morning. Albert and Violet arrange by phone to leave their apartments—they live three blocks apart—at nine-thirty on the dot and meet on Sixth Avenue, Violet to hand over Albert's mail, Albert to hand over Violet's Chinese laundry, which he will have picked up en route. "J 954, green," she says, speaking through a handkerchief to disguise her voice.

When the exchange has taken place, Albert says, "Violet, when are you going to let me come over and get some more of my books?"

"Albert, I told you that leaves holes."

"Holes, holes. You think I don't have any holes in my house?

My whole life's full of holes."

"You're not preying on the weakness of women anymore?"

"Actually, Violet, I'm feeding on my own."

"Oh, Albert, you'll utterly consume yourself. There'll be nothing left."

"No, the reverse. I've finally figured out what's going to happen to me."

"Which is?"

"I'm going to become more of what I am. I'll make a deal with you, Violet. If you let me have two shopping bags full of books I'll put new bulbs in your ceiling fixtures for you. No, you like living in the dark. If Kant lived in the dark, you can live in the dark. Do you want me to string up a rope to help you find the can, or wherever it was he went, hand over hand, as though nightly condemned to scale the same terrible peak, pondering the interaction between the things he bumped into and himself?"

Albert takes the train to Connecticut to see his twenty-eight-year-old girl friend, the Human Dynamo. She finishes telling him off in her driveway. "You don't play tennis, you don't snow-ski, you don't water-ski, you don't ride a bicycle, you're the last one off the train, you *plod* across the parking lot. Albert, we have nothing in common."

"I seem to have little in common with anyone," he says, failing to heave himself out of her BMW on the first try.

He stands beneath the pines in front of the converted pool house she is renting. Before she turns off the headlights, he sees it is beginning to snow.

"And you huff and puff when you make love," she says, taking his arm. "You should see your face."

"What would I see?"

"Strain," says the Human Dynamo. "Anguish. Despair."

As she lets him in, it strikes Albert that if they stopped seeing each other he'd be stuck with an odd number of eggs. Three weeks ago, when he moved into his own place, she stayed over and had an egg for breakfast. As Albert always has two, there has been an odd number in his refrigerator ever since. Albert foresees this haunting disparity continuing indefinitely; an old man, he opens the refrigerator and sighs, knowing that yet again he will be confronted with five eggs or eleven. On the other hand, he reflects that if he hadn't got separated he never would have known how much he valued symmetry.

"The special tonight is spaghetti," the Human Dynamo announces, setting a pot of water on the stove.

Albert is sitting at the kitchen table in one of Uncle Arthur's overcoats, listening to the news and snipping frost-blackened leaves off a miserable avocado plant. The Human Dynamo keeps her thermostat at fifty-five—the lowest possible setting—to stimulate the circulation; her house is full of stunted or vestigial plants. Albert breathes through his mouth—a practice Kant considered insalubrious—to find out if he can see his breath. It plumes from his mouth like a comic-strip balloon in which nothing is written.

"If you're all that cold, stand by the stove," she says.

He joins her next to the steaming pot. They are enveloped in a column of romantic vapor. Slipping his hands beneath the Human Dynamo's turtleneck, Albert listens to the boiling spaghetti. The sound is of a dozen pens industriously scratching, and he feels his life has become a mockery.

Albert does not believe in causality. Nor does he have any truck with destiny, chance, or sortilege. However, he dabbles in numerology to the extent that he has an "operative number"; this is the term he uses to distinguish it from a lucky number, inasmuch as he does not invoke it for divine audition or to solicit good fortune, but to carry out a pattern. Three, ten, and one hundred are common examples of what might be called operative numbers. We often perform acts in threes or on three, or count to ten or one hundred before taking, or abandoning, action.

Albert's number is thirty-one. In the morning, he counts silently to thirty-one before getting out of bed—or to sixty-two or to ninety-three; in certain situations multiples are admissible. (Albert weighed one hundred and eighty-six pounds until recently, when he went on a diet. Alas, one-fifty-five is beyond reach.) Going to work, he chooses the subway exit where thirty-one steps

lead to the surface; these he ascends with uncharacteristic jaunti-
ness. At his desk he downs his cup of coffee in thirty-one rapid,
intense sips. Before retiring, he does thirty-one sit-ups, thirty-one
push-ups, reads thirty-one pages, and turns out the light.

Now, making love to the Human Dynamo, Albert executes
one hundred and twenty-four strokes.

"I can see you moving your lips," she says midway.

Albert awakens early and sits up in bed. Chin in hand, he contemplates the Human Dynamo, whose back protrudes from the
disordered covers like the ivory hilt of an ornamental dagger that
had been thrust at him in the night and missed. So had Sardanapalus surveyed the tumult and wreckage of his life.

Albert goes to the window; it is still snowing. The pool house
is built on a rise; a narrow brook emptying into a pond runs at
the bottom of the lawn. These are now frozen. Movement in the
second growth on the far side of the brook catches his eye. At first
he thinks a little old man is emerging from the wood, carrying
each foot to the ground and setting it firmly down, the way Kant
got around in his last years. When the man gets clear of the trees,
Albert realizes that he is in fact an upright and prodigious bird, a
great blue heron stalking through the mottling snow. Albert regards its resplendent, metrical approach. As Japanese screens are
meant to be viewed while one is seated on the floor and lose something when seen from a standing position, so Albert fears he is too
high up to appreciate what is unfolding and rushes downstairs to
the kitchen. However, when he gets to the kitchen window, the
bird is gone, its tracks filled in with snow.

"Kant was a bird watcher," the Human Dynamo says when
Albert returns to the bedroom. She is standing naked by the window, looking out. "He could distinguish them by their songs. You
never sing, Albert," she adds, getting back in bed. "How can you
expect anyone to know who you are?"

"I'm being painted," Albert tells Violet on the phone.

"I thought you said it didn't need painting."

"I was mistaken. Peach depresses me. So do hundreds of little
ducks."

"What are you talking about, Albert?"

"The wallpaper. They waddle from right to left. It's perverse."

"I don't follow you."

"Like words, life flows from left to right. You open a book with your left hand, you close it with your right. Commuter trains arrive from the left and depart to the right, except at Jamaica, Croton-Harmon, and 125th Street. When men kiss women's breasts, they invariably elect to kiss the nipple to their left first. In the morning you put on the left sock before the right and at night you take them off in the same order. Consider their shape and you will agree that too often they serve as parentheses—which, by the way, Schopenhauer deplored—enclosing yet another day's digression."

"All very well, Albert, but why did you call?"

"To ask whether you'd let me stay with you when they do my bedroom."

"If you bring your pillows."

Several nights later, Albert, wrapped in another of Uncle Arthur's overcoats, plods up Sixth Avenue, a pillow under each arm. This, he thinks, is how I'd have carried my children, if I had had any. When I married Violet her kids were too big to tuck under the arm and break into a run. Emotions have a left-right flow, too, but rarely preserve their character en route, wishes forming at the left and straggling off as disappointments at the right.

7

The Human Dynamo says, "Are Jewish people always sad when they pack?" She is lounging on Albert's bed, watching a World Team Tennis match on television without the sound, which Albert won't let her turn up because life is hard enough—admittedly, he has told her, a state of affairs he doesn't expect her to recognize at twenty-eight. Off to Miami in the morning, he is traipsing back and forth between his dresser and his suitcase, carrying a shirt or a little pile of underwear, as though they were relics he was bearing in a religious procession. "You're slowing down," the Human Dynamo says. "You misjudged the pace."

Albert inwardly concurs. He has rated his life incorrectly; he is forty-five, the finish line is within sight, and there is too much ground to make up.

"I'm going to rephrase my question," the Human Dynamo announces. "Are all Jewish people sad when they pack?"

Balling a pair of socks, Albert decides he's not so much sad as disquieted and wonders why. All that comes to mind is that the pool will be full of shrieking children or drained for repairs and he won't be able to go swimming. Albert is haunted by the spectre of empty pools; they figure in his dreams—immense, freshly dug graves. This, he realizes, is an anxiety unlikely to afflict many of his fellow-men, and thus sets him dubiously apart.

"I'm going to descend from the general to the particular," the Human Dynamo says. "Did you ask Violet to console you while you packed?"

One night a week later, back from his trip, Albert stares out of his bedroom window. This overlooks a yard in which he once saw an ovenbird circumspectly walking beneath a rank rose of Sharon bush, so that for a moment he had the unsettling impression he was deep in the country rather than on the third and top floor of a Federal house in the Village. Before he and Violet split up six months ago, they rented the apartment in the elevator building two blocks away, which I have described; she has continued to live there with Barney, Emily, and Josh. From his bedroom, Albert can see a corner of Violet's building, if not the windows of her apartment. If he could look in, Albert fancies he would behold events that happened far in the past, as though the brightly lit windows were heavenly bodies, and learn whatever lessons history teaches.

"Oh, God," his mom had said when Albert told her where he had moved. "You can hear her hair dryer from there. Couldn't you have put more ground between yourselves?"

"It wasn't premeditated," Albert said. "It was a supervenient turn of events. If you visualize the marriage as a ship that has broken up, you will see us as two shipmates clinging to opposite ends of a large piece of flotsam."

"I see you as two idiots awash on a delusion," his dad said.

"Be that as it may," Albert said, "it also means I can walk Josh now and then." Under the terms of the separation agreement, Violet got Josh, so he wouldn't have to climb stairs; Albert got the Boston fern.

Before he gets into bed to read, Albert goes into the little bedroom giving off his and transfers the fern from the windowsill to a pedestal table. This way, when he looks up from his book he can see the fern and its reflection; he has hung a mirror behind the table for just this purpose. Besides augmenting the green, reposeful rise and fall of the fronds, which, when faintly agitated by a draft, enhance the illusion that the plant is a fountain, the mirror extends his vista since it appears to afford a view of an empty room beyond it rather than reflecting the one in which he lies unseen. All that is visible in the mirror is an oblong of white wall. If it were not for the venous hands holding the book, Albert thinks, he would be merely a pair of incorporeal eyes by means of which words evenly flowed, maintaining their spacing, to an immaterial brain. Albert reflects that he is doing little more than placing himself in the way of the endless stream of words, which by and large pass through him like cosmic rays.

Albert's gaze is drawn to his fern; this, luxuriant, sits on the pedestal table like a green Persian cat. How much we have in common, he muses: silence, self-containment, seeming contemplativeness. Man may be a thinking reed, Albert acknowledges, but he wonders whether others have as appallingly few thoughts as he does—not vagrant notions or impressions but carefully mediated achievement. Violet used to accuse him of secrecy, of mocking her, when she asked him what he was thinking and he said "Nothing." But this was nearly the case.

Albert has a sudden, sentimental urge to take the fern in his arms. Every morning, in fact, he does so, picking it up like a cat, or a baby, or perhaps a human head, and carrying it into the bathroom to get the benefit of the humidity when he takes his shower. Anyone who hasn't lifted a cat or a baby for a while will find them surprisingly heavy; the same perhaps holds for a human head. If, of course, you could just carry the fern itself, it would be as nothing, as weightless as the thoughts of a lifetime; it's the burden of the compacted earth that astonishes.

A sudden, obscure, conceivably oracular utterance startles Albert, for three reasons: first, although it is apparently in English, he can't grasp what was said; second, he doesn't know who said it; lastly, he doesn't know where the speaker is. This is the order of his concern. Albert doubts whether someone else in his position would have established the same hierarchy. It is probably things like this that set him apart from his fellow-men, he decides.

At any rate, he eventually finds by his side another man's wife, whose presence he has forgotten, muttering in her sleep. He slips a hand under her head and hefts it.

"What are you up to now, Albert?" she says.

"I'm weighing your head."

"What do you think—is it a keeper?"

Albert glances at his alarm clock. "Will you excuse me?" he says, getting out of bed. "I've got to intercept Mills."

Every night at eleven, Albert's landlord, Mills, who with his family occupies the parlor and second floors, leaves the house to jog through the streets of New York, returning at midnight.

Standing on the sidewalk in his raincoat, pajamas, and slippers, as if he has been evacuated because of a fire or gas leak, Albert peers toward Fifth Avenue, waiting for Mills to materialize. In a few minutes he comes into view, pounding down the middle of the street in his burnt-orange sweatsuit with the white competition stripes. When he passes in front of his house, he arches his chest and throws up his arms, as though breasting a tape or invoking a greater authority.

"Mills, a word," Albert says, stepping off the curb.

"Gotta warm down," Mills gasps, swiveling his head, shaking out his arms, capering toward Sixth.

Albert trots alongside. "It's about the bulbs, Mills."

"Bulbs?" Mills pants.

"They're out again. Three of the five in the chandelier in the vestibule that are supposed to resemble little flames, the one in the entranceway, and one of the two flanking the front door that are stipulated by the Housing Maintenance Code. Mills, I realize we belong to two extreme schools of thought respecting dead bulbs, neither of which perhaps is socially desirable. You are indifferent to them almost to a perverse degree. I, on the other hand, am traumatized by dead bulbs—particularly in ceiling fixtures. My gaze is fatally drawn upward in the manner of cinquecento saints whenever I pass beneath them. Wait a minute—I lost a slipper."

Having reached the corner, Mills turns and jogs back to where Albert is forlornly hopping about and offers him his shoulder so he can put on the slipper without stepping on the pavement with his bare foot, which would mortify his mom. Albert's mind retains the impress of such things.

"I'm going to take care of the bulbs right away," Mills says.

"You've made these promises before," Albert says. They are climbing the stoop. Submissively noting the dark coach lamp, Albert forces his gaze higher. Wisteria, in whose thick coils innumerable sparrows presumably sleep, engulfs the façade, as though, Albert muses, centuries had passed since he got out of bed and the building had fallen into picturesque decay. "No one forced you to convert it into a multiple dwelling," he tells Mills.

"I didn't know you subscribed to free will, Albert," Mills says.

Albert hangs up his raincoat and climbs back into bed, brushing against a bulky object he can't place. Withdrawing to the edge of the bed, he considers this encounter. Given that my life is a demonstration of Hume's discontinuous present, he thinks, what we have here might equally be a prie-dieu, an incomplete set of *Notable British Trials*, or my dad. Albert reaches out: she has slipped his mind for the second time.

"Would you accommodate a fantasy of mine?" she says.

"Just my métier," Albert says sadly. "What would you like me to be, a weak-hitting third baseman or a poet *manqué*?"

In a few moments, the phone rings.

"I just wanted to let you know there's nothing in this house to read."

"Who am I speaking to?" Albert says.

"You're speaking to Violet, who's been through two marriages, and both times all the books have gone. Here I am, a fairly literate person, and all I've got on my bookshelves is junk."

"But you got the jelly cupboard and the Gabon funerary figure and the seashells."

"And you got the apothecary jars and the ashtray from the Colony and the pie cupboard *and* all the Elizabeth Bowens."

The next morning, Albert walks down Sixth Avenue, carrying a dead iris that hadn't fully opened. He goes into Mother Nature's Creative Gardens, where he buys his flowers.

"Has Mother let you down again, Albert?" Donald, the

proprietor, asks, addressing him from between two great lilac branches, which he has parted.

"It never unfurled, Donald."

"Didn't say 'Ah'—is that what you're telling me, Albert?" Donald says, scrutinizing the shriveled petals. "Did I ever tell you you're the only customer I have who returns flowers?"

"It seems to be a recurring theme," Albert says. "I recently returned a loaf of raisin bread to Jefferson Market—"

"What was wrong with it?"

"No raisins. They told me it was a first. Donald, I sometimes think it's things like this that set me apart from my fellow-men. Are you going to give me a refund or another flower?"

"What did Jefferson give you?"

"Another loaf. There weren't any raisins in that one, either."

"I think you've been singled out by Providence, Albert."

"These lilacs any good?"

"Please don't shake them, Albert. You shake quince, you shake dogwood, you don't shake lilacs. They're too big for you anyway. They'll tip your pot over."

"I can manage."

"Albert, listen to me. You're not going to be able to handle them. I happen to know that these lilacs are beyond your capability. They're going to get the upper hand. You want me to pick up the *Post* and read 'MAN WRESTLES GIANT LILAC, LOSES'?"

"Albert, they're out of the question."

It's his mom, advancing, withdrawing an iris from a vase to see if its stem is split.

"Are you coming from your knee therapy at St. Vincent's or your body-language class at the New School?" Albert asks.

She turns to Donald. "My son has a poor grasp of reality," she says in a confidential tone. "He overextends his bounds."

"Only in little things," Albert says. "Insofar as great issues are concerned, I know my place."

"Are you coming to dinner?" his mom says. "I'm making Tou Goo Gai Kew."

"My mom has taken up Chinese cooking," Albert tells Donald.

"I've *taken* Chinese cooking," his mom says. "Now I'm taking *advanced* Chinese cooking." Albert wonders what lies in store for him at seventy-five. Lately he has the feeling that he is not so much pursuing his destiny as furiously racing alongside it, the way cars race trains in old movies.

After dinner, Albert settles into his dad's chair at one end of the living room; his mom and dad draw up bridge chairs. While his mom tells him she is thinking of having his comforter restuffed, Albert looks past her at the bookcase at the other end of the room, where a large photograph of him and Violet embracing beneath the pines in Wellfleet is propped, and discovers he has his arms around Shakespeare. A *Hamlet* paperback has been placed to obliterate Violet, the Droeshout portrait on the cover coinciding with her hidden face.

"While I'm at it," his mom is saying, "I'm going to have it re-covered, but definitely not in satin."

"What's wrong with satin?" his dad asks.

"Satin is slithery. Don't you find it slithers off, Albert?"

"Slides," says his dad, compulsively hitching a trouser leg. " 'Slithers' implies volition."

"Your dad is always squelching me, but he can't snuff out my artistic flame. Don't you find it slips off, Albert?"

"I don't mind," says Albert, regarding Shakespeare and himself—Shakespeare somewhat quizzical, as though having second thoughts about their collaboration, he with a lunatic grin. "It gives me something to do in the middle of the night."

"Whatever do you mean?" his mom asks.

"Groping for the comforter. It's almost as though it's some vast, rudimentary invertebrate, which, no matter how assiduously trained, instinctively seeks its natural habitat on the floor when its master is asleep."

"Cotton," his mom pronounces, biting into an after-dinner mint.

"What about cotton?" his dad says.

"Cotton will put an end to all that."

"The way you've so neatly put an end to Violet?" Albert says, gesturing toward the bookshelf.

"Why should she be on display here?" his mom says. "She's not a part of our lives."

Albert reflects that nowadays he is barely part of his own life. It undeviatingly extends without seeming to require his presence. He plays a minor role, if any, like that of a page turner at a recital.

Not so much quizzical, Albert decides, reappraising Shakespeare, as speculative, as though Shakespeare were considering the disrepair of his own life; of course, it's hard to tell with gentiles. Or perhaps he was only listening to a pine warbler. High above, one was periodically singing, Albert recalls, rending their hearts, when the shutter fell.

Albert and the Human Dynamo take the noon balloon to Boston to see the sixth game of the World Series. In the Ritz, she says, "Which do you think is bigger, your whizzer or a World Series ticket?"

"I'd say it's a tossup," he says.

"I'd say you have delusions of grandeur."

"If I have any delusions," Albert says, "they are ones of insignificance."

"Not from there," the Human Dynamo says. "Come on, you've got to play fair."

"So my father has told me. Last night, while we were having Ton Goo Gai Kew, he said, 'You're fondling your silverware again. If you fondle it here where mother and I can overlook it or forgive you because you're our son, you'll fondle it when you're dining out where it will reflect falsely on your rearing.' "

"Let's face it, Albert, you just don't measure up."

"It wasn't a fair test. I digressed."

Albert and the Human Dynamo fly to L.A., rent a car, and drive into the dun hills above El Toro, where she will go to tennis camp while he reads *Historia Animalium* by the pool.

One afternoon she suddenly looms above his chaise in her tennis clothes, furiously weeping. He closes Aristotle on a finger and motions her to one side, because she is blocking his sun. "I thought the 'B's were doing the overhead between three and five," he says.

She glares at him, then stalks off toward the road that winds higher into the hills. He follows her progress. Now and then, she is hidden from view; each time she reappears, she is more remote, smaller. It is his wish that she should vanish altogether. What business has he seeing someone so young?

When she has been out of sight an hour, he goes to their unit. Opening the door, he hears her tearfully chanting, " 'Point with relaxed arm, chin up, hit ball in front of body, hit up and through ball, snap wrist . . .' " She is standing naked by the kitchenette counter, practicing overheads, and he is charmed anew.

"Don't cry," he says. "You're a darling girl."

"But I can't do overheads," she wails.

"Surely that's nothing to cry about."

"Don't Jewish people ever cry?"

"At the movies," he says, recalling that Violet used to accuse him of being afraid to succumb to his emotions except in the Greenwich or the Waverly.

By and by, they get on the bed. Lying sideways toward the end, Albert considers Aristotle's boar, which, in its declining years, "finding itself unable to accomplish the sexual commerce with due speed, and growing fatigued with the standing posture, will roll the sow over on the ground, and the pair will conclude the operation side by side of one another."

And, Albert concedes, at literary allusions as well.

The next week, Albert runs into Violet on his way to the laundromat and tells her about the comforter.

"I'll say one thing about that old puff," she says. "I spent many a night of our marriage sewing the panels where they were ripped. Like the Turks plastering over St. Sophia, your mother's striving to efface every last vestige of my artistry."

"I never saw you sewing it up."

"I did it when you were off on your trips, unable to sleep for fear the pool would be full of kids or that they were about to let the water out. Then, as now, you never spared a thought for me or your stepchildren."

"I did. I do. Yesterday, I brought each of you a bottle of multi-vitamins with minerals."

"Don't worry. We're not going to contribute to your load of moral accountability by dropping dead of scurvy. What have you got in that shopping bag—one of your perpetually ailing plants?"

"My laundry. But since you mention it, mushrooms are growing in my philodendrons."

"It's probably a consequence of the lugubrious atmosphere in which you live. Milton says you always look as if you're going to cry."

"Who's Milton?"

"He folds at the laundromat to put himself through N.Y.U. nights."

Albert finds Milton folding primrose facecloths in the back of the laundromat. "This here's a vast, untapped mine of the human comedy," he says, indicating the ranks of throbbing washers. "If you want to look into the heart of man, look at his laundry. A case in point. This particular customer's load invariably contains two bath towels—one his, one his old lady's. No hand towels, no facecloths; they don't use them. However, in this bundle spread out before me what do we find but *three* bath towels, *two* hand towels, *two* facecloths. Now, from long acquaintance with the customer's laundry, I know he's a reasonably fastidious dude, but for a while back what do we get for two weeks running but *one* bath towel minus the few feminine garments that aren't of delicate fabric construction that are customarily in the bundle. For the last couple of weeks, I'm folding the stuff you see before you minus the feminine garments per the previous two weeks.

"Now I'm going to give you the fruits of my protracted labors in the human vineyard. Since they dried themselves with individual bath towels, the *one* bath towel two weeks running indicates to me his old lady cut out on him. If it was for only a week, she's ten-twelve to be in Jersey, visiting her mother. For two weeks he's a lost soul, going to Jefferson to buy a nice piece of haddock for dinner, watching a little Channel 13, take half a Valium, and so to bed. Time passes, and in accordance with the great cycle of nature, life begins anew. He starts calling up chicks from days of yore. To make a long story short: *three* bath towels, *two* hand towels, *two* facecloths."

"And me and Violet?"

"A painful case. I can't help recollecting how you used to lug in those big five-dollar, six-dollar loads. Now the two of you show up with these dainty little bundles. Albert, after folding someone's stuff week after week you get a certain rapport going with the garments, a very warm, personal feeling. Those items originally came in here together, Albert, and they belong together. Whenever it's humanly possible, I throw yours and Violet's in the same machine. It gives me good vibes to see them being agitated en masse in the wash cycle, tumbling amongst one another in the dryer's warm embrace."

Albert finds himself looking into one of the dryers. Behind the glass door, clothes appear and reappear, seemingly striving with death-defying leaps to reach an unattainable objective: to be something more exalted than garments, Albert guesses. He recalls the long hairs, so reminiscent of Violet's, that from time to time he would find coiled upon his underwear when he was putting his laundry away, and how their presence posed a tender mystery he never attempted to solve or charge with meaning, wary of the trap of Keats's egotistical sublime. A narrow escape, since they could well have been hers.

"Now more are out," Albert tells Mills in the Eighth Street Marboro. Heads down, they had been slowly circling the long table of dollar remainders, Mills clockwise, Albert counterclockwise, and gently collided. "Four in the chandelier, both coach lamps."

"Words, Albert, words," Mills says.

"Near darkness," Albert says.

Mills flips open a book. "I'm talking about *these*. All of them jammed in there. And there and there. We've been overrun with words, Albert. We're repeating ourselves."

"Dr. Johnson approved of the superfoetation of the press," Albert says.

"A man could still hope to read everything then. Now what do we have? Word pollution!" Mills slams the book shut, as though stemming the tide.

Albert says, "I once read about a prisoner who wanted to write a book but had nothing upon which to write it except the pages of a book, so he wrote in the spaces between the lines of print. This is interesting, but odd. On the face of it, one would more likely have paper than a pen or pencil. There are more sheets of paper in the world than writing instruments."

"Whether at a given time there are more blank sheets than ones densely covered with writing is problematical," Mills says.

"Besides," Albert says, "you would need an awful lot of pencils to write a book, and if you had access to a steady supply, it would seem that you could obtain writing paper, as well."

"To a lesser degree the same holds for ballpoints or ink for fountain or steel pens," Mills says.

"It could be, of course, that the prisoner wrote his book with, say, the bristles from his toothbrush dipped in his life's blood," Albert says.

"How much blood do you think it would take to write a decent-sized book?" Mills asks. "More than the five quarts in the human body?"

"Now, suppose the book he is so laboriously interlineating is one he himself wrote," Albert says. "Suppose further that it is autobiographical, as is the work in progress. In this case, he must resist the temptation to revise and amend his published volume, for if he does so at all extensively he will run out of room in which to write the new book. And being daily faced with the expression of old wastes, slack, and follies, his imperfect art like blighted acanthus leaves embellishing them, he must remember to turn aside when overcome, so that his tears don't dissolve what he has just written."

"We are in agreement then that his writing in pencil is farfetched," Mills says.

They decide to walk home together. It is evening, the air the blue of a black duck's speculum. On the way, Albert says, "To take it a step further, I have unresistingly become the prisoner of my own life. I have watched it close in, confine me, become as drab, uniform, and unyielding as the walls of a cell."

"Though conventionally narrow, the cell is immeasurably long," Mills says, "so from where you sit you cannot see either end."

"It is as though the book of my life were already written on an immense scroll in two crenellated lines of type, which immure me," Albert says.

"Prisoners traditionally write on the walls of their cells to those—or for those—who will come after them," Mills says. "If a prisoner were told that after he was executed his cell would be demolished, would he still write on the walls?"

"Yes, because he wouldn't believe them."

"That they were going to pull down his cell or that they were going to put him to death?"

Climbing the stoop, contemplating the lifeless coach lamps, Albert adds, "Insofar as I am imprisoned in the book of my life, which I am told will end (as I was told it began), I am, in effect, writing on the walls of my cell—merely, and compulsively, explicating my own text."

Mills opens the door. "Lenin exhorted, 'Ceaselessly explain,' " he says.

Flinging up an arm, like one of the beseeching figures in Titian's "Adoration," to draw Mills's attention to the chandelier, Albert cries out in the murky vestibule, "The public areas are your responsibility."

"And Ovid said," Mills goes on, " '*Scripta ferunt annos.*'"

Albert is awakened by the crash. At first, he imagines it is the shutter falling in the woods in Wellfleet; next, Mills slamming the book shut in Marboro.

"What happened?"

The question is as alarming as the crash. Once more Albert reaches out in the dark, reflecting that, having attained an age when his surroundings should be depressingly familiar, he seems increasingly to be feeling his way, whether toward momentous swimming pools or overmastering lilacs. And once again he encounters another man's wife.

He strives to look into the little bedroom, but he cannot see over the brow of the re-covered comforter, which, steadfast, folded in four, looms at the foot of the bed.

"Will you excuse me?" Albert says, getting up and heading into the little bedroom in his bare feet. He unexpectedly steps on earth. He crouches in the dark, fingering the damp soil, the cold fragments of the broken pot, the papery fronds. Extending a hand, he locates the pedestal table lying on its side, the place where one of the legs had snapped off. He must have set the pot down off center, and its unfailingly surprising weight, augmented by solicitous waterings, caused the leg to give way.

"What happened?" she says, crouching beside him, so that as he in turn picks up and lets drop the dirt, the shards, the fronds, he finds himself occasionally lifting her tumbling hair as though she, too, has come to grief.

"Shouldn't we stick it in something, or something?" she says.

A naked man and woman, Albert muses, huddled over a dying fern in the middle of the night as though re-enacting some ancestral sorrow—it's ten-twelve this affecting tableau has not been seen in New York since the turn of the century, when such affecting representations were more prevalent.

He dusts off his hands and rises. How quickly remorse is replaced by a sense of relief. Violet, his stepchildren, Josh, now the fern—one more thing he won't be encumbered by, have to take care of, be responsible for. Why is Violet weeping? When will Emily unlock her door? Is it true Barney put Josh in the refrigerator? Are the tips of the fronds dying in consequence of the great cycle of nature or because he is over-watering—or not watering enough? All that remains between him and seclusion, Albert realizes, are the philodendrons and the mushrooms.

"Oh, my God, what's that?" she says, having got up and bumped into what appears to be a severely stunted live oak festooned with Spanish moss. It is Albert's clothes dryer draped with socks. "Oh, it's a clothes dryer."

"Actually, it's a calendar," Albert says. "When I hang my socks up to dry, I count them and divide by two to discover how many days have gone by since I last washed them. Inevitably, more time has passed—or time has passed more quickly, I'm not sure it's the same thing—than I realized. A forcible reminder of the impermanence of our earthly mansions. By the same token, the Aztec Sun Stone, which archeologists believe to be a calendar, is in reality half of a giant waffle iron used on certain ceremonial occasions—the other half, which would make its purpose clear, being still unearthed."

So, too, Albert acknowledges, that while water, air, finally earth—or, everlastingly, fire—delineate us, we are molded and stamped by our responsibilities. The prospect of growing old among furled irises, raisinless bread, and slowly drying socks brings tears to Albert's eyes, which the other man's wife fails to detect, for Albert is now lying on the very edge of the bed—a habit he got into when he was married; that way, he could sleep with a hand on Josh's back to comfort him if he had bad dreams or awoke believing they had all gone away and left him.

After making sure she is asleep, Albert calls Violet.

"I just wanted to let you know that my life has become palindromic."

"Who am I speaking to?" Violet says.

"You are speaking to Albert, who is afraid his life makes as much sense backward as forward."

"Or as little," Violet says.

Because he has a lunch date, Albert goes to the Y before work instead of at noon and finds the pool full of old men and women—none, apparently, under seventy. They are swimming so slowly and in so many directions that he gets the impression they aren't making any progress, or, collaterally, that they have no destinations but are merely rocking back and forth like boats at their moorings. Like appalled Dante, Albert stares down at them from the deck. Except for the sound of an occasional wavelet breaking over the gutter, the pool is preternaturally silent; the swimmers' faces are composed, serene, their strokes and kicks so feeble or languorous they seem barely sufficient to keep them afloat.

"Do you get this bunch every morning?" Albert asks the lifeguard.

"From eight to twelve. Senior Citizens' A.M. Swim."

Taking note of the hours, Albert returns to the locker room; he will lower himself in at the shallow end twenty-five years hence.

Albert says, "Do gentile people always skip when they read?" He is unpacking, traipsing back and forth between the suitcase and the dresser, carrying a shirt or a little pile of underwear, as though putting away the costumes after another unsatisfactory performance of his life. The Human Dynamo is lying on her back on Albert's bed, holding an open book above her head, letting the pages slip one after another from under her right thumb, her arms uplifted, as were Michelangelo's on his scaffold and, as Walter Benjamin pointed out, Proust's upon his sickbed while holding his pages in the air. When Jews open a book, Albert reflects, they resolve—are condemned—to read every word. But the mind strays, being susceptible to such questions as why every now and again an odd number of socks graces the clothes dryer and why it is that no other creature except man can recall the past at will.

8

In the preface to *The Tragic Muse,* Henry James says that all we see of the artist in triumph "is the back he turns to us as he bends over his work." But what is our view of him in anything less than that state . . . ?

Albert lubricates the male ferrule with sebum from the side of his nose, and puts his spinning rod together. He fits the reel foot into the rod seat, twists the retainer rings and screws them down tight. Then he strips out the seventeen-pound test mono, gently threads it through the guides, and checks the line for frays and nicks. He slips the line through a one-ounce egg sinker and the eye of a snap swivel, twists it five times, passes it through the loop formed by the first twist, and draws it tight. Next he opens the swivel and slips the snell loop of a wire-snelled 7/0 long-shank bluefish hook into the swivel and snaps it shut. He fixes the hook in an envelope upon which "Compliments of Mr. Al E. Mohny" is written and goes to his bedroom window. Opening the bail, he lowers the rig into the garden three stories below, where Violet is sitting with Skippy Mountjoy.

Paying out the line, Albert reflects on the contingencies awaiting all of us. For example, having recently purchased his first pair of reading glasses, he discovered the other night that he had inadvertently worn them while masturbating.

When she has calmed down, the Human Dynamo declares that the only conceivable reason Albert told Violet the garden apartment was available was that he had run out of material. She tells this to him on the telephone toward the end of a long, heroic, even Wagnerian conversation. Because the Human Dynamo lives in New Canaan and Albert in New York, they talk on the phone nearly every night, largely about what she had for dinner and whether he needs to bring bread.

In the winter, Albert visits the Human Dynamo Wednesdays, because she skis weekends; in the summer, he visits her Saturdays, because on weekdays she plays tennis after work until it is too dark to see the ball. When he tells her their relationship is absurd, she says, "Why don't you take up tennis [or skiing], so we could have fun together?" Do you know Donatello's "Dead Christ with Angels"? One of the piteous, attending cherubs has clapped a chubby hand to its cheek—nowadays, curiously, a gesture associated with Jewish people, as the Human Dynamo calls us. This is Albert's attitude when he is told he should take up tennis (or skiing) at forty-six.

Because the Human Dynamo doesn't eat bread, she considers it extravagant to buy a whole loaf so Albert can have toast for breakfast on Thursday (winter) or Sunday (summer). If she goes to her parents for dinner, she filches a slice for him; otherwise, he has to bring one with him on the train, wrapping it in foil and slipping it into his jacket pocket.

Like other clandestine acts, carrying a concealed slice of bread is to a degree thrilling, and invests the bearer with a sense of mission, self-importance, and romance. Returning to his office from the Y one Wednesday afternoon, Albert reckons he may be the only person walking the streets of New York with a slice of Sprouted Wheat in his pocket. Chances are that at that very moment more bombs are being conveyed in this fashion, and with the terrorist, Albert shares the unendurable need to let someone in on the secret.

"Excuse me, sir. Perhaps you've noticed this slight bulge in my pocket. Pat it for a moment and see if you can guess what I have in here?"

"A paperback?"

"No."

"An eight-track of The Grateful Dead?"

"Uh-uh."

"A very small ant farm?"

When Albert informs the Human Dynamo that as a consequence of reminding him to bring bread or, for example, asking him to solve such moral dilemmas as whether she has the right to insist that Kurt, a BMW dealer and former beau with whom she is dickering for a new car, throw in cocoa mats, his phone bills are averaging more than a hundred dollars a month, she says, "I'm worth it. You give *her* five hundred dollars a month."

Albert also gives Violet his dying quince. Unlike the alimony checks, he doesn't lower the branches from his window on fishing line, but carefully carries them downstairs, avoiding the sprinkler system, as though he were participating in a multi-level production of *Macbeth*, so they won't shed petals all over the runners. Violet has told him she can't afford fresh flowers because her lawyer let Albert's lawyer—his father, *her* ex-father-in-law—put one over by not taking into account the fact that she has to pay taxes on her alimony, so that instead of getting five hundred a month, she only gets two hundred and eighty-three dollars and thirty-three cents. Whatever, Albert recalls that when he was married to her, the apartment was full of moribund chrysanthemums and asters standing in dark, faintly fetid water. Albert often wondered why she didn't get rid of them. Was it because of neglect or because of a yearning for the wild, rank, and tangled associated with her rural upbringing? "Willows, old rotten planks, slimy posts and brickwork, I love such things." Constable was another such fancier.

Once Albert threw out several boughs that were so ancient they had come to resemble antlers, being covered with a velvet-like growth. When Violet learned what he had done, she burst into tears; the branches were from the magnolia that grew beside the house in which she had been born, and she had broken them off for a memento when it was put up for sale. Their marriage had been characterized by such sensational episodes, as had that of her parents. Following Violet's appearance on the kitchen table, upon which stage her nine older brothers and sisters had previously made their entrances, the midwife, piqued that Violet's father had been so heedless as to make his wife suffer through ten pregnancies one after the other, thrust the afterbirth at him, which he flung in the fireplace. Albert has tried to imagine what *his* dad's reaction would have been if he had been handed his, Albert's, afterbirth.

To make up for putting the magnolia down the incinerator, Albert bought Violet a print of a sprig of small magnolia, or white bay. This now hangs with other floral prints above her bed. Whenever Albert comes bearing his old quince—or, at other seasons, forsythia, dogwood, pendulous, ashen lilacs—and puts the branches in a vase by her fireplace, Scotch-taping them to the mantelpiece so they won't tip the vase over, he notices anew that the prints are hanging crooked. This disarray is especially poignant. When he and Violet were married, he kept the pictures straight; now their obliquity seems to him symbolic of her inability to cope without him and gives rise to tender sentiments, though she might very well be unaware that the prints are dazzlingly crooked, considering rectitude unimportant.

This last reflection gives Albert pause. He visualizes himself going critically about his apartment, nudging prints of walruses, flounders, and orioles into line; making sure the telephone sits squarely on the telephone table, but a little off center to improve the composition; and arranging the overlapping magazines on the coffee table so that they describe a gentle, jagged arc. In the right angles he recognizes his dad's influence, in the curves his mom's.

During the eleven years of his marriage, Albert tried to instill in his stepchildren this sense of order and fitness, this artistic vision, if you will. He believes he had failed, as he had in inculcating his store of practical and moral precepts, until the other evening when Emily, who is now twenty-three, came to dinner. While waiting for her ice cream "to turn to mush," she wandered about the living room. "Your dictionary is open to 'p,' " she suddenly announced. Although her tone was gloating, Albert had the impulse to take her in his arms. How many times had he told her and Barney to leave the dictionary open to "m" after looking something up? *It had sunk in*! Solicitously kneading her ice cream with a tablespoon, which keeps getting bent out of shape, so that he has to keep straightening it (surely a parallel can be drawn with the examined life), Albert recalls his dad's explanation, which he had automatically passed on—what did he know of physics?—that the spine would be ruined if the dictionary was left open to any letter other than "m," especially those at the beginning or end of the alphabet. *Ruined*! How often his dad had invoked that fate, whether in respect to Albert's posture as a result of slouching about all over the place, or to the chairs he insisted on tipping back at the dinner table.

Albert goes over to the dictionary and clutches it with both hands, his left thumb on the page headed "Mainstay," his right on the one headed "Make," the fingers of his left hand on "Collegium," those of his right on "Tortive," as though passionately grasping two hanks of hair to force a lover's head closer or, as he had done years ago, to fling his disobedient stepdaughter from him.

Albert stands before the dictionary, shaking it, as if once and for all to put his dad's theory to the test or to punish the words, to scatter them into unintelligibility for failing to serve him, for not bending to his will—or to express his ardor for them.

It has been said that words are stones, compact and uncompromising, picked up from civilization's communal rubble, hacked out of its great, repetitive designs; it has been said that words are bright, lightly tossing buoys, marking definitions lying far below. In the first case, writing is like building a wall; in the second, it is a series of deep, baffling dives. And it has been said that words butter no parsnips.

"What are you doing?" Emily says apprehensively.

What *is* he doing? Albert releases his hold and smooths out the pages, as though the dictionary were a pillow upon which he would later gratefully lay his head.

But I left Albert fishing from the window. Surely, no angler will have better luck. It is gusty, darkening, early spring. The air through which the white envelope—addresser Mr. Al E. Mohny—flutters down is palest lavender, the color, Albert recalls from his life with Violet, that cornflowers turn if they're not thrown out. She and Skippy are seated at a glass-topped table, in which overarching California privet is reflected, the images of the tossing branches more tempestuous than their actual counterparts, either because they are concentrated, like a stormy sea funneled against rocks, or because an image is in a sense art, which heightens. Drinking iced tea, Violet and Skippy are unaware of the descending envelope, now hovering ominously a few feet above their heads.

As Skippy begins laughing—immoderate laughter that from time to time awakens Albert in the middle of the night—the telephone rings. Albert turns the reel handle to snap the bail shut, lays the rod on the floor, and answers the phone. It's the Human Dynamo, who left the courts early on account of the wind. "Should I name my car 'Yogurt'?" she says.

She explains that she is going to register her new BMW in Vermont so she won't have to pay the local property tax, and is thinking of getting vanity plates.

"It can't be more than six characters."

"Have you considered anything else?"

" 'Sundae,' 'Banana,' 'Raisin,' 'Gopher,' 'Muffin.' "

"Does it have to be comestible or small and furry?"

" 'Squeak,' 'Oh Wow,' 'Breezy.' What do you think, Albie?"

"I think we ought to get a WATS line."

"No, *really*."

"I *really* think you should call it 'Virtue,' after your age."

"Huh?"

"The ancients regarded twenty-eight as the perfect number because it equals the sum of all its divisors and therefore signifies virtue. I think a good many motorists would find it uplifting."

"Do you think you're too old for me?"

"I think I'm too old for myself," Albert says, imagining driving along the South Dixie Highway in the prolonged summer twilight, his plates emblazoned MISERY or CRISIS or SORROW.

After he's hung up, Albert returns to the window and begins reeling in. By then it is dark, the wind has died; Violet and Skippy are either sitting quietly under the privet or have gone inside. Albert has the impression that while he was on the phone, line had been taken out and that he is fishing in an abyss. What had he expected to catch? To what use could he put a fragment of the past? Aubrey wrote of seeing a mower using an arm off the monument of a lord in a ruined abbey nearby to whet his scythe.

"While preparing my income tax," Albert's dad, who is now eighty, says, "I was made aware of a haunting fragrance."

"I think 'haunting' is too theatrical for daisies," Albert's mom says, biting into a brownie, "Jasmine. Frangipani—"

"I think 'was made' is too literary, particularly for the Upper West Side," Albert says. "What's wrong with 'became'? I became aware—"

"I have become aware that I am surrounded by *petit stinquers*," his dad says, frenchifying, his habit in a tight spot.

Albert is having dinner at his parents', which he does every Friday.

"At any rate," his dad goes on, "the fragrance unexpectedly wafted across my calculations. I looked up, puzzled. It was—" He indicates the daisies, which, with an arrangement of gourds, make up the centerpiece. "It was evocative."

Albert waits for him to say of what, but his dad's lips are compressed. He turns to his mom to see if there is a secret and she shares it. She, too, is looking at him expectantly. Albert detects that she is on the verge of smiling, but is unsure whether it would be appropriate. In the moments in which his dad is apparently dwelling on the evocation the scent of daisies gave rise to and his mom is evidently trying to again come to terms with the fact that the man to whom she has been married for more than fifty years has memories of idyllic interludes from which she is forever excluded, Albert recalls reeling in his line until the bare hook appeared above the sill.

"Jake's coming back," he announces to change the subject.

"Jake?" his mom says.

"Josh's litter brother," Albert says.

"They're those dogs," his dad says to his mother.

Shortly after they were married, Albert and Violet had bought two dachshund puppies, Josh and Jake. When they were four, Jake inexplicably began attacking Josh. Albert and Violet decided they would have to separate them, and advertised to find a new home for Jake. The ad was answered by a childless couple named White. Albert took Jake in a taxi to their apartment in the West Eighties, in which rows of nearly identical cacti were set out beneath indistinct landscapes featuring morose cows. Albert showed Mr. White, a short man with a frequent, perhaps facetious laugh, how to clean Jake's ears; he hadn't seen him since. Josh now lived with Violet, as I've mentioned. In the morning, when Albert went for the *Times*, he took Josh along, forgotten down by his ankles; when he delivered his withering bouquets, he would dandle him on his knees, like the infant he never had, contemplating the graying muzzle, preposterous in this context, scarred by Jake's teeth: part dog, part child, part god.

"I began to have pangs," Albert tells his parents. "I felt I had cast Jake out of my life, disposed of him. I wanted to see him again before he died. I called the Whites up. Dialing, I had a premonition I would be too late. Mrs. White answered. 'How's that 'ittle doggie doin' after all these years?' I said. 'He's fine,' she said. 'He was a great comfort to Mr. White at the end.' It turned out the 'ittle hubbie had died three years ago. I didn't know what to say. I was entranced by the irony. The upshot is she's going to Corfu for ten days and would be delighted to have Jake visit me while she's away."

"For the life of me, I don't know why you go out of your way to encumber yourself," his mom says.

"You persist in dwelling in the past," his dad says.

"Installing Violet right under your feet," his mom says. "How are you ever to go forward?"

"I seem to be swept along," Albert says. "I'm going to be in *Who's Who*."

"In the Northeast?" his dad says. "I'm in the Northeast. *Who's Who in the Northeast*. I've been in there for ages."

"*In America*," Albert says, feeling that it may be an uncharitable remark.

"I'm in the morgue," his dad says.

"I'm in the morgue, too," his mom says.

Albert envisages the two slim manila envelopes of brittle, yellowing clippings nestled side by side in a filing cabinet, closer than their subjects are in life.

"I'm clearing the decks," Albert's dad says abruptly, rising, as though realizing that in weighing his accomplishments he had kept his thumb on the scale and that there is no time to lose if he wants to swell his envelope. He begins scooping up plates.

"I'll do it," Albert's mom says, also rising.

They face each other warily across the littered table like wrestlers before a match.

"I'm restoring some order," his dad says.

"You're terrible," his mom says.

"You're the second person who's called me that today."

"Who was the first?" she says.

"Albert's Violet."

"I never—"

"I was riding the down escalator at the bank, when I noticed her rising toward me on the up escalator. I greeted her. 'You're a terrible man,' she said."

"I never—"

"I wanted to ask her what she meant, but we were rapidly drawing apart. When I reached the bottom I got on the up escalator. When I reached the top she had vanished. Albert, do you have any idea what she meant?"

"The tax on the alimony, probably."

"But she was represented."

"I never—"

"Please sit down," Albert says. "*I'm* going to clear the table."

"Do you think I'm terrible?" his dad asks, slowly lowering himself, reaching behind with one hand, as though uncertain whether his chair might have been whisked away, that his life might have turned out to be some sort of practical joke.

"Violet tends to divide people into friendlies and hostiles," Albert says. "I believe it has to do with coming from a large family where you had to fight for hind teat." Once again he imagines his dad, a young man not unlike himself at thirty-three, but appalled, not knowing what to do with his, Albert's, afterbirth.

"It's not your dad's fault that she didn't have better representation," Albert's mom says.

Albert collects the teacups and heads for the kitchen.

"Don't dispose of the lemon," his dad sings out. "There are one or two squeezes left."

"Why don't you take more dishes with you?" his mom calls after him. "Then you won't have to make so many trips."

Pushing open the swinging door, Albert thinks: But I want to keep going back and forth; that way I can postpone whatever is going to happen next: e.g., that the last of the argyle socks Violet bought him during the course of their marriage and sedulously darned would get a hole in it and he would have to throw it out. Albert thinks of himself as a balloon, whose mooring lines are being cast off one by one, so that one day he will unexpectedly, fearfully, stately rise.

Returning from his parents, Albert runs into Skippy Mountjoy walking Josh.

"What was the blue-plate special tonight?" Skippy asks, falling in alongside him. "Roast capon or brisket?"

"Know my every move, don't you, Skippy?"

"Josh clues me. Dog's very deep. Ver-ry deep. Ver-ry 'ittle gets by 'ittle Josh. Fridays Mom and Dad, Saturdays Human Dynamo, except in the winter when it's Wednesdays and the Knicks are Saturdays, as well as Tuesdays, when they're at home. Josh tells me Jake's coming for a visit. Think they'll mix it up?"

"No. Jake was always the aggressor. I'm convinced it had to do with territory. Josh never had a sense of territory. Besides, the territory no longer exists."

"Care to draw any parallels vis-à-vis you, me, and Violet?"

"Only if you do, Skippy."

"Oh, no, I pass. Never touch the stuff. More in your line— analogizing, metaphorizing. No izing on my cake. Right, Josh? Dog's got unimagined depths. You, you've got imagined depths. Right, Albie? Surface another story."

They pass beneath the sycamores that border the sidewalk at intervals, treading on the fretted shadows of their foliage. Albert has the impression the shadows are duckweed and that they are walking on water.

"What do you mean?"

"You're in a rut."

"I'm not in a rut, Skippy. I lead a contrived life."

"V8, schav, three-quarters of a pound of ground round, Sprouted Wheat and applesauce every night is a poor contrivance, then. Allow me to give you my recipe for red-wine court bouillon."

They have reached the gate to the three steps leading to Violet's apartment. Skippy unlatches it and Josh bounds down. Albert turns to climb the stoop. Taking out his keys, he tells Skippy, "Send it up on the line sometime."

As he approaches his landing, Albert hears his telephone ringing. He pounds up the remaining stairs, unlocks the door, and runs for the phone.

"It's me." It's the Human Dynamo.

"Yes, what is it?" Albert says, out of breath.

"Oh, Albert, a bird pooped on my new car."

When Albert gets into bed, he puts on his glasses, but doesn't read. Instead, he wonders whether by nature the contrived life precludes what were once called "the good parts"; e.g., "This book has a lot of good parts" or "Did you get to the good parts yet?" If he puts a quarter in a Times Square peep show, invariably an innocuous segment of the loop appears; a blonde and a brunette in a convertible driving along a palm-lined street, making little *moues* as they try to find the house where the mixed foursome will take place. Albert is almost convinced that no matter how many quarters he spends, he will never get to see the good parts, that in episode after episode the girls will continue to circle through the streets, becoming more and more fretful—the acting here godawful—at their inability to find the right address, that it will gradually become dark, the lights come on, the girls' eyes, the convertible gleaming lustrously beneath the palms. . . .

Albert takes off his glasses and folds the earpieces. They make two little clicks when they strike the frames. He is charmed by the sound. What a satisfactory way to denote the conclusion of yet another day, like the detonation of a remote sunset gun. To think that until recently his days ended unceremoniously. In a sense, these minute, faintly melancholy salutes constitute good parts, too, he supposes.

Several hours later, Albert's bedroom door opens. The light from the landing discloses a little boy of two or so. He is wearing a brown velveteen suit. A spray of quince and leather-leaf fern is pinned to his lapel. He makes a hieratic sign. "Behold," he says, "I show you a mystery." As he totters toward the bed, Albert sees that his eyes are red, glowing, like a dog's in a flash photograph.

"Jakie!"

Extending his arms, Albert recalls walking him and Josh, how they vibrantly anchored him to the ground, gave him a sense of place and intention.

The next morning, Albert is awakened by the phone.

"It's me." It's Violet.

"Yes, what is it?"

"Oh, Albert, a squirrel's eating my babies'-breath."

"It has been said that the greatest single discovery in the history of thought is the invention of a symbol for nought," Albert says. He is sitting at Violet's desk, writing out her alimony check. "It would make a nice couplet, if I worked at it."

"We would've made a nice couple if you had worked at it," Violet says, Scotch-taping to her mantlepiece the quince he brought downstairs. She steps back to examine her handiwork. As if on cue, a few pink petals flutter pathetically to the hearth. "And if it's such a great invention, why don't you add another to the check?"

"I hear you passed my dad on an escalator and called him a terrible man," Albert says, taking off his shoes and climbing up on Violet's bed.

"Because he is."

Albert straightens the floral prints above her pillows, then begins jumping up and down on the bed.

"Violet, do I look like a high-bouncing ex-lover?"

"You look like someone who has shafted me."

"I'll set up an appointment for you with my accountant. Maybe he can scheme up some deductions."

"Timmmberrrr!" Violet cries.

On the way up, Albert sees the Scotch tape ripping loose, the quince going over. He springs off the bed, catching the branches before they bring the vase down. The last of the blossoms litter the hearth.

" 'In a drear-nighted December,'" Albert quotes, picking them up, "Too happy, happy tree / Thy branches ne'er remember / Their green felicity.' I have to go."

"It's Saturday, isn't it?"

"I'm catching the five-oh-five."

"Don't go. When you're here, I think of you up there. It's like you're sitting on my head. When you're away, I have no top."

"But it's Saturday."

He backs toward the door, the blossoms filling his cupped palms, not knowing where to put them.

"Albert," Violet says, holding out her hands, "why don't you take up bowling so we can have fun together?"

He gently tips the petals into her hands.

Albert hears the telephone ringing as he climbs the stairs.

"It's me." It's the Human Dynamo. She's sobbing.

"What's wrong?"

"The form came from the Vermont Motor Vehicle Bureau."

"And—"

"And Albie, it says you're only allowed to have *five* characters."

"And—"

"And all I can think of is 'Peach.' I had such good names for my car."

"We'll discuss it at dinner."

"Don't forget to bring bread."

On the five-oh-five he reinvisages the South Dixie Highway at twilight. This time his plates bear ENNUI, GUILT. A few miles beyond Port Chester, the train comes to a halt. Five or ten minutes pass and there is still no announcement about pantographs or stalled trains ahead. Then the doors slide open. Several passengers, Albert among them, jump to the ground and walk forward along the roadbed. It is a mild, clear evening. The engineer and the conductors are standing in front of the head car, gazing down. Joining them, Albert sees that they are at the rim of a vast abyss. Its interior is largely in shadow, the very depths filled with a bluish haze out of which protrude vividly colored eminences of sandstone and shale, suggesting minarets, turrets, steeples, spires. Albert pictures the Human Dynamo waiting forlornly at the station in her new BMW. If he can descend into the abyss and then scale the other side, he can get a cab at Greenwich.

He lowers himself over the edge and plunges down a rocky slope. After he has gone a way, he looks back. He can no longer see the rim. Raising his eyes higher, as though contemplating a Tiepolo ceiling, he descries not whirling, apotheosizing figures but a cloudless sky being drained of light. He continues picking his way down; on the more level stretches the little evening primrose *Oenothera pterosperma* displays its pink blossoms. My life has been one long interruption, he muses, between what I intended to do and what I never got around to doing. While composing "Intimations," Wordsworth was interrupted by the arrival of Mr. Olliff's load of dung, and went to work in the garden. But he finished it.

Slipping and sliding on the scree in his suède loafers, Albert loses his footing and fetches up against a hoodoo. Brushing himself off, he discovers he is carrying something in his jacket pocket. What does he have in there? A pack of cigars? A bundle of love letters? A well-folded Speedo swimsuit? He fishes out the object and unwraps it. For some unfathomable reason, a slice of bread.

9

Albert once knew a woman who designed women's gloves. Paper cutouts of hands—left or right, he couldn't tell which; either sufficed—were strewn throughout her apartment. At another time, he went with a woman who did illustrations for advertisements of women's shoes. Her apartment was littered with shoes—one of a kind, left or right; she had no need for pairs. While Albert was married, the apartment in which he and Violet lived was awash with tears. Like subatomic particles whose existence is confirmed by photographs of their tracks, the fugitive existence of these tears was often made evident to Albert only by the rapidly drying streaks on his wife's cheeks. The tears, he noted, had trickled from her left eye as well as her right. "Being married to you," she once told him, "you need both barrels."

Albert and Violet have been separated for three years. During the first two, her tears had dried up, the transeunt cause, himself, having been removed, although not very far. Indeed, separation is a particularly apt word to describe their situation, Albert living, as I have previously noted, on the third, and top, floor, Violet in the garden apartment.

From his bedroom window Albert can look down into the garden, which he has paid a young man who hoped to serve mankind by combining ecology with the law to do over, as Violet's forty-eighth-birthday present. This humanitarian cut back the privet and planted Hosta beneath it, uprooted a large ailanthus in favor of a crab apple, and put in a bed of annuals, a border of day lilies, a rosebush that never leafed, much less budded, and, at Violet's insistence, several tomato plants. He told her these were going to be very iffy, because the garden got so little sun, but Violet was adamant. The great contending themes of her life were a yearning for her rustic upbringing and *nostalgie de la boue*; in this case the former held sway.

As predicted, the tomato plants fared poorly; further, they were ravaged by squirrels. Skippy Mountjoy, who came by to work on his sonnet sequence under the privet, enclosed the plants with chicken wire, but the squirrels swarmed up and over the netting. He then laid a heavy cardboard poster of Dürer's "Feast of the Rose Garlands" on top of the wire enclosure. This kept the squirrels out but plunged the plants into near-total darkness.

As far as Albert can tell, the poster has never served a decorative purpose. Violet told him that when Barney was an infant it had been used as a gate to keep him from tumbling downstairs. While Albert was married to Violet, they had penned in Josh and Jake with it. Now, when Albert gazes out his bedroom window, what catches his eye is this weather-beaten *Rosenkranzbild*, resplendent with the roses the nearby bush never produced. The poster is askew, Skippy not having aligned it to be viewed from Albert's vantage.

Albert tells Violet on the phone one day, "If that thing's going to hit me in the eye every morning when I open the curtains, the least you can do is straighten it out."

"That's just like you," she says. "You're not satisfied having the world spread out at your feet, it has to be at right angles."

Notwithstanding, Albert shortly sees Violet go into the garden. "To the left!" he shouts out the window. "A little more. More. Too much. Back to the right. Hold it!"

Albert reflects that he and Violet are communicating at longer and longer range. While a few years ago they were murmuring in one another's ears, now they speak on the phone, shout out windows, leave notes for each other under the carpet in Unit 40 of the Sun 'n Sea Motel on Key Biscayne. Albert and Violet had honeymooned there fifteen years before and have often gone back since; now, of course, they go to Florida separately, but they cling to their old unit. When neither of them is there, Albert envisions solitary middle-aged men like himself doing push-ups on the carpet, spent lovers out-flung upon it as though they have fallen from great heights, the maids raking it to make the nap stand up, all unaware of the tender messages beneath them, and he is put in mind of the numberless generations of Anatolian herdsmen and charcoal burners who have gone about their business ignorant of the poems, correspondence, and bills of lading impressed into clay tablets that have lain buried for millennia under their feet.

At times, Albert stands by his open window at night, singing "Da-da-da." (According to the Human Dynamo, when Jewish people don't know the words to songs they go "da-da," while gentiles go "la-la." She is given to this kind of generalization. Violet is a generalizer, too, although of a different sort; e.g., "The reason you don't have any friends is that you don't really like people. You just like those parts of them that suit your purposes. Which is why all of us who became involved with you are maimed." Why is it, Albert thinks, that I, who never draw inferences, invariably wind up in the dark with my arms around women who make generalizations?)

Sometimes, as Albert stands and sings, the dark garden seems to him to be flooded, with just the topmost branches of the privet projecting from the water, and the blistered poster a raft upon which a desperate swimmer might try to haul himself, only to find it wouldn't support the weight of a child. A notion comes to him: except for those Bibles in which bullets become embedded, works of art don't save lives.

In the morning, as Albert looks down into the garden while waiting for Violet to answer the phone, it seems to have dwindled overnight, withered, as though time has suddenly tightened its grip, or that he is viewing it from higher up than the third story, from that fancied height which the imagined lovers he has envisioned on the motel carpet have cast themselves.

"Elite," Albert says when Violet picks up the receiver. This is short for Elite Dog-Walking Service and means that he is coming downstairs to walk Josh. Similarly, Skippy Mountjoy is the Acme Dog-Walking Service, or Acme, it being his pleasure to take Josh out between *abab* and *cdcd*.

One autumn morning, when Albert arrives to walk Josh, he becomes aware of a pungent, almost acrid odor he can't identify. Although not that of burning leaves, it correspondingly stirs the emotions, evoking pathetic feelings and a sense of impermanence—*lacrimae rerum*.

"What's cooking?" Albert asks Violet.

"Credit cards," she says from the bathroom.

Albert enters. She is sitting in the tub, in several inches of soapy water, dreamily shaving her legs; Josh is curled on the bathmat. She is rosy, and the water has a bluish tinge, the blue of infants' veins, and gently heaves with her motions. Vapor has condensed on the medicine-cabinet mirror, so that Albert can't find his reflection. The airport is closed in, the plane is in a holding pattern, and he is unable to see out the bleary window. During the last years of their marriage, this had seemed an appropriate metaphor, and, in a sense, he is still waiting for permission to land. Now the amplitude of gentle curves—Violet bending to her shins, Josh on the bathmat, the bell graph of his life—nearly brings him to tears.

"They're ashes," Violet says.

Ah! He recalls the four of them crowded about the stove, Barney and Emily taking turns holding an expired Master Charge in the flame, raptly watching it blacken, melt, blister, vanish. Families have these rites or ceremonies. Another of theirs had been the watering of the fern: the procession to the bathroom to "The Washington Post" march ("la-la"s from Violet, Emily, and Barney; "da-da"s from Albert); the lowering of the fern into the tub (all hum "Taps"); and the spraying. This last had been enhanced by manipulating the plastic sprayer so that it emitted an uncannily human moan, which sent the children into peals of laughter.

"I'm consolidating my position," Violet says.

"What?" He isn't paying attention. Despite their ministrations, the fern hadn't flourished. Like tea leaves in the bottom of a cup, adumbrating pinnules littered the tub. Kneeling before it after the others had borne the fern away, Albert devotedly gathered them up and, as his dad would say, disposed of them.

"They were too much of a temptation," Violet is saying. "I can't afford them anymore. American Express, Visa, Master Charge—I consigned them to the flames, as your father would say. How is your father, by the way? Is he still being oracular?"

"Yesterday he told me there were seventeen chairs in his proctologist's waiting room. I said, 'You counted them?' He said, 'I did.' 'But why?' 'It helped pass the time. Didn't I ever tell you about my propensity for enumerating?' I said he hadn't, and what else did he count? 'Members of orchestras,' he told me. I expressed my amazement, and was forced to reconsider all the time I had spent in his company. Untold occasions when he must have been secretly totting things up swam into view. 'There's a lot about me you don't know,' he said."

"But you," Violet says, "you're an open book, aren't you?"

Tugging Josh along Sixth Avenue, Albert tries to recall if he has ever represented himself that way. An open book is not like an open door or a disrobed woman; for all practical purposes, it discloses only two pages, a fraction of its contents, and the odds are against these being in themselves particularly revelatory—"the axe," as Kafka said, describing the proper function of books, "for the frozen sea inside us." Masturbatory practices aside, Albert wonders whether he leads a secret life. (The Human Dynamo once inquired of him whether, in fact, he even led what is commonly construed as a *life*. It was late at night and they were in Forest Hills, walking along a leafy, deserted street to her BMW, he having prevailed upon her to leave the stadium in the middle of the fourth set of an interminable baseline match between Vilas and Orantes that threatened to end at daybreak. It proved to be an unpopular move. "When was the last time you examined your motives?" she shrieked. "Have you ever considered the consequences of your acts? What is your guiding principle? Never to venture more than a hundred yards from a bathroom?" Albert didn't reply. He was concentrating on avoiding her handbag, which she was swinging at his head. He was a practiced hand, in his marriage to Violet having dodged hard rolls, tangerine sections, and a platter of linguine with white clam sauce.)

Shortly after Albert leaves Josh off and returns to his apartment,

he notices that Skippy is in the garden. The perspective is unsettling, like that of Raphael's "The Glorification of the Sacrament"
or Mantegna's "The Dead Christ," and brings to mind the view
from the roof of the dome of St. Peter's, to which he climbed years
ago. From there, the great statues of the saints—which, when looking up at them from below, he assumed to be erect—appeared, like
swimmers on the mark, to be on the verge of launching themselves
into the square. So much depends on one's vantage point, Albert
reflects—where you are standing. We rely on conventions, the way
things are supposed to be, for most of our understanding, and thus
tend to skip the hard parts—endeavoring to find hidden truths, to
elucidate mysteries, to recognize a cry for help; even the road to
self-knowledge becomes paved. In this respect, poets are no more
often seen from above than whales from below, until someone
wields Kafka's splintering axe.

Albert takes up the binoculars with which he watches birds,
and trains them on Skippy's notebook to see if he can make out
what he is writing. Albert reads: "The perusal of literary compositions across a state line, with intent to appropriate them for one's
own use, is a Federal offense, punishable by no less than . . ."

Withdrawing from the window, Albert goes to the bathroom.
Above the tub is a skylight. As though he is in the Pantheon or
Texas Stadium, a shaft of sunlight sometimes unexpectedly illu-
minates him while he is taking a shower, and he feels as if he is
being singled out . . . but for what? Lately, Albert has come to
the conclusion that if it is possible to absorb the unhappiness of
others, that will be the mission he will undertake. Like the old-
clothes man who in his youth trudged the streets, head expectantly uplifted, crying "Old clothes! Old clothes!" and retrieved the
bundles that housewives flung from the windows, he will cry out
"Sorrows! Sorrows!" and wait below with open arms.

"Fire!" a voice cries, awakening Albert and the Human Dynamo, who is sleeping over. He gets out of bed and rushes
downstairs. The vestibule seems to be ablaze, and a black youth
of sixteen or so is dancing wildly about the flames. When Albert
gets closer, he sees that what is burning is a stack of firewood that

Mills keeps behind the front door, and what the boy is doing is trying to grab some of the fiery logs so he can throw them onto the sidewalk. Albert joins in, but the flames are too intense; in addition, the wall against which the wood is stacked has caught fire. Recalling that the hose used to flush the sidewalk is hooked on the top rung of the ladder leading to the basement, Albert runs down the stoop, heaves open the basement doors, and passes the hose up to the boy. When the fire is out and the boy (was he a firebug?) gone, Albert turns to put the hose away and notices for the first time that the Human Dynamo is standing on the sidewalk. Alongside her, but somewhat apart, is Violet, wearing a robe that his mother had insisted on giving him but that he had had no use for; Skippy Mountjoy, dressed in an old raincoat of Albert's that Violet had altered and given to Skippy; and Josh, whose leash Skippy is holding. Looking down at them from the top of the stoop, Albert is struck by how short, even stumpy, Violet and Skippy are compared to the Human Dynamo and himself. It is almost as if they are members of a different race—one among which, like an anthropologist or missionary, he has dwelt but whose mysteries he hasn't penetrated; they are sharers in a tribal history from which he is excluded. His hand-me-downs seem to point up his own inadequacies; they wear them the way savages wear top hats—not for their civilizing effects but for panache.

They stand motionless, expressionless, staring at him, as though about to be photographed on the banks of a tributary of the Orinoco. Towering above them, Albert feels that something is expected of him. Again, what? To take notes? To forgive them? To allow *them* to forgive *him*? The Human Dynamo, for her part, is looking at him as if to say, After tagging along all these years, is this my reward—an obscure confrontation in the smoky, reeking dark? Have you dragged me here to be a witness to your failure to involve yourself with people?

Albert's eyes are tearing—not, he feels, from emotion this time, but from the smoke, whose volumes rise all about him. He is on the verge of disappearing, he thinks, or rather they are. Although he can now begin all over again, a long, dark line, like that scorched in the grass by a powder train, will inescapably connect him with the past.

There is a momentary rent in the smoke, revealing Josh. How old and scuffy he is, like Barney's football, which had been kicked around the P. S. 41 schoolyard for years. Albert realizes he has not paid Josh much attention since becoming separated from Violet; the dog is merely a vague presence down there at the end of the leash, a warm, trusting neck about which Albert fastens and unfastens a collar. Had he neglected Barney in the same way?

"Josh is losing his fuzz," Albert says to Violet.

"Acme had nowhere to stay, Elite," he hears Violet say.

This time, the stench of ashes reminds Albert of dead campfires, and thus of summer camp and his youth—the woods sloping down to the lake, the blue foothills on the far shore, which he never reached, the bluer mountains beyond. These unattained peaks at times come to mind when he goes downstairs in the morning to take Josh for a walk. Albert invariably finds him asleep in the chair by Violet's bed, and he gropes for him in the dark among the folds of his blanket, trying to determine which is Josh's front end, which his rear. While doing so, he glances at the bed, and is reassured by the gentle swell of the covers that indicate Violet's sleeping form; it is a landmark that enables him to maintain his bearings, to complete the familiar circle of his horizon. But some mornings another range—steeper, more massive, jagged—looms behind her, as though the earth has shifted overnight and new features have been upthrust.

In these instances, when Josh is following him to the kitchen for his biscuit, Albert often comes upon the visitor's shoes. They are slip-ons—large, black, scuffed. Usually, one will be upright, one on its side, and they are never together; Albert has the impression that they have been kicked off in an access of passion or that their wearer has met a violent end—an explosion, a hit-and-run.

It is Albert's practice on weekends to buy the *Times*, a brioche, and a bunch of flowers while walking Josh, and to leave them, agreeably arranged, on Violet's dining-room table. Whenever he sees in her bed what looms like a toppling wave or the greater half of a dictionary unequally open, he buys an extra brioche. For some reason, the addition of a second roll poses an almost insuperable obstacle to putting together a satisfactory still life, and he will stand in the dining room for long minutes, fussing with its components. Once he recalled his mom's dismay upon glancing at his and his dad's dinner plates. "I've turned the asparagus the wrong way!" she had cried. Holding the extra brioche aloft, as though it is a chess piece he isn't sure where to set down—or, indeed, if it is the right piece to move—Albert thinks, Perhaps I am better suited to be a mother. Indeed, toward the end of the marriage the roles were ill-defined; Violet was assuming the father's part while he was learning the mother's. But time ran out on them, and in the uncertainty and confusion Barney slipped through the net.

One night, looking down on the privet jutting from the dark pool of Violet's garden, Albert is put in mind of Pompeii and his mom. In respect to the former, how its excavators uncovered what they believed to be the mast tops of the city's stranded fishing fleet but which deeper digging proved to be a cypress grove; in respect to the latter, how at a recent Friday dinner he had noticed her uncharacteristically staring off into space. Albert asked her what she was looking at. Albert's dad, sitting alongside her on their couch, responded, " 'Gazing upon Broadway's busy scene,' " and they both smiled. Albert said they had him there all right, and that he sure was in the old dark. His dad explained that fifty years ago, when Albert's mom appeared on the Broadway stage, the lead of a Sunday feature on her began, "Gazing upon Broadway's busy scene . . ." Albert asked how come he had never heard this before. "As I believe I told you," his dad said, "there's a lot about us you don't know." Among them, Albert later realizes, is what his mom was looking at.

These speculations, indicating once again the fallibility of presuppositions, lead to the reflection that although figures diminish as the space between them and the observer grows, time can magnify. Thus Barney now looms larger than in life, whirling out of the darkness like the Black Monk, towering unsteadily in the garden, so that his terrified face is at Albert's window—huge, pale, unshaven, mutely appealing—as it was when Barney last kissed him goodbye. When Barney told him over the phone from Wisconsin, a month before he returned to New York and disappeared,

forever, from LaGuardia—he was found a month after his twentieth birthday in the Hudson River—that he was running twenty
miles a day, that he was going to win the marathon at the Moscow
Olympics, why hadn't Albert made the connection and realized
that Barney was losing his mind? Was it because there was the
possibility, however remote, that he was a prodigy, that he *would*
win, that he would make something of his life?

"Did you remember the alimony?" Violet asks Albert.
She is lying in the tub, with only her head above the surface. Gazing upon her submerged form, Albert recalls that Augustine had
gone to a certain public bath after his mother's death because he
had heard that its name was derived from the Greek for driving
sadness from the mind, but that "the bitterness of sorrow could
not exude out of my heart."

"As my dad would say," Albert says, producing the check
from his pocket, "I prepare my trousers the night before."

Once, when Albert asked him to run through this nifty little
procedure, his dad had said, "Before retiring, I remove the contents of the pockets—coins, my keys, penknife, and so forth—of
the trousers I'm wearing and transfer them to the pockets of the
trousers I've set out for the next day—"

" 'What's the big hurry?' I always ask him," Albert's mom
said, chiming in. "And do you know what he tells me? 'I am the
foe of disorder.' "

"While doing so," his dad went on, "I glance at the memoranda I've jotted down in the course of the day and put in my pockets. Some of these I may transfer from pocket to pocket as many as
a half-dozen times until the operative date of the matter I have to
remember, when I dispose of them. I recommend you follow my
example."

In his mind, Albert sometimes reverses this process of his
dad's, so that the foe of disorder, interminably rummaging in his
pockets under Albert's mom's skeptical gaze, becomes progressively younger each day, as does she, while he transfers their contents, until Albert's mom vanishes and the young man who is to
become his dad, having arrived at his wedding eve, is alone with

his little pile of belongings and memoranda, one of which, reading "Wedding, 11 a.m., June 25," he methodically tears into many
pieces.

"And how *is* your father?" Violet asks, lifting an arm to take
the check. To Albert, this seems a prodigious occurrence—the pale
arm unexpectedly rising, dripping, from the depths, like that of
the Lady of the Lake.

Prodigies! Is this what the pinnules foretold, these mournful
interludes in this vaporous place? After the fern's decline, Albert
recalls, everyone else lost interest in it, and the spraying ceremony
was no longer observed; it was left to him to lug the diminished
plant to the tub and dutifully sprinkle its few remaining fronds. As
he usually took care of the fern after his morning shower, while he
was still naked, at night he often discovered several pinnules entangled in his pubic hair. These evoked vague longings, as though
they were evidence of pagan revels in which he had been permitted
to take part, on the condition that all memory of them would be
erased.

"Limping," Albert replies at last. "He told me that he and his
secretary were walking down the corridor to his office, and that he
was imitating her rather emphatic step by stamping his feet on the
marble. 'But I was not entirely satisfied with the amount of noise I
was making,' he told me. 'I had failed to reproduce her tread.' 'So
what did you do?' I asked. 'I leapt in the air,' he said. 'And when
you came down?' 'I fell.' 'You got carried away,' I said. 'Even I go
to extremes,' he told me."

Albert envisions his eighty-one-year-old dad at the height of
his leap, in the long, dim corridor faced with marble the color of
old bones, striving to free himself from time's grip; and he also
sees Barney, momentarily suspended in the dark over the river—
Albert has persuaded himself that it had lain entrancingly, dark
and darker, full of speculative gleams, in the path of his headlong
flight from reality—seeking surcease from *his* torments. Fifteen
years before—thin, white, naked, aloft—Barney soared past the
door of Albert and Violet's bedroom on his way to the bathroom.
"Don't look!" he cried in midair, but Albert, dazzled, could not
avert his eyes. Now—shouldering the blame for Barney's death in
the same spirit with which he yearned to circle under less specific

griefs—he realizes that this time he had turned aside, and that Barney had passed from view forever.

As though with aching arms, Albert bears upraised the memory of that first frantic leap, just as the massive "Feast of the Rose Garlands" was conveyed through snowy mountain passes, for when Rudolf II, the Holy Roman Emperor, acquired it he deemed it too precious to be transported by a carriage, which might overturn, and had it bundled in rugs and carried upright across the Alps from Venice to his citadel in Prague by relays of strong men.

10

Albert tells Dr. Nederlander that everything women say to men can be reduced to ten basic expressions, all of which begin with "Why don't you . . ." Dr. Nederlander nods noncommittally. Albert goes on to say he arrived at this when the Human Dynamo said to him, "Why don't you ever take me dancing?"

"Why don't you?" Dr. Nederlander asks.

"That's irrelevant in this context," Albert says. "It struck me that Violet had said the very same thing, as had a number of girls I knew before I married her."

"Aha! *Das Aha-Erlebnis*!" Dr. Nederlander murmurs.

"As you will," Albert says. "Another of the Top Ten is 'Why don't you make love to me anymore?'—which, of course, is why I'm here."

"Of course," Dr. Nederlander says, perhaps, Albert detects, a little doubtfully.

Here is a six-story building with a good address on the East Side, in which Dr. Nederlander has had an office since he gave up his apartment on West End Avenue and moved to New Jersey, where he tramps about his property playing his accordion or systematically cutting down trees with his power saw. Make that *offices*, as Albert discovered when he started going to him again after a lapse of five or six years. His initial shock had been the first-floor waiting room, which resembled the Port Authority Bus Terminal, being dismally crowded with lounging blacks and ethnics. As he further discovered, the upper stories were divided into cubicles identically furnished, down to the Utrillos on the walls, through which he could hear disharmonious and unrewarding lamentations. If, like a doll house, the façade was missing, Albert felt sure that an array of fifty therapists would be revealed, nodding in concert as though obedient to a central baton, their fifty patients straining on their couches as though trying to burst the bonds that tied them to themselves—a struggle in several ways reminiscent of C——'s.

"Hey, what is this," Albert said during his first session, "some kind of plain-pipe-rack Berggasse 19?"

"I believe we have the odd podiatrist," Dr. Nederlander said.

The cubicles gave off corridors at whose turnings Albert might suddenly be confronted with psychiatric couches standing on end, like rearing horses, so that their ripped cambrics were revealed; in much the same manner, those who had reclined on them over the years had bared their rent psyches, although, Albert acknowledged, it was their particular natures that the former disclosed their undersides while vertical, the latter while horizontal. This insight set off unspecified reverberations, like the buzzings and rattlings behind his back whenever he typed; Albert was never able to determine which objects in his living room produced the noises, because, as he told Dr. Nederlander, when he stopped typing to investigate, they ceased vibrating.

"I may be on the verge of a major epistemological breakthrough," he said.

"Turn your desk around, Albie."

"Dr. Nederlander, that's like asking me to turn my life around, and if I could do that, I wouldn't be here."

Each Thursday evening, when Albert has his appointment, the receptionist directs him to a different office. She presides over a great board equipped with buzzers and lights, by means of which, like an air-traffic controller, she brings the patients safely up and down, making sure that two troubled souls don't violate one another's space in their venturings above. Although Albert is always told where to find Dr. Nederlander, he nonetheless has the impression they are playing a gloomy game of hide and seek, and that there is some sort of therapeutic benefit to be derived from his ability to track Dr. Nederlander down.

"Why can't I make love to her anymore?" Albert asks.

"Why were you able to make love to her for so long?" Dr. Nederlander shoots back.

"Why don't you knock off the sophistry?"

"Everything patients say to their therapists can be reduced . . ."

More is to come. Lying on his back at the bottom of the room at first light—the Human Dynamo had removed the frame of the bed so that the box spring rested on the floor—this is what Albert is thinking. There is so much emptiness between them and the ceiling, which, because the uncurtained windows are set high in the wall, is the brightest part of the room, resembling the surface of the sea seen from below. Indeed, at high tide there are traceries of moving water on the ceiling; the Human Dynamo now lives in Fair Haven, a community of a hundred homes guarded by two decapitated plaster lions and a speed bump, which extends like a gnarled finger into Long Island Sound.

Albert has been going with the Human Dynamo for five years, or since shortly before he separated from Violet, and he has been ineluctably sinking. In the converted pool house in New Canaan, which she was renting furnished when Albert met her, she slept in a high maple bed, presumably Early American. This her landlord, a retired investment banker in his eighties, subsequently removed, replacing it with one several inches lower. (An involved story went with this exchange. The Human Dynamo told it to Albert in bed during a rain delay in the Yankee game they were watching on television, but he hadn't paid attention. He was thinking of the Headless Landlord, as years later he would dwell on the Bodyless Ex-Lovers. Albert occasionally caught glimpses of him at night in the windows of the house across the pool—that is, of him from the waist to the neck. "He's extremely tall," the Human Dynamo had said when Albert first marveled at the apparition. The bedroom reeked of chlorine; the still black water of the pool promised the concealment of ever greater prodigies. "I think the magic is going out of our relationship," Albert had said.)

When the Human Dynamo rented the second-floor apartment in the two-story house in Fair Haven, she and Albert perforce lay as entwined as wisteria in a single bed with a wicker headboard belonging to her landlady, which was lower still, until Albert gave her a check to buy a king-size. This turned out to be built even closer to the floor; moreover, the extra width permitted them to lie addorsed on either side, a waste of bedclothes stretching between.

"You know," Albert said upon awakening one morning, "at times I get the impression we're guarding a national monument or something. But commemorating what?"

"The battlefield upon which we lost our lyricism," she murmured.

He was on one elbow, gazing down at her pretty face, whose shape always reminded him of home plate. "That doesn't sound like you," he said.

"That's because almost from the start you discouraged my intelligence."

One evening, when Albert came up from New York to see her, he found that she had taken the bed frame apart and put it away, leaving him stranded.

"What's going on around here?" he asked.

"I'm trying to bring you down to my level," she said.

Reviewing his gradual descent, Albert felt that the beds had been whisked out from under him the way magicians remove tablecloths without disturbing the settings.

Albert turns his head to look out the windows. As always, what he sees are three oblongs of sky. It is early morning and they are as pale as clam shells; the view is without perspective and, Albert feels, is more expressive of disappointment than promise. An egret emerges in the window to his right, by its whiteness revealing the sky to be greyer than Albert thought, fills the frame, its wings stately folding and unfolding, passes from view, reappears in the middle window, vanishes, crosses the window to Albert's left, and disappears. The last he sees of it is its trailing yellow legs, their intricate reticulations. Albert reflects that its progress was such that it might have been pulled from off stage, like the swans in *Swan Lake*. So undeviating has his own passage become, he speculates, that he, too, may as well be at the mercy of some great windlass in the wings.

Albert is unresistingly drawn into sleep. He is awakened by a bird singing "The Colonel Bogie March."

"Did you ever hear a bird whistle the opening bars of 'The Colonel Bogie March'?" he whispers in the ear of the Human Dynamo, who is still sleeping.

"Where?"

"Am I to infer that you *have* heard one, but elsewhere?"

"What?"

"I am trying to determine from your response whether in fact there *is* a bird that whistles 'The Colonel Bogie March,' which you've had occasion to hear, but that Fair Haven is outside its range, or whether—"

"Oh." This a groan.

"Oh, *what*?"

"Oh, you're being Talmudic again."

"It was just a simple Q. & A."

"Albert, you've got to come to grips with the fact that we're separated by a profound socioreligious gap."

"I thought it was a metaphorical battlefield."

"Now *this* is what I call a metaphor," Albert tells the Human Dynamo that night. They had walked to the end of the pier extending from the Fair Haven beach, and down the flight of stairs to the float, upon which they are now sitting. However, since it is low tide, the float isn't floating; it is resting on the mud. "Us," Albert goes on, beginning a vague but comprehensive gesture. How much of the view, or their predicament, he intended to encompass, the Human Dynamo could only infer, because he suddenly arrests his arm, extends it, and points out over the Sound. Where a foot or so of water covers the bottom is a train of little gleams. It advances, shimmering, toward the beach, becoming gradually extinguished at the rear as it is kindled in front, so that it remains the same length. "What is it?" Albert says in awe.

"A duck."

Straining his eyes, he realizes that the scene is not uniformly black, as he assumed, that at the head of the train is a yet blacker object, which resolves itself into a duck, and that the glimmering train is its wake, this or that light from shore being reflected in the rippled surface of the Sound. As the egret defined the day, the duck set forth the night. And how, Albert thinks, is he determined? When he was vacationing in Key Biscayne not long ago, the girl who took care of the motel pool told him one morning that the previous evening she and her husband had tried to reach him to have dinner with them at this little Indian place. She had even called the health-food restaurant where he ate every night, hoping he might be able to join them for jellabees and coffee. "But they don't know my name," Albert said. She was idly vacuuming the pool, the great hose hitched around her waist like Minos' tail. "I asked them," she said, "if there was a grey-haired man eating alone."

Albert visualized the long row of diners at the counter, bent over their spinach soufflés, as if inclined in prayer—the dim, conceivably ecclesiastical light and the virtuous thoughts to which mung bean sprouts and seaweed give rise strengthened this impression—and for the first time it struck him that at forty-eight he might well be the oldest among them. Did he really stick out? He had never thought of himself as being all *that* grey. For that matter, he never thought of himself; that is, of the figure he cut. Pursuing this line, he concluded that he never considered himself as being older than those who were in fact younger than he, like the Human Dynamo, who was now thirty-two; he only seemed to be aware of the age of older people. How long, he wondered, with a more precipitous sinking feeling than he had experienced *in re* the beds, would that be the case?

Peering into the dark, he recalls that the day he was leaving Key Biscayne to return to New York, the girl gave him a loaf of zucchini bread she had baked. His secretary recently presented him with a half-dozen homemade rugelach, and one of the copy readers at the office had given him a miso cupcake. What was it about him that produced this sudden outpouring of baked goods? Did he seem forlorn or undernourished? A wave of self-pity, like the swell of the incoming tide now gently rocking the float, agitates him.

"How come you never bake any cookies for me?" Albert asks the Human Dynamo.

"I don't give sympathy," she says. "I give advice."

Holding hands, they wend their way back to her house. The curving streets are overarched by trees, intensifying the darkness. Albert feels there is something charmed about the scene—the deep silence, the leafy vault, the winding way. He imagines them as seen from above, through gaps in the foliage. Fondling his scaly tail, Minos—again!—broods in a dormer window, and stays his hand.

A hurtling cyclist, unseen until the last moment because he (or she) has no light, nearly crashes into them and vanishes, and Albert is put in mind of the first time he encountered the Human Dynamo. Along with one of his fellow editors, he was taking part in the New Canaan Christmas Bird Count, poking about some hedges bordering Weed Street, which were supposed to harbor a winter wren. She passed by on her bicycle, furiously pedaling, her ass tilted heartbreakingly to Heaven. (Like a Hassid, Albert mused at the time, watching her diminishing figure through his binoculars, she intimately links Heaven and earth independent of ritual mediation.)

"Not home," the editor said, backing out of the hedges. "What you got there?" He raised his binoculars. "You ought to put that on your life list," he said. The editor knew her slightly; they had bought their BMWs from the same dealer, and had met at the three-thousand-mile check. Albert called her and took her to dinner and a George Segal movie, the first of many of his they went to together.

"Do Jewish people—" the Human Dynamo said on the way to her car.

"We're not Jewish *people*," he said. "We're just Jews."

"Do *Jews* think of George Segal in terms of his Jewishness?"

"What do you mean?"

"I mean, is going to a George Segal movie a Jewish experience?"

"Not like going to the bathroom, if that's what you mean."

When gentiles go to the bathroom, he reflects later that evening, observing the Human Dynamo leaning tranquilly back against the tank, her purple panties with the yellow competition stripes about her ankles, her arms folded across her chest, they look as though they are riding on a cross-country bus. Jews sit behind closed doors, hunched forward as if condemned to occupy the corners of pediments, chins in their right hands, left forearms across corresponding thighs, expressive of their inveterate sadnesses.

When she joins him in bed, they watch a Yankee game.

"If you'd stop waving it around," she says, "I could see what was happening."

"But nothing's happening."

"Something's *always* happening. Don't project your inertia on the Yankees."

"But they're changing pitchers."

"Marcus Aurelius said, 'All things take place by change.'"

"Marcus Albertus said, 'But not always for the best,' " Albert says, closely observing the *tableau vivant* on the mound. If they weren't wearing baseball uniforms, he thinks, would anyone know what they were up to? If the attitudinizing figures in "The Apotheosis of Henry IV" were dressed as New York Yankees, would Rubens's painting be merely absurd, or would it still resplendently evoke transitoriness and tragedy? If the Human Dynamo and he, naked and outsprawled on the bottom of this darkened room, like drowned men, were on display, would those who viewed them be able to discern that they were drifting apart? Or would there have to be a label on the frame?

Unlike, say, the GNP, Albert reflects as Gossage warms up, relationships between men and women don't rise and fall; they are at their height at the outset, and inevitably decline. Did he cry out "Stop the car!" on the access road of the Bridgeport airport five years ago in a desperate attempt to preserve that flourishing moment, that *tempus beatum,* to arrest the decay? At any rate, the Human Dynamo stopped her BMW, he flung open his door, she flung open hers, and they ran around to the back of the car, where they embraced. How marvelously true to life it was that they met by the trunk! If Albert were George Segal, she Glenda Jackson or Susan Anspach or Jane Fonda, he would have raced to the back of the car and she to the front; then, skidding, nearly losing their balance, he would have torn around to the front and she to the back. Next Albert to the back, she to the front . . . .

Another night, tide in, water lapping at the sea wall, they walk on top of it in single file, their nostrils full of iodic and melancholy odors; on their right are the lawns of the houses fronting the Sound.

"You're sure we're not trespassing?" Albert says to the Human Dynamo, who is in the lead.

"I always walk here when there's no beach."

At that moment, a terrier materializes on the wall in front of her and starts barking. Spotlights go on, illuminating the lawn, the wall, themselves, the water; next, living-room lights. Through a picture window, Albert sees a woman approaching, peering out.

"Of all the *nerve*," she says in a braying whiskey voice. "Just what do you think we pay our dues to the Association for, I ask you? Of *all* the nerve. Of all *the* nerve."

The lights, the barking dog, the coarse voice sounding as though it were issuing from a loud-hailer, makes Albert feel as though he has been detected sneaking across a border. He turns and begins to retrace his steps. Looking over his shoulder he sees that the Human Dynamo hasn't moved. She is standing on the wall in her BMW racing team jacket, her hair extraordinarily blond in the stark light.

"*Of* all the nerve." There, she's rung all the changes, Albert notes. As far as he can tell, she is alone; evidently her appeals are to a higher authority—the same party, he supposes, who wields the inexorable baton in Dr. Nederlander's office building. If he hadn't been with the Human Dynamo, there would have been no alarm, he concludes. It was he and his kind that the headless lions were intended to menace, the pedimental fugitives who made her kind wait outside the bathroom door at country inns. If he were George Segal, he'd caper about the lawn, scratching his flanks like a chimpanzee, telling her and her Association where they could put their cute little peninsula—mixing invective with wit, of course, so it would play.

"Just how do you expect us ever to make love again if you keep lying on your back staring at it in wonder?" the Human Dynamo says when they are in bed.

"But you went and turned the Yankee game on."

"We used to make love when the Yankees were playing."

"But they weren't any good then. It didn't matter if they won. They were background music. [La-dah-dah-dah-*dum*.] Now every game is *crucial*."

Awakening in the middle of the night, Albert hears a tennis game in progress—the faint pops of the ball striking the rackets. Fair Haven's two clay courts are only a block or so away, but he hadn't been aware that there were lights for night play. Pop, pop. Pop, pop. Albert neither plays tennis nor skis—another battlefield separating him from the Human Dynamo, whose unrelenting pursuit of these sports and cycling gave rise to her name. Pop, pop. Pop, pop. No one is playing tennis, he realizes. The pops are the exhalations of the Human Dynamo's breath. This discovery strikes him as being almost unbearably poignant: the image that comes to mind is of her being unable to find a partner and so reduced to playing interminable sets of tennis with herself in her sleep. Poignancy will be my ruin, he thinks. As other men are undone by avarice, ambition, grand passions, he will sink—is sinking—under a burden of tender sorrows, which, like snowflakes, singly are nearly weightless, but heaped on a roof can buckle it. An example of reverse *lacrimae rerum*, he reflects, would be his dwindling supply of argyle socks. In this case, the fewer that remain in his sock drawer, the more affecting the emotion.

Tap. Pop. Tap. Pop. Tap, tap. Pop. Taptaptap. Pop.

Now it's raining, Albert says to himself. A hell of a doubles match.

"I heard it," the Human Dynamo says, awakening.

"I know, it's raining."

"Not the rain. Howard."

"Howard? Oh yes, good old Howard. One of those space salesmen you hit with."

"Howard's a parrot."

"I'd never have guessed."

"He lives next door."

"I always said Fair Haven didn't let just anyone in."

"Howard whistles 'The Colonel Bogie March.' "

"Another mystery down the drain," Albert says sadly. "Life never lives up to the expectations that its theme music promises."

"*Our* lives, Albie."

"As you keep saying, we've got nothing in common."

"Well, do we?"

"Yes. Although we're incompatible, we're incapable of breaking up."

Albert's hotel room in Madison is on the third floor, overlooking the lake, which is unexpectedly vast, sealike, the far shore barely discernible. The hotel is built right on the water, so that when he stands back from the picture window, he can't see the shore below; the impression is that the hotel rises out of the lake, its foundation green with algae, at which long, shadowy fish languidly nibble. This romantic illusion is heightened by the lurid colors the evening sky imparts to the water, the wave-tossed surface, and, as it becomes darker, bats perilously veering by the window.

Albert had come to Madison to see Greta, with whom Barney was living before he fled to New York. He had paid for her plane ticket so she could come to the funeral, but he hadn't gotten the chance to speak to her about Barney then; he told her he would fly out to Madison sometime—she was a phys ed major at the university—and they would talk.

Now Albert is sitting on one of the twin beds in the hotel room, speaking on the phone to the Human Dynamo in Fair Haven.

"Then we played a little nine-ball."

"Who won?"

"She did."

"But you weren't really trying. You were attempting to dazzle her by making like George Segal with the massé and jump shots."

"I was trying. I always try to do my best, you know that."

"You don't always try to be nice to the Dynamo."

"That may be because Albie finds it hard to relate to people who take refuge in the third person."

"You're so out of touch with your own feelings, to say nothing of mine, that I sometimes think it's the only way to reach you."

"Barney taught her."

"Taught her what?"

"To shoot pool. He taught me, too. He could run the table.

That's his legacy. Greta and I are his disciples. And she's now older than he ever was. I can't rid myself of the feeling that we're leaving him farther and farther behind. It's almost as if he is trapped somewhere and struggling, and that through neglect or a lack of application we're not doing our best to find and free him, as we failed to come to his aid when he was alive."

"What else did she tell you?"

"That he didn't eat or sleep, that he roamed about all night. Days were consumed in sentences, weeks in paragraphs. The more she said, the less I recognized him. He kept changing shape; he dwindled away. Before long she was talking about someone I never knew. It was as if she were telling me her dreams, and I found myself not listening."

"I told you you shouldn't go. But by then it was too late. You tell me everything after it's taken place. Letting Violet take the garden apartment in your building because you felt sorry for her, flying to Madison because you felt sorry for yourself. It's as if I'm reduced to writing letters to the editor. You've put me on the fringes of your life. I can't improve our relationship from there."

Neither of them say anything for a while. At last, she goes on. "Then what did you do and what did she do?"

"We bought frozen yogurts."

"Did you sleep with her?"

"What makes you say something like that?"

"You're always wanting to complete circles."

In the dark, the lake sounds like a running toilet. Albert feels overwhelmed by wetnesses, greennesses, stoninesses; the bats trying to penetrate the picture window, the fishes' slow undermining, Barney streaming with the tide. His coffin was so unexpectedly light, the pallbearers, the huge, loping kids he'd played basketball with, nearly lost their balance when they lifted it to leave the church.

The declivity on the other bed appears to Albert like the settled surface of a grave into which the earth has been newly shoveled.

"If we were spies," Albert says to the Human Dynamo, "we could pass on state secrets and no one could overhear us."

"But we're not," she says. "We're ex-lovers, and no one is listening to us because we no longer have anything new and interesting to say."

They are standing in the surf off the coast of South Carolina, with the water up to their necks, so that their heads appear to be bobbing on the surface like floats come loose from fishermen's nets.

"As far as anyone can tell," Albert says, "we don't have any bodies. I suppose it's because we don't have any more use for them, like our tails."

"You can't see us hanging upside down from a branch, chattering to each other? It does sometimes seem we've been together millions of years."

"What I can see is us in your BMW going to LaGuardia the morning after I made love to you for the first time."

"That was at least a *thousand* years ago. The last time, too, I wouldn't doubt. Same millennium, anyway."

At least, Albert thinks, because she had been wearing a miniskirt, and he had kept his hand on the inside of her revealed thigh all the way down the Merritt. It had been so early in the morning—she was catching the first flight to Detroit—that there wasn't any traffic. She must have driven eighty-five miles an hour the whole way. But, Albert reflects, surface diving, no matter how fast she drove how many times, they would never arrive at the airport in time to prevent Barney from plunging off.

In the underwater murk, he gently takes hold of the Human Dynamo's ankles and yanks her down. Whether her burbled utterance is a laugh or a shriek, he can't tell, but, watching the bubbles issuing from his mouth—each, he fancies, conveying a letter to the surface, like an SOS tapped on the hull of a disabled sub—he knows that his blub-blub-blub is, "Now we no longer exist."

That night, Albert awakes in their hotel room to find himself, like a dog scrabbling at the earth after a buried bone—not a specific bone, necessarily, but one of the hoard of numberless bones strewn and intermingled and forgotten that the earth encloses—tearing at his forehead with his fingernails, as if trying to uncover a thought, a system of thought, from the great disorderly pile locked inside.

"What have you gone and done now?" the Human Dynamo says in the morning, seeing the terrible gash, the dried blood on the pillow.

"I was trying to remember."

"Remember what?"

"That's it."

"Albie," she says, reaching out, possibly to smooth his hair, "ex-lovers can love each other, can't they?"

"Maybe that was it."

"Was what?"

"The answer to your question."

If Frege were right, Albert reflects, when he wrote that thoughts cannot be created but only grasped, all that came to hand were the birds twittering on the plane to Charleston. He had been half asleep when he heard the first one. Someone's bringing his caged bird south on his lap, he concluded, and has taken the cloth off. Then he heard another, and still another. Must be a big bird show going on somewhere.

"Plane's full of little twittering birds," he muttered to the Human Dynamo, who was sitting alongside him.

"What ever are you talking about?"

"Listen."

"I am listening."

"Then don't you hear them?"

"Albert, what I hear are those little electronic games."

"I bet George Segal would have something to say at a time like this."

"But it wouldn't be that still more magic is going out of our relationship."

"I knew it would happen," Albert tells Dr. Nederlander the next time he sees him.

"I'm not going to guess, Albie."

"You're not going to have to, I'm going to tell you. I open your office door and I catch you with your hand inside an analysand's blouse. Don't talk, *I'm* the one that's paying. That's right, wrong office, wrong therapist, probably not a therapist at all because they don't mess around, it has to be one of the podiatrists. But what does it *mean*?"

"What does *what* mean?"

"Hey, this is your bag, Doc. Me bursting into the wrong office."

"Albert, everything you do doesn't have to have significance."

"Yes, but *something* has to. Remember how when I used to see you before, we talked about my rut, how you wanted me to rent a car and go antiquing in Connecticut, anything that was *different*?"

"You *ought* to be an antiquarian," Dr. Nederlander says. "You really like circling back."

"To where?"

"To Violet, the Human Dynamo."

"Barney. I keep dreaming about him. Last night he confessed he'd been hiding in Mamaroneck. He said he thought I'd punish him for running away. Oh, do I have a good one for you. This morning I went down to Violet's to walk the dog. I got the collar and the leash and was on my way out when I heard her calling from her bed. 'You forgot something,' she said. 'What did I forget?' I said. 'You forgot the dog,' she said. I had, and I was half out the door. I've got to be on the verge of a major phenomenological breakthrough."

"Which reminds me, what about all the buzzing and rattling?"

"I've got a new carpet. *Alles schläft.* Now *you* tell *me* something, Dr. Nederlander. Is the ceiling of this office higher than the others, or did you bring your power saw to the office and cut down the legs of the couch?"

"I'll give you a lift to the subway," Dr. Nederlander says, rising. "I'm late for this course I'm taking."

"What's that, 'The Psychopathology of Narcissistic Tranquillity'?"

"No, 'Small Gasoline Engines.'"

Crossing Central Park, Albert says, "Every time I go to Violet's to walk the dog, I'm overwhelmed anew."

"You do get easily overwhelmed."

"You would too, if half the furniture down there was yours. How would you like to be on permanent loan exhibition. It's a fucking marriage museum!"

"You told her she could hang on to the furniture because your apartment was furnished."

"I said it, but it was because I felt sorry for her. You think I'm a nice guy, don't you, Dr. Nederlander?"

"I think you deserve the all-around camper award, Albie."

Albert looks out the car window at the perspective of dark solemn domes of foliage, like the swelling prominences of a Middle Eastern city. Serene visions and contemplations of mosque and Moorish give rise to their joint near-homophone, morose; this in turn calls to mind a week he spent with the Human Dynamo at a Western ski resort, mood taking precedence over conflicting angularity. She had made a terrific scene one foggy morning before the lifts opened, crying out that she would have to kill herself in front of him for him to realize how far he had let her down.

"Don't you remember the girl who lived in the pool house?" she said, waving her roaring blow dryer about, as though it were the weapon with which she was going to do herself—or him—in. "Can't you see what you've done to her?"

"What have I done?" he said, evading a blast of hot air.

"You left her alone."

Albert regretfully acknowledged that he had heard this line before, too, from Violet, and the theme and thrust of his life suddenly stood revealed: he was irresistibly drawn to disillusionment—and disillusioning—because it was from the rubble of dashed hopes that he fashioned his slight and sentimental art.

Her tears nearly dried, the Human Dynamo insisted he accompany her to the tram terminal, so he could watch her ascend the mountain. In a din of clattering boots and skis, they shuffled forward in the line that snaked around and around the barriers, as though proceeding to the tellers' windows in some stony, infernal bank. At one point, he was asked to step aside, for he didn't have a ticket. The tram arrived, emerging from the fog. As the attendant flung open the gates and the skiers surged forward, he heard above their jocular mooing someone calling his last name. He turned and saw it was the Human Dynamo. She had never used it before. She was in high gear, hurtling down Weed Street. In the distance, two middle-aged men were peering into the shrubbery, as though in its crepuscular recesses they had at last found, as Dr. Johnson wrote of Pope's grotto, "a place of silence and retreat, from which he endeavoured to persuade his friends and himself that cares and passions could be excluded."

Later, swimming laps in the pool at the lodge, the vapor rising from the superheated water commingling with the descending mist, so that he was all in whiteness, snowflakes settling coldly on his arms and back, Albert imagined the tram rising, swaying, vanishing. When she got to the top of the mountain, she was going to ski down the other side, a tiny, determined figure against the enormity of the slope—so much like Violet on the expanse of sheets, he recalled when, despairing, she clenched herself into a miserable ball—and never come back.

Turning to Dr. Nederlander, Albert says, "You know, Tolstoy said that playing the accordion diverts men from realizing the falsity of their goals."

"You want me to turn on the Yankee game?" Dr. Nederlander says.

11

Such is the allure of the written word that if we could see through walls we would be appalled by what met our gaze: thousands, *tens* of thousands of haunted men and women in lonely kitchens, second bedrooms, and sun porches, hunched over typewriters, striving for literary fame, the faint, intermittent clatter as mournful as rain spattering on fallen leaves, which, Kafū the Scribbler tells us, is a stronger agent to move men's hearts than cataracts. Now and again, Albert has been afforded glimpses of a number of these undaunted souls—Skippy Mountjoy, bowed beneath the privet, for one—engaged in what Dr. Johnson called "the epidemical conspiracy for the destruction of paper." So have we all. You may apprehend Albert in the window, third floor front behind the pot of morning-glories, given to self-dramatization, wondering whether he is repeating himself, and smoking a cigar.

Years ago, Albert was taken by a mutual friend to meet a man named Parsons who edited the house journal of an oil company. He lived on the outskirts of El Paso with his wife and three children, and had written five novels before breakfast, none of which had been published. He said he had high hopes for No. 6, then in progress. His wife, seated beside him on the sofa, ambiguously squeezed his hand. After drinks, Parsons took Albert on a tour of the house; his kids tagged along. Albert towered above them, swaying slightly, like the image of a saint in a religious procession.

That, he regretfully gathered, was his role there: He was that venerated figure, the published writer, who might bless or favor Parsons' ineffectual art, his interminable pages. They paused at the door of Parsons' study; it was in the back, commanding a prospect of the desert. Parsons made a diffident gesture, indicating an irregular pile of manuscript that, picturesquely illuminated by the light from the hall, rose from a bridge table like the stump of a ruined marble column. Albert envisioned him at his electric typewriter, the cold blast from the air conditioner ruffling a stack of second sheets, faint with hunger, his inspiration failing, staring at the desert as though hoping that an *Erlebnisträger*, a carrier of experience, would stumble into view and unfold his strange and profitable tale.

Garrulous wayfarers never ring Albert's bell; idly cleaning his typewriter keys with an old toothbrush dipped in rubbing alcohol or laying his cheek against the cold top plate, he tries to recall what has happened to him recently that might move men's hearts. Only one thing that hasn't happened before comes to mind; perhaps this is by design, perhaps a result of a kind of resignation. Not long ago, while talking on the telephone to Violet, he mentioned that he varied his bedtime. "You live so dangerously," she said.

Now and again, Albert wonders what became of Parsons. If life had gone on as before, he would have finished No. 12 or 13 by now. But perhaps he threw in the towel midway through No. 8 and took up, say, jogging instead. Albert visualizes him, pounding through the neighborhood before daybreak, eyes brimming with tears in acknowledgment that the world wasn't at fault for not recognizing his literary merit, but that he had little or none, his wife glancing out the kitchen window in anticipation of his ungainly finishing sprint. Albert pictures, too, Parsons' abandoned typewriter, like Ozymandias' shattered visage, drifted over with the sand that somehow sifts through shut windows in places such as El Paso.

But give him his due; whatever else they lacked, presumably his pages were—are?—coherent. Would Albert could say the same about those so unremittingly typed by his old college roommate Emory Bates on his three ancient office machines in Coconut Grove. These monumental contraptions are arrayed on a long table as though on display in an exhibit commemorating the Industrial Revolution. Emory has a wheeled typing chair, and, Albert gathers, if the muse deserts him at one typewriter, he propels himself in front of another. At such urgent moments, he must appear like a figure in one of Rubens's more tumultuous compositions—his full, fair beard and long hair flying, his glasses pushed to the top of his head like an uplifted visor.

Emory has been keeping what he calls a journal for five years— ever since he became aware that he was vanishing. "Why don't I have an effect on people anymore?" he asked Albert at the time. "I'm becoming invisible." He sold his health-food store and began typing. Each day got at least a single-spaced page, often two, so that by now he has written more than two thousand pages. These cannot be read; this is not to say they are unreadable, which is pejorative. It is just that the writing is so condensed, so private, so allusive that they are all but unintelligible. They might as well be in cipher. (Suppose you were the first to crack Pepys's or Schlegel's code and found it concealed a laundry list.) Nonetheless, Emory has convinced himself that it is inconceivable that there is nothing of value in two thousand pages. Specifically, it is inconceivable that there isn't a book that can be made into a movie. When on the subject, he skips over whatever this entails so he can get to the part where he steps from the limousine for the premiere. "I've been thinking of wearing a Glenurquhart suit with gray, bronze, and red decorations," he once told Albert, "a blue-jean blue chambray shirt, and a burnt-orange silk tie."

Two thousand pages! Emory yanks at the handle of a filing cabinet drawer, which, because of the great weight of what is within, rolls irresistibly, even majestically, open to its full length, and steps aside so that Albert can view the contents. Instead of two thousand pages, his naked body could be lying there—pale, puffy, careworn—for the journal is not only his life's work, it is also his life. "I find I can't recall anything earlier than nineteen seventy-three," he told Albert on his last visit. "It is as though the past does not extend back beyond the first page of my journal."

It was on this occasion that Emory informed Albert he had appointed him his literary executor. They were in the sleeping porch where he batted out the journal. The room was full of greenish

light; Emory lives in an old frame cottage hemmed in by a mul-
tifariousness of leaves. In that light, the function of the typewriters, which now protruded from the table like coral heads, seemed
mysterious, inexplicable; they could have been obsolete and di-
lapidated contrivances for making buttonholes. Emory, too, his
eyes enlarged behind his glasses, conferring heroic proportions to
his entire frame as well as suggesting the marine, in the respect
that refraction makes fish, bare feet appear larger underwater, was
ruined, mythic, tinged with green—in Albert's fancy algae on marble or, more simply, *verde antico*—as though, with his streaming
beard and locks, he was not so much Poseidon, tilted in rage on
the seabed, as his statue, which, having tumbled through vertigi-
nous fathoms, was implanted at a fearful angle, eyes, mouth eternally open, stupendously imploring, unable to drown.

"You'll know what to do with it," he went on. "I don't want
it falling into the wrong hands. In addition, I would like you to
deliver the eulogy at my funeral." Emory had also convinced himself that he would die young, unappreciated, before he had the
chance to emerge from the limo. "I want you to tell them I was
intelligent."

He rested a hand on one of the typewriters, as one would lay a
hand on the head of a faithful setter or a bust of Aristotle. "Maybe
the shirt should be orange and the tie blue," he said. "What do you
think?"

When Buddy Bloom went to the premieres of his movies he
wore a safari jacket and Adidas, no socks. But producing movies didn't gratify him; it is Buddy's conviction that you can't be
a success in life unless you write a book. Buddy stopped making
movies and wrote an autobiographical novel, *Foreign Bodies*, in
his beach house in Malibu. He sent Albert a Xerox of the MS for
his comments. Albert wrote back, telling him it wasn't half bad—
it wasn't—but that the protagonist was like somebody played by
George Segal, and that Buddy Bloom's life was more interesting
than George Segal's.

The next time Albert was on the Coast, he had dinner with
Buddy. After Buddy took a sip of his white-wine spritzer, Albert asked him what was happening with the book. Buddy told
him someone had put him on to this old lady, a German who did

freelance editing, and the upshot was she moved in with him so they could whip *Foreign Bodies* into shape.

"I was the first on my block to have a live-in editor," Buddy said. "She could parse the shit out of a sentence, but she wouldn't let up. I'd say, 'What say we knock off so I can clear the head by shooting a *bissel* bumper pool?' and I'd take off for the game room. She'd be right behind me in her fuzzy yellow slippers, popping Tic Tacs and carrying on about my transitions. 'Mr. Bloom,' she'd say, 'your rhythms are too predictable, like a bad dance band from the thirties. A ricky-tick, a ricky-tick, a ricky-tick. Ve *must* wary dem. Ve *vill* wary dem.' 'Before ve undertake dat, Frau Gelberman,' I told her, '*I'm* going to valk on the beach and *you're* going to stay in the house and comb out your schlippers.' 'Mr. Bloom,' she told me, 'the vorld vould not haff *Wallenstein* if Schiller had goofed off by valking on de bich.' 'Frau Gelberman,' I told her, 'there is no bich in Weimar.' 'Mr. Bloom,' she told me, 'you are haffing schport mit me.'

"I was haffing it up to here with her was what I was haffing. I had to get rid of her. But she wouldn't go. So I went. Late one night, after she had gone to bed with a cup of Ovaltine and a couple of chapters, I packed a bag, tippy-toed out of the house, put the Lamborghini into neutral, and pushed it down the Colony until I was out of earshot. Then I drove into the desert and watched game shows in motels. Two days later, I called up. 'Gelberman.' I hung up. I called again the next day. 'I know it's you, Mr. Bloom,' she said this time. 'You can run away from me, but you can't escape your obligations to posterity.' She underestimated me. I drove to the airport, took a plane to New York, and stayed at the St. Regis for a week. Flying back, I had the awful feeling I might find Frau Gelberman's skeleton on my deck, manuscript pages interspersed with bones, but the house was empty."

A year later, as Albert was about to step off a curb at Columbus Circle, he stayed his foot. Stenciled on the pavement was the following: FOREIGN BODIES. A BLOCKBUSTER OF A NOVEL BY BUDDY BLOOM. Buddy always had a flair.

Albert's foot hovered over *Foreign Bodies* in May; now it is October, and nighthawks are swooping about the floodlit tower of the Kismet Hotel and Country Club like lost souls. (I fear Frau

Gelberman would decry this transition as an unseemly metasta-sis.) Albert is in Las Vegas waiting for Bruce Bleibtraub to arrive from Rancho Mirage, so they can go over *Preferential Treatment*, his novel in progress. Like all the enterprises Bruce has involved Albert in over the years, this one started with a phone call in the course of which he said, "I'd like you to do me a special favor." In the past, these favors ranged from Albert using his connections to get him a ringside seat for the second Ali-Frazier fight to pick-ing up a birthday cake Bruce ordered for his daughter, who lived with her mother in Westport, where they didn't know *bupkis* about baking cakes, and sticking it in Albert's refrigerator so Bruce could come by for it after his show because the bakery was closed when he got off the air and he was going up to Connecticut first thing in the a.m.

Until he decided that only writing could fulfill him and went to Rancho to work on his novel, Bruce had a talk show on an FM station and did voice-overs for TV commercials. When the cam-era girl in the Kingdom of the Deep, the Kismet's gourmet sea-food restaurant, where Albert and Bruce ate on Bruce's last night in town, asked him what he did for a living, he said, "I'm an air personality" and grinned prodigiously. To his mind, it was all pre-posterous: his livelihood; the net festooned with corks, Japanese glass floats, and blowfish strung over their heads in whose dusty meshes Albert feared they would become entangled and hauled off for a moral accounting; the camera girl's half-revealed breasts, quivering like quennels of pike—everything but his writing.

When Bruce called he was prepared to fly to New York with the MS: Albert had the wild notion he was going to buy two tick-ets and get adjoining seats, one for *Preferential Treatment*, the way athletes have been known to travel with massive trophies, musi-cians with valued instruments. He was elated when Albert told him he was going to be in Vegas, and they could get together there. He insisted that Albert read the MS beforehand—a problem, as he wouldn't entrust it to the mails. Bruce has little faith in public serv-ices and leaves nothing to chance. For example, he went to great lengths to seek out the meteorologist who forecast for Rancho, cul-tivated his friendship, took him and his wife out to dinner, because the public forecast was insufficiently detailed for his purposes.

"A solution has presented itself," Bruce told Albert when he called the next day. "The parent company that owns the station I worked for is having a convention in Los Angeles, and one of my former colleagues who is attending is more than willing to hand-carry the MS to your office when he gets to New York. I'm driving up this evening to effect the transfer." Knowing Bruce, Albert was sure this arrangement had been set up by a phone call asking for a special favor; and, knowing Bruce, Albert visualized the transfer being effected on a deserted street corner in Beverly Hills, say Rodeo and Elevado.

Albert wasn't clear what function he was supposed to perform *in re Preferential Treatment*—anything, he supposed, from correcting Bruce's spelling to hailing him as a genius.

"Ees not half bad," is what Albert tells him by the Kismet pool, where they are reclining on adjoining chaises, brushing away flies; the air is scented with mown grass and piña coladas. Whenever Bruce solicited Albert's opinion, he addressed him in the guise of a Puerto Rican super or a Chinese laundryman, and expected him to reply in kind; Albert gathers this charade softened anything less than unqualified praise. "But the hero is like somebody played by George Segal," Albert goes on, "and Bruce Bleibtraub's life is more interesting than George Segal's."

This isn't a stock reply; that's the way both MSS strike Albert; it must be in the air. Whether Bruce's life is more interesting than Buddy's is a subject to which Albert doesn't address himself; suffice it to say both are more interesting than his. For instance, Bruce often regales Albert with tales of making love with one of his pretaped shows booming out of the Marantzes for background music, of threesomes he videotaped, of his affairs with famous movie stars who, in long, murmurous phone calls in the middle of the night, tell him all the outtasight things their Abyssinian cats have done lately, like mistaking the bowl of grass for kitty litter.

"I know there's a motion picture in it," Bruce says, "but does eet have literary merit?"

"Eet, uh, ees—how you say eet?—eet has, uh, affecting moments." In fact, affecting moments, effectively transferred.

On the way out of the Kingdom of the Deep, Bruce says, "I'd like you to do me a special favor."

Characters in books Albert has read frequently expostulated—those in Buddy's and Bruce's are no exception—but until now never in Albert's life has he uttered what he considered at the time to be an expostulation. "But Bruce—" he expostulates.

"What I'd like you to do is drive me to an adult book store," Bruce says.

As they head down the Strip in Albert's rent car, Albert wonders whether their outing has any connection with his failure to extol *Preferential Treatment*.

"You turn right on East Charleston and go one point one miles," Bruce says.

"How do you know all this?"

"I asked the cab driver on the way in from the airport."

After they have gone point seven miles, Bruce says, "I think we better stop and ask someone."

"Bruce, we haven't gone far enough."

"He could've been wrong. There's a gas station, why don't you stop and ask?"

"If we go a mile and a half, and we haven't come across it, we'll ask."

"Help," Bruce says, "I'm a prisoner in a Chinese metaphor factory! What we have here is you all over—going on too long, hanging in there when it's dead and buried to make obscure, self-serving points. Your marriage was playing to an empty house its last two years. I tell you, we passed it already. It's dark out. Any minute, we'll be in the fucking desert already."

"We've only gone nine-tenths of a mile, Bruce. He said one point one."

"He said it, but he was a shmuck. He had those shmucky allergic-to-smoke signs all over the cab. Stop the car. We need directions. We got to ask somebody who isn't an obvious shmuck. Please, I beg of you, stop!"

Albert pulls over to the curb. Traffic streams silently beyond the closed windows. The arctic blast from the air conditioner blows between them, separating them like a wall of ice. Like Buddy and me, Albert thinks, we don't have much in common, anyway; I'm fascinated by their energy, I suppose they're intrigued by me because I have certain abilities that cannot be energetically attained, and, in a sense, to them I am an *Erlebnisträger* from a more languid world who, once rid of the meshes, would cite, in defense of the charge that he was repeating himself, the morning-glory, which resplendently reiterates itself without approbation.

"Metaphors," Albert says, "we got metaphors up the ass! No way you can function by yourself, Bruce. You need a cast of thousands to stage your life, and everything has to be set up in advance, arranged, assured. You've got to know where you are at all times. Me, I do things on my own hook, catch-as-catch-can, stumbling upon dirty books, what my mom trustingly calls human relationships, whatever. Given, a lot of times I come up empty, but there's something to be said for finely distributed sadness, the way darkness imbues the summer sky in a flat place, say Hackensack. It may not lead to an interesting life, but I think it's conducive to a life lived to be put down on paper. That's what's wrong with your hero, Bruce. He's predictable."

"Ah, so," Bruce says, peering intently out the car window, as though straining to will the adult book store into being. "Velly intelesting. But case is, helo of *Plefelential Tleatment* modeled after you."

As though peering through walls, Albert wills into being the manuscript on the bridge table in El Paso, which, successively tinged with violet, with rose, with peach, has grown to a nearly sublime, a precarious height, like those rocky, toppling eminences upon whose summits artists of the late eighteenth century carefully placed tropic birds. He summons up, too, his friend Emory Bates propelling himself, a legless man on a dolly, from one typewriter to another; Buddy pushing the burnished Lamborghini along the Colony, ears pricked for the nemesic flop-flop of Frau Gelberman in the night (But at my back I always hear / Time's fuzzy slippers hurrying near).

Albert wishes it were possible to put his hands gently on theirs, as so many years ago his piano teacher put hers on his, press their fingertips to the typewriter keys, and whisper, "This is the way it is done, this is the way it is done." The impulse brings to mind his forging the endorsement on Barney's income-tax-refund check, which arrived after he was found in the Hudson not far from where, years before, Roger Russek told Albert that integrity had gone out of the world; evidently snagged, his body had been immersed a month. Albert copied the signature from a college application blank Barney had never completed, As he duplicated the signature, Albert discovered how painstakingly, almost devoutly, Barney had written it. Here he had ascended, there he had swooped down; now, like an aviator doing aerobatics, he had inscribed the glorious loop of the "y." As he reproduced the signature, Albert felt Barney's hand on his, guiding the pen, as if telling him, "This was me, this was who I was." If Barney had lived, his signature would have become more ragged—he would have learned to dash it off. So, in a sense, he, too, was an author *manqué*, if only of his name.

Dancing has much the same appeal as the written word. Who doesn't yearn to dance like Fred Astaire? A friend of mine once rapturously described to me Astaire descending the great staircase in the Racquet Club, his little, swift, deft, jaunty, lilting steps. He said Astaire flowed down the marble steps like water. His recitation took a good five minutes and toward the end tears stood in his eyes. (Upon reading this, my friend tells me I am mistaken. Astaire wasn't going downstairs, he was going up. So much apter, that. I rerun it in the cinema of my mind: water gloriously ascending.)

Years ago, on Ponce de Leon, in the Gables, on one of those interminable summer evenings of MISERY and SORROW, Albert noticed a pretty girl of eighteen or so waiting for a bus. The air was still and uniformly lavender, she was wearing white shorts and a pale-yellow T-shirt and she was languorously dancing by herself, beguiling life's monotony away. As far as Albert could see, the city was otherwise deserted; no one was on the sidewalk, there was no traffic; the impression was the bus would never come and that if he parked at a distance and watched, all that would happen would be that finally, astonished, he would realize it had become dark.

Albert only saw the girl twice, once in passing, once as a tiny, solitary, vaguely swaying figure in the rearview mirror, but she beckons to him still, inviting him to join in her wanton dance, mocking his inability to accept, to lift his feet off the ground. "I write the World," Byron said. "I sketch your world exactly as it goes." But, Albert acknowledges, Byron also took part, he briefly leapt in the air, the world he devoted himself to roughing out revolved beneath him, he came down in a different place.

Another example. While he was at the Kismet, waiting for Bruce Bleibtraub, Albert often had occasion to pass the hotel fur shop. This seemed to be open at all hours. Albert gathered this was to accommodate impulse buyers; who knows, a highroller from the New York junket might cash out at 3 a.m. and have an urge to buy a lady friend a palomino fox jacket or a three-quarter wolverine. But only once did Albert see a customer in the store. Usually when he looked in, a woman in her mid-fifties, evidently the proprietress or manager, would be sitting at a reproduction Louis table reading a newspaper. At times she was joined by a man of the same age in doubleknits and a styled hairpiece glittering with spray. The proprietor? The one time Albert saw them with a customer, the man tore coat after coat from their hangers and flung them on the carpeted floor to disclose, as the bucket of water dashed on the unpolished marble slab revealed its variegations, the striping, the definition, the uniformity of flow, the lushness of the skins.

More than once Albert saw these two unattractive people elaborately embracing among the baum marten, fitch and mink, as though demonstrating to window-shoppers that their love was unaffected by the lack of custom. On one occasion, while in each other's arms, they executed a few accomplished dance steps. A waltz it was, slow and sweeping. Their eyelids drooped, their lips parted. As they whirled among the racks of furs, they drew further and further apart, until they were barely touching, being joined only by the lightest application of fingertips, so it appeared that they were about to fly apart. But, Albert recognized, like the time he tied Violet's tie, at that moment they never were more tightly bound.

And once, in an Irish bar, Albert saw two old biddies get up and dance to the jukebox. Sweeter, more piercing than a pine warbler singing on a hot, clear summer day, that—my standard of comparison.

Why are those four men dancing on the mountain pass? What a scene it is! All is white and terrible. Wind is shrieking in their ears, driving snow into their eyes like so many nails, plugging their nostrils, battering them about the body, buckling their knees. So why persist in dancing? I will tell you. Look more closely and you will see they are carrying something. It rises from their midst like a great, taut, white sail, which, catching the full brunt of the wind, slams them this way and that as they stumble toward waiting arms, toward Prague. So, too, we twist and turn, trying to keep a tight grip on what we value, but no one waits down the road to assume our burden.

Guitar and flute play a *gigue* in A minor, andante *con moto*. The melody is taken up by the celli restating the guitar accompaniment pizzicati, as the oboe replaces the flute motif, *con tristezza*.